STORM STALKER—

The Herald pursued an icy apparition through the storm-torn forest, a creature that was now wolf, now wind, now an unholy amalgam of both. It glared back over its shoulder at him through snow-swirls that half obscured it, baring icicle fangs and radiating cold and evil.

Talia was somewhere ahead of him, when he looked down he could see her tracks—but he could not seem to spot her through the curtains of snow that swirled around him. He realized then that the wind-wolf was stalking *her*—

The Herald quickened his pace, but the wind fought against him, throwing daggers of ice and blinding snow-swarms into his eyes. The thing ahead of him howled, a long note of triumph and insatiable hunger. It was outdistancing and outmaneuvering him—and it would have Talia before he could reach her. He tried to shout a warning—

ARROW'S FLIGHT

Mercedes Lackey

DAW BOOKS, INC.
DONALD A. WOLLHEIM, PUBLISHER

1633 Broadway, New York, NY 10019

DAW Book Collectors No. 720.

*For Carolyn
who knows why*

First Printing, September 1987

3 4 5 6 7 8 9

PRINTED IN THE U.S.A.

The Kingdom of Valdemar
(Reign of Queen Selenay)

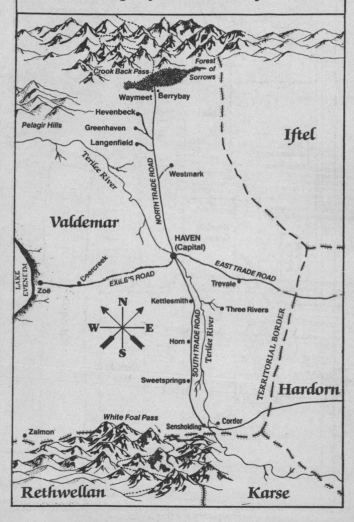

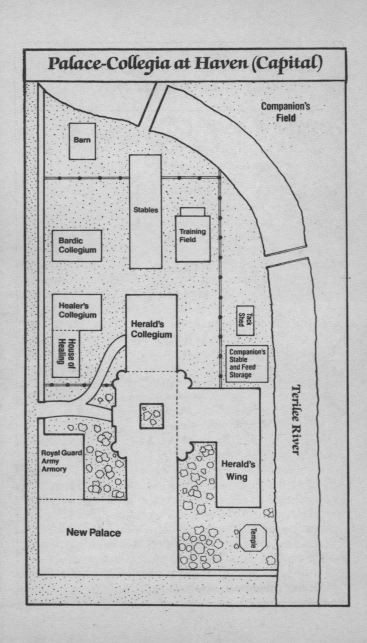

Palace-Collegia at Haven (Capital)

Companion's Field

Barn

Stables

Training Field

Bardic Collegium

Healer's Collegium

House of Healing

Herald's Collegium

Tack Shed

Companion's Stable and Feed Storage

Terilee River

Royal Guard Army Armory

Herald's Wing

New Palace

Temple

Prologue

Long ago—so long ago that the details of the conflict are lost and only the merest legends remain—the world of Velgarth was wracked by sorcerous wars. The population was decimated. The land quickly turned to wilderness and was given over to the forest and the magically-engendered creatures that had been used to fight those wars, while the people who remained fled to the eastern coastline, there to resume their shattered lives. Humans are resilient creatures, however, and it was not overlong before the population once again was on the increase, and folk began to move westward again, building new kingdoms out of the wilderness.

One such kingdom was Valdemar. Founded by the once-Baron Valdemar and those of his people who had chosen exile with him rather than facing the wrath of a selfish and cruel monarch, it lay on the very western-and-northernmost edge of the civilized world. In part due to the nature of its founders, the monarchs of Valdemar welcomed fugitives and fellow exiles, and the customs and habits of its people had over the years become a polyglot patchwork. In point of fact, the one rule by which the monarchs of Valdemar governed their people was "There *is* no 'one, true way.' "

Governing such an ill-assorted lot of subjects might have been impossible—had it not been for the Heralds of Valdemar.

The Heralds served many functions; they were administrative overseers, dispensers of justice, information gatherers, even temporary military advisors; answerable only to the Monarch and their own circle of peers. Such a system might have seemed ripe for abuse—it would have been, but for the Companions.

To the unknowing eye, a Companion would seem little more than an extraordinarily graceful white horse. They were far more than that. Sent by some unknown power or powers at the pleading of King Valdemar himself, it was the Companions who chose new Heralds, forging between themselves and their Chosen a mind-to-mind bond that only death could sever. While no one knew precisely *how* intelligent they were, it was generally agreed that their capabilities were at least as high as those of their human partners. Companions could (and did) Choose irrespective of age and sex, although they tended to Choose youngsters just entering adolescence, and more boys were Chosen than girls. The one commonality among the Chosen (other than a specific personality type; patient, unselfish, responsible, and capable of heroic devotion to duty) was at least a trace of psychic ability. Contact with a Companion and continued development of the bond enhanced whatever latent paranormal capabilities lay within the Chosen. With time, as these Gifts became better understood, ways were developed to train and use them to the fullest extent to which the individual was capable. Gradually the Gifts displaced in importance whatever knowledge of "true magic" was left in Valdemar, until there was no record of how such magic had ever been learned or used.

So the governing of Valdemar evolved; the Monarch, advised by his Council, made the laws; the Heralds dispensed the laws and saw that they were observed. The Heralds themselves were nearly incapable of becoming corrupted or potential abusers of their temporal power; the Chosen were by nature remarkably self-sacrificing—their training only reinforced this. They had to be—there was a better than even chance that a Herald would die in the line of duty. But they were human for all of that; mostly young, mostly living on the edge of danger—so, it was inevitable that outside of their duty they tended to be a bit hedonistic and anything but chaste. And only seldom did a Herald form a tie beyond that of brotherhood and the pleasures of the moment—perhaps because the bond of brotherhood was so *very* strong, and because the Herald-Companion bond left little room for any other permanent ties. For the most part, few of the common or noble folk held this against them—knowing that, no matter how wanton a Herald might be on leave, the moment he donned his snowy uniform he was another creature altogether, for a Herald in Whites was a Herald on duty, and a Herald on duty had no time for anything outside of that duty, least of all the frivolity of his own pleasures. Still, there *were* those who held other opinions . . . some of them in high places.

Laws laid down by the first King decreed that the Monarch himself must also be a Herald. Thus it was ensured that the ruler of Valdemar could never be the kind of tyrant who had caused the founders to flee their own homes.

Second in importance to the Monarch was the Herald known as the "King's (or Queen's) Own." Chosen by a special Companion—one that never seemed to age (though it was possible to kill him) and was always a stallion—the Queen's Own held the special position of confidant and most trusted friend and advisor to the ruler. Thus the Monarchs of Valdemar were assured that they would always have at least one person about them who could be trusted and counted on at all times. This tended to make for stable and confident rulers—and thus, a stable and dependable government.

For generations it seemed that King Valdemar had planned his government perfectly. But the best-laid plans are still capable of being circumvented by accident or chance.

In the reign of King Sendar, the kingdom of Karse (that bordered Valdemar to the south-east) hired a nomadic nation of mercenaries to attack Valdemar. In the ensuing war, Sendar was killed, and his daughter, Selenay, assumed the throne, herself having only recently completed her Herald's training. The Queen's Own, an aged Herald called Talamir, was frequently confused and embarrassed at having to advise a young, headstrong, and attractive female. As a result, Selenay made an ill-advised marriage, one that nearly cost her both her throne and her life.

The issue of that marriage, the Heir-presumptive, was a female child whom Selenay called Elspeth. Elspeth came under the influence of the nurse Selenay's husband had brought from his own land, and became an intractable, spoiled brat. It became obvious that if things went on as they were tending, the girl would never be Chosen, and thus could never inherit. This would leave Selenay with two choices; marry again (with the attendant risks) and attempt to produce another, more suitable Heir, or declare someone already Chosen and with the proper bloodline to be Heir. Or, somehow, salvage the Heir-presumptive. Talamir had a plan—one that it seemed had a good chance of success—which involved sending the child into fosterage in a remote province, away from the influence of the nurse and Court, with those who could be counted upon to take no nonsense from her.

Then Talamir was murdered, throwing the situation into confusion again. His Companion, Rolan, Chose a new Queen's Own—but instead of picking an adult or someone already a full Herald, Chose an adolescent girl named Talia.

Talia was of Holderkin—a puritanical Border group which did its best to discourage knowledge of outsiders. Talia had no idea what it meant to have a Herald's Companion accost her, and then (apparently) carry her off. Among her people, females held very subordinate positions, and nonconformity was punished immediately and harshly. And since Talia herself was ill-suited to a subordinate role, she was constantly being told that everything she said or did was wrong at best, and evil at worst. She was ill-prepared for the new world of the Heralds and their Collegium. The one thing she *did* have experience in was the handling and schooling of children, for she had been the teacher to her Holding's younger members from the time she was nine.

But she managed—to find a true home among the Heralds, *and* to civilize the Brat. Now the year-and-a-half of Field duty awaited her—and a trial she never dreamed of having to pass.

One

Thwack!

The flat of Alberich's practice-blade cracked against Talia's ill-guarded side. She hadn't seen the blow coming, she truly hadn't. That had *hurt*, and she would lay money on having a bruise despite the padded jerkin that had absorbed most of the blow. The practice blades may have only been wood, but Alberich tended to wield them all the harder for that.

"Faugh!" he spat in disgust, and came at her again before she had recovered from the last blow. This time he connected with her knife-arm, right at the elbow. She yelped, the arm went numb, and she lost her blade entirely.

The hawklike eyes glared at her with no trace of pity, and the scar-seamed face was a demonic mask as he passed judgment on her performance.

He was at least in his mid-forties, if not older, but he hadn't lost a fraction of his edge or agility in the five years Talia had known him. She was panting with exertion—he might as well have been taking a leisurely stroll. His well-worn, dark leathers (he was the only working Herald in Talia's experience who never wore Whites) showed not so much as a tiny sweat stain. The afternoon sun pouring down on all

of them had made him look as thin and insubstantial
as a shadow. And he had been just as hard to catch.

"A pity it is that Skif is not here to see you. Die of
laughter he surely would!" he growled. "Eighteen
you are—one would think you eight. Slow, clumsy,
and stupid! Paugh! Had I been a real assassin—"

"I would have died of fright before you touched
me."

"Now it is jokes! This is a battle-practice—not a
comedy. If I wish amusement, I shall find a jester.
Once again—and correctly, this time."

Once she was ready to drop with exhaustion, he
turned his attention to Elspeth. Now that both of
them deserved special tutelage he had changed the
hour of their lessons to one shared by no one else, so
that he could give his full devotion to the Queen's
Own and Heir-presumptive. Rather than being held
on the training grounds outside, the two had their
drills in the salle. This was a barn-like building with
a sanded wooden floor, lined with mirrors, with high
clerestory windows to admit the maximum amount
of light. Lessons were always held here during in-
clement weather, but it was too small for mass prac-
tices and classes for the combined Heraldic-Bardic-
Healer's Collegium students. Only those "privileged"
to receive private lessons with Alberich took those
lessons habitually in the salle.

Now that his attention was off her, Talia found
her thoughts drifting back to her surprise of this
afternoon.

Talia tugged and wriggled impatiently until she
had succeeded in getting the supple, soft, white leather
tunic over her head. Pulling it into place over the
white raime shirt and leather breeches, she finally
turned to admire the effect in the polished metal
mirror in front of her.

"Havens!" she laughed, not a little surprised, "Why
don't the Grays ever look like this?"

"Because," a harsh voice drawled from the next room, "You youngsters would have your minds on anything but your studies if they did!"

Talia laughed, turned back to the mirror, and preened. Today was the anniversary of her first class at Herald's Collegium—a fact that she'd forgotten until Keren and Sherrill (senior Heralds both, and instructors at the Collegium as well as Talia's long-time friends) arrived at her room with their arms full of white uniforms and wearing broad grins.

For the Heraldic Circle had considered—for less than five minutes, all told—had voted—and had passed Talia into full Herald status with the rest of her year-mates—no surprise to anyone in the Collegium, though by tradition the trainees were not to know when they were to be evaluated until the evaluation had already been made *and* they had passed.

Keren and Sherrill had claimed the right to give her the good news.

They didn't even give her a chance to think, either—just appeared at her door, swept her up one on either side, and herded her down the long, dark wood-paneled hall of the Collegium dormitory, down the stairs to the first floor, and out the double doors at the end.

From there they had taken her off to the Seneschal's office to claim her new quarters. Now she stood in the bedroom of the suite she'd chosen, marveling at her reflection.

"I look like a real grownup for a change!"

"That *is* the general idea," Sherrill laughed richly.

She cocked her head to one side, regarding the tiny, slender figure in the mirror. Her unruly red-brown curls were as tousled as ever, but somehow gave an impression now of being tumbled the way they were on purpose. The huge, deep-brown eyes that had been utterly guileless seemed somehow wiser; the heart-shaped face no longer so childlike. And all that change wrought by the magic of a new uniform!

"Talia, your head is going to swell like a spongetoad in rainy season if you're not careful." Keren interrupted her train of thought a second time. By craning her neck to peer around the doorframe Talia could see the riding instructor grinning sardonically from where she was sprawled on the wooden-backed, red-cushioned couch in the other room.

"Don't you know what the Book of the One says?" Sherrill added piously over her mate's shoulder. " 'Great pride shall earn equal humiliation.' "

Talia left her bedroom to join them. They were lounging comfortably in her sparsely-furnished outer room, sharing the lone couch.

"I suppose you're both going to claim that you never spent so much as a minute in front of the mirror when you first got *your* Whites," Talia taunted, strolling toward them with her hands clasped behind her back.

"Who? Me?" Sherrill replied in artificial innocence, lifting an airy hand and batting thick black lashes over wide hazel eyes. "And feed my vanity? W-e-l-l, maybe a *little*."

"I happen to know for a fact that you spent half the day there. I'm told you were trying every hairstyle you could twist that black mane of yours into, seeing which one went best with the new outfits," Keren countered dryly, running her fingers through her own close-cropped, graying brown hair.

Sherrill just grinned and crossed her legs elegantly, leaning back into the cushions. "Since I can't claim equal knowledge of what you did on that august occasion, that's hardly a fair blow."

"Oh, I did my share of mirror-gazing," Keren admitted with mock reluctance. "When you're as scrawny as a sapling and flat as a boy, it's rather astonishing to see yourself in something that actually flatters you. I swear I don't know how they do it— it's the same pattern for everybody, and not that dissimilar from the Student Grays—"

"But Lord, the difference!" Sheri concluded for her. "I don't know of *anybody* who doesn't look fantastic in their Whites. Even Dirk manages to look presentable. Rumpled, but presentable."

"Well, what do you think of me?" Talia asked, turning on her toes in front of them, and grinning impishly into Keren's eyes.

"What do I think? That you look fabulous, you young demon. Keep fishing for compliments, though, and I'll likely dump you in the horse trough. Have they told you anything about your internship?"

Talia shook her head, and clasped her hands behind her again. "No. All they said was that the Herald they want to pair me with is in the field, and they won't tell me who it is."

"That's pretty much to be expected. They don't want you to have time to think of things to impress him with," Sherrill replied. Suddenly her eyes sparkled with mischief. "Oh, but I can think of *one* prospect that would give Nerrissa a litter of kittens!"

"Who?" Talia asked, head to one side.

"Kris and Dirk are due back in the next few weeks, and Dirk got the last greenie—as you should know, since it was Skif—so it's Kris' turn next! Nessa would *die!*"

"Sheri, it's *only* my internship assignment."

"A year and a half Sector-riding, most of it spent alone together, and you say it's *only* an assignment? Talia, you must have ice water for blood! Do you have any notion of the number of hours Nessa—and half the females of the Circle, for that matter—spend on their knees praying for an assignment like that? Are you sure you don't have leanings our way?"

Talia chuckled, and wrinkled her nose at them. "Quite sure, darlings. Just what is Kris' attraction for Nessa, anyway? She's got most of the males of the Circle panting at her heels as it is."

"The lure of the unattainable, or so I would surmise," Keren supplied, lids half-closed lazily with only a glint of brown iris showing. "He hasn't taken a vow of chastity, but he's so circumspect about his dalliances you'd never know it. It drives Nessa wild, and the harder she chases, the faster he runs. She's as caught up now by the chase as by the face."

"Well, she can chase him all she wants. *I* am not at all impressed by Kris' handsome face," Talia replied firmly.

"Or the gorgeous body—?" interjected Sherrill.

"*Or* the gorgeous body. Nessa can have all the gorgeous bodies in the Circle, for all I care. Holderkin men are handsome specimens, and I can do without them—my father could have given Kris stiff competition in his younger days, and I've told you what kind of a petty tyrant he was. And my late-but-not-lamented brother Justus was actually handsomer, if you favor blonds, and he was the foulest person I've ever known. I'd rather have a good heart and plain packaging."

"Yes, but Kris is a Herald—" Sherrill pointed out, tapping one long finger on her knee for emphasis. "That guarantees the good heart without having to settle for a homely exterior. No handsome, smiling bastards in *our* ranks—"

"Sheri, this is all sheer speculation. Until I find out who I'm interning with, I refuse to worry about the subject," Talia replied firmly.

"You are no fun at all."

"I never said I was."

"Hmm. Dirk's interning that scalawag Skif—" Keren said thoughtfully. "You and Skif were very thick there for a while. In fact, as I recall, you and *he* had a rumor or two floating about your heads. Is that why you aren't interested in Dirk's partner?"

"Maybe," Talia smiled enigmatically. The fact that their "romance" had been entirely without any result was Skif's secret—and hers. The streak of ill-luck and accident that had plagued their meetings had not had any effect on their friendship: except that

they had never managed to be more than just that—
friends. Oddly enough, though, except for a brief
period of anxiety when word had come that Skif had
been hurt during his first three months in the field,
Talia had thought less of Skif, and more of his
counselor. To her own amazement—and for no reason, logical or fanciful that she could think of—when
her thoughts strayed in the direction of the former
thief and his internship assignment, it was in Dirk's
direction that they tended to wander. This was an-
noying; she'd met the man all of three times in her
life, and had never been in his company for more
than an hour or two at most. Yet, that homely face
and those wonderful blue eyes kept lingering stubbornly in her thoughts. It did *not* make sense.

She shook her head to free it of those fanciful
images. She had little enough time, and had none to
spare in daydreams.

"Well, this little wardrobe change of yours ought
to surprise little Elspeth," Sherrill said, changing the
subject.

"Oh, Lady Bright—" Talia sat down with a thump
on one of her cushions, joy extinguished. It almost
seemed to her at that moment that the bright sun-
rays pouring through her windows had dimmed.
"Poor Elspeth—"

"Something up?" Keren asked, one eyebrow rising.

"Just the usual."

"What's usual? You know I don't get around the
Court."

"Intrigue rising beyond gossip. She's almost fourteen and still not Chosen; there's muttering in the
Court that she's still the Brat under the skin and
she'll *never* be Chosen. In Council meetings one or
more of the Councilors is usually trying to pressure
Selenay into naming an Heir—'pro tem,' as they put
it—"

"Who?" Sherrill asked in alarm, sitting straight up.
"Who's stirring up the water?"

"You know I can't tell you that! Anyway it isn't just *those* particular Councilors; it's more than half of the Court. Elspeth doesn't say much, but it's got her very depressed, poor baby. Their timing couldn't be worse. She's already moody enough with the normal adolescent woes, and this has got her in near-tears on a regular basis. When I'm not getting my shoulder soggy, I keep finding her at Companion's Field whenever she's free, sort of lurking—"

"Hoping any minute to be Chosen. Gods, no wonder she's wearing a long face whenever I see her. What's Rolan got to say about this?"

"Be damned if I know!" Talia gifted Keren with a look of exasperation. "*You* know he doesn't Mindspeak me in words."

"Sorry," Keren winced, "I keep forgetting."

"He's worried, but it could be as much over the machinations and power-maneuverings at Court as anything else. The current candidates are Jeri, Kemoc, and your oh-so-lovely Kris."

"Wonderful people in and of themselves," Keren observed, "But with some not-so-wonderful relatives lurking in the family trees. One would think Kris' uncle Lord Orthallen would have his hands full enough as chief Councilor without wanting to be the Heir's uncle—"

"*That* man will *never* have enough power to satisfy him," Talia snapped bitterly.

Keren raised an eyebrow at the outburst, and continued. "Kemoc's horde of lazy cousins would swarm the Court, looking for sinecures—and Kemoc's such a soft touch he'd try to manage it. And Jeri—Lady Bright! Her *mother!*"

"We'd have a battle royal every day between Jeri and Lady Indra over how Jeri's Council votes should go. I wish her husband would lock her away. Or buy a gag for her."

"Amen. Pity none of them come without baggage.

Not my idea of a fun situation. And poor catling caught in the middle."

Talia sighed in agreement. "Speaking of no fun, I'd better scramble. Alberich informed me in no uncertain terms that my new status does not exempt me from his special lessons. I have the sinking feeling that he intends to slap my inflated pride down to pre-student levels, and probably with the flat of his blade."

"Can I watch?" Keren asked wickedly.

"Why not? Elspeth's always there, and there's nothing like being worse at something than a thirteen-year-old girl to really deflate your opinions of yourself. Well, that ought to reinflate *her* self-esteem a bit. Ah, me, it's a pity to have to get these lovely new clothes all over dirt and sweat—"

As they descended the cool darkness of the spiraling staircase, Keren and Sherrill in the lead with their arms casually linked, Talia reflected that bringing them together was probably the best thing she'd ever done. The bond between them was easily as strong as the one Keren had shared with Ylsa—and had Ylsa lived, they might very well have formed one of the relatively rare, permanent threesomes. There was no doubt that they were very good for each other. Poor Ylsa . . .

Talia's chosen living quarters were at the very top of her tower at the end of the Herald's wing. The suites in the four towers were seldom used—probably because they were more than a bit inconvenient. The walk up and down the darkened stone staircase was a long one, but she felt that the view (and the privacy) were worth it.

But the trudge was likely to bring complaints from Talia's friends—and Keren voiced the first of many.

"I'll tell you one thing, my fine young Herald," Keren grumbled a little when they finally reached the ground floor. "Visiting with you on a regular basis is going to keep your friends in shape. Why you chose to roost with the birds is beyond me."

"Do you truly want to know why I chose that particular suite?" Talia asked with a grin.

"Say on."

"Pray remember, if you will, what my Gift is—I'm an empath, not a mindspeaker. Either of you remember who my neighbor was?"

"Mm. Destria, wasn't it?" Sherrill replied after thought. "Turned out to be a good Field Herald, despite her—ah—"

"Randiness," Keren supplied with a hint of grin. "That girl! Anything in Grays *or* Whites, so long as it was male! Havens, when did she ever have time to study?"

"Then you both know about her habit of 'entertaining' with great frequency and—um—enthusiasm. What I couldn't shield I could most certainly hear! Between her nocturnal activities and Rolan's, I got a quite thorough education, let me assure you! That's when I swore my privacy was worth any inconvenience. I don't want to eavesdrop on anyone else's fun ever again, and I certainly don't want anyone eavesdropping on mine!"

"Talia, I don't believe a word of it," Sherrill giggled. "What could you possibly have to fear from eavesdroppers? You're practically a temple virgin compared with the rest of us!"

"You ought to believe it, since it's all true. Well, here's where we part company. Wish me luck—I'm going to need it!"

Pity that they hadn't wished her luck—she might have gotten a few less bruises. Talia fanned herself with a towel while she paced back and forth to keep from stiffening up, and watched Elspeth with unforced enjoyment. The girl was a pleasure to observe, moving through the sparring bout with the grace and agility of a dancer, and making it all seem effortless and easy. She was much better even than Jeri had been at her age, but then she had had the benefits of four years of Alberich's remorseless training; Jeri had only had the finest arms-tutors money could obtain. No amount of money could buy Alberich's expertise.

She ran through the assigned exercises with careless grace. Then, at the end of a bout, she unexpectedly executed one of the spin-and-tumbling-rolls that Alberich had been trying to train into Talia—a move that was *not* one Alberich had been teaching *her*. And she scored a kill on him.

He stared at her in startled amazement for a long moment, as both Talia and Elspeth waited breathlessly for the roar of disapproval they were certain would come.

"Good!" he said at last, as Elspeth's jaw dropped in surprise. "Very good!" Then, lest she dare to grow careless because of the compliment, "But next time must be better."

Despite this unexpected kudo, Talia found when she brought Elspeth a damp towel at the conclusion of the lesson that the girl was subdued and depressed.

"What's wrong, catling?" she asked, seeing how like her mother Elspeth was, despite the brown hair and eyes rather than Selenay's blond and blue. At this moment the shadow on her face matched the one the Queen wore when troubled. She *knew* the answer already, but it would do the girl good to talk it out one more time.

"I can't do anything right," Elspeth replied unhappily, "I'll never be as good as you, no matter how hard I try."

"You can't be serious—"

"No, really, look at you! You spent half your life on a backwoods dirt-farm; now you can't be told from Heralds that were highborn. You got good marks in your classes; I'm abysmal in all of mine. And I can't even manage to be Chosen. . . ."

"I suspect it's the last that's eating at you the most."

Elspeth nodded, the corners of her mouth drooping.

"Catling, we're two different people with wildly different abilities and interests. In the five years I've been here I've never once managed to earn a 'good' from Alberich, much less a 'very good'! I'm still so stiff when I dance that they say it's like dancing with a broom."

"Oh, huzzah, I'm a marvel of coordination. I can kill anything on two legs. That's a *terrific* qualification for being Heir."

"Catling, you've *got* the qualifications. Look, if I live to be two hundred, I will *never* understand politics. Think back a minute. At the last Council meeting, I could sense that Lord Cariodoc was irritated, but *you* were the one who not only knew why and by whom, but managed to placate the old buzzard before he could start an incident. And your teachers assure me that though you may not be the best in your classes, you aren't the worst by any stretch of the imagination. As for being Chosen, catling, thirteen is only the *average* age for that. Think of Jadus—he was sixteen and had been at Bardic for three years! Or Teren, for Lady's sake—a man grown and with two children! Look, it's probably only that *your* Companion just hasn't been old enough, and you know very well they don't Choose until they're ten or better."

Elspeth's mood seemed to be lightening a bit.

"Come on, love, cheer up, and we'll go see Rolan. If riding him will bring some sun to your day, I'm sure he'll let you."

Elspeth's long face brightened considerably. She loved riding as much as dancing and swordwork. It wasn't often that a Companion would consent to bear anyone but his Chosen; Rolan had done so for Elspeth in the past, and she obviously counted those moments among the finest in her life. It wasn't the same as having her own Companion, but it was at least a little like it. Together they left the training salle, and headed for the wooded enclosure that was home to the Companions at the Collegium (part-nered, unpartnered, and foals) and that also held the Grove, that place where the Companions had first appeared hundreds of years ago.

And although she took pains not to show it, Talia was profoundly worried. This situation with Elspeth's status hanging fire could not be maintained for much longer. The strain was telling on the Queen, the girl, and the Heraldic Circle.

But Talia had no more notion of how to solve the problem than anyone else.

Talia woke with a start, momentarily confused by the strange feel and sounds of the room in which she found herself. She couldn't see a blessed thing, and over her head was a rattling—

Then she remembered where she was; and that the rattling was the shutter of the window just over the head of her bed. She'd latched it open, and it was rattling in the high wind that must have begun some time during the night.

She turned over and levered herself into a kneel-ing position on her pillow, peering out into the dark-ness. She still couldn't see much; dark humps of foliage against barely-lighter grass. The moon was less than half full, all the buildings were dark, and clouds racing along in the wind obscured the stars and the moonlight. The wind smelled of dawn though, and sunrise couldn't be far off.

Talia shivered in the chill, as wind whipped at her; she was about to crawl back under her warm blan-kets when she saw something below her.

A person—a small person—hardly more than a dim figure moving beyond the fence of Companion's Field, visible only because it was wearing something light-colored.

And she knew with sudden surety that the one below was Elspeth.

She slid out of bed, wincing at the cold wood under her feet, and grabbed clothing by feel, not waiting to stop to light a candle. Confused thoughts tumbled, one over the other. Was the girl sleepwalking? Was she ill? But when she reached unthinkingly and tentatively with her Gift, she encountered neither the feel of a sleeping mind, nor a disturbed one; only a deep and urgent sense of *purpose*.

She should, she realized in some dim, far-off corner of her mind, be alarmed. But as soon as she had touched Elspeth with her Empathic Gift, that sense of calm purpose had infected her as well, and she could no more have disobeyed its promptings than have launched into flight from her tower window.

In a dreamlike state she half-stumbled out into the middle room, fumbled her way to the door, and cautiously felt her way down the spiraling staircase with one hand on the cold smoothness of the metal railing and the other on the rough stone of the wall beside her. She was shivering so hard her teeth rattled, and the thick darkness in the stairwell was slightly unnerving.

There was light at the foot of it, though, from a lamp set up on the wall. The dim yellow light filled the entranceway. And the wood-paneled corridor beyond was lighted well enough by farther wall-hung lamps that Talia felt safe in running down the stone-floored passageways to the first door to the outside she could find.

The wind hit her with a shock; it was a physical blow so hard that she gasped. It nearly wrenched the door out of her hands and she had to struggle for a moment she had not wanted to spare to get it closed behind her. She realized that she had gotten only a hint of its force from her window; her room was sheltered from the worst of it by the bulk of the Palace itself.

She found herself at the exterior bend of the L-shaped Herald's wing; just beyond her bulked the Companion's stables. Elspeth was nowhere in sight.

More certain of her ground now than she had been in the unfamiliar wing of the Palace, Talia would have run if she could, but the wind made that impossible. It plastered her clothing to her body, and drove unidentifiable debris at her with the velocity of crossbow bolts. She couldn't hear anything now with it howling in her ears; she *knew* no one would hear her calling. Now she became vaguely alarmed; with the wind this strong and in the dark, it would be so easy for Elspeth to misstep and find herself in the river—

She mindcalled Rolan for help—and could not reach him—

Or rather, she could reach him, but he was paying no attention to her whatsoever; his whole being was focused on—what it was, she could not say, but it demanded all his concentration; for he was absorbed in it with such intensity that he was shutting everything and everyone else out.

It was up to her, then. She fought her way around the stables toward the bridge that led across the river to the main portion of Companion's Field. It was with incredible relief that she spotted the vague blur of Elspeth ahead of her, already across the river, and headed with utter single-minded concentration in the direction of—

There was only one place she *could* be heading for— the Grove.

Talia forced her pace to the fastest she could manage, leaning at an acute angle into the wind, but the girl had a considerable head start on her, and had already entered the Grove by the time she had crossed the bridge.

The pale blob was lost to sight as the foliage closed around it, and Talia stumbled over the uneven ground, falling more than once and bruising hands and knees on the stones hidden in the grass. The long grass itself whipped at her booted legs, tangling her feet with each step. She was halfway to the Grove when she looked up from yet another fall to see that it was—gods!—*glowing* faintly from within.

She shook her head, blinking, certain that her eyes were playing tricks on her. The glow remained, scarcely brighter than foxfire, but unmistakably *there*.

She started to rise, when the entire world seemed to give a gut-wrenching lurch, disorienting her completely. She clutched at the grass beneath her hands, as the only reality in a suddenly unreal world, the pain of her bruised palms hardly registering. Everything seemed to be spinning, the way it had the one time she'd fainted, and she was lost in the darkness with the wind wailing in a whirlwind around her and the Grove. There was a sickening moment—or eternity—when *nothing* was real.

Then the world settled, and normality returned with an almost audible *snap;* the wind died away to nothing, sound returned, the disorientation vanished, all in the space of a single heartbeat.

Talia opened her eyes, unaware until that moment that she'd been clenching both eyes and jaw so tightly her face ached. Less than five feet away stood Elspeth, between the supporting shoulders of two Companions. The one on her left was Rolan, and he was back in Talia's awareness again—tired, though; very tired, but strangely contented.

Talia staggered to her feet; the gray light of the setting moon was lightening the sky, and by it, she could make out the girl's features. Elspeth seemed dazed, and if the contrast between the dark mass of her hair and the paleness of her skin meant anything, she was drained as white as paper.

Talia stumbled the few steps between them, grabbed her shoulders and shook her; until that moment the girl didn't seem to realize she was there.

"Elspeth—" was all she managed to choke out around her own nerveless shivering.

"Talia?" The girl blinked once, then dumbfounded her mentor by seeming to snap into total wakefulness, smiling and throwing her arms around Talia's shoulders. "Talia—I—" she laughed, almost hysterical with joy, and for one brief moment Talia feared she'd lost her mind.

Then she let go of the Herald and threw both of her arms around the neck of the Companion to her right. "Talia, Talia, it happened! Gwena Chose me! She called me when I was asleep, and I came, and she Chose me!"

Gwena?

Talia knew every Companion in residence, having spent nearly as much time with them as Keren, and having helped to midwife many of the foals. *That* name didn't belong to any of them.

And that could only mean one thing; Gwena, like Rolan—and unlike any other Companion currently alive—was Grove-born. But why? For centuries only Monarch's Own Companions had appeared in the Grove like Companions of old.

Talia started to say something—and abruptly felt Rolan's presence overwhelming her mind, tinged with a feeling of gentle regret.

Talia shook her head, bewildered by the sensation that she'd forgotten something, then dismissed the feeling. Elspeth had been Chosen; *that* was what mattered. She remembered the mare vaguely now. Gwena had always been one of the shyer Companions, staying well away from visitors. All her shyness seemed gone, as she nuzzled Elspeth's hair with possessive pride. Rolan, who had been supporting Elspeth on the left, now paced forward in time to give Talia a shoulder to lean on, for her own knees were going weak with reaction, and she felt as drained as if she'd had a three-candlemark workout with Alberich. Birds were breaking into morning-song all around them, and the first light of true dawn streaked the sky to the east with festive ribbons of brightness among the clouds.

"Oh, *catling!*" Talia released her hold on Rolan's mane and flung both her arms around Elspeth, nearly in tears with joy.

It did not occur to either of them to wonder why no one else had been mustered out of bed by that imperative calling both of *them* had answered—and why no one else had noticed anything at all out of the ordinary even yet.

Talia managed to convince Elspeth—not to go back to her bed, because that was an impossibility—but to settle with Gwena in a sheltered little hollow, with a blanket purloined from the stable around her shoulders. Talia hoped that when her excitement faded the child would doze off again; the gods knew she'd be safe enough in the Field with her own Companion standing protective guard over her. She wished devoutly that she could have done the same, but there were far too many things she had to attend to.

The first—and most important—was to inform the Queen. Even at this early hour Selenay would be awake and working, and likely with one or more Councilors. That meant a formal announcement, and not what Talia *really* wanted to do, which was to burst into Selenay's chamber caroling for joy.

However pleased Selenay would be, *that* sort of action would only give the Councilors a very poor impression of the Queen's Own's maturity.

So Talia stumbled back to her room again, through the sweet breeze of a perfect dawn, through bird choruses that were only a faint, far echo of the joy in her heart, to get redressed. And this time, as neatly and precisely as she could manage, cringing inwardly at the grass stains left on the knees of the pair of breeches she'd just peeled off. *Then* she walked—

walked—decorously and soberly down through the silence of the Herald's wing to the "New Palace" wing that held the suites of Queen and Court.

As usual, there were two blue-clad Guardsmen stationed outside the doors to the Royal chambers. She nodded to them, dark Jon to the right, wizened Fess to the left; she knew both of them well, and longed to be able to whisper her news, but that wouldn't do. It wouldn't be dignified, and it would absolutely shatter protocol. As Queen's Own, she had the right of entry to the Queen's chambers at any time of night or day, and was quickly admitted beyond those heavy goldenoak doors.

As she had expected, Selenay was already hard at work in her dark-paneled outer chamber; dressed for the day in formal Whites, massive desk covered with papers, and both Lord Orthallen and the Seneschal at her shoulders. She looked up at Talia's entrance, startled, blue eyes seeming weary even this early in the day. Whatever brought those two Councilors to her side, it did not look to be pleasant. . . .

Perhaps Talia's news would change all that.

She clued Selenay to the gravity of her news by making the formal half-bow before entering, and that it was good news by a cheerful wink so timed that only Selenay noted it. Protocol demanded exactly five steps across that dark-blue carpet, which took her to exactly within comfortable conversational distance of the desk. Then she went to one knee, trying not to flinch as her bruises encountered the floor. Selenay, tucking a strand of gold hair behind one ear and straightening in expectation, nodded to indicate she could speak.

"Majesty—I have come to petition the right of a trainee to enter the Collegium," Talia said gravely, with both hands clasped upon the upright knee, while her eyes danced at the nonsense of all this formality.

That got the attention not only of Selenay, but of

both Councilors. Only highborn trainees needed to have petitions laid before the Crown, for becoming a Herald often meant renouncing titles and lands, either actual or presumptive.

Talia could see the puzzlement in the Councilors' eyes—and the rising hope in Selenay's.

"What Companion has Chosen—and what is the candidate's name and rank?" Selenay replied just as formally, one hand clutching the goblet before her so tightly her knuckles went white.

"The Companion Gwena has Chosen," Talia barely managed to keep from singing the words, "And her Choice is the Heir-presumptive, now Heir-In-Right, the Lady Elspeth. May I have the Queen's leave to enter the trainee in the Collegium rolls?"

Within the hour Court and Collegium were buzzing, and Talia was up to her eyebrows in all the tasks needed to transfer Elspeth from her mother's custody to that of the Collegium. Elspeth spent the day in blissful ignorance of all the fuss—which was only fair. The first few hours were critical in the formation of the Herald-Companion bond, and should be spent in as undisturbed a manner as possible. So it was Talia's task to see to it that when Elspeth finally drifted dreamily back through the gates of Companion's Field, everything, from room assignment to having her belongings transferred, had been taken care of for her.

And toward day's end it occurred to Talia that it behooved her to take dinner with the Court rather than the Collegium. The Queen might make dinner the occasion for the formal announcement of choice of Heir.

She finished setting up Elspeth's class schedule with Dean Elcarth, and sprinted to her quarters and up the stairs as fast as her sore knees would permit. After a quick wash, she rummaged in the wooden wardrobe, cursing as she bumped her head against one of the doors. After making what she hoped was an appropriate selection, she dressed hastily in one of the velvet outfits. With one hand brushing her hair, half-skipping as she wedged her feet into the soft slippers that went with it, she used the other hand to snatch the appropriate book of protocol from among the others on her still-dusty desk. While wriggling to settle the clothing properly and using both hands to smooth her hair, she reviewed the brief ceremony attendant on the coronation of the Heir. She shot a quick look at herself in the mirror, then took herself off to the Great Hall.

She slipped into her seldom-used seat between Elspeth and the Queen and whispered "Well?"

"She's going to do it as soon as everyone arrives," Elspeth breathed back. "I think I'm going to die. . . ."

"No you won't," Talia answered in a conspiratorial manner, "You've been doing things like this for ages. Now *I* may die!" Elspeth was relaxing visibly now that Talia was there to share her ordeal.

Talia had only taken meals with the Court a handful of times since she'd arrived at the Collegium, and the Great Hall never ceased to impress her. It was the largest single room in the Palace, its high, vaulted ceiling supported by slender-seeming pillars of ironoak that gleamed golden in the light from the windows and the lamp- and candle-light. There were battle-banners and heraldic pennons that went clear back to the Founding hanging from the rafters. Talia's seat was at the table placed on the dais, which stood at right angle to the rest of the tables in the Hall. Late sunlight streamed in through the tall, narrow windows that filled the west wall, but the windows to the east were already beginning to darken with the onset of nightfall. The courtiers seated along the tables below her were as colorful as a bed of wild-flowers, and formed a pleasing grouping against the panels and tables of golden ironoak.

When the Great Hall was filled, the Queen arose

as the stewards called for silence. It would have been possible to hear a feather fall as she began. Every eye in the Hall was riveted on her proud, White-clad figure, with the thin circlet of Royal red gold (it was all she would wear as token of her rank) encircling her raival-leaf golden hair.

"Since the death of my father, we have been without an Heir. I can understand and sympathize with those of you who found this a disquieting and frightening situation. You may rejoice, for all uncertainty is at an end. This day was my daughter Elspeth Chosen by the Companion Gwena, making her a fully eligible candidate for the position of Heir. Rise, daughter."

Elspeth and Talia both rose, Elspeth to stand before her mother, Talia to take the silver coronet of the Heir from the steward holding it. She presented it to the Queen, then retired to her proper position as Queen's Own, behind and slightly to Selenay's right. She was pleased to note that although Elspeth's hands trembled, her voice, as she repeated her vows, was strong and clear. Elspeth caught her eyes and held to Talia's gaze as if to a lifeline.

Elspeth was frightened half to death, despite her lifelong preparation for this moment. She could clearly see Talia's encouraging expression, and the presence of the Queen's Own gave her comfort and courage. For one panicked moment halfway through her vows, she forgot what her mother had said just the instant before. She felt a flood of gratitude when she noticed Talia's lips moving, and realized that she was mouthing the words Elspeth had just forgotten.

There was more to it than just having a friend at hand, too—with her mental senses sharpened and enhanced by having been Chosen, Elspeth could dimly feel Talia as a solid, comforting presence, like a deeply-rooted tree in a wild windstorm. There would always be shelter for her beneath those branches, and as she repeated the last words of her Oath, she suddenly realized how vital that shelter would be to one, who as ruler, must inevitably face the gales; and more often than not alone. There was also, distinctly, though distantly, the sense that Talia loved her for herself, and as a true friend. And that in itself was a comfort. As she finished the last words and her mother placed the silver circlet on her head, she tried to put all her gratitude to her friend in the smile she gave her.

As the Queen placed the coronet on her daughter's hair, a spontaneous cheer rose that gladdened Talia's heart. Perhaps now the Brat could be forgotten.

But as they resumed their seats and the serving began, the unaccustomed dainties of the Queen's table suddenly lost their appeal as Talia realized that there was yet another ceremony to be endured, one about which she knew nothing. As soon as the powers of the Kingdom could be gathered there must be a great ceremony of fealty in which the Queen's Own would play a significant role. Talia reached blindly for her goblet to moisten a mouth gone dry with panic.

Then she took herself firmly in hand; Kyril and Elcarth, as Seneschal's Herald and Dean of the Collegium, would surely know everything about this occasion—and just as surely would be aware that Talia *didn't*. There was no need to panic. Not yet, anyway.

The meal seemed to be progressing with ponderous slowness. This was Talia's first High Feast—and it seemed incredibly dull. She sighed, and the Queen caught the sound.

"Bored?" she whispered out of the corner of her mouth.

"Oh, no!" Talia replied with a forced smile.

"Liar," the Queen replied with a twinkle. "No one but a moron could avoid being bored by all this. You sit and sit, and smile and smile, till your face and backside are both stiff. Then you sit and smile some more."

"How do you manage this day after day?" Talia asked, trying not to laugh.

"Father taught me a game; Elspeth and I play it now. What are we doing this time, catling?"

"We're back to animals," Elspeth replied, as her mother nodded to an elderly duke in response to some comment he'd mumbled. "You try and decide what animal the courtiers most remind you of. We change each time. Sometimes it's flowers, trees, rocks, landmarks—even weather. This time it's animals, and *he's* a badger."

"Well if he's a badger, his lady's a watchdog. Look how she raises her hackles whenever he smiles at that pretty serving girl," Talia said.

"Oh, I'd never have thought of *that* one!" Elspeth exclaimed. "You're going to be good at this game!"

They managed to keep straight faces, but it wasn't easy.

Talia sought out Kyril the next day before the thrice-weekly Council meeting to learn that she had three weeks in which to prepare for Elspeth's formal investiture. He and Elcarth pledged to drill her in all she needed to know, from protocol to politics, every day.

The Council meeting in itself was something of an ordeal. She and Elspeth had seats on the far end of the horseshoe-shaped Council table, almost opposite Selenay and the empty place beside her. That empty chair was the seat of the Queen's Own, but Talia could not, under law, assume that place until she had passed her own internship. She and Elspeth had voice on the Council, but no vote. Elspeth's own voting rights were in abeyance until *she* passed internship. The Councilors tended to ignore them because of that lack of voting rights—but not today.

No, today they interrogated both Talia and Elspeth with an ill-concealed eagerness that bordered on greed. How soon did Talia think she'd be out in the field—could the internship be cut back to a year? Or given the importance of her position, and her lack of experience, should it be extended past the normal year-and-a-half? Could Elspeth's education be rushed? What should she be tutored in besides the normal curriculum of the Herald's Collegium? Did *she* feel ready for her new position as Heir? And on and on . . .

From most of the Councilors Talia only received a well-intentioned (if irritating) eagerness to help "the children" (and she cursed—not for the first time— her slight stature that made her seem barely an adolescent). But from others—

Lord Orthallen, one of Selenay's closest advisors (as he had been to her father) regarded both of them with a cool, almost cold, gaze. And Talia felt very like a prime specimen of some unusual beetle on the dissecting table. She got no emotional impressions from him at all; she never had. That was profoundly disturbing for one whose Gift was Empathy— and even more disturbing was the vague feeling that he was not pleased that Elspeth had at last been Chosen.

From Bard Hyron, speaker for the Bardic Circle, she got a distinct feeling that all this was happening far too quickly. And that not enough caution was being exercised. And that *he* didn't quite trust *her*.

Lord Gartheser's feelings were of general displeasure over the whole affair, but she couldn't pinpoint why. There was also a faint overtone of disappointment; he *was* related to Kemoc, one of the three other contenders for the position. Could that be all, though? Or was there something deeper in his motivation?

Lady Wyrist was downright annoyed, but why, Talia couldn't fathom. It might have been simply that she was afraid that Talia would favor her own relations, the Holderkin, who lived in the area Wyrist spoke for. She could hardly know that there was small chance of *that!*

Orthallen was the one who bothered her most, but as the meeting broke up, she knew she would mention this to no one. She had nothing of fact to report; and she and Orthallen had bad blood between them over his treatment (and near-expulsion) of her friend Skif from the Collegium. She knew better than to give Orthallen so powerful a weapon if he *was* an enemy as to seem to be holding a grudge. Instead she smiled sweetly and thanked him for his good wishes. Let him think her an innocent idiot. Meanwhile she would make sure to have one eye on him.

But soon, very soon now, *she* would be gone, on her year-and-a-half internship, and that would take her entirely out of the current intrigues at Court. It would also make it impossible for her to deal with any of it. If Gartheser, Orthallen, or any of the others had deeper schemes, there would be no one near Elspeth who could detect the shadow of the scheming.

She would be gone—and who would watch them then?

Two

Three weeks to the investiture. Only three weeks, but they seemed like three years, at least to Talia.

There was an elaborate ceremony of oaths and bindings to memorize, but that wasn't the worst of it. Talia's main function at this particular rite would be *apparently* to perform the original duties of Heralds, the duties they had held in the days before Valdemar founded his kingdom, to announce each dignitary by name and all ranks and titles before escorting him or her to the foot of the Throne.

This was, of course, the lesser of her twin functions. In reality the more important would be using her empathic Gift to assess—and, one hoped, neutralize—any danger to the Queen and Heir from those about to come within striking distance of them. The full High Court ceremonial costumes included a wide variety of instruments of potential mayhem and assassination.

There was one small problem with this; Talia was farmbred, not highborn. The elaborate tabards of state that a highborn child could read as easily as a book were little more than bewildering patterns of gold and embroidery to *her* eyes. And she would be dealing with nobles who were very touchy over their titles, and apt to take affront if even the least and littlest were eliminated.

That meant hours closeted in Herald Kyril's office, sitting until her behind went numb on one of the hard wooden chairs he favored, memorizing plate after plate from the state book of devices until her eyes were watering. She fell asleep at night with the wildly colored and imaginative beasts, birds, and plants spinning in mad dances behind her eyes. She woke in the morning with Kyril's voice echoing out of her dreams, inescapably drilling her.

She spent at least another hour of every day in the stuffy Council chamber, with the Councilors engaged in pointless debate about this or that item of protocol for the coming ceremony until she wanted to scream with frustration.

Elspeth, at least, was spared this nonsense; *she* had quite enough on her plate with her new round of Collegium classes and duties. For the next five years or so, once the ceremony was complete, she would be neither more nor less important nor cosseted than any other trainee—within certain limitations. She would still be attending Council sessions once she'd settled in, and certain High Court functions. But these were far more in the nature of duties rather than treats—and were, in fact, things Talia reckoned that Elspeth would really rather have foregone if she'd had any choice in the matter.

When Talia had taken the opportunity to check on her, the girl seemed well-content. She was surely enjoying the new-found bond with her Companion Gwena. Keren had told Talia that every free moment saw the two of them out in the Field together, which was exactly as it should be.

But there was one unsettling oddity about the Council sessions that kept them from sending Talia to sleep—an oddity that, in fact, was contributing to an uneasiness ill-suited to the general festive atmosphere that hovered over Court and Collegium.

Talia was catching Councilors and courtiers alike giving her bewildered, almost fearful glances when they thought she wasn't watching. If it had not happened so frequently, she might have thought she was imagining it, but scarcely a day passed without someone watching her with the same attention they might have given to some outre creature that *might* prove to be dangerous. It troubled her—and she wished more than once for Skif and his talents at spying and subterfuge. But Skif was furlongs away at very best, so she knew she'd have to muddle along beneath the suspicious glances, and hope that whatever rumors were being passed about her (and she had no doubt that they *were* about her) would either be put to rest or come to light where she could confront them.

Another goodly portion of each day she spent helping to train a young Healer, Rynee, who was to substitute for her while she was gone on her internship circuit. Rynee, like Talia, was a mindHealer; she could never replace Talia, not without being a Herald herself, but she could (and would) try to keep her senses alert for Heralds in stress and distress, and get them somewhat sorted out.

And last, but by no means least, there were exhausting bouts with Alberich, all with the express purpose of getting both Talia and Elspeth prepared for any kind of assassination attempts that might occur.

"I really don't understand why you're doing this," Elspeth said one day, about a week from the date of the ceremony. "After all, I'm the one who's the better fighter." She had been watching from a vantage point well out of the way, sitting cross-legged on one of the benches in the salle, against the wall. Talia was absolutely sodden with sweat, and bruised in more places than she cared to think about—and for a wonder, Alberich wasn't in any better condition than she.

Alberich motioned to Talia that she could rest, and she sagged to the floor where she stood. "Appearances," he said, "partially. I do not wish that any save the Heralds should know how skilled you truly are. That could be the saving of your life, one day. Also it is tradition that crowned heads do not defend themselves; that is the duty of others."

"Unless there's no other choice?"

Alberich nodded.

Elspeth sighed. "I'm beginning to wish I wasn't Heir, now. It doesn't look like I'm going to be allowed to have *any* fun!"

"Catling," Talia panted, "If this is your idea of *fun*—you're welcome to it!"

Elspeth and Alberich exchanged rueful glances that said as plainly as words, *she'll never understand,* and made shrugs so nearly identical that Talia was hard put to keep from laughing.

Finally the day arrived for the long awaited—and dreaded—rite of Elspeth's formal investiture as Heir. The fealty ceremony was scheduled for the evening with a revel to follow. Talia, as usual, was running late.

She dashed from her last drilling session with Kyril to the bathing-room, then up to her tower suite, taking the steps two at a time. She thanked the gods when she got there that one of the servants had had the foresight to lay out her gown and all its accoutrements, else she'd have been later still.

She donned the magnificent silk and velvet creation with trepidation. She'd never worn High Court ceremonials in her life, though she'd helped Elspeth into her own often enough.

She faced the mirror, balancing on one foot while she tied the ribbons to the matching slippers around the ankle of the other.

"Oh, bloody hell," she sighed. She knew what a courtier ought to look like—and she didn't. "Well, it's going to have to do. I just wish . . ."

"You wish what?"

Jeri and Keren rapped on the side of the tower

door and poked their heads around the edge of it. Talia groaned; Jeri looked the way she *wished* she looked, gowned and coiffed exquisitely, every chestnut hair neatly twisted into a High Court confection and precisely in place.

"I wish I could look like you—stunning, instead of stunned."

Jeri laughed; to look at her, no one would ever guess this lady was nearly the equal of Alberich in neatly dissecting an opponent with any weapon at hand. "It's all practice, love. Want some help?" Her green eyes sparkled. "I've been doing this sort of nonsense since I was old enough to walk, and mama usually commandeered all the servants in the house to attend *her* preparations, so I had to learn how to do it myself."

"If you can make me look less like a plowboy, I will love you forever!"

"I think," Jeri replied merrily, "that we can manage at least that much."

For the next half hour Talia sat on her bed in nervous anticipation as arcane things happened to her hair and face while Jeri and Keren exchanged mysterious comments. Finally Jeri handed her a mirror.

"Is that *me*?" Talia asked in amazement, staring at the worldly sophisticate in the mirror frame. She could scarcely find a trace of Jeri's handiwork, yet somehow she had added experience and a certain dignity without adding years or subtracting freshness. Replacing her usual disordered tumble of curls was a fashionable creation threaded through with a silver ribbon.

"Do I dare move? Is it all going to come apart?"

"Havens, no!" Jeri laughed, "That's what the ribbon's for, love. It isn't likely to happen this time, praise the Lord, but you know very well what your duty is in an emergency. The Queen's Own is supposed to be able to defend her monarch at swordpoint, then calmly clean her blade on the loser's tunic and go right back to whatever ceremony was taking place. That's why your dress is ankle-length instead of floor-length, has no train, and the sleeves detach with one pull—yes, they do, trust me! I ought to know; I supervised the making of it. It's been a long time since we've had a female Monarch's Own, and nobody knew exactly how to modify High Court gear to suit. At any rate, you could work out now with Alberich without one lock coming loose or losing any part of the costume you didn't want to lose. But don't rub your eyes, or you'll look like you've been beaten." She gathered her things. "We'd better be moving if we don't want to get caught in the mob."

"And you'd better take care of the important part of your costume, childing," Keren warned as they started down the stairs.

Talia had not needed the reminder. The rest of her accessories were already laid out and waiting. A long dagger in a sheath strapped around her waist and along her right thigh that she could reach—as she carefully determined—through a slit in her dress was the first weapon she donned. Then came paired throwing knives in quick-release sheaths for both arms—gifts from Skif, which he had shown her how to use long ago. Even Alberich admitted that Skif had no peer when it came to his chosen weapons. Lastly, were two delicate stilettos furnished with winking, jeweled ornaments that she inserted carefully into Jeri's handiwork.

No Herald was ever without a weapon, especially not the Queen's Own, as Keren had reminded her. The life of more than one Monarch had been saved by just such precautions.

Just as Talia was about to depart, there was a knock at her door. She opened it to find Dean Elcarth standing on her threshold. Towering over him, fair and raven heads side by side, lit by the lantern that cast its light beside her door and looking like living representatives of Day and Night, were Dirk and Kris. Talia had not heard that either of them had returned from the field, and surprise stilled her voice as she stared at the unexpected visitors.

"Neither of these gallants seems to have a lady," the Dean said with mischief in his eyes. "And since you have no escort, I thought of you immediately."

"How thoughtful," Talia said dryly, finally regaining the use of her wits, and knowing there was more to it than that. "I don't suppose you had any other motives, did you?"

"Well, since you *are* interning under Kris, I thought you might like to get acquainted under calmer circumstances than the last time you met."

So Kris *was* to be her counselor. Sheri had been right.

"Calmer?" Talia squeaked. "You call *this* calmer?"

"Relatively speaking."

"Elcarth!" Dirk exclaimed impatiently. "Herald Talia, he's teasing you. He asked us to help you because we know most of the people here on sight, so we can prompt you if you get lost."

"We also know who the possible troublemakers are—not that we expect any problems," Kris continued, a smile warming his sky-blue eyes. "But there's less likely to be any trouble with two great hulking brutes like us standing behind the Queen."

"Oh, bless you!" Talia exclaimed with relief. "I've been worried half to death that I'll say something wrong or announce the wrong person and mortally offend someone." She carefully avoided mentioning assassination attempts, though she knew all four of them were thinking about how useful the pair would be in *that* event.

Kris smiled broadly, and Dirk executed a courtly bow that was saved from absurdity by the twinkle in his eyes as he glanced up at her.

"We are your servants, O fairest of Heralds," he

intoned, sounding a great deal like an over-acting player in some truly awful romantic drama.

"Oh, don't be ridiculous." Talia flushed, feeling oddly flattered and yet uncomfortable, "You know very well that Nessa and Sheri make me look like a squirrel, and the last time you saw me, I was passing out at your feet like a silly child and probably looked like leftover porridge. Among. friends my name is Talia. *Just* Talia."

The Dean pivoted and trotted down the staircases, seemingly very pleased with himself. Kris chuckled and Dirk grinned; both of them offered her their arms. She accepted both, feeling dwarfed between the two of them. There was barely enough room for all three of them on the stairs.

"Well, you devil, you've done it again," Dirk said to his partner over her head, blinking as they emerged from the half-dark of the staircase into the light of the hall. "I get a scrawny ex-thief with an appetite like a horse for my internee, and look what you get! It's just not fair." He looked down at her from his lofty six-and-a-half feet, and said mournfully to her, "I suppose now that you've gotten a good look at my partner's justifiably famous face, the rest of us don't stand a chance with you."

"I wouldn't go making any bets if I were you," she replied with a hint of an edge to her voice, "I *have* seen him before, you know, and you don't see me falling at his feet worshiping now, do you? My father and brothers were just as handsome. No insult meant to you, Kris, but I've had ample cause to mistrust handsome men. I'd rather you were cross-eyed, or had warts, or something. I'd feel a great deal more comfortable around you if you were a little less than perfect."

Dirk howled with laughter at the nonplussed expression on his friend's face. "That's a new one for you, my old and rare! Rejected by a woman! How's it feel to be in *my* shoes?"

"Odd," Kris replied with good humor, "distinctly odd. I must say though, I'm rather relieved. I was afraid Elcarth's mind was going, assigning me a female internee. I've only seen you once or twice, remember, and we weren't exchanging much personal information at the time! I thought you might be like Nessa. Around her I start to feel like a hunted stag!" He suddenly looked sheepish. "I have the feeling I may have put my foot in it; I hope you don't mind my being frank."

"Not at all. It's my besetting sin, too."

"Well, you seem unexpectedly sensible. I think we'll do all right together."

"Provided that *I* haven't taken a dislike to *you*." Talia was just a little nettled at his easy assumption that she would fall swift prey to his admittedly charming manner. "Haven't you ever been told not to count your eggs till the hens lay them?"

From the look on Kris' face, that possibility hadn't occurred to him, and he was rather at a loss to deal with it. Dirk didn't help matters by becoming hysterical.

"She's got you there, old boy!" he choked. "Stars be praised, I've lived to see the day when it's *you* that gets put in his place, and not me!"

"Oh, Bright Havens, don't worry about it," Talia said, taking pity on him. "We're both *Heralds,* for pity's sake! We'll manage to get along. It's just for a year and a half. After all, it's not as if somebody were forcing me to *marry* you!"

Kris' expression was indescribable when Talia spoke of being "forced" to marry him as if it were something distasteful.

"I'm fairly sure you didn't insult me, but that certainly didn't sound like a compliment!" he complained forlornly. "I'm beginning to think I prefer Nessa's attitude after all!"

By now they'd had to stop in the middle of the hall, as Dirk was doubled over and tears were streaming down his face. Both of them had to pound on his back in order to help him catch his breath again.

"Holy—Astera—" he gasped. "This is something I never expected to see. Or hear! Whew!" He somehow managed to look both contrite and satisfied at the same time. "Forgive me, partner. It's just that seeing *you* as the rejected one for a change—you should have seen your own face!—you looked like you'd swallowed a live toad!"

"Which means that nothing worse can happen to him for the rest of the week. Now look, none of this is getting us to the ceremony," Talia pointed out, "and we're already running late."

"She's right again," Dirk said, taking her arm.

"What do you mean, 'again'?" Kris asked suspiciously, as they hurried to the Great Hall.

Fortunately, their arrival at the door of the Great Hall prevented his having to answer that question.

Dirk had been having a little trouble sorting out some very odd feelings from the moment that Talia had answered her door. The last time he'd seen the Queen's Own, she'd fainted from total exhaustion practically at his feet, after having undergone a considerable mental and emotional ordeal. He had learned afterward that she had experienced at firsthand the murder of the Herald-Courier Ylsa, and saved Ylsa's lifemate Keren from death-willing herself in shock. Then, without a pause for rest, she had mentally guided him and his partner to the spot where Ylsa had been slain. This slight, fragile-seeming woman-child had aroused all of his protective instincts as well as his admiration for her raw courage. He'd carried her up to her room himself, and made certain she was safely tucked into her bed; then left medicinal tea ready for her to brew to counteract the inevitable reaction-headache she'd have when she woke. He'd known at the time she'd exhausted all her resources—when he heard the whole story later in the day he'd been flabbergasted at her courage and endurance.

And she was so very frail-looking; it was easy to feel protective about her, even though her actions gave lie to that frail appearance. At least, he'd thought at the time that it was only his protective instincts that she aroused. But the sight of her this time had seemed to stir something a bit more complicated than that—something he wasn't entirely sure he'd wanted to acknowledge. So he defused the situation as best he could, by clowning with Kris. But even while he was bent double with laughter, there was a vague disquiet in the back of his mind, as though his subconscious was trying to warn him that he wasn't going to be able to delay acknowledgment for long.

Talia was refusing to allow her nerves to show, but they were certainly affecting her despite her best efforts. She was rather guiltily hoping Kris had realized that she had been taking some of that nervousness out on him.

The Great Hall, tables cleared away, and benches placed along the walls, with every candle and lantern lit, gleamed like a box made of gold. The courtiers and notables were dressed in their finest array, jewels and silver and gold ornaments catching the light and throwing it back so that the assemblage sparkled like the contents of a highborn dame's jewelbox. Prominent among the gilded nobles were the bright scarlet of Bards, the emerald green of Healers, the bright blue of the uniforms of high-ranking officers of the Guard and Army, and the brilliant white of Heralds. Each of those to be presented wore over his or her finery the stiff tabard, heavy with embroidery, that marked a family or Guild association. The men and women of the Guards standing duty in their sober midnight-blue and silver ringed the walls, a dark frame for the rest.

The Queen's Own and her escorts assumed their places behind the thrones, Talia in her place behind and to Selenay's right, Kris and Dirk behind and to

either side of her. Talia had a feeling that the three
of them made a very impressive and reassuring sight
to those who had come here fearing to see weakness.

But there was uneasiness, too—the uneasiness she
had been sensing for the past three weeks, magni-
fied. And she could not, for the life of her, fathom
the reason.

The ceremony began; Talia determined to ignore
what she could not change, and did her best to
appear somehow both harmless and competent. She
wasn't sure just how successful she was, but some of
the background of general nervousness *did* seem to
decrease after a while.

She tried to will some confidence into the young
Heir, who was beginning to wilt under the strain.
She tried to catch her eyes and give her a reassuring
smile, but Elspeth's expression was tight and nervous, and her eyes were beginning to glaze.

For Elspeth was not faring as well as Talia. The
ceremony demanded that she respond to each of her
new liegemen with some sort of personalized speech,
and about halfway through she began running out
of things to say.

Kris was the first, with his musician's ear for ca-
dence, to notice her stumbling and hesitating over
her speeches. As the next worthy was being brought
before her, he whispered, "His son's just presented
him with his first grandchild."

Elspeth cast him a look of undying gratitude as
she moved to receive this oath. As the gouty lord
rose with difficulty from his knees, she congratu-
lated him on the blessed event. The gentleman's
expression as he was escorted away was compounded
of equal parts of startlement and pleasure, for he'd
no notion that anyone knew other than the immediate members of his family.

Elspeth decided at that moment that Kris was fully
qualified for elevation to sainthood, and beamed

quickly at both of the Heralds before the next notable arrived.

Dirk caught on immediately and supplied the information for the next. Kris countered with intelligence for the following two. Elspeth began to sparkle under the gratified looks of the courtiers, reviving as quickly as she'd wilted; and Kris and Dirk began to keep score in the impromptu contest. The Queen seemed to find it all she could do to keep a straight face.

Finally, the last dignitary made his oath, and all three Heralds took their places with the Circle to swear their oaths en masse. The Healer's and Bardic Circles followed them, then the various clerics and priests made vows on behalf of their orders and devotees.

And the long ceremony was at last complete—without a mishap.

The Queen's party retired from the dais, leaving it to instrumentalists of the Bardic Circle, who immediately struck up a dance melody.

Talia joined Elspeth in the window-alcove furnished with velvet-padded benches that was reserved for the Queen's entourage. "What were you three up to?" she asked curiously. "I was too far away to hear any of it, but you certainly seemed to be having a good time!"

"These two Heralds that came as your escort—they were wonderful!" Elspeth bubbled. "I ran out of things to say, and they told me exactly what I needed to know. Not big things, but what was most important to them right now—the lords and so forth, I mean. Then they started making a contest out of it, and that was what was so funny, them arguing back and forth about how much something was 'worth' in points. Mother could hardly keep from laughing."

"I can imagine," Talia grinned, "Who won?"

"I did," Kris said from behind her.

"You wouldn't have if I'd thought of the sheep first," Dirk retorted.

"Sheep?" Talia said inquisitively. "Sheep? Do I want to know about this?"

Dirk snickered, and Kris glared at him.

"It's perfectly harmless," Kris answered, with just a hint of irritation. "When Lady Fiona's husband died, she and Guildmistress Arawell started a joint project to boost the fortunes of her family and Arawell's branch of the Weaver's Guild. They imported some sheep with an especially soft and fine fleece much like lambswool from outKingdom—quite far south. They've finally succeeded in adapting them to our harsher winters; the spring lambing more than doubled their flock, and it seems that everyone is going to want stock or fabric of the wool."

"That's not what we came here for," Dirk said firmly. "Sheep and discussions of animal husbandry—keep your filthy thoughts to yourself, partner!—"

"*My* filthy thoughts? Who was the one doing all the chortling a few minutes ago?"

"—do not belong at a revel. I claim the first dance with you, Talia, by virtue of the fact that my partner is going to have you all to himself for a year and more."

"And since that leaves me partnerless," Kris added, "I would very much like to claim our newest Chosen for the same purpose."

"Mother?" Elspeth looked pleadingly at the Queen. Kris' stunning good looks had made more than a slight impression on her, and that he should want to dance with her was a distinct thrill.

"My dear, this is *your* celebration. If you want to ride your Companion around the Great Hall, you could even do that—provided you're willing to face the Seneschal's wrath when he sees the hoofmarks on his precious wood floor."

Without waiting for further permission, Kris swept the girl into the dance.

Dirk lifted an inquisitive eyebrow at Talia.

"Oh, no," Talia laughed, "You don't know what you're asking. I dance like a plowboy, I have no sense of rhythm, and I ruin my partner's feet."

"Nonsense," Dirk replied, shaking unruly blond hair out of his eyes. "You just never had the right partner."

"Which is you? And I thought Kris was vain!"

"My dear Talia," he countered, swinging her onto the floor, "Truth can hardly be considered in the same light as vanity. I have it on the best authority that my dancing more than compensates for my looks."

Shortly, Talia was forced to admit that he was absolutely correct. For the first time in her experience, she began to enjoy a dance—it was almost magical, the way they seemed to move together. Dirk didn't seem displeased by her performance either, as he yielded her to other partners with extreme reluctance.

Kris, on the other hand, despite yearning glances from nearly every young woman present, danced only with women far older than himself, or with Elspeth or Talia.

"I hope you don't mind being used like this," he said contritely, after the sixth or seventh dance.

"Used?" she replied, puzzled.

"As a shield. I'm dancing with you to keep from being devoured by *them*," he nodded toward a group of Court beauties languishing in his direction. "I can't dance just with beldames, Elspeth has to take other partners, and the only Heralds I can trust not to try to carry me off are Keren, Sheri, and you. And those other two don't dance."

"It's nice to know I'm wanted," she laughed up at him.

"Did I just put my foot in it again?"

"No, not really. And I don't mind being 'used.' After all, by now they all know we're assigned together, so they'll assume we're getting acquainted. You can avoid people without anyone's feelings being hurt."

"You *do* understand," he said, relieved. "I hate to hurt anyone's feelings, but they all seem to think if they just throw themselves at me hard enough, I'll *have* to take one of them—short-term, long-term, it doesn't seem to matter. Nobody ever seems to wonder what *I* want."

"Well, what *do* you want?" Talia asked.

"The Collegium," he replied to Talia's amazement, "That's where most of my time and energy go—and where I want them to go. I do a lot of studying on my own: history, administration, law. I'd like to be Elcarth's replacement as Dean and Historian when he retires, and that takes a lot of preparation. I don't have much free time—certainly none to spend on games of courtly love. Or shepherd-in-the-hay."

Talia looked at him with new respect. "That's marvelous; Elcarth's job is the hardest and most thankless I can think of. In some ways, it's even worse than mine. You might just be the one to handle it. I don't think you can serve the Collegium and still give another person a—a—"

"The amount of attention a decent pairing needs," he finished for her, "Thank you—do you know, you're the first person besides Dirk who didn't think I was out of my mind?"

"But what would you do if you *did* find someone you wanted?"

"I don't know—except that it isn't likely to happen. Face it, Talia, Heralds seldom form permanent attachments to anyone or anything. We're friends, always, and sometimes things get more intense than that, but it doesn't last for long. Maybe it's because our hearts are given first to our Companions, then to our duty—and I guess there aren't too many of us with hearts big enough for a third love. Non-Heralds don't seem to be able to grasp that. Not too many

Heralds do, for that matter. But look around you—
Sherrill and Keren are the *only* lifebonded couple I
can think of, and I wouldn't be willing to settle for
less than what they've got. Which is why I'm hiding
behind you."

"You can't hide forever."

"I don't have to," he replied whimsically. "Just till
the end of the revel. After that, I'll be safely in the
field, accompanied solely by the only person I've met
who thinks I'd be better off cross-eyed and covered
with warts!"

Dirk reclaimed her after that; it was during that
dance that she noticed that the number of white-clad
bodies was rapidly diminishing. "Where's everyone
gone?" she asked him, puzzled.

"It's not often that we get this many of us together
at one time," he replied, "so as people get tired of
dancing, we slip off to our own private party. Want
to go?"

"Bright Havens, yes!" she replied with enthusiasm.

"Let me catch Kris' eye." He moved them closer to
where Kris was dancing with a spritely grandmother,
and tilted an eyebrow toward the door. When Kris
nodded, Dirk arranged for them to end the dance
next to the exit as the musicians played the final
phrase.

Kris joined them after escorting his partner to her
seat. "I like that one; she kept threatening to take me
home, feed me 'proper'—and then 'train me right,'
and I know she wasn't talking about dancing or
manners!" He laughed quietly. "I take it Talia's ready
to go? I am."

"Good, then we're all agreed," Dirk replied. "Talia,
go get changed into something comfortable, find
something to sit on, and an old cloak in case we end
up outside. If you play any instruments, bring them,
too—then meet us in the Library."

"This is like the littles' game of 'Spy'!" she giggled.

"You're not far wrong," Kris answered, "We go to

great lengths to keep these parties private. Now hurry, or we'll leave without you!"

She gathered her skirts in both hands and ran lightly down the halls of the Palace. When she reached her tower, she again took the steps two at a time. She paused only long enough in her room to light a lamp before unlacing her dress and sliding out of it. Even though she was in a hurry she hung it up with care—there was no use in ruining it with creases. She changed into the first things that came to hand. She freed her hair from the ribbon, letting it tumble around her face while she carefully stored My Lady in her case, and stuck her shepherd's pipe in her belt. She slung the carrying strap of the harpcase over her shoulder, an old, worn wool cloak from her trainee days over all, picked up one of her cushions, and was ready to go.

Well, almost. Remembering what Jeri had said about the cosmetics, she stopped at the bathing room at the base of the tower for a quick wash, then ran for the Library.

When she swung open the door to the Library, she discovered that the other two had beaten her there— but then, they probably didn't have several flights of stairs to climbs.

Kris was all in black, and looking too poetic for words. Dirk was in mismatched bluish grays that looked rather as if he'd just left them in a heap when he'd picked up his clean laundry (which, in fact, was probably the case). Both of them looked up at the sound of the door opening.

"Talia! Good—you don't dawdle like my sisters do," Dirk greeted her. "Come over here, and we'll let you in on the secret."

Talia crossed the room to where they were standing; the first study cubicle.

"The first to leave always meet here to decide where we're going to convene," Dirk explained, "And they leave something telling the rest of us where that is. In this case—it's this."

He showed her a book left on the table—on harness-making.

"Let me guess," Talia said. "The stable?"

"Close. The tackshed in Companion's Field; see, it's open at the chapter on the special bridles we use," Kris explained. "Last time they had to leave a rock on top of a copy of a religious text; we used the half-finished temple down near the river because we'd met too often around here. A bit cold for my liking, though I'm told those currently keeping company enjoyed keeping each other warm."

Talia smothered giggles as they slipped outside.

The windows of the tackshed had been tightly shuttered so that no light leaked out to betray the revelry within. Both fireplaces had been lighted against the slight chill in the air and as the main source of illumination. The three of them slipped in as quietly as possible to avoid disturbing the entertainment in progress—a tale being told with some skill by a middle-aged Herald whose twin streaks of gray, one at each temple, stood out startlingly in the firelight.

"It'll be quiet tonight," Kris whispered in Talia's ear. "Probably because the Palace revel turned into such a romp. Our revels tend to be the opposite of the official ones."

Heralds were sprawled over the floor of the tackshed in various comfortable poses, all giving rapt attention to the storyteller. There seemed to be close to seventy of them; the most Talia had ever seen together at one time. Apparently every Herald within riding distance had arranged to be here for the fealty ceremony. The storyteller concluded his tale to the sighs of satisfaction of those around him. Then, with the spell of the story gone, many of them leaped up to greet the newcomers, hugging the two men or grasping their hands with warm and heart-felt affection. Since they were uniformly strangers to Talia, she shrank back shyly into the shadows by the door.

"Whoa, there—slow down, friends!" Dirk chuckled, extricating himself from the press of greeters. "We've brought someone to meet all of you."

He searched the shadows, found Talia, and reaching out a long arm, pulled her fully into the light. "You all know we've finally got a true Queen's Own again—and here she is!"

Before anyone could move to greet her, there was a whoop of joy from the far side of the room, and a hurtling body bounced across it, vaulting over several Heralds who laughed, ducked, and protected their heads with their arms. The leaper reached Talia and picked her up bodily, lifting her high into the air, and setting her down with an enthusiastic kiss.

"Skif?" she gasped.

"Every inch of me!" Skif crowed.

"B-but—you're so *tall!*" When he'd gotten his Whites, Skif hadn't topped her by more than an inch or two. Now he could easily challenge Dirk's height.

"I guess something in the air of the south makes things grow, 'cause I sure did last year," Skif chuckled. "Ask Dirk—he was my counselor."

"Grow? Bright Stars, *grow* is too tame a word!" Dirk groaned. "We spent half our time keeping him fed; he ate more than our mules!"

"You've done pretty well yourself, I'd say," Skif went on, pointedly ignoring Dirk. "You looked fine up there. Made us all damn proud."

Talia blushed, glad it wouldn't show in the dim light. "I've had a lot of help," she said, almost apologetically.

"It takes more than a lot of help, and we both know it," he retorted. "Well, hellfire, this isn't the time or place for talk about work. You two—you know the rules. Entrance fee!"

Dirk and Kris were laughingly pushed to the center of the room, as the story teller vacated his place for them. "Anybody bring a harp?" Kris called. "Mine's still packed; I just got in today."

"I did," Talia volunteered, and eager hands reached out to convey the harp, still in the case, to Kris.

"Is this—this can't be My Lady, can it?" Kris asked as the firelight gleamed on the golden wood and the clean, delicate lines. "I wondered who Jadus had left her to." He ran his fingers reverently across the strings, and they sighed sweetly. "She's in perfect tune, Talia. You've been caring for her as she deserves."

Without waiting for an answer, he began playing an old lullaby. Jadus had been a better player, but Kris was surprisingly good for an amateur, and much better than Talia. He made an incredibly beautiful picture, with the golden wood gleaming against his black tunic, and his raven head bent in concentration over the strings. He was almost as much a pleasure to watch as to listen to.

"Any requests?" he asked when he'd finished.

" 'Sun and Shadow,' " several people called out at once.

"All right," Dirk replied, "But I want a volunteer to sing Shadowdancer. The last time I did it, I was hoarse for a month."

"I could," Talia heard herself saying, to her surprise.

"You?" Dirk seemed both pleased and equally surprised. "You're full of amazing things, aren't you?" He made room beside himself; and Talia picked her way across the crowded floor, to sit shyly in the shadow he cast in the firelight.

"Sun and Shadow" told of the meeting of two of the earliest Heralds, Rothas Sunsinger and Lythe Shadowdancer; long before they were ever Chosen and while their lives still remained tangled by strange curses. It was a duet for male and female voice, though Dirk had often sung it all himself. It was one of those odd songs that either made you hold your breath or bored you to tears, depending on how it was sung. Dirk wondered which it would be tonight.

As Talia began her verse in answer to his, Dirk

stopped wondering. There was no doubt who'd trained her—the deft phrasing that made the most of her delicate, slightly breathy voice showed Jadus' touch as clearly as the harp he'd left her. But she sang with something more than just her mind and voice, something the finest training couldn't impart. This was going to be one of the magic times.

Dirk surrendered himself to the song, little guessing that he was surpassing his own best this night as well. Kris knew, as he accompanied them—and he wished there was a way to capture the moment for all time.

The spontaneous applause that shook the rafters startled both Dirk and Talia out of the spell the music had wrapped them in. Dirk smiled with more than usual warmth at the tiny female half-hiding in his shadow, and felt his smile returned.

"Well, we've paid *our* forfeit," Kris said, cutting short the demands for more. "It's somebody else's turn now."

"That's not fair," a voice from the back complained, "How could any of us possibly follow *that*?"

Someone did, of course, by changing the mood rather than ruining it by trying to sustain it. A tall, bony fellow borrowed Talia's pipe to play a lively jig, while two men and a woman bounded into the center to dance to it. That seemed to decide everyone on a dancing-set; Talia reclaimed her pipe to join Kris, someone with a gittern, and Jeri on tambour in a series of very lively round dances of the village festival variety. As these were both strenuous and of an accelerated tempo, those who had felt lively enough to dance were soon exhausted and ready to become an audience again.

Those who didn't feel up to entertaining paid their "entrance fee" in food and drink; Talia saw a good many small casks of wine, cider, and ale ranged along the walls, and with them, baskets of fruit, sausages, or bread and cheese. Stray mugs and odd cups were always accumulating in the tackshed, especially during the hot summer months when Heralds and students were likely to need a draught of cool water from the well that supplied the Companions' needs at this end of the Field. These handy receptacles were filled and refilled and passed from hand to hand with a gay disregard for the possibility of colds or fever being passed with the drink. Like Talia, most of the Heralds had brought cushions from their quarters; these and their saddles and packs were piled into comfortable lounges that might be shared or not. A few murmurs from some of the darker corners made Talia hastily avert her eyes and close her ears, and she recalled Dirk's earlier comments about Heralds "keeping each other warm." From time to time some of these rose from the dark, and either left for more private surroundings or rejoined those by the two fires. And over all was an atmosphere of—belonging. There was no one here that was not cared for and welcomed by all the rest. It was Talia's first exposure to a gathering of her fellows under pleasant circumstances, and she gradually realized that the feeling of oneness extended outside the walls as well—to the Companions in the Field, and beyond that, to those who could not be present this night. Small wonder, with such a warmth of brotherhood to bask in, that the Heralds had deserted the main revelry for this more intimate celebration of their joy at the Choosing of the Heir. It was enough to make her forget the strange uneasiness that had been shadowing her the past three weeks.

As soon as she could manage it, Talia retrieved Skif from a knot of year-mates who seemed bent on emptying a particular cask by themselves.

"Let's go up to the loft," she said, after scanning that perch and ascertaining that none of the amorous had chosen it themselves. "I don't want to disturb anybody, but I don't want to leave, either."

The "loft" was little more than a narrow balcony that ran the length of one side and gave access to storage places in the rafters. Talia noticed immediately that Skif—*very* uncharacteristically—kept to the wall on the stairs, and put his back against it when they reached the loft itself.

"Lord and Lady, it's good to see you!" he exclaimed softly, giving her a repeat of his earlier hug. "We weren't sure we'd make it back in time. In fact, we left all the baggage and the mules back at a Resupply Station; took only what Cymry and Ahrodie could carry besides ourselves. I've missed you, little sister. The letters helped, but I'd rather have been able to talk with you, especially—"

Talia could sense him fighting a surge of what could only be fear.

"Especially?"

"—after—the accident."

She moved closer to him, resting both her hands on his. She didn't have to see him to know he was pale and white-knuckled. "Tell me."

"I—can't."

She lowered her shields; he was spiky inside with phobic fears; of storms, of entrapment; and most of all, of falling. In the state he was in now, she doubted he'd be able to look out a second-story window without exerting iron control—and this from the young man who'd led her on a scramble across the face of the second story of the Palace itself, one dark night!

"Remember me? What I am? Just start at the beginning; take it slowly. I'll help you face it down."

He swallowed. "It—it started with a storm; we were caught out on the trail in the hills. Hills, ha! More like mountains! Gods, it was dark; rain was pouring down so hard I couldn't even see Cymry's ears. Dirk had point, the mules were next, I was tail—it was supposed to be the safest place. We were more or less feeling our way along; sheer rock on one side of us, ravine on the other."

Talia had herself in half-trance, carefully extending herself into his mind. He was fighting down his fear as he spoke and beginning to lose to it.

"The trail just—crumbled, right under Cymry's hooves. We fell; there wasn't even time to yell for help."

Gently, Talia touched the fear, took it into herself, and began working away at it. It was like knife-edged flint, all points and slicing surfaces. As softly as flowing water, and as inexorably, she began wearing away at it, dulling it, muting it.

"We ended up wedged halfway down. Cymry was stunned; I'd broken my arm and most of my ribs, I think; I don't remember much. It hurt too much to think, and where I was stuck, there was a flood of water pouring down the wall like a young waterfall. You know I don't Mindspeak too well, and Dirk's Gift isn't Mindspeech anyway; I couldn't get hold of myself enough to call for help that way, and it was impossible to be heard over the storm."

He was shaking like a reed in a windstorm; she put her arm around his shoulders; supplying a physical comfort as well as the mental. "But Dirk found you," she pointed out.

"The Gods alone know how; he had no reason to think we were still alive." The tension was rapidly draining out of him as Talia shielded him from the phobic memories; not enough to make him forget, but enough to make them less real, less obsessive. "He got ropes around both of us and anchored us where we were; used something to divert the water away from me, and stayed with us, hanging on with his teeth and toenails, until the storm was over. Then he got blankets over us and sent Ahrodie off for help while he got me back up to the trail. I don't remember that part at all; I must have blacked out from the pain." His voice sounded less strained.

The fear was nearly conquered now; time to diffuse the rest of it. "You must have looked like a drowned rat," she replied with a hint of chuckle. "I know you have a fetish for cleanliness, but don't you think that was overdoing it a bit?"

He stared at her in surprise, then began to laugh, shakily. The laughter was half tears as the last of the tension was released. Hysterics—yes, but long needed.

She held him quietly until the worst passed, and he could see past the tears to her face, childlike in the half-dark.

The paralysis of fear that Skif had lived with on a daily basis for the past several months had all but choked the voice out of him as he tried to tell Talia what had happened that awful night. He'd suffered nightmare replays of the incident at least one night a week ever since. It had taken all of his control to repeat it to her—at least at first. But then, gradually, the words had begun to flow more freely; the fear had slowly loosed its grip on him. As he neared the end of his narrative, he began to realize what Talia had done.

It was gratitude as much as release that shook the tears from him then.

"You—you did it to me, didn't you—fixed me like you did with Vostel and the rest of them—?"

"Mm-hm," she nodded, touching his hair in the dark. "I didn't think you'd mind."

"No more nightmares?"

"No more nightmares, big brother. You won't find yourself wanting to hide in a closet during storms anymore, and you'll be able to look down over cliffs again. In fact, you'll even be able to tell the story in a week or two without shaking like a day-old chick, and it should make a good tale to earn the sympathy of a pretty lady with!"

"You—you're unbelievable," he said at last, holding her tightly.

"So are you, to have been coping with all that fear all this time, and not letting it get the best of you."

They sat that way for some time, before the mur-

mur of voices below them recalled them to their surroundings.

"Hellfire! This is supposed to be a party, and you're supposed to be enjoying it," Skif said at last.

"I am, now that you're all right." She rose to her feet, and gave him a hand up. "Well, I'm going back to the singing, and it seems to me that your year-mate Mavry is looking a bit lonely."

"Hm. So she is," he replied, peering down into the lighted area. "Think I'll go keep her company. And—heart-sister—"

"No thanks needed, love."

He kissed her forehead by way of reply, then skipped lightly down the stairs of the loft and took himself off to the other side of the room, where Mavry willingly made a space for him beside her.

Talia rejoined the musicians just in time for Dirk to claim her for another duet. She had to plead a dry throat before they'd let someone else take the floor.

She didn't notice the passing of time until she caught herself yawning hard enough to split her head in half. When she tried to reckon up how much time had passed, she was shocked.

Thinking she surely *must* be mistaken, she slipped over to the door to look out to the east. Sure enough, there on the horizon was the first hint of false dawn. True dawn was less than an hour away.

She collected her things, feeling suddenly ready to collapse. Dirk, half-propped on a backrest of saddle and several old saddleblankets, seemed to be asleep as she slipped past him, but he cracked an eyelid open as she tried to ease herself out.

"Giving up?" he asked softly.

She nodded, stifling another yawn with the back of her hand.

"Enjoy yourself?" At her enthusiastic nod, he smiled, another of those wonderful warm smiles that seemed to embrace her and close everything and everyone else outside of it. "I'll be heading back to my own bed before long. About this time things start to break up on their own. And don't worry about being expected on duty today. No one will be up to notice before noon at the earliest—look over there." He cocked an eyebrow to his left. Talia was astonished to see the Queen, dressed in old, worn leathers, sharing a cloak and resting her head in easy intimacy on the shoulder of the middle-aged storyteller. And not far from her sat Alberich, finishing the last of a wineskin with Keren, Sherrill, and Jeri.

"How did Selenay and Alberich get in without my noticing?" Talia asked him.

"Easy. You were singing at the time. See, though? You won't be missed. Have a good long sleep—and pleasant dreams, Talia."

"And to you, Dirk," she said.

"They will be," he chuckled, and closed his eyes again. "They most assuredly will be."

Three

Talia didn't usually sleep long or heavily. Perhaps the cause was that she'd drunk more wine than usual, or perhaps it was just the incredibly late hour at which she'd sought her bed. At any rate, it took having the sun shine directly into her eyes to wake her the next morning.

Since the window of her bedroom faced the east, she'd positioned her bed with the headboard right under the windowsill. That way she always had the fresh air, and her face should remain out of the sunlight until well after the time she normally rose. No matter how cold the winter, she'd never been able to bear the slight claustrophobia that closed shutters induced in her, so the glazed windows themselves and the thin fabric curtaining them were all that stood between her eyes and the sun's rays, and the windows themselves were open, with the curtains moving slightly in the breeze.

As she squinted groggily through the glare, she realized that it must be nearly noon, and as if to confirm this, the noon warning bell at the Collegium sounded clearly through her open window.

Well, the wine she'd indulged in last night had given her a slight headache. She muttered something to herself about fools and lack of judgment

66

and pulled her pillow over her head, tempted to go right back to sleep again. But a nagging sense of duty, (and, more urgently, a need to use the privy) denied her further sloth.

She'd been so tired last night—this morning?—that all she'd been able to do was peel off her clothing, leave it in a heap on the floor, and fall into bed. Now that she felt a little more awake, her skin crawled with the need for a bath. Her hair itched. Her mouth didn't bear thinking about. She groaned. It was definitely time to get up.

She sighed, levered herself out of bed, and set about getting herself back into working condition.

Sitting on the edge of the bed, she rubbed her eyes until they cooperated by focusing properly, then reached for the robe hanging on one of the posts at the foot of her bed. She wrapped it about herself, then collected the clothing on the floor. The soiled clothing went into a hamper; the servant who tended to the Heralds in this section of the wing collected it and sent it to the laundry as part of her duties—and *that* was a luxury that was going to take some getting used to! She'd been lowborn and at the bottom of her Holderkin family's pecking order as a child, and once at the Collegium had fallen naturally in with the tradition that trainees tended to their own needs and shared the common chores. She had become habituated to doing the serving, and not to being waited on herself!

The warmth of the smooth wood beneath her feet was very comforting, and she decided then that she would *not* have any floor coverings in her new quarters. She liked the way the sunwarmed boards felt to bare feet, and she liked the way the wood glowed when the sun touched it.

She rummaged in her wardrobe, and draped a new, clean uniform over one arm, then bundled her bathing things into the other arm and headed for the door.

The bathing-room shared by the other tower occupants was on the bottom floor; that was another disadvantage of having selected a tower room. It was a long walk, and seemed longer for the thinking about it. Talia was the only current occupant though. The other rooms were either unclaimed or their owners were out on circuit. So at least there wasn't going to be any competition for the facilities.

Talia saw a note waiting for her on her door as soon as she opened it. Rubbing her temple in response to the ache behind her eyes, she wondered who could be the early riser after the revelry of the previous night. She took it down and began to skim through it as she headed down the stairs. What she read caused her to stop dead and reread it thoroughly.

It was from Kyril.

I realize this is notice so short as to be nonexistent, he wrote, *but we've had an emergency since last night. The Herald currently riding one of the Northern Border Sectors has had an accident, and we have no one free who knows anything about the area to cover it. Dirk can't—he's already assigned to another Border Sector that needs a Border-bred Herald too badly to reassign him elsewhere. The closest we can come is this—since Dirk is a native of that area, Kris has visited up there fairly often; and you're of Borderer upbringing. Since you haven't been assigned a circuit yet, it seemed to me that assigning it to you as your internship with Kris would solve our problems very neatly. However, this means that you two will have to start as soon as we can get you on the road north; tomorrow, I hope. Please report to me right after the noon meal—or as soon as you read this note!—for a briefing and some final information.*

Her first thought was an irreverent and irrelevant one. She *knew* Kyril hadn't left the revel before her—how *could* he have been awake and ready to handle crises so blasted early in the morning after? Her next was more to the point. Tomorrow! She hadn't expected assignment with so little warning. There wasn't any time to waste; she ran downstairs to the bathing-room. The last thing she wanted to do was give Kyril an impression of carelessness or incompetence.

A good hot bath did a great deal to revitalize her; a dose of willowbark tea took care of the ache in her head. She couldn't do much for the half-cloudy feeling of her mind, but she hoped that being aware that she wasn't quite at her best would compensate for that. Rather than take the time for a full meal she begged cheese, bread, and fruit from Mero. She was far too keyed up to eat much, anyway. This would be the first time that she would meet with Kyril as an equal; up until now, even though she had her Whites, it had still been very much a teacher-student relationship.

She took a few moments of precious time to consult with Rolan before seeking Kyril. It was frustrating not to be able to speak with him in words—but simply Mindtouching with him gave her an added measure of calmness. He reassured her that Kyril would never have expected her to report any earlier than this, and prevented her from changing at the last minute into one of her formal uniforms. And beneath it all was the solidity of knowing that he stood ready to help her if she truly found herself out of her depth on this assignment. Feeling a good bit more confident, she skipped down the tower steps and entered the Palace proper.

A few moments later she had made her way to the administrative area. She paused outside the door of the Records Room—which served as Kyril's office—for a moment to order her mind and calm herself. She pulled the doeskin tunic straight, smoothed her hair; took a deep breath, knocked once and entered.

The Records Room was as neat as Dean Elcarth's office was cluttered. Sun streamed in through the two windows that looked out into the gardens on the west side of the building. Both of them were wide open, and flower-scent wafted in through them. The room was crammed as full of bookshelves as it was possible to be. Kyril's desk stood just under one of the two windows, to take full advantage of the light. Kyril himself was leaning in the window frame, absently watching courtiers stroll in the gardens, and obviously waiting for her. She noticed something anomalous on his desk as he turned from the window to greet her; a quiverful of white arrows.

"Sir?" she said softly; and he turned to smile greeting at her.

Kyril was pleased to see that Talia was looking alert and ready for practically anything. In the past few weeks of working with her, he had come to truly believe all that her Collegium teachers had claimed for her. The Queen's Own was always an outstanding person among Heralds, but Talia bid fair to be outstanding among the ranks of her own kind. He could not for a moment fathom why her reputation, even among her fellow Heralds, was one of being a sweet, but somewhat simple creature. He wasn't altogether certain that *he* would have been able to manage the feat of memorizing all the Kingdom's familial devices and titles in the three weeks she'd taken. Perhaps it was because she was so shy, even yet, and seldom spoke without first being spoken to. Perhaps it was because of her ability with children in general, and the Heir in particular—a strong maternal instinct was not necessarily coupled in anyone's mind with a high intellectual level.

Then again, there weren't too many even among the Heralds who had been her teachers who had seen the *real* Talia. She had not allowed very many of them to come within arm's length, as it were. Kyril was just sorry he had had so little time for her; and he sometimes worried a little about that strange Gift of hers. Empathy that strong—and having seen her exert herself, he *knew* it was very strong—was far more the Gift of Healers. He had been relieved when she'd begun spending so much time with the

Healers; *they* would know how to train her properly, if anybody would. If he had only had the time—if Ylsa hadn't been killed—

But Talia seemed to have everything perfectly under control, and if even her own peers tended to underestimate her, that surely wasn't going to harm her any.

Perhaps, though, that tendency to dismiss her lightly was not altogether a bad thing. Kyril had been dealing with Court and Council on a daily basis for something like twenty years, and being underestimated could be a potent and very useful weapon. People might not see past the guileless eyes, and tend to let their tongues run on longer leads in her presence. No, that reputation of hers might well be a very *good* thing for all of them. Certainly the disturbing rumors he'd heard lately about her would not survive much longer if people began comparing the tales of machinations with her reputation as a sweet and uncomplicated innocent.

"Sit, sit," he waved at a chair, taking one himself. "You look none the worse for your late night. I remember *my* first Herald's revel; I thought my hangover was going to last for the next week! I trust you enjoyed yourself." He smiled again as she nodded shyly. "It's the first chance I had to hear you sing. Jadus used to make us all curious, boasting about your abilities. He was certainly right about you! Last night—to tell the truth, I've heard Bards that didn't give performances that moving. You're as good as Jadus claimed, maybe better." She blushed, and he chuckled. "Well, that's neither here nor there. I am very sorry about all the hurry, but we don't like to leave Border Sectors without a Herald for very long; in this case, it's not that there's potential for trouble, but that the people of the Sector feel isolated enough as it is, particularly in winter. They need to know that they're as important to the life of this Kingdom as the capital Sector itself." He regarded her steadily; her answer to his speech would tell him a great deal.

The eyes that met his squarely held faint surprise.

"I—I thought there was always potential for trouble in a Border Sector, sir," Talia ventured. "There're raiders, bandits—lots of problems even if the people themselves never cause them."

"In the general run of things that's true, but the Border in this Sector runs through the Forest of Sorrows, and that's no small protection."

"Then the tale of Vanyel's Curse is true?" Talia was amazed. "Sorrows *does* protect the Kingdom? But . . . how?"

"I wish I knew," Kyril replied, musing half to himself, "They knew things, those old ones, that we've forgotten or lost. They had magic then—real magic, and not our mind-magic; the Truth Spell is just about all we have left of that. Vanyel's Curse is as strong in Sorrows as the day he cast it with his dying breath. Nothing that intends ill to this Kingdom or the people in it lives more than five minutes there; I've seen some of the results with my own eyes. I used to ride Northern myself, back in the days when I was still riding circuits, and not Seneschal's Herald. I've seen bandits impaled on branches as if on thrown spears. I've seen outlaws who starved to death, buried to their waist in rock-hard earth, as if it opened beneath their feet, then closed on them like a trap. What's more—and *this* is what was more frightening than the other things—I've seen barbarian raiders dead without a mark on them, but their faces twisted into an expression of complete and utter terror. I don't know what it was that happened to them, but my guess is that they were truly frightened to death."

Talia shook her head wonderingly. "It's hard to believe. How can a curse know someone's intent?"

"I can't explain it, and neither can any of the old chronicles. It's true nevertheless. You, or I, or any of the people of the Sector can walk that forest totally without fear. A baby could walk through there totally unharmed, because even the forest predators leave humans alone in Sorrows—well, that's the only anomalous thing about the area. The religion is fairly ordinary, the people follow the Lady as Astera of the Stars, and the God as Kernos of the Northern Lights; there's no anti-woman prejudice. In fact, because of Sorrows, we often have females riding circuit there alone. The Herald you're replacing is a woman, in point of fact. You may know her, she was two year-groups ahead of you—Destria."

"Destria? Havens—she isn't badly hurt, is she? What happened?"

"The injury is fairly serious, but not life-threatening. She was trying to rescue half a dozen children during a flood—it's a hard land, Talia, that's the main problem with it—and broke both legs."

"Thank the Goddess for Companions."

"Amen to that; without hers she'd have lain in sleet-born water for hours, probably died of exposure. No, Destria's Sofi managed to get not only her Herald but all the children to safety. All's well there except for the injury. So, that's the gist of the situation, and as I said, I apologize for the short notice. I hope you don't mind too much."

"Not at all sir," Talia replied, "After all, I had even less notice when I was Chosen, didn't I?"

"Good for you!" Kyril chuckled. "Well, now we come to the reason why I asked you to come here, instead of meeting you for lunch or asking you to meet with both Kris and myself to be told about this. I'm sure you realized a long time ago that there were things we wouldn't teach you until you got your Whites. What I'm about to show you is the best-kept secret of the Heraldic Circle. Haven't you ever wondered why all Heralds are required to become archers?"

"I never thought about it," she confessed, looking

puzzled. "It does seem a little odd, now that you mention it. We don't fight with the royal Archers in battle; when we do fight, it's mostly sword or hand-to-hand. We usually don't have to hunt to feed ourselves riding circuit; we carry supplies or depend on the shelters. So why do we have to learn bow?"

"So that you have an excuse to carry arrows wherever you go," Kyril replied. "Not everyone has the kind of mind-reach I have; Lady knows things would be much simpler if they did, because there are plenty of times when the ordinary means of passing information wouldn't do at all. We have to have a foolproof, unambiguous method of passing simple messages, but it has to be impervious to tampering. That's why the Arrow-Code was developed, and thus far no one has broken it. And it all starts with this— "

With skillful and practiced fingers, he carefully broke barbs from the fletchings of a plain white arrow he pulled from the quiver. Talia could see that he was being very precise about which barbs he broke from which fletchings, yet when he was through, it looked as if the arrow had simply been handled too roughly.

"So *that's* why all our arrows are fletched with mud-gannet feathers!" Talia said, enlightened.

"Right. They're nowhere near as suitable as goose, but the barbs are so thick, heavy, and regular it's possible to have the fletching on every arrow we carry absolutely identical—*and* it's possible to literally count barbs for the code. Now this is my pattern. It's registered here, among the secret Records, and even there it's in an encrypted form for added security. Outside of those Records, only four people know it—the Queen, the Seneschal, Elcarth, and Teren, who used to be my partner. Only the Queen, the Seneschal, and Elcarth know how to translate the ciphers we've written the patterns in besides myself. When your internship is over, you'll be given the encryption key as part of what you need to know as Queen's Own. Only two people know every pattern by heart; myself and Elcarth. Now you know why one of the primary prerequisites of both our jobs is a perfect memory!"

Talia smiled, and bit her lip to keep from chuckling.

"This pattern identifies the message carried by the color of the banding on the arrow as coming from me and no one else. Now—" He took a second arrow from the quiver, and broke the barbs in a second pattern. "—this is *your* pattern. When I'm satisfied that you can reproduce it in the dark and behind your back, I'll give you a general idea of the rest of the code."

She was slightly nonplussed to discover that Kyril meant that literally. It took several hours before she could perform that simple task without seeing the arrow she was working on, and without truly thinking about it, with a speed and accuracy that contented him. Meanwhile, the sun crept across Kyril's desk, and her stomach began reminding her that it had been a long time since her last real meal.

Finally Kyril pronounced her competent, and allowed her to give her tired fingers a rest while he explained the remainder of the code to her.

"The rest of it," he told her, "is a bit more complicated, although we've done our best to make the colors mnemonic to the message. Kris will drill you on the full code on your way to your sector, but in general, this is what the simple banding of one color means. White means there's nothing wrong—'all is well, come ahead.' It's usually used just to identify that there's another Herald about, and who it is. Green calls for a Healer to be sent, purple for a priest, gray for another Herald. Brown tells the receiver to watch for a message; there's trouble, not serious, but something that requires elaboration, and something that may delay the Herald sending it in keeping his schedule. Blue means 'treachery.' Yellow calls for military aid, the number of yellow bands on the arrows tells how many units—if you send every yellow-ringed arrow you've got, and we know exactly how many you have, we know to send the entire Army! Red means 'great danger—come with all speed.' Then there's black."

He paused, his eyes holding Talia's. "I pray to Heaven that you never have to send a black arrow, Talia. Sending any black-ringed arrow means there's been or will be death or catastrophe. And there's a variant on the code for black you should also know now rather than later. The black arrow intact except for the fletching pattern means 'total disaster, help or rescue needed.' Break the arrow, send the pieces, and it reads 'disaster, all hope gone. *Do not attempt rescue.*' Remove the head, and it means that the one whose pattern is in the fletching is dead. The broken arrow, the headless arrow—those can actually be of any color so long as the fletching pattern's there. Those are the two we'll always understand—and the ones we never want to see."

Talia felt a peculiar chill thread her backbone, and suddenly the hot, sunny day seemed unaccountably gray and chill. She shook off the feeling, and repeated Kyril's words back to him, verbatim.

"That's all there is," he said, satisfied. "You're as well prepared as any of us is for his first assignment— and you're one of the best Heralds the Collegium has ever turned out. You ought to do just fine, even though this is going to be a tough assignment. Good luck to you, Talia; I look forward to seeing you in another year and a half."

She took her leave of him and despite her hunger, decided it would be a good idea to hunt up Kris. The first place she looked for him, given the situation, was the tackshed. After all, he was only just in from fieldwork; his first move should be to see that needed repairs had already been made to his Companion's gear. That was exactly where he was, in company with Dirk, checking over his harness and tack.

As alert as a wild thing to any hint of movement, Dirk was the first to notice her. "It's our songbird!" he said genially, favoring her with one of those smiles that was almost an embrace. "I expect you have the word? And Kyril's given you the code?"

She nodded, feeling oddly shy, then searched for Rolan's never-used traveling equipment. It was similar to the tack he'd worn when he'd found her, except that the bridle bells were removable, and the saddle was a bit more complicated. Besides the usual girth, it had breast and rump bands like those on warriors' saddles, a far larger number of the snaffles by which objects could be fastened to the skirting, and an arrangement of rings and straps that made it possible for a rider—ill, injured, or unconscious, perhaps—to be belted securely into his seat.

Talia rarely ever bothered with saddle or bridle around the Collegium, but she knew from experience, both her own and Rolan's, that it would mean a great deal in the way of comfort on a ride of more than an hour (for both of them) for her to use the saddle. And as her near-fatal escapade in the river had shown, the otherwise useless reins on the bridle had other functions than guiding her Companion. Had Rolan been wearing his bridle, she could have twined her arms in the reins and let him tow her to shore, for instance.

"Everything in good order?" Kris asked. She nodded an affirmative, feeling awkward and tongue-tied now that she was less than twenty-four hours away from a long journey spent mostly in his company.

"Kris and I haven't taken care of requisitioning your supplies yet," Dirk said, giving her an encouraging, lopsided grin, as if he sensed how she was feeling, "We were waiting for you to catch up with us."

"We?" Kris lifted an eyebrow at his partner. "What's this 'we' all about? She happens to be *my* trainee, you know."

"And who's the one who can't ever remember how many furlongs it is to his Sector, and whether or not you need high-energy rations, or even *where* he's going, half the time?"

"Your guess is as good as mine—I don't know of anybody answering that description," Kris grinned.

Dirk heaved a heavy sigh. "No gratitude, that's what it is. All right, sieve-head, let's you and *your* trainee get over to the Quartermaster and show her how it's done."

They arranged themselves with Talia walking between them, and strolled out of the Collegium area of the Palace to the area reserved for the Guard. That is, *they* strolled—Talia had to stretch her legs no small amount to keep up with them. All the time she was constantly aware of the little, warm, sidelong glances Dirk kept throwing at her when he thought she wasn't watching. She wasn't used to being under such intense scrutiny, and it made her a little—not uneasy, precisely—*unsettled* was perhaps the better word.

Like the Heralds, the Guard had their own area of the Palace, although they had nothing that was quite like the Collegium. They did have a training center, and a communal barracks, as well as officer's quarters, and they maintained a number of small rooms as offices. Since the needs of the Heralds and the Guard were quite similar in some areas of supply, the Quartermaster of the Guard also dispensed initial supplies to outbound Heralds. Any other supplies were taken care of at special Resupply Stations in the field.

The Offices of the Guard were entered by a door directly under the shadow of the wall that encircled the entire Palace/Collegium complex. There were a dozen or more officers seated at desks literally crammed together in the relatively small room, all busy with piles of paperwork, but Kris and Dirk seemed to know exactly where they were going. Talia followed as they threaded their way through the maze, while the officers whose work they inadvertently disturbed gave them either glares or friendly winks. Their goal was a desk at the very rear, whose occupant, a grizzled old veteran, looked rather out of place among the younger, obviously townbred officers. He seemed to be hard at his paperwork, but looked up and grinned broadly at the sight of them.

"Wot, ye tired of our faces alriddy?" he jeered. "Or is't ye've got somebody's daddy 'twould like t' see if Heralds bleed red?"

"Neither, you old pirate," Kris replied. "We've got a gap to fill up North, and Kyril, in his infinite wisdom, has decreed that we're best suited to fill it."

The man's face grew serious. "Ah didna hear the' Bell—"

"Relax, Levris, it wasn't fatal," Dirk assured him. "A pair of broken legs, or so I'm told. Talia, this is Levris, he's the Quartermaster of the Guard, and as such, those of us on circuit see a lot of him."

The wizened man stood, took her hand like a courtier, and bowed gracefully over it. " 'Tis a pleasure," he said gravely, while Talia blushed. "An' a privilege. Ye be Queen's Own, I'm thinkin'—"

"Absolutely right," Kris said, corners of his mouth twitching. "She's my internee."

"Oh, so?" Levris let go of Talia's hand, rested both hands on his hips, and gave him a stern look. "Ye'll not be tryin' any of yer seducin' tricks on her, m'lad, or if Ah come t' hear of it . . ."

Now it was Kris' turn to blush, and Dirk's to hide a grin.

Talia decided to come to his rescue. "Herald Kyril surely wouldn't have assigned us together if he thought there was any harm in the pairing," she pointed out. "And this is *duty*, not a pleasure-jaunt."

"Well, an' that's true," he admitted reluctantly, seating himself again. "So—what Sector?"

"North Border, Sorrows Two," Kris told him, "And since we won't be meeting the outgoing Herald, we'll need the whole kit."

"By t'morrow, Ah s'ppose? And ye'll be wantin' the special rations. Ye might give a man some warnin', next time!" he grumbled, but there was a twinkle in his eye.

"Sure, Levris. We'll make certain to schedule our broken legs from now on—*and* make certain it's convenient for you."

"See that ye do, then," he chuckled; then pulled out a half-dozen forms, and had Kris and Talia sign them all. That done, he shooed them out the way they had come.

"That's all there is to it," Kris said as they returned to the Collegium side. "He'll have everything we'll need ready for us in the morning."

"Provided Herald Sluggard can be persuaded to rise that early," Dirk grinned.

"Now that you've checked over your harness, all you need to do is pack your personal things," Kris continued, ignoring him. "Keep in mind that where we're going it gets cold sooner than here, stays that way for longer, and the cold is more intense. The leaves are already falling up there, though they've just started to turn here. We'll plan on staying mostly in Waystations near the villages; we won't want to get too far from other people if we can help it."

"Nevertheless," Dirk warned both of them, "You'd better also plan on having to spend several nights alone in the wilderness. I lived in that area; you didn't. The villages are far apart, and winter storms can spring up out of nowhere. You may get caught without a Waystation near, so pack the emergency supplies; if you don't use them, there's no harm done, but if you need them, you'll be glad you have them. Plan for the worst possible snow you've ever seen—then overplan."

"Yes, O graybeard," Kris made a face at him. "Holy Stars, Dirk, I visited with your family up there often enough! The way you're fussing, you'd think both of us were green as grass and totally untrained! Talia's no highborn fragile flower, she's a Borderer, too, even if she's from farther south than you."

"Well, better I should remind you needlessly . . ."

"Stow it and rope it down, granther! We'll be *fine!* Anyone would think you were my keeper, not my partner." Now Kris cast a sly, sidelong glance at Talia, who was feeling distinctly uncomfortable. "Or is it someone else you're worrying about?"

From the surprise on Kris' face, even he hadn't expected the blush that reddened Dirk's ears.

"Look," Dirk said hastily, "I just don't want you two to get into any trouble. You owe me for too many lost bets, and I'd rather not have to try to collect from your lord father! Is there anything else you'd like advice for, Talia?"

"N-no," she stammered. "I don't think so, anyway. I thank you both. I'd better get back to my quarters and pack."

"Don't forget—take nothing but Whites!" Dirk called after her. "You're on duty every minute in the field. And nothing fancy! It'll only get ruined."

He needn't have said that, about "nothing fancy," she thought a little resentfully. *After all, I'm not some silly townbred chit.* And then she wondered for a fleeting instant why his good opinion of her should seem so important.

Dismissing the thought from her mind, she ran back up the tower stairs and ransacked her wardrobe, laying everything white she could find on the bed. That way she wouldn't overlook a tunic or other article that she might find herself in need of out in the field.

She packed nothing but the doeskin, with the summer and winter changes both—but she packed every stitch of those she had.

Though from the way Dirk talks, she thought wryly, *you'd think it never got warm up there.*

She added a repair kit for leather and one for harness, and then for good measure added a sealed pot of glue, just in case. There'd been times enough back on the Holding when she was on sheep-watch that she'd needed a pot of glue, and not had one to hand. She packed her sewing kit, and a brick of hard, concentrated soap—the special kind that you needed for use on Whites to keep them pristine— just in case it ever became necessary to do her own repairs and cleaning of her clothing. Certainly the village laundrypeople normally tended those jobs, but you never knew. She added a small metal traveling lamp, and extra wicks, because she'd never seen a lamp in the Waystations, and if they stayed more than one night, lamplight was easier on the eyes than firelight. Then her personal gear, her weapons, a precious book or two, some writing supplies. Her bedroll was next, and all the extra blankets she could find; with them, two extra towels besides the others she carried, and a pair of thick sheepskin slippers. Rolan's gear was all with his tack, but just the same she packed a vial of ferris-oil. He liked it; it was good for his hooves and coat and kept the insects away.

Even when she'd packed everything as compactly as she could, it still bulked distressingly large. She stared at the clumsy packs in near-despair, trying to think of something she dared leave behind. Kris would surely think she was an idiot for wanting to bring all this stuff!

"Good packing job," Keren said from the open door behind her, "I intended to come up here and help you cut down on the flotsam, but it looks like I'm not needed."

"Is that meant ironically or seriously?' Talia asked, turning to greet the more experienced Herald with relief.

"Oh, seriously. My counselor made me repack three

times for my interning trip, and I never did get my packs down that small—I kept thinking of things I was sure I'd miss. Know what? I ended up sending most of them back here."

"But how is Rolan ever going to carry all this, the supply pack and me, too?"

"Easy, he won't have to. You'll each have a packbeast, probably a mule. Well, maybe not; you're going north, they may give you chirras. Didn't anybody tell you that? You're riding circuit, not carrying messages, so you don't need speed. You can easily hold your speed down to match your packbeasts' without sacrificing anything."

Talia heaved a sigh of relief. "Nobody told me. Kris either assumed that I knew, or left it out deliberately to keep me from overpacking."

"Well don't go crazy now that you know," Keren warned.

"I won't. In fact, other than begging a couple more blankets and a pillow from Supply, packing all three pairs of my boots, and adding a bit more in the way of towels and soap and the like, there's only one thing more I want to add." Talia tucked her third pair of boots into a pack, tied it shut, and turned to the hearthcorner. There, where she'd left her last night still in her carrying case, was My Lady. She opened the case, detuned the strings for safety in traveling, and added her to the pile.

"Good notion," Keren said. "You may be snowbound at any time, and that'll keep you from tearing out each other's throats from boredom. Not only that, folks up there seldom see a Bard except in summer. You'll be like gifts from the Gods."

"Keren—I'll—" Talia suddenly had a lump in her throat. Now it came home to her; she was leaving, leaving the only place that had ever felt like home, and the only friends she'd ever had. "—I'll miss you."

Keren reached out and hugged her shoulders.

"Don't you worry. You'll be fine, I know you will. Kris is a good lad, if a bit too conscious of his own good looks. Little centaur—I'll miss you, too. But don't you dare cry—" she warned, caught between a chuckle and a tear, "—or *I'll* start! Come on, we've just enough time to catch the end of supper, and you must be ready to chew harness."

Supper was rather subdued; nearly everyone had long since eaten and gone, and of those that were left Talia really knew only Keren well. Talia kept glancing around her, realizing how much she was going to miss this place, that had been her first *real* home.

She had expected that Keren would leave her afterward, but to her surprise, the older woman insisted that she come with her to Keren's rooms. She was even more surprised when Keren insisted Talia precede her through the door.

Then she saw who was waiting for them there; almost more people than would fit into the room: Elcarth, Sherri, Jeri, Skif, Teren—even Alberich. Devan made a brilliant patch of green among the Whites in his Healer's robes; the students were well represented by Elspeth. Keren pushed her into the room from behind as she hesitated on the threshold.

"You really didn't think we'd let you go without a proper good-bye, did you?" Skif teased as Talia stared in dumb amazement. "Besides, I know you—you were all set to mope away your last night here alone. Goose! Well, we're not having any of *that!*"

Since that was exactly what she'd expected to be doing, Talia blushed rose-pink, then stuck her tongue out at him.

Skif, knowing very well how prone Talia was to isolating herself just when she needed others the most, had accosted Keren as soon as the news of Talia's assignment had gotten to him. The two of them had put their heads together and quickly put together this little "fare-thee-well" party, designed to keep her from falling into a last-minute melancholy. When Skif saw the expression on Talia's face as she'd realized what they'd done, he felt more than repaid for his effort.

He did his level best the whole evening to project how much his "little sister" meant to him, knowing she'd pick it up. The warmth in her eyes made him feel that he'd at least begun to give her an honest return for the help she'd given him last night. In some ways he was just as glad now that they'd never become lovers, for there was nothing that could have been more satisfying, in the long run, than the open, loving relationship they had instead. He had more than a suspicion that she felt the same.

"So, songbird, how about a tune or three?"

While it wasn't precisely as festive as the celebration the night before had been, everything had been geared to setting her mind at rest and making her feel confident about the morrow. Each of them, with the exception of Devan and Elspeth, had faced the same moment—and each knew some way to make the prospect a positive one. There was a great deal of laughter, plenty of absurd stories, and a palpable aura of caring. They sent her off to bed in good time to get a full night's sleep, and she left with a smile on her face.

Kris answered the tap on his door late that evening, expecting to see Dirk; in fact, he'd already gotten out a bottle of wine and two glasses, figuring that his partner wouldn't let the evening pass without coming by for a farewell drink and chat. He got a fair shock to find his uncle, the Councilor Lord Orthallen, standing in the dim hallway instead.

He managed to stammer out a surprised greeting, which Orthallen took as an invitation to enter. The silver-haired, velvet-robed noble wore a grave expression on his still-handsome, square-jawed face, so

Kris had more than a faint suspicion that his visit was *not* just to bid farewell to his nephew.

He directed his uncle to the most comfortable chair in the room and supplied him with the glass of wine intended for Dirk before taking the chair opposite him.

"Well, uncle?" he said, deciding he was too tired to dance diplomatically around the subject. "What brings you here? I know it wasn't just to bid me a fond farewell."

Orthallen raised one eyebrow at his bluntness. "I understand you have the new Queen's Own as your internee."

Kris shrugged. "It's no secret."

"How well do you know her?"

"Not at all," he admitted. "I've seen her twice, worked with her once. She seems nice enough—quite well balanced, all told. Her Gift is an odd one, but—"

"*That* is exactly what is worrying me." Orthallen all but pounced on the opening. "Her Gift. From all anyone has been able to tell me, it *is* a very unusual one for a Herald, much less the Queen's Own. It seems to be one that the Heralds themselves know very little about, and I'm not entirely happy that an inexperienced child should be in her position with a power so . . . out-of-the-ordinary."

"Rolan Chose her," Kris replied warily. "That should be proof enough that she's capable of handling it."

"Yes, but—*emotions*—it's such a volatile area. No black-and-white there, only gray. There are rumors in the Court . . ."

"Such as?"

"That she has fostered an unnatural dependence in the Heir. After all, the child *is* vulnerable to that sort of thing. It was her unnatural dependence on that foreign nurse, Hulda, that led to her nearly being disallowed in the first place. And there are other rumors."

Kris bit back an angry retort; best hear his uncle out. "Go on."

"That Talia has used her power to influence the Council; you can imagine for yourself how easy that would be. If a Councilor were wavering . . . it would be very easy to nudge his emotions, make him feel happier about one side or the other. Or not even that . . . simply *sense* that he is wavering, and *use* that knowledge to persuade him in a more ordinary fashion. By knowing how Councilors stood, it would make it quite simple for her to manipulate them just by tone of voice. . . ."

"That's absurd! *No* Herald would ever use her Gift in any such fashion!"

"So *I* have maintained," Orthallen replied smoothly, "But—the only others Gifted with Empathy are the Healers; Healers put it to very specific and humanitarian use. There is no corresponding protocol of use among Heralds. And, nephew—what if she truly were not aware she was using her abilities? These powers are not material properties one can weigh or measure or hold in one's hand. What if she were doing this sort of thing without even realizing it?"

Kris felt as if he had been hit with a pail of cold water. "I—I suppose it's just barely possible. I don't think it's at all likely, but I can't dismiss the notion out of hand."

Orthallen rose, a satisfied smile creasing his lips. "That is what I hoped you would tell me. I'm counting on you, nephew, to lay these phantoms of doubt to rest. You'll be with her night and day for the next eighteen months, and I'm sure you will be able to tell me on your return that all these rumors are no more than smoke."

"I'm sure I will, uncle," Kris replied, letting him out—but not at all sure in his own mind.

It was just false dawn when Talia woke, and she dressed as quickly as she could, discovering that someone had left a breakfast tray for her outside her door. She had only just finished it when a Guardsman tapped discreetly on the doorframe, explaining that he was there to help her carry her packs down. With his aid she managed to get everything down to the tackshed in one trip.

Bright light from oil lamps along the wall dazzled her eyes as she entered. Waiting in the very center was Rolan; his harness was piled beside him. Next to him was a second Companion stallion, and Talia could see Kris' legs behind him as she and the Guard approached. Tethered beside the strange Companion were two most unusual pack animals.

Talia had never seen chirras before except in pictures, for their heavy coats made summer at the Collegium far too uncomfortable for them. Rather than keep them there, the Circle had a northern farm where they were bred and stabled, and only brought them down on rare occasions like this. Had this been within the normal order of things they would have taken mules from the Collegium stables for the first part of the journey. Then they would have met the Herald they were replacing at the edge of her Sector and exchanged their mules for her chirras.

Talia discovered that pictures and descriptions were inadequate to convey the charm of the northern beasts. The chirras were as tall at the shoulder as a horse, but a much longer neck put their heads on a level with the head of a human on horseback. Instead of hooves they had doglike, clawed feet, except that the feet were almost round and far bigger than Talia would have expected from the overall size of the animal. Both chirras were creamy white with black markings; one had a little cap-like spot on the top of its head, and a matching saddle-marking on its back, the other had a collar of black fur that ran around its throat and down its chest. Their ears were large, resembling rabbit ears, but rounder, with tips that flopped over. Their ears were set on the tops of their skulls and faced forward. Their faces were vaguely rabbit-like. Their brown eyes were very large, gentle, and intelligent. When Talia approached them with her hand held out to them, they scrutinized her closely, then politely took turns whuffling her palm.

Kris was already halfway through his inspection of the beasts and their gear.

"Kind of cute, aren't they? Anybody ever tell you how they manage to live through those blizzards? They've got three layers of fur," he said, bent over and adjusting the girth of the pack-harness, half-hidden by the chirra's bulk. "The outermost is long and coarse, and pretty much waterproof—even frost won't form on it. The middle layer is shorter, and not quite so coarse. The inner layer is what they shed every year; it's dense, very soft and fine, and is what does most of the work of keeping them warm. We'll have to groom them very carefully every night to keep all that fur from getting matted, or they'll lose the warming and waterproofing effect."

"Why are their feet so big?"

"To hold them up on the snow; they'll be able to walk on snow crusts that the Companions will break right through." He moved to the front of his and picked up its forefoot while it whiffled his hair. "Look here—see all the hair between the toes? If you think their feet look big now, wait till they spread them out on snow. You'd think that hair wouldn't make any difference, but it does, like the webbing on snow-shoes. I much prefer chirras over mules in any kind of climate that they can tolerate. They've got sweet tempers, and they're really quite intelligent. If a mule balks, you can't tell half the time if he's being stubborn, or if there's really something wrong. A chirra never balks *unless* there's something wrong."

The chirra next to Talia stretched out his neck and nudged her hand, obviously wanting to be petted. "How much can they carry?" she asked, complying by scratching behind the chirra's ears. It sighed happily and closed its eyes in content.

"Almost half their own weight—as good or better than a mule. Well, look at the packs they're bringing now, and you can see."

Talia was astonished at the size of the pack the stablehands were loading on the chirra she was scratching. It didn't seem the least bit uncomfortable.

Kris looked it over, then eyed the packs Talia had brought down from her room. "They've left enough leeway for you to load those on him as well, Talia. Don't worry, he's smart. If it's going to be more than he can carry, he'll just lie down until we lighten the load."

To her relief, the chirra showed no sign of wanting to lie down after her packs had been strapped on top of the supplies. Kris saw to the distribution of the rest of the supplies and his own belongings, while Talia made sure the chirra's harness was firm, but comfortable, with nothing twisted or binding.

She harnessed Rolan herself, then double-checked her work, and asked him in an undertone, "You don't mind traveling with these beasties, do you?"

He seemed pleased that she had asked the question but conveyed the impression that he was quite pleased with the packbeasts. Without words, Talia got the distinct impression that the chirras, sporting those thick, warm coats, would be more than welcome company on cold winter nights.

She fastened the lead rope of the chirra to the back of Rolan's saddle, and mounted. Kris mounted a fraction of a second later. "Ready?" he asked.

"As ready as any internee, I guess."

"Then let's go."

Four

Kris took the lead; they had to go single file in the city. Talia and Rolan followed his chirra out of the gates of the courtyard, past the Collegium and Palace buildings, gray and silent in the early morning light, then down the cobblestoned road to the iron gates leading to city streets themselves, the road she'd ridden up five and a half years previously. She looked back over her shoulder for a last glimpse of the dear, familiar stone buildings, and wondered what she'd be like when she saw them again.

The guard at the gate let them out; it was scarcely an hour until dawn and the streets were not yet crowded. They followed the long spiral outward, passing first through the residential areas that were nearest the Palace—huge buildings belonging to the highest ranked of the nobly-born, some nearly rivaling the size of Bardic or Healer's Collegium, though not that of the Palace itself. Then, crowded far more closely together, the homes of the rich—merchants and craftsmen and Guild officials. Unlike the Palace and the edifices of the nobles, which were the same gray granite as the city walls, these buildings were wooden. Since land within the walls was at a premium, they crowded so closely the eaves touched— and when there was a need to expand, the only direction to take was *up*, which sometimes produced some very strange results. Most of these houses had been constructed of ironoak, a wood nearly as tough and indestructible as steel, but that was where any similarity among them ended. They had been built to some highly individual styles, and often had been added to in years and styles varying wildly from the original. Had the spiraling main street not been wide enough for three carriages, it would never have gotten any sun; as it was, riding through this district so early in the morning was rather like riding down a canyon with sides carved in the most fantastic of shapes. Talia had to fight to keep from giggling as she passed some of these houses, for Skif—to "keep his hand in," or so he claimed—had often paid uninvited visits to the upper stories of some of these places. He'd usually left unsigned notes to be found later, chiding the owners for their lack of security. That was *one* prank the Provost-Marshal would *never* have forgiven him if it had been discovered.

After the street took a sharp right-angle turn, the purely residential district came to an end. Now the lower stories of the buildings were devoted to shops and the work-places of fine craftsmen, or offices, with an occasional expensive hostelry. The upper floors were comprised of apartments or lodgings. At this point they began encountering what little traffic there was this early in the morning. Nearly the only people about were the farmers who had brought their produce in to market, for the only cityfolk moving were those who were buying fresh supplies for their inns. Talia and Kris were able to move at a brisk pace, not having to stop for traffic more than once or twice. The streets were so quiet at this hour that *they* were the chief sources of sound; the ringing of the Companions' hooves, the chime of their bridle-bells, and the click of the chirras' claws on the cobblestones.

It took them nearly an hour to reach the Northern gate; the farther from the center of the city they went, the less wealth was displayed. There were no slums within the Old City; those were outside the city gates, huddling against the walls as if in hopes that those sturdy stone structures might shelter them from the elements. It was in one such district that Skif had grown up, the rather odd section along Exile's Road that led into the West. Talia had never been there; she had seldom been out of the Old City, much less into the New. The one time she'd asked to be taken there, Skif had turned white, and refused. She'd never asked again.

Nor would she go anywhere near that section this time, for Kris' chosen route led past the warehouses and the shipwrights, after crossing over the River just inside the Old City walls and exiting through the North Point Gate. Here there was no activity at all; workers had not yet arrived, and deliveries to the warehouses had yet to be made. So once again, they rode in silence after a sleepy Guardswoman waved them on their way.

Beyond the gate the road widened and changed from stone to that odd substance that wasn't stone and wasn't clay. Talia hadn't thought about it in years, but it occurred to her now to wonder just what it was that paved some of the roadways of this Kingdom.

"Kris?" she called, and he motioned to her to ride up alongside him, now that they were out of the city.

"What *is* this stuff?" she asked, pointing to the surface of the road.

He shrugged. "Another lost secret. Some of the roads leading to the capital are paved with it, a few all the way to the Border; but any roads made later than Elspeth the Peacemaker's time are just packed gravel at best." He saw she was looking about her with unconcealed curiosity. "Haven't you ever been out of the city before?"

"Not very often since I was Chosen," she replied, "And never in this direction."

"Didn't you even go back home for holidays?" he asked, astonished.

"My parents weren't exactly pleased with me, even—or perhaps especially—when they learned I was Chosen," she replied dryly. "Not to put too fine a point upon it, they disowned me. In Hold terms, that means they denied the very fact of my existence. I spent all my holidays here, with Jadus while he was still alive, then with Keren and Ylsa, or with Gaytha Housekeeper and Mero the Collegium cook."

"You've been rather sheltered, then."

"At the Collegium, yes, except for the first year. Not at the Hold, though. Know anything about Holderkin?"

"Not much," Kris admitted. "They seemed so dull, I'm afraid I've forgotten most of what I learned about them as a student."

"Whether or not it's dull depends on whether you were born male or female. Holderkin are originally from outKingdom—Karse, if you're curious. They fled from religious persecution; their religion is based on a dominating, ruling God and a passive, submissive Goddess, and the Karsites are monotheistic. That was . . . oh, two generations ago. They are very secretive, and very intent on maintaining their ways intact. Men have some choice in their lives; women are given exactly two choices—serve the Goddess as a cloistered, isolated votary under a vow of silence, or marry. You make that choice at the mature age of thirteen, or thereabouts."

"Thirteen!" Kris looked aghast.

"Hellfire, Kris, life is hard on the Border! *You* ought to know that, with your partner being a Borderer. There were raiders every winter I can remember. The land is stony and hard to farm. Holderkin don't believe in going to Healers, so a lot of simple injuries and illnesses end in death. If you're not wedded by fifteen, you may not leave any offspring—and they need every working hand they can get."

"You sound like you *enjoyed* that kind of life—like you approve of it!" Kris was plainly astonished by her attitude.

"I hated it," she said flatly. "I hated every minute that I didn't spend reading or daydreaming. Rolan's Choosing me was the only thing that saved me from a forced marriage with some stranger picked out by my father. I think that the way they confine themselves, their children, and most especially their minds is something approaching a crime. But *most* of the Holderfolk I knew seemed content, even happy, and I have no right to judge for them."

"Fine; you don't judge for them, but what about others who are unhappy as you were, with no Rolan to rescue them?"

"A good point—and fortunately for those would-be rebels, one Elcarth and Selenay thought of after hearing my story. The Holderfolk got their landgrants on condition that they obey the Queen and the laws of this Kingdom. Shortly after I arrived at the Collegium, Selenay had a law passed through the Council that Heralds must be allowed free access to children at all times, in order that they can be certain that the children of this Kingdom are properly educated in our laws, history, and traditions. Heralds whose Gift is Thought-sensing go right into the Holdings now. Anyone willing to sacrifice family ties and standing as I did is free to leave with them, and they make sure the unhappy ones know this. The amazing thing to me is that there was very little objection to the practice after the initial outrage died down. I suppose the Hold Elders are only too pleased that their potential troublemakers are leaving on their own."

Kris seemed a bit bemused. "I can't imagine why anyone would *not* want to leave conditions like that."

Talia shook her head sadly, remembering. It wasn't quite true that she hadn't gone back to the Hold— she had, once, last year. She'd gone back in the hopes of rescuing her sister Vrisa—to discover Vris had changed, changed past all recognition. Vris was a Firstwife now, with status, and three Underwives to rule. She'd regarded Talia as if she were a demon— when she thought Talia wasn't looking, she'd made holy signs against her. In point of fact, she looked and acted enough like Keldar, the Firstwife who'd done her best to break Talia's rebellious spirit, to have been Keldar's younger self. She not only didn't want rescue, she'd been horrified by the idea.

"Kris, it's not my choice to make," she answered wearily, "it's theirs. All that I care about is that the ones like me now have the option I didn't have before I was Chosen—to escape."

Kris looked at her with curiosity. "Just when I think I have you neatly categorized, you say or do something that turns it all upside down again. I'd have bet that you'd have been willing to lead an army into the Holds to free the women, given the chance."

"Maybe when I didn't know as much about people as I do now," she sighed.

They rode on in silence. The sun rose on their right, turning the sky pink, rose and blue, casting long shadows across their path from the buildings. Before long they had passed beyond the edge of the New City, and there was nothing before them but the occasional farmhouse. Cows were gathering outside barns, lowing to be milked. Now they saw people working; and a light breeze carried to them the smell of cut grain and drying hay, and the sounds of birds and farmbeasts.

"Tell me about yourself," Kris said, finally. "When you're tired of talking, I'll tell you about me. Start with what it was like on the Hold, before you were Chosen."

"It's boring," she cautioned him.

"Maybe—but it's part of you. As your counselor, I need to know about you."

He did his best to keep his opinions to himself while she talked, but he frequently looked surprised by some of what she told him, and actually horrified once or twice. He had, she thought, a hard time conceiving of a culture so alien to his own, so confining and repressive. Talia herself spoke in a kind of detached tone. She felt very distant from the Holderkin and all they meant now. She could think of them without much animosity; as something foreign.

It was noon when she finally grew tired of explaining Hold customs to Kris. She paused for a long drink from her waterskin, suddenly aware that her mouth was very dry, and said firmly, "I think I've talked enough."

"More than that; it's time to break for lunch," he replied. "While we keep to this pace the chirras can go on indefinitely, so whether or not we break depends on whether or not we want to take a rest from riding. How are you feeling?"

"Like I'd like to get off for a while," she admitted, "It's been a long, long time since I spent this many hours riding."

"I'm glad you said that." His answering smile was completely ingenuous and quite charming. "I'm not all that fond of eating in the saddle unless there's no choice. As soon as I spot a place where we can water the chirras and our Companions, we'll take a rest."

They found a Waystation within the half-hour. This one was watered by a well rather than a stream; they took turns hauling up enough water to satisfy the four-footed members of the party, then tethered the chirras so that both Companions and chirras could graze for a bit while they ate their own lunch.

They ate in silence, and Kris seemed to be in no great hurry to move on afterward. He lay back in the soft grass instead, thoughts evidently elsewhere, though he glanced over at Talia once or twice.

Kris was worried, though he was taking pains not to show it. His uncle's words kept coming back to him, and he could not, in all conscience, dismiss them. He'd made a number of assumptions about his trainee, most of them based on her apparent youth and inexperience—and now what she'd told him seemed to indicate that she was anything but inexperienced, and certainly was *not* the simple creature he'd pictured to himself. This child—no, *woman;* he began to wonder now if she'd ever had anything like a "childhood" as he knew the meaning of the term— had been functionally the Queen's Own long before she ever attained her Whites. But she was so tiny, and so guileless, and so very innocent-seeming, that you forgot all about that, and tended to think of her as much younger than she really was.

He didn't think any of that surface was a deliberate act—but he also couldn't tell what lay below the surface, either.

Was she capable of the kind of deliberate misuse of her Gift that Orthallen had described?

"I've got to ask you a question," he said at last. "And please, I don't mean this as any kind of insult. There are some rather unpleasant rumors circulating the Court, and I'd like to know the truth. Have— have you ever used your Gift to influence Elspeth?"

Her reaction was far more violent than he would have expected. *"No!"* she shouted, sitting bolt upright, and actually startling Companions and chirras into shying. "How can you even *think* such a thing?"

Her eyes were hot with anger; her face as white as her uniform.

He met that angry gaze as best he could, acutely aware of how still it was, of the grass under his hands, of the sun on his head. "It's a rumor, I told you; I have to know."

"I have never—I *would* never—do anything like that to anyone. It's—the whole idea is perverted," she choked. "Dammit, I *knew* there had to be some odd things being said about me. I mean, I could tell, people were acting very strangely when they thought I wasn't looking. But this! It's—it's disgusting. Does Elspeth know about this?"

"Not so far as I know—" He broke off at the sudden, pained look she gave him.

She rose to her feet, abruptly. "I've—I've got to go back; I can't leave her to face that alone."

"That's just what you can't do," he said, jumping up and catching hold of both her arms. "Don't you see? If you did that, you'd just be *confirming* the idea in people's heads. Besides, you've been given an assignment, and a set of orders. It's not up to you to decide whether or not you're going to obey them."

She buried her face in her hands for a moment; when she took her hands away he could see her fighting to exert control over herself. "All right," she said, sinking back to the ground, "You're right. You said that there were other rumors. What are they?"

"That you've been using your Gift to influence other people—specifically Councilors on crucial votes. The kindest version of that rumor says that you're not doing it consciously, that you don't realize you're doing it."

"Good God. How am I supposed to answer *that* one?"

Kris didn't have an adequate reply, so he continued. "Another rumor is that you're using your Gift just to *read* people, then using the knowledge of their emotional state to manipulate them into doing what you want."

"Goddess. That's almost close to the truth . . ."

"Again, the kindest version is that you don't realize that you're doing it. People are frightened; your Gift isn't one they've seen outside of a Healer;

Mindspeakers have an ethical code they understand, but *this*?"

"So far as I know, there *is* no ethical code," she said, and looked up at him. Her eyes were full of a pain he didn't understand, and a confusion he wished he could resolve. "Is that all?"

"Isn't it enough? They say you're young, you're inexperienced—some say *too* young to be in the position of power that you are, and to be wielding such a strange mindGift."

"As if," she replied bitterly, "I have any choice in the matter."

And she did not speak to him again until long after they had mounted up and gotten back on the North Road.

Kris bore with her lack of communication up to a point, but finally decided to try and break the deadlock himself. He Mindtouched Tantris, asking him to move in closer to Rolan, until he and Talia were almost knee to knee.

"Just exactly how *does* your Gift work?" he asked, unwilling to bear the tense silence.

"I feel emotions the way Farspeakers hear words," she replied, after turning in her saddle to give him a sober look, one that seemed to be weighing him for some quality. "If the emotions are connected with something strongly enough, I See that. If they're twisted or wrong, or very negative, sometimes I can fix them, like a Healer with a wound. Ylsa said it's a pretty rare Gift to see crop up alone, that it's usually tied up with the Healing Gifts. As you know."

"Interesting," he replied as casually as he could. "So *that's* how you were able to lead me to where Ylsa died. Most Heralds are Mindspeakers, you know, and most of the rest are Farseers, like me. Only a few of us have odd Gifts like yours and Dirk's. And Griffon's— brrr!—that's one I wouldn't want." The sun lost some

of its warmth for him as he thought of the demonstration Griffon and Dirk had given him. "Firestarting
is a terrible burden, and it's so easy for the power to
get out of control . . . and when it does, well, you
end up with barrens like at Burning Pines. And it
isn't really useful at all except as a weapon. I hope
his being born with it now doesn't mean something;
Heralds with the really odd Gifts tend to appear
when there's going to be a need for them. The last
Firestarter was Lavan Firestorm, and you know what
his era was like—" He flushed, beginning to realize
that he was pontificating—but, damn—he wanted to
get her mind off the rumors so she'd act normally
again. "Sorry. I tend to get carried away when I start
discussing Gifts. It's a hobby of mine, one I share
with Kyril. It's fascinating to see what kinds of Gifts
we have, and to try and see if there are patterns."

"Really?" She perked up a little, a bit more color
coming into her cheeks. "Has anybody else ever
had my kind of Gift before?"

"Not that I'm aware of among the Heralds, but I
must admit that I've only looked into the Gifts of
living Heralds, or the really spectacular ones of the
past. I can't say that I've ever heard of that ability to
Heal the mind, except in a true Healer, but it wouldn't
surprise me much to discover that this one's the Gift
that distinguishes the Queen's Own from the rest of
us. And you seem to have it mostly by itself, and
maybe much stronger even than in Healers. Probably the others *have* had it, but not so strongly that
anyone noticed it. Nobody seems to have made a
study of the Monarch's Own—not like they have
with the more ordinary Gifts. And now that I think
about it, your primary job is to ensure the mental
stability of the Monarch—an ability like the one you
have could come in very useful if something *really*
went wrong." He was doing his best to imply that he
believed her—that he was certain the rumors weren't

true. He only wished that he really *could* be that certain.

"I can see that." She was silent, and seemed to be thinking hard. Late afternoon sun was gilding everything, and the early breeze had died. The chirras' eyes were half-closed in the drowsy warmth, and the few sounds to either side of them were those of farmworkers cutting hay and grain, and insects droning in the grass. "So you See, and Dirk Fetches?"

"Right. That's why we work together, and generally don't ride Sectors except when we're shorthanded, the way we have been lately. To put it bluntly, we're Selenay's thieves." He laughed a little. "If I know what I'm looking for, I can generally find where it is from several miles away—more, if I get a 'ride,' like I got from you. Once I know exactly where it is and can fix the location in my mind, Dirk can read the location to Fetch whatever it is to where *we* happen to be. That's how he retrieved Ylsa's arrows."

"That seems to be a lot harder than it sounds . . . rather wearing, too, from the little I've seen."

"Gods, that's an understatement. In a lot of ways, it would be less tiring to run on foot to where it is, get it, and run back. And the heavier the object, the more difficult it is to Fetch. We haven't tried anything much larger than a building brick—and that gave him a reaction-headache that lasted for a week. I was pretty surprised when he had enough energy left to carry you to your room after retrieving those arrows."

"Aha!" She seemed please that it had been Dirk who had cared for her. "A mystery solved! I've wondered about that for the last two years. So *he* was the one!"

"He was like a hen with one chick—wouldn't let me do more than trail along, and I was in better shape than he. Said that with all those girls in his family, he knew better than I did what to do with a sick one."

"Can he work with anyone but you?"

"We don't know; he's never tried, since he gets such a good 'fix' from me. Probably, though. One Farseer's a lot like another."

"How long have you two been working together?" she asked curiously.

"Since we both got our Whites. That was another year they were shorthanded, and sent us both out to intern with the same counselor—Gerick. Well, you know Gerick, he's absentminded; he left a small, but valuable ring at one of the Waystations—it was the Queen's gift to one of the Guildmasters. Rather than spend two hours going back for it, Dirk offered to try Fetching it. I Looked for it, found it had rolled under the bed while we were packing, and gave Dirk the location. That was when we discovered that I gave him the clearest 'fix' he'd ever had to work from. He Fetched the ring, no problem; we started working as a team, and we've been doing things that way ever since."

"It's just that you seem so unlike each other, I find it hard to imagine you two staying together."

Kris laughed, pleased to have gotten onto a safe subject. "You might be surprised. Underneath that jester mask he wears, Dirk's a very serious gentleman. And we have pretty much the same taste in music, reading, even food. . . ."

"In women?" she teased.

"Well . . . that, too," he admitted with a reluctant smile. "And it's really pretty unfair. Poor Dirk—it doesn't matter if he finds the lady first. Once she's seen me she usually goes all 'sisterly' on him. He's mostly pretty good-natured about it, but if I were in his shoes, I'd be damned annoyed!"

"Well, he knows you can't help it. You were born looking like an angel, and he . . . well, he wasn't, and that's all there is to say."

"It's still not fair. You'd think that at least *one*

woman would figure out that Dirk the man is worth
ten faces like mine."

"I expect someday someone will," Talia replied
noncommittally, avoiding his eyes. "Where is he
from?"

Her reply was just a bit too casual; her attempt at
nonchalance immediately set off mental alerts in Kris'
mind, especially following all those questions about
his partner. Part of him followed up on the puzzle
while he answered her question. He had a very faint
suspicion, too tenuous to be even a guess. It was
rather like trying to remember a name he'd forgotten. It would probably take a while before he had
enough information to make a surmise . . . but now
he'd be subconsciously watching for clues.

"The Sector right next to ours, Sorrows One. He's
got a huge family up there. He used to haul me
home with him for holidays—still does when we're
free. Three of his married sisters and their families
live with their parents and help run the farm. It's
like a madhouse; people everywhere, babies and cats
constantly underfoot. It's marvelous madness though.
They're wonderful people, and there's never a lonely
or dull moment."

He smiled half to himself as he recalled some of
those visits, his earlier thoughts gone on the breeze.
Dirk's family—they should have been gypsies! All of
them crazy, and all of them delightful. He'd been
looking forward to another Midwinter Festival with
them, but it obviously wasn't going to be *this* year.
Well, there was always another time.

Talia's next question broke the strange, apprehen-
sive chill he felt at that thought.

"What about you?"

"Well, let me think. My father is Lord Peregrine;
I'm the second son, but my brother is ten years older
than I am, and I have nephews and nieces that aren't
much younger than you. My parents are both very
wrapped up in matters of state, so I was left pretty

much in the hands of my tutors, back on the family estate."

"I think I know your father; he's one of the Seneschal's chief assistants. And your mother?"

"She organizes the resupply of the Waystations. I think she would have liked to have been a Herald, but since she wasn't Chosen, this is the closest she can get."

"Weren't there any children your own age on the estate?"

"Not many; their parents seemed to think mine would be angry if their offspring were allowed to 'contaminate' me. I spent a great deal of my time reading."

"Like me—only you didn't have to hide to do it!" she laughed.

"You're wrong there! My tutors seemed to think that my every waking moment should be spent learning something serious, dull, and practical. I had a hiding place up in the oldest tree in the garden. I fixed it up until it was quite impossible to see me from the ground. I smuggled my tales and poetry up there, and escaped at every opportunity." A breeze that stirred the leaves of the trees lining the road to either side of them seemed to chuckle at Kris' childish escapes. "Then, when I was twelve, my parents took me to Court. I don't think it ever entered their heads that the Collegium stood on the same grounds." He smiled. "Even if they'd forgotten, though, I hadn't. I hoped—but when no Companion met me at the Palace gate, I gave the dream up. I was supposed to be presented at Vernal Equinox Festival, and I can remember everything, right down to the fact that one of my boot-lacings didn't quite match the other. I was standing next to my father, outside, in the gardens, you know—when there was an unexpected visitor to the Festivities."

Tantris shook his head, making the bells on his bridle sing. Kris chuckled, and reached forward to scratch behind his ears. "I knew what the appearance of a Companion meant, and I kept looking around to see who he had come to Choose. I nearly went out of my mind with happiness, when I finally stopped craning my head around and found he was standing right in front of *me!* Then, when I looked into his eyes. . . ." His voice trailed off.

"It's not like anything else, is it?" Talia prompted softly. "and it isn't something you ever lose the wonder of."

"That it's not," he agreed, speaking half to himself. "and I knew then that I'd never be lonely again. . . ." He shook off the spell, and became matter-of-fact. "Well, my parents were both very proud. They had me installed at the Collegium before I had a chance to turn around. Oddly enough, it's easier to deal with them now that I'm an adult. My father can relate to me as an equal, and I think that my mother forgets half the time that I'm one of her offspring. I really don't think they ever knew what to do with a child."

"They probably didn't, especially with so much time between you and your brother."

"Dirk has no notion how much I envy him his family," he sighed.

"You think not?" Talia smiled. "Then why does he keep bringing you home with him?"

"I never thought about that."

They rode silently for a mile or so.

"Talia, do you ever miss your family?"

"Not after I found other people who really cared about me. I was the scarlet jay among the crows with them; I was more of an outsider among my own family than I ever was at the Collegium. One of those pretty brothers of mine used to steal my books, and call me 'Herald Talia' to make me cry. I'd like to have seen his face when I was Chosen."

"Do you ever think about going back?"

"You know, that used to be a daydream of mine,

that I'd somehow magically become a Herald—remember, I didn't know about being Chosen—and I'd come back dressed in my Whites and covered in glory. Then they'd all be envious, and sorry that they were mean to me."

"And now?"

"Well, I went back long enough to try and 'rescue' the sister I'd been closest to only to find she had turned into a stranger. I didn't go any farther into the Holdings, just turned around and came back home. I didn't want to see any of them again. Why bother? My parents pretended I was an outsider, my sibs were either afraid or contemptuous; Heralds are very immoral, you know. What is it Mero's Book says? About how the people you grow up with react to your fame?"

" 'No one honors a saint on his hearthstone.' "

"It's true, too. I'm resigned to letting things rest as they are, knowing that my example shows misfits that there *is* an escape."

He didn't seem inclined to further conversation, so she turned her attention back to those unsettling rumors.

Poisonous, that's what they were. Ugly, and poisonous.

And true? said a niggling little doubt.

She wanted to deny any truth to it at all—vehemently. But could she? In all conscience, could she?

The business about Elspeth—no, she could not believe she'd been fostering dependence in the child, not even unconsciously. Once Elspeth had begun acting like a human being again, she'd been pushing her toward *independence*, driving her to make her own decisions and take responsibility for the results.

But the rest—oh, insidious. For a Mindspeaker, it was obvious when he was projecting; it sounded to the recipient a great deal like the Mindspeaker's normal voice, but as if the words were coming from deep inside his own ear. But when *she* projected—would anyone be able to tell she was doing so?

She could tell; sending emotion cost her effort and energy.

But if she were excited or agitated—would she notice the energy expense?

Did she even need to be doing it while she was awake? What about when she was *asleep*? How could she possibly be sure what her irrational sleeping mind was doing?

And what about simply reading people's emotional states? Was she transgressing by doing so, and acting on the knowledge?

How could she *avoid* doing it? It was like seeing color; it was just *there* unless someone was deliberately shielding.

Doubt followed doubt in an insidious circle, each feeding on the one preceding it, until Kris broke the silence.

"This is our first stop—this close to the capital they won't be hungry for news, and it's very unlikely they'd need us to work in any official capacity. Still, it's only good manners to repay them in some way for their hospitality. Small villages don't see trained Bards oftener than once a month, so they're very receptive to even amateur music. Would you be willing to sing if I played?"

"Of course," she replied, grateful for the interruption. "It's only fair that I share the work. Did you notice that I brought My Lady?"

"No!" he exclaimed with delight. "You'll let me play her? I have a smaller traveling harp with me, but it hasn't half the range or the tone of My Lady."

"I let you have her the other night, didn't I? You'll have to retune her. I detuned the strings so they wouldn't snap if the weather changed suddenly." She smiled shyly. "I have good instrument etiquette. Jadus taught me quite well, I assure you."

"He couldn't do otherwise when it came to music. He's the one who taught me in the first place."

"Really? I wonder why he didn't leave her to you?"

"That's easy enough to answer. I didn't take the time to keep him company the way you did," Kris replied with a slightly shamed expression. "He may have given me a little of his skill, but he gave his harp where he'd given his heart—to a lonely little girl, because she'd given him her own."

The village came into view before a surprised Talia had time to form a reply. Children swarmed upon them, chattering and calling questions that both Heralds fielded with chuckles and smiles. Older children ran ahead to alert their elders that there were two Heralds taking the road north, who were clearly planning on spending the night.

Long before they reached the inn at the center of the village square, a crowd had gathered to meet them. The village itself was a large one, with cobblestoned streets and white-plastered buildings of two and even three stories high. Rather than thatched, the roofs were tiled—something Talia had read was more common the farther north one went. With all the shutters thrown open, soft yellow light gleamed through the windows of the houses, as the sun set and candles and lamps were lit.

As Kris had indicated, this village was close enough to the capital that Heralds stopped with fair regularity. Heralds traveling to their Sectors were housed in inns rather than the Waystations, unless they were caught without other shelter, and inns got back a percentage of their taxes for every Herald they entertained. It was possible for an inn on a busy road to be rebated all of its tax if enough Heralds stayed there—and that made Heralds welcomed and sought-after guests.

Under all those strange eyes, Talia regained an outward control, at least; putting on her "public" face and pushing her self-doubts into the back of her mind. It would not do for these people to see her disturbed.

The Innmaster himself welcomed them at his front step and escorted them to the stables. Stablehands tended to the chirras, but the Heralds themselves cared for their Companions. Kris chuckled once or twice—apparently at something that Tantris "said" to him—and Talia felt a tiny twinge of jealousy at their ability to Mindspeak one another.

Once back inside, the Innmaster escorted them personally to their quarters, and gave Talia and Kris small rooms on the second floor—rooms scrupulously, almost painfully clean. Their rooms adjoined one another and each boasted a window, a small table, and a narrow bed that looked surprisingly comfortable.

They were courteously given the use of the bathhouse without anyone pestering them. But once they joined the rest of the guests in the common room for supper, the questions began. The dark-paneled common room overflowed to near-bursting with villagers; tallow-dips in sconces on the walls cast a dim but clear light, so it was easy to see and be seen. The air was seasoned with a pleasant aroma of bread and roasting meat and wood smoke. Though the furnishings were only rough wooden tables and benches, they, and the floor, were sanded smooth and scrubbed clean. The Heralds took their places at a table near the fire, and the rest of the guests gathered around them.

Kris took it upon himself to try and answer them, but when it seemed as if he'd never get more than a mouthful of dinner before it got cold, Talia took her own turn. As Kris had told her, the common people were very well informed this close to the capital: what they wanted most was detail. Much of what they wanted to know centered on the new Heir, a subject Talia knew very well indeed. She satisfied them enough that eventually she and Kris were able to finish their dinners in peace.

Talia had brought My Lady down with her; while Kris tuned her, she took the time to answer questions from a different source—the children. They seemed to sense that this Herald would not brush them off, ignore them, or give them light answers. They had a thousand questions concerning Heralds and what it took to be one.

Some of the questions gave her pause for thought.

"Why don't Heralds ever stay in one place?" one young boy asked. "We always have the same priest—why don't we keep the same Herald?"

"For one thing, there just aren't enough of us to send one to each village, or even one to each group of villages," Talia told him. "For another—tell me, what will happen when your priest grows old and retires, or perhaps dies?"

"They'll send us a new one, of course."

"And he'll be a stranger to all of you. Do you think he'll fit in and be accepted right away?"

"No." The lad grinned impudently. "A lot of the grannies won't really trust him until he's been here for years—if then."

"But a Herald has to have your trust right away, don't you see? If you come to trust the person more than the office, the way you do with your priest, there would be trouble for every new Herald in a Sector."

The boy looked thoughtful at this. "So you move all the time, to make sure it's the job that stays important, not the person doing it. I bet if you stayed in one place too long, you'd get too bound up with the people to judge right, too."

A little startled by this observation, so very accurate, she sent a fleeting thought toward the stable.

Since she wasn't in trance, Rolan couldn't give her more than a vague feeling—but the impression was that he had already noted this boy, and it was very

probable that the child was going to receive a hooved
visitor in the next year or two.

Armed with this knowledge, she answered the rest
of this boy's questions with special care and watched
him afterward. She noted that he seemed to be the
mentor and protector of some of the little children,
urging them forward to talk to her when he knew
that they were too shy to go alone. He wasn't above
his share of pranking about, she noticed with relief,
but his tricks were never those that could *hurt*
anyone.

Kris soon had the harp in tune; Talia let him take
center stage alone for a while, knowing how much the
approving attention would please him. The guests
and villagers were loud in their appreciation, and
only when Kris was glowing from their applause did
Talia add her voice to the harpsong.

The host of the inn eventually decreed they'd tired
the Heralds out long enough, and mock-ordered
both of them to their beds. Talia was just as pleased;
she was feeling the effects of a long day in the
saddle, and she thought of her pillow and warm bed
with longing.

When they mounted the next morning, just as the
sun arose, Talia winced a little as she climbed into
her saddle.

"Sore?" Kris asked with a slight smile.

She groaned faintly. "Before this trip is over I'll
probably be in agony. I didn't realize I was this badly
out of riding trim. I may never be able to get my
legs closed again."

"That would make some people happy," he teased,
and ducked as she threw an apple core left from her
breakfast at him.

"Just for that, maybe I won't give you this." He
held up a pouch that jingled faintly.

"Why? What is it?" she asked, curiosity aroused.

"When I picked up our expense money, I *thought*

perhaps you might have forgotten your stipend," he replied, tossing the pouch over to her. "'You had, so I drew it for you. You're a full Herald now, remember? You earn a stipend."

"Bright Havens!" Her hand flew to her head in embarrassment. "I *did* forget."

"Don't feel badly. After five years of no pocket money, most of us forget. I did. But it comes in very handy, especially when you happen to be at a fair, and see something you just *know* So-and-so would love. Or, for that matter, that *you* can't live without."

"It's a good thing I've got you for a counselor," she replied ruefully. "I'd probably have left my own head back at the Collegium."

Kris just chuckled as he led the way out the gates of the inn onto the road.

As they traveled northward, the road changed from the strange, gray material to packed gravel, to clay, to finally a simple raised and cleared strip between the trees, all the grass worn down by travelers and their mounts and carts.

As the roadway changed, so did the landscape to either side. Farms covered more area—and there were greater stretches of uncultivated land between them, from wide meadows to nearly virgin forest.

The weather changed, growing slowly, but steadily, worse. It rained almost every day, in a steady, penetrating shower. And soon the rains lasted all day, never becoming less than a drippy drizzle, so that the chill water soaked through even their oiled-wool cloaks. The chirras whined in protest at being made to travel at all, and they rode enveloped in miasmas of soggy leaves and wet wool. By the time they reached their chosen resting place each night, they were aching with cold, sodden clear through, and longing for hot wine, hot food, and hotter baths.

Talia's mood was at one with the weather. Her mind kept running in circles on the same subject.

Was she misusing her Gift? How could she tell? What were the ethics of Empathic sensing, anyway?

From time to time, long skeins of waterbirds called from overhead, flying south, high and fast, their cries coming down on the wind like the calls of lonely spirits. The lost calls echoed in Talia's mind long after they'd passed; sad callings for the answers to questions that could not *be* answered.

And when, at dismal day's end, they saw the lights of the next village and heard the cheerful noise of the inn, those were welcome sights and sounds indeed.

And yet for Talia, the sight of the inn became a prospect she almost dreaded. She found herself scanning the faces of those around her, seeking almost obsessively for some sign that *she* was influencing their moods.

The only interruption to her rounds of intense self-scrutiny came when Kris drilled her in the intricacies of the Arrow Code, or coaxed her into some kind of conversation while they rode.

The farther north they came, the farther apart the villages were. Finally there was little choice as to which village they would rest in overnight; often there would be only one within striking distance. The cultivated areas began to be fewer, the woods and forests thicker and showing less evidence of the hand of man. At long last the weather cleared a bit; the rain stopped, although most days were overcast. At the beginning of the trip, the workers they saw in the fields had hailed them cheerfully, then gotten on with what they were doing. Now almost invariably the farmfolk called them to the roadside and offered them a drink of sweet cider or cold spring water in exchange for a bit of news. This evidence alone made it plain that they were on the very edge of the Kingdom, for at this time of year, there wasn't much time left to get the last of the crops in; and it took a great deal to pull a farmer's attention away from that goal, even for the little time it took to drink a glass and pass a trifle of information.

Talia was just as glad that they met with so few people. Her circling self-doubts were beginning to have an effect on her; her shields were wearing thin and she could feel the press of Kris' emotional state just beyond them—though *he* was trained to mind-block without thinking about it. With ordinary folk it was far worse.

It didn't help her doubts at all that to sense that *he* was still uneasy about *her*.

Kris had done his best to shove his uncle's words into the back of his mind, but he wasn't overly successful. He wanted to bring up the subject with Talia again, but hadn't dared. She seemed edgy and pre-occupied in general—and nervous whenever they were around large groups of people, although he doubted that anyone but another Herald would have noticed the nerves behind her "public" face. So he tried to keep the conversation going on other topics.

But behind it all were the unanswered questions. *Was* she misusing her Gift? Was she doing so without realizing it?

And—much more sobering—was she using it to manipulate him?

It was distressing, because he was coming to like her—like her a great deal, more so even than the usual hail-fellow good comradeship that was the norm among Heralds. They were very much alike in many ways. It was horrible to have to suspect a friend of something so insidious.

Because she was becoming that—a friend of the same order as Dirk.

"You know . . ." he said one day, out of the blue, "you're like the sister I never had."

"You're like the brother I wish I had . . ." she replied without seeming to think about it. "That I might have had if Andrean hadn't died in that raid.

He was the only one of my sibs who was kind to me, excepting Vrisa. If I'd had you instead of Justus and Keltev, things might have been easier."

"They also might have turned out a lot differently. Would you have been willing to run away if life had been more pleasant?"

"A good point," she conceded. "Probably not. And then where would I be?"

He grinned, while Tantris shook his head mirthfully and made his bridle bells ring. "If what you've told me is true, six years married, and the mother of as many children."

She grimaced, and shifted in the saddle with a creak of leather. "Thank you, no. Hectic as it is, I like the life I'm leading now. Speaking of which, don't we cross into our new Sector today?"

He pulled the map they'd been given out of a pocket on the front of his saddle, consulted it, and peered around under the lowering sky, looking for landmarks. Finally he spotted one, a cluster of three flat-topped hills off to the west of the road. "We'll cross the border before nightfall, and we'll be staying tonight at our first Waystation."

"Because—" she put on a somber mien. "—Heralds do not stay at inns in the Sector they serve, unless weather prevents them from reaching a Station; this insures that they keep a proper distance and maintain impartiality with the people of their Sector.' I remember."

"You certainly do!" he laughed, cheered by her apparent return to good humor. "That's old Werda to the life!"

"And that's also the reason we either buy the supplies we run out of outright, or wait until we reach a Resupply Station; assuming they're not in the Waystation. Right?"

"High marks; completely correct." He looked about him at the falling leaves, at trees whose branches were almost bare. "I'm sorry that this isn't going to be an easy beginning for you. This is a bad time of year to start riding this Sector. There's going to be snow in the next couple of weeks. Trainees usually aren't faced with conditions this hard at the beginning of their internships."

"I'm Borderbred, remember? *This* is a lot more like the kind of life I was bred to than my life at the Collegium. I'll manage."

"You know," he said soberly, "I know you'll do your best. I know you'll try your hardest. That's all anyone can ask. I trust you. Talia."

At least, he thought to himself, *I think I do.*

Five

The boughs of the nearly-leafless trees arched above them, skeletal hands reaching for the gray sky. The road continued before them, a leaf-carpeted tunnel through the bleak, gray-brown forest. The sodden leaves had been flattened by so many rains that the Companions didn't even kick them up; the dense mat only served to muffle the sounds of their hooves. There were no birds, only the occasional sound of a branch cracking somewhere off in the shadows of the underbrush.

Talia and Kris rode well past sunset and on into the dark to reach the Waystation Kris intended to use as their first stop in their new Sector. With the last rays of the sun went the last hint of warmth; as the last dim, red light filtered through the branches, a cold wind began to sigh among them. Kris took the lead, but it was Tantris, with the superior night-sight of Companions, who was really picking out their way, through cold and dark that was enough to drive just about any other consideration from human minds. Talia was strongly considering unpacking her heavy cloak and was definitely glad that all Waystations, however small or primitive, had fireplaces. The wind had a sharp bit to it, and carried a hint of snow along with the cold.

This Station, as it loomed up out of the shadows in front of them, did not appear to be all that small. Hopefully, it was not primitive either.

One thing was always the first order of business, no matter how late the hour, nor how foul the weather, when Heralds opened a Waystation. Talia dismounted, felt along Rolan's saddle, and took out her firestarter and tinderbox. After no little fumbling and cursing, she managed to get a tiny flame going in the tinder. Protecting it carefully from the wind, she removed a small, fibrous bundle from one of the packs; it had a waxed wick sticking out of it, which she lit at the tiny flame. While Kris pulled off the packs and saddlebags, she tossed it inside and shut the door. He left the packs at her feet, and took Companions and chirras around to the side of the building. While she waited, she shivered in the cold wind, and started a little when an owl cried in the distance. The little, homely sounds Kris was making in the lean-to stable were very welcome against all that dark, with the wind sighing in the boughs of the trees.

She nursed the tiny fire she had going; if it went out, the whole rigamarole was to do over again. When she had counted to one hundred, slowly, she opened the door again. The Station was full of a pungent, oily smoke that was now being swiftly drawn up the chimney with the help of the draft from the open door. And any vermin that had been within the Station were either dead or fled.

Talia hauled the packs and bedrolls inside, then began to get them set up while Kris ducked inside long enough to get grain for the Companions and the chirras who were now in the stabling at the side of the building. She took a rushlight from her saddlebag by feel, and lit it from her bit of tinder. To her immense relief, the place seemed to be quite sturdy, and well maintained and supplied. She threw the bedrolls into the twin bedboxes, then proceeded (wistfully wishing for just a touch of Griffon's Gift) to get a fire going. It took several false starts, but eventually she managed to get a respectable blaze on the cold hearth. Once the flames were high enough to provide illumination as well as warmth, she extinguished the light she'd lit; no sense in wasting what wasn't really necessary, and the rushlights took up so much space in the packs that they didn't carry many of them. She unpacked some of their food supplies and unsealed the vermin-proof cendal-wood bins the Station staples were kept in to put together a reasonable meal, then took two of the larger pots outside to the well to get water for washing and cooking.

Kris seemed to be taking overly long with bedding down the chirras and Companions; she'd managed to heat enough water for both of them to wash, had fixed a meal, and had cleaned herself up and changed into a worn shift and old breeches she kept for sleeping in before he finally appeared. She was about to chide him for being so slow, when she realized that he'd dawdled on purpose.

"Kris, you don't have to be so thrice-blessed chivalrous, you know," she said instead, feeling his reticence sharply, and being irrationally irritated by it. "All the children on the Holdings sleep in the same room until they're thirteen, and you know very well I've shared Waystations and tents with my whole year-group while we were in training. I can't possibly have something you've never seen before—and the same goes for you."

"I'm ... just not used to having a woman as a partner," he said.

"Then stop thinking of me as a woman," she yawned, bundling herself into her bedroll and blinking at him sleepily through the firelight. Her irritation was gone as quickly as it had come, once she'd reinforced her shielding—although the fact that she'd had to do the latter bothered her; she shouldn't have *needed* to.

"That's easy for *you* to say!" he retorted.

"Then pretend I'm Keren, with no interest in men whatsoever. Because if you don't, one of these evenings I'm going to find an ice statue waiting outside the door—and it'll be you!"

He chuckled, and admitted that she just might be right.

Her heart pounded a little the next day as they approached their first village of their Sector. There was no telling what reception awaited them—or what requests. This far from the capital, a village often didn't even boast its own priest, but shared one with several other villages; and the only representatives of Kingdom law were the Heralds.

Her shields were so very thin; she'd discovered that last night. She couldn't fathom why; shielding had always been second-nature, nearly instinctive—and now they seemed to be eroding, slowly, inexorably. She was frightened by the loss of control and was afraid to tell Kris, afraid her confession would simply reinforce his own doubts about her, and create more stress than she already had.

As they rode in, it appeared as though the entire population of the area had asssembled to meet them. Talia thought they must have had lookouts posted, perhaps for the last week or so, waiting for the Heralds they knew were replacing the injured one. The emotional atmosphere—which she felt in spite of her best efforts to shield—was tense, with no hint of why. The village was a small one, single-storied houses of gray wood and darker gray stone, topped with tile roofs, all clustered about a central square. There were no bright-painted shutters here; the wind-driven ice of winter storms would have etched the paint off in a single season. The inn was so small it obviously had no guest-rooms; those overnighting would have to sleep in the common room on the benches when the inn closed for the night. There was no sign of damage to any of the buildings, no hint of disorder; whatever had these folk anxious had nothing to do with their material life. The village folk, though—*they* were dressed in gaudy colors, as if for a festival. So why the feeling of apprehension so thick she could almost smell it?

"Thanks be to the Lady, you've finally come!"

A plump woman who reminded Talia for all the world of a hen bustled forward, pushing before her a young couple of about sixteen or so until they stood less than a foot from Kris' stirrup. Both were dressed in heavily embroidered finery, and the girl was roundly pregnant. They clutched each other's hands as if they were afraid, and neither of them would look at the Heralds. Talia was puzzled beyond her own worries. What was it that could be wrong— that she hadn't sensed?

"The priest took sick and hasn't been able to make his rounds since eight weeks ago," continued the plump woman, tucking a stray strand of hair behind the girl's ear, "and in any case, he hasn't been here since before Midsummer. There hasn't been anyone to marry these two in all that time!"

"Were they properly year-and-day handfasted?" Talia asked, knowing the Border custom, meant to ensure fertility before a permanent bond was made.

"Bright Stars, yes—the priest did it himself last Midwinter!" the woman exclaimed impatiently, while the other villagers nodded in agreement.

Enlightenment dawned on Talia, though Kris was obviously still perplexed about the reason for their obvious apprehension.

"You're both still willing?" he asked. Both gave a very shy assent, but one obviously unforced.

"They're just victims of very bad timing," Talia whispered to him. "And they're afraid we'll disapprove—maybe even refuse to wed them—because they left the formal ceremony so long. They should have wedded as soon as they knew she was with child, but I'll bet a pretty they were so busy with planting that they put it off until after Midsummer, assuming the priest would get here in plenty of time— except that they hadn't counted on him falling ill. Poor babies! They're terribly in awe of us, and they're afraid we'll make difficulties for them because they didn't take care of it right away. We'd be within our right to do so . . . by the letter of the law."

"But not by the spirit," Kris whispered back, relieved that it was so simple. "Well, since everyone's agreed," he said loudly enough for everyone to hear, smiling broadly, "what's holding up the celebration?"

There was a general sigh of tension vanishing, and trestle tables and food began appearing as if conjured by a spell. Before very long the square had been transformed and a proper wedding celebration was in full swing. To save them any further embarrassment, Kris took the young couple off to one side and witnessed their vows, signing their wedding contract as officiating Herald in lieu of a priest.

The young couple returned to enjoy their feast, their shyness nearly gone. They were obviously comforted on two counts: that the Heralds had made no difficulty over the lateness of their vows, and that now their firstborn would have no taint of illegitimacy about it.

The remainder of that day they spent in relative idleness, since there was no use whatsoever in trying to get any official business conducted. The press of people was putting a considerable strain on Talia, but she thought she was succeeding in keeping the strain from showing, even to Kris. She sat mostly on the edge of things, speaking pleasantly when spoken to, but letting Kris take the lion's share of the attention.

And she was even more worried than when they'd first entered this village; her shields hadn't been this fragile since before she'd learned the full use of her Gift. Virtually *anything* would bring them down, and she had to expend ridiculous amounts of energy to put them back up again.

If only she'd never heard those filthy rumors. . . .

The thought of the rumors brought her back full circle to her self-doubt and fear, and the press of emotions became almost painful, until she finally resorted to an old expedient; drinking enough wine to blur the edges of her sensing, and make it all bearable. It was rather too bad that it left her sober enough to negotiate the dark path back to the Waystation with no trouble at all—for that meant she was still sober enough to think.

They returned the next day, ready for business. The people of the village had no grievances that needed settling, but they were eager to hear the news from the capital and the other towns of the Sector. The common room of the inn, dark and smokey as it was, was the only "public" room in the whole village, so that was where they conducted their business. The village storyteller—who doubled as the clerk—sat drinking in every word they spoke, and making copious notes, for it would be his duty to repeat all that the Heralds related for those who were absent from the village, or for those small holders who seldom came to town.

They gave the morning to the decisions of the Queen and Council, how and why those decisions had been reached, and what, if any, laws had been passed to uphold and enforce those decisions; and the afternoon they spent relating the news of the Court and events of major importance to the entire Kingdom—all of which took them until darkness fell, and they returned to the Station again.

This day had lain easier on Talia's wire-taunt nerves, for there was nothing to excite anyone's emotions in the dry news they recited, and even if there had been, the storyteller/clerk was too intent on memorizing every word to allow his feelings to intrude.

When the two of them returned to the Waystation, Talia made herself a cup of double-strength shamile tea, a strong soporific. She was determined to get to sleep, and to sleep deeply, thinking perhaps weariness was part of the cause of her troubles.

But her dreams were uneasy, and she woke feeling more drained than she had been when she'd gone to sleep.

They spent the third day on the reports of the headman and clerk, and taking the verbal news of the village to be passed on up the line. Kris would carry the headman's written reports until they came to a center of population large enough to boast a messenger, or until they arrived at a Resupply Station, at which point he could send what he had collected south to the capital, together with his own observations on the probable truth or falsehood of the information contained in them.

That was Kris' job. Talia remained in the background the entire time, hoping to be noticed as little as possible, for it seemed that the strain was worst when she was interacting with someone.

But that evening at the Waystation, Kris insisted on hearing Talia's opinion on the reports they'd been given, and the reliability of the headman and clerk who had given them.

"They seemed honest to me," she told him, hoping he had no notion of how much she *had* sensed, against her will. "I didn't have any feeling they were trying to mislead us, hide anything, or hold anything back. As far as I can judge, the only mistakes in their records are honest errors. They were quick enough to correct them, in any event, when you pointed them out."

"Good," Kris said with satisfaction. "That tallies with what I saw. I'm just as glad; I hate calling people out—even when it's blatantly obvious that they're lying to me." He noted both their observations on the cover page of the reports, and sealed them in a waterproof wrapper.

To Talia's relief, he had not seemed to note how much strain she was under.

"I didn't realize we took tax records, too," she said, attempting to distract herself—and him—with questions about routine.

"Always, in Border Sectors; almost never in the interior. We take a duplicate of what they're supposed to give the taxmen when they come next spring. This way, if some disaster should destroy their records, they have at least a partial reckoning on file. It's to their advantage, since if there's a disaster of that magnitude, the village may have lost quite a bit more than the records, and the Queen will be able to judge what aid to give them based on what would have been taxed."

She did not make the same mistake with the tea this night, but instead lay in the darkness of the Station, staring up at the blackness above her head, listening to Kris' quiet breathing and going back to her earliest lessons in shield-discipline. She thought, when she finally was weary enough to sleep, that she might have reinforced her shields enough to carry her through the final day.

The fourth day they went over the clerk-storyteller's accounts of what they'd told him, making corrections or elaborations as required. When the fifth day dawned (much to Talia's relief), they were back on the road again; headed through the village on their way out, but not to do more than pick up their laundry and visit the village bathhouse.

By the time they were well past the village and out into the wilds, it was growing noticeably colder, and both of them were wearing their heavier winter cloaks. The trees were now totally barren of leaves, and the warm, friendly scents of autumn were gone from the wind. Although it seldom rained anymore, the skies continued to be overcast—a featureless slate-gray. They crunched their way through a carpet of dead, brown leaves that had collected on the roadway. Most of the birds and beasts were gone, hibernating, or in hiding now; the loss of foliage and cover made them cautious and quiet, those that were left. The Heralds seldom saw more than the occasional rabbit or squirrel, and never heard much besides the wind in the naked boughs of the trees and the scream of a crow or two. The Companions' bridle bells made a lonely chime against the silence of the sleeping forest.

So far as Talia was concerned, that was all to the good; at least she wasn't having to be continually on guard against her shields failing. But her nerves continued to fray; and as they traveled onward through the bleak woods, she wasn't sure which was worse, being alone in this gloom-ridden wilderness, where the gray and empty forest only fed her depression, or being surrounded by people, with shields slowly going to pieces.

Kris wasn't much happier; he kept wondering if— and how much—of his general feelings of approval toward Talia were manufactured. Was she consciously or unconsciously augmenting them? He was beginning to examine every nuance of feeling, trying to detect if *she* had had a hand in it.

He liked her—Bright Havens, he *wanted* to like her, she was so much like him in so many ways. She was a good partner, taking on tasks without complaining, without needing to be prompted, striving to be a full equal and pull her own weight . . . and yet, and yet . . .

Yet there were those rumors, and his own feelings that he could well have been tampered with without his ever noticing it. "No smoke without fire?" Perhaps. It was so damned hard to tell . . . and the way she was withdrawing wasn't helping.

*   *   *

The next stop was two days distant, which meant an overnight stay in a Waystation midway between the two villages. Kris was no longer even thinking of his partner in terms of being female; *now* the strain on his nerves was because of his suspicions. They repeated their routine of the first night; Talia readying the shelter while Kris took care of the four-footed members of the party. His night-vision was much better than hers; it only seemed logical. And it gave him a chance to consult with Tantris without her around.

Tantris was puzzled, and worried. *:I haven't felt anything, little brother, but . . .:*

"But?" Kris asked aloud.

:I am not certain that I would. Rolan is disturbed, and refuses to discuss it.:

"Great."

:He is senior to me, as you are senior to Talia. If he does not wish to discuss the private affairs of his Chosen, that is his business, and his right.:

"I know, I know. Look, at least tell me if you pick up anything, all right?"

:You have my word.: his Companion replied, *:but I think perhaps . . .:*

"Perhaps what?"

:You need more expert aid,: came the reluctant reply.

"Tell me from where, and I'll get it! There isn't anybody in the Circle with a Gift like hers—and I rather doubt that Healer's Empathy is identical."

:True,: came the sigh in his mind, and after that, he could coax nothing more out of Tantris on the subject.

It troubled him deeply. If a *Companion* didn't feel up to the problem . . .

And they did not even have time to reach the gate of the next village before they were met on the road by two different parties demanding justice.

They saw it coming easily enough. "Steady," Kris said as they rode into a press of farmers in heavy brown homespun, who crowded up against the sides of the Companions with their petitions. Talia went pale and strained, and sat Rolan's back absolutely motionless and with lips tightly compressed. Kris did his best to sort out the arguments, then finally lost patience and sharply ordered them all to hold their tongues.

When the clamor died down, he finally managed to ascertain that there were two aggrieved parties, both as alike to his eyes as a pair of crows—brown hair, thick brown beards, nearly identical clothing of brown homespun. After listening to both sides, and putting up with each one interrupting the other until he was ready to take a stick to both of them, he decreed that the argument was moot until third parties could be questioned.

The dispute was a trivial one by *his* lights, over a cow and her calf. The facts were that a bull had somehow made its way into a field containing a cow in season; not surprisingly, the calf resulted. The calf was quite plainly the offspring of the bull in question, nor did the cow's owner deny this. What *was* under dispute was how the bull had gotten at the cow in the first place.

The cow's owner claimed angrily that the owner of the bull had allowed it to stray, and that it had found its own way there, and thus he had incurred no stud fee. He pointed to the damage done to his hedges, and inquired with self-righteous wrath if anyone thought he'd ruin his own enclosure to save himself the fee.

The bull's owner claimed just as vociferously that the owner of the cow had enticed the bull into the pasture with the express purpose of saving himself the stud fee.

Kris felt absolutely helpless; this was *not* an area in which he had any expertise at all. He glanced entreatingly at his internee, who was farmbred, after all, and should have *some* notion of how to sort it out. Talia was looking a bit white around the lips and eyes, but otherwise seemed in control. He nudged Tantris up beside her, and whispered, "All right, trainee—you know more about this sort of thing than I do. Got any ideas?"

She started just a little; possibly only someone watching for reactions would have noticed it. "I . . . I think so," she said, slowly. "It's like a dispute we had once back at Sensholding."

"Then take over. *I'm* out of my depth."

She asked a few questions of the disputants, then went among the rest of the villagers, making inquiries into the habits of each of the parties in question. It was generally agreed that, while the owner of the cow was parsimonious, he was far too stingy to have ruined his own fences just to save a stud fee. And the bull's owner had a habit of allowing it to stray, being too lazy to fix breaks in his own enclosures until after the beast had escaped yet another time.

But then she surprised Kris by asking a source he never would have considered—some of the children gathered at the edge of the crowd. After sidelong glances to be certain that no one was likely to tell them to hold their tongues, they told Talia that this particular cow was *never* kept in the field where the bull had supposedly found her. She was quite valuable, and her owner always kept her where he could keep an eye on her.

Talia returned to the disputants.

"This is my first judgment;" she said, slowly, and with an oddly expressionless tone. "There is no doubt that your bull *did* stray, and since it is quite probable that it did the damage claimed to the fences, you owe this man for the repairs he had to make."

The owner of the bull looked extremely disgruntled; the cow's owner gloated. Talia did not allow him to gloat for long.

"You, on the other hand," she told him—not quite looking at him, "have never kept your cow in that particular field. You must have seen that the bull had broken in, and decided that since the damage was already done, you might as well save yourself the stud fee. So you moved your cow to the field where the bull was. Because of this, my second judgment is that you owe him half the stud fee he would normally have charged you."

Now both of them looked chagrined.

"All things considered, I should think that you are probably even."

They grudgingly agreed that this was the case.

"Don't you leave yet!" she said, turning to the owner of the bull, and showing a little more animation. "You have been letting a potentially dangerous animal roam loose. My third judgment is that anyone who finds your bull roaming and confines it in a safe place for you to take home is entitled to have his cows serviced for nothing to pay him for his trouble. *That* should induce you to take better care of your stock in the future."

The grins creasing the faces of the rest of the villagers made it clear that they considered Talia's rulings to have been equitable and appropriate—and they were certainly popular. Kris smiled and gave her a little nod of approval; she smiled back, tentatively, some of the strain gone from around her eyes.

With children ranging along before and behind them, they continued down to the village itself, which was a slightly larger version of the first village they had served, and actually boasted a "town hall" of sorts. It was there that they set up shop in the single large room that served as a meeting hall, behind an ancient and battered marble-topped table that might well be the oldest object in the village. It was an improvement on the common room of the inn in that it wasn't as smoky or cramped; but the fireplace did little to heat it, and Kris found himself hoping that they would be able to deal with their business and be on their way before he got frostbitten feet and fingers.

But another dispute for arbitration landed on them almost immediately; a problem of the location of the boundary between two neighboring farms. The farmers themselves were not overly concerned about the matter, as they were old freinds and had settled the problem over the years by sharing equally both the work and the fruits of the fields in question. They confided to Kris, however, that they feared this could not continue for very much longer; both had more than one son to be provided for, and they feared that tempers were already growing heated on the subject among their offspring. Kris, after a glance at Talia showed him she had no opinion in this matter, agreed that the matter should be settled now, before it developed into a full-blown feud. He promised that they would attend to it as soon as they had discharged their other duties.

The disputants were obliged to be content with that. Kris called for the village records, and while each of them took a turn at relaying the news and the laws, the other searched the records provided by the village clerk for clues to the ownership of the properties in question.

Regrettably, the clues were few, and contradictory. It seemed that both claims were equally valid.

Talia was increasingly reluctant to take any part in the affairs at hand. Her shielding was disintegrating, slowly, but steadily; she was positive of that now. What was worse, she was no longer certain that she was able to keep her own feelings from intruding and influencing those around her, for her instinct-level control over projection was going, too. Kris was trying to put her at ease, but she could sense his own doubts as clearly as if he were shouting them aloud.

And when, the night before they were due to

leave, they discussed the problem of the disputed fields at length in the privacy of the Waystation, she was keeping herself under such tight control that she knew she was going to have a reaction-headache from the strain.

"The problem is that the stream they used as the original dividing line has changed its bed so many times that I can't see any way of reconstructing what it was originally," Kris sighed. "And you can't cast a Truth Spell on a stream!"

She hesitated a long moment, drawing invisible patterns on the hearthstone of the Station with a twig. "Do you suppose they'd settle for dividing it equally? You've talked with them more than I have."

"Not a chance," Kris replied flatly, firelight casting ever-changing shadows across his face. "I've talked with the eldest sons, and they're just about ready to come to blows over it. The fathers would be perfectly willing, but the children would never stand for it, and it's the children who will make trouble if they're not satisfied."

"I can't see making this an all-or-nothing proposition," she sighed, after a long pause.

"Neither can I," Kris stared into the flames, thinking. "Among the highborn the way to settle this would be to marry two of the younger children, then deed the land in question to them."

"There's not enough land there to support even one person, much less a family," Talia felt impelled to point out, "even if we could find two of the children willing to marry."

Kris played absently with one of the arrows from his quiver—then looked down at it suddenly, and smiled in inspiration. "What about the hand of Fate?"

"What do you mean by that?"

"Suppose we each took a stand on the opposite sides of the area and shot arrows straight up—then drew a line between where they landed for the new border. If there's no wind tomorrow, where they fall is going to be pretty much at the whim of the Lady. Do you think that would satisfy everyone?"

"That . . . that's no bad notion," she said, thinking hard. "Especially if we have the priest bless the arrows, pray over the fields, that sort of thing. It wouldn't be human decision anymore; it would be in the hands of the gods—and who's going to dispute the will of the gods? I think both families will be willing to abide by it. Kris, that's a wonderful idea!" She sighed, rather sadly. "I wouldn't have thought of that."

"You did *fine* yourself, earlier," he said, more forcefully than he had intended. "I was totally out of my depth."

"Well, I don't like the idea of anyone allowing livestock to roam at will. Out here on the Border if cattle or hogs get into the forested areas, they're likely to go feral, and then you've got a real problem on your hands."

"Hmn. I knew dogs gone wild could be a problem, but I never knew livestock could." Kris filed that piece of information away for future reference.

"It's a fairly serious problem," she replied absently. "When domestic animals go feral, they have no fear of man the way wild animals do, and what's more, they're familiar with how people act. There was more than one person among Holderkin killed or maimed by feral stock."

"Well, I repeat, you did fine. You shouldn't be afraid to put your say in. That's what this internship is all about."

"I—" she started, then shrank back into herself.

"What?"

"Nothing," she replied, moving back into the shadows where he couldn't read her expression. "I'm just tired, that's all. We should get some rest."

That withdrawal troubled him badly . . . but there didn't seem to be anything he could do about it.

*   *   *

On their way out of town the next day, they stopped to acquire the clerk and the priest; when they presented their solution to the two families in question, both sides were heartily in favor of it. The farmers themselves were willing to agree to any solution to the problem that would defuse the potentially explosive situation between their children. The children of both families were equally certain that the gods would be with them when the arrows flew.

For something that had been under dispute for so long, the end came almost as an anticlimax. The priest blessed arrows, bows, Heralds, fields, families—anything that could possibly pertain to or be interested in the problem. ("If it moves, I'm blessing it," he told the Heralds with a twinkle in his eyes. "And if it doesn't move, I'm praying over it!") Talia and Kris each took a stand on the exact midpoint of the northern and southern boundaries of the disputed plot and launched their arrows; the priest marked the landing point of one, the clerk of the other. The landing places were permanently designated with stone cairns and newly-planted trees, the new border was made and drawn on the maps and deeds. Both sides professed themselves satisfied. The Heralds went on their way.

But by now Talia was so withdrawn that Kris could not read her at all; she might as well have been a statue of a Herald. She seemed to have wrapped herself in a cocoon of self-imposed isolation, and nothing he could do or say seemed to be able to break her out of it.

And as for himself, he found himself wondering if both those disputes hadn't been solved a little *too* easily. It would have been child's play for her to have nudged the disputants ever so slightly into a more friendly—or at least less antagonistic—attitude toward one another. And once she was gone, if that was indeed what she had done, the quarrels would break out all over again.

Had he been overly impressed with the way she had handled the first case? Had she been adjusting *his* attitude?

There was simply no way of being sure . . . no way at all.

Talia was coming to realize that all her control had been on a purely instinctive level; that she really didn't *understand* how her own Gift worked. The training Ylsa had given her was the sort given to Mindspeakers, and in the face of this disintegration of control, very little of Ylsa's teaching seemed directly applicable to her current problem. The Healers she'd worked with had never said anything to her . . . perhaps because they'd seen the control and assumed it was conscious rather than instinctive.

For that matter, her Gift might not be much like theirs except in effect. They certainly didn't use *their* Empathy as primary Gift; it was used mostly as an adjunct to Healing.

They certainly weren't confronted with the ethical considerations she found herself facing. When they weren't Healing, they simply shielded. And they didn't work with law and politics.

She longed to tell Kris—and feared to. It would only make things worse, and what could he do, after all? His Gift wasn't even of the same type as hers, and what training he had been given could hardly apply to her.

So she said nothing, endured in miserable self-doubt, and did her best to reverse a situation that was moving increasingly out of control.

Six

There was little of note in any of the towns and villages they passed through on their meandering way to the Border. The worst that they encountered were three cases where the village headmen were obviously trying to cover something up; twice they were lining their own pockets with tax money, once the headman was deliberately omitting his farms and those of his kin from the survey and tax rolls. In all three cases they actually *did* nothing when the cheats were uncovered; that was not their job. Instead, they noted these facts on their reports. When the taxmen arrived in the spring, they would come armed with the truth, and the guilty parties would find themselves paying a stiff penalty. This kept the onus of tax enforcement off the Heralds.

One thing was notable: the farther north they went, the greater the distance grew between communities, and the smaller the communities were. Now it was taking nearly a week's ride to pass from village to village.

Talia remained withdrawn and silent, responding only when spoken to, and never volunteering any opinion. She seemed to warm up a little when they were between villages. She'd talk to Kris then, on her own; she even could be persuaded to sing a little.

But as soon as they came within a day's ride of a populated area, the shutters came down, and she locked everything and everyone outside. When she spoke, she had an odd, flat, indifferent quality to her tone. She reminded Kris of himself the first time he'd walked the two-rope bridge on the obstacle course; there was that kind of tautness underneath the mask, as if she expected to fall at any moment. Tantris could tell him nothing, but even Rolan seemed unusually on edge.

There was one other thing to observe about the countryside; these northernmost communities were not only smaller, but they kept themselves behind palisades of strong logs, with gates that were barred at night. There were wolves and other wild beasts prowling the winter nights—and some of those beasts were on two legs. The Forest of Sorrows didn't keep everything out of this Sector, and couldn't prevent outlaws from coming in from the three directions other than the forest Border. Talia and Kris rode with all senses alert and their weapons loose and to hand now, and they bolted the Waystation doors at night.

All of which *might* have accounted for Talia's nerves; except that she supposedly came from Border country herself, and should be used to keeping watch for raiders. Still, Kris reasoned, it *had* been a long time, and she had never been part of the defenders—she had been part of what was being protected.

But that wouldn't account for Rolan's nerves. The Companions were both combat-trained *and* combat-experienced; they were more than guard enough for themselves, their Chosen, and the chirras. Kris watched Talia—unobtrusively, he hoped—and worried, and wondered.

They progressed through several towns and villages; Talia was beginning to feel as if she were falling to pieces, bit by bit. Her shields were eroding to the point where she had very little control over them, and nearly everything was getting through; she *knew* she was not only reading, she was inadvertently projecting, because *Rolan* was becoming as nervous as she was. Her only defense was to withdraw into herself as much as possible, and Kris seemed bound and determined to prevent *that*. She felt lost, and frightened, and utterly alone. There was no one she could turn to for help; Kris himself had said that he thought her Gift was unique. She was certain now that *he* couldn't give her any advice on how to handle it; his own Gift *was* very nearly the kind that could be weighed and measured. Hers wasn't even necessarily detectable. And now it was becoming utterly unpredictable. Her feeling of panic and entrapment grew.

Finally they reached the town of Hevenbeck, very nearly on the Border itself. Tailia's unhappiness was a hard knot within her now; the petty problems of the townfolk seemed trivial at this point.

In the previous village they'd had some of their messages catch up with them; one of them had been a brief note to Talia from Elspeth. She'd said only that she was doing well, hoped Talia was the same, and that Talia wasn't to worry about her. And that added to Talia's troubles. She had no notion of what prompted the note, or what could be happening back at the capital at this moment. Elspeth was in her first year as a trainee; like Talia she was the only girl in her year-group. She was probably confused—most certainly overwhelmed—and just entering adolescence to top it all off. *And* she would be having to cope with all the rumors Talia already knew, and whatever had sprung up in her absence. It was quite likely she needed Talia more now than she ever had since she'd been the Brat.

Not to mention the effect of the rumors on the rest of the Heralds.

Would they, like Kris, be tempted to believe them?

Or would they dismiss them out of hand and ignore the matter—leaving Elspeth to face them alone?

How was Selenay getting along without her? What if the Queen was turning to Orthallen for advice—Orthallen, whom Talia somehow *could not* bring herself to trust?

She was so engrossed in trying to hold control and deal with these other worries that had begun occurring to her that she was paying scant attention to the petitioners before her—a grim and straitlaced couple who reminded Talia unpleasantly of her own Holderkin relatives.

They were dressed in clothing of faded black and dusty brown; carefully mended and patched as if they were two of the town's poorest inhabitants, although Talia and Kris had been informed by the headman that they were actually one of the wealthiest couples Hevenbeck boasted. Their mouths were set in identical disapproving grimaces as they harked over their grievances in thin, whining voices.

Those voices irritated her no end; their petty spitefulness rasped at her through what was left of her shields, like having sandpaper rubbing over a sunburn. She was grateful when Kris interrupted them.

"You're quite certain this girl is responsible for the missing poultry? There's no chance it could be foxes or other vermin?"

"Our coops are as tight as our house, Herald," the man whined. "More so! She's done it; done it in spite of the good wages we've paid her and the comfortable job she's had with us. I don't doubt she's been selling them—"

"But to whom? You said yourself no one in town will admit to buying fowl from her."

"Then she's been eating them!" the woman retorted. "Greedy she is, that I know for certain—"

Talia forced herself to turn her attention to the serving maid; her garb was even more threadbare than her employers, she was thin and pale, and looked ill-used. She certainly didn't look to Talia as if she'd been feasting on stolen chickens and geese!

The girl briefly raised her eyes—and a disquieting chill threaded Talia's backbone at the strange blank, gray gaze. Then she dropped her regard again, and Talia dismissed her misgiving as another manifestation of her lack of control over her Gift. She wanted away from them all; they made her skin crawl, and all she wanted was to have this nonsense over with so that she could retreat back into the relatively safe haven of the Station.

She spoke without thinking about anything except getting rid of them.

"I can't see where you have any proof of what you're claiming," she interrupted sharply, "and I can't see why you're bringing it before Heralds—"

"Talia, you haven't been listening," Kris said in a low, warning voice. "It isn't just the missing birds—though that's all they seem to be worrying about. There's other things—the runes on their doorstep in blood—the—"

"Kris, this is *ridiculous!*" she exploded. "All they want is an excuse to dismiss that poor child without her wages! Havens, Keldar used to pull that filthy trick once every year—hire some pathetic wench and dismiss her on some trumped-up excuse before her year's wage came due!"

"Talia," Kris said after a pause, his voice full of reluctance, "I hate to have to pull rank on you, but I'm going to have to insist—because you can work Second-stage Truth Spell and I can't. I want you to cast it on all three of them in turn."

"I can't believe you're wasting Truth Spell on something this petty!"

"That's an order, Herald."

She bit her lip at the cold tone of his voice, and obeyed without another word. The First-stage Truth Spell only revealed whether or not the speaker was telling the truth. Second-stage *forced* him to tell it.

Much to her surprise, when Kris questioned the couple at some length while she held the spell on them, their story was the same.

Then she transferred the spell to the timid-seeming servant-girl—and mouse became a rabid weasel.

The girl underwent a complete personality change when Talia's spell touched her mind. She stared at her employers, eyes bright and feral, a fierce snarl twisting her lips. "Oh, yes," she hissed softly. "*Oh* yes, I've been taking their birds. It's little enough for all they've done to me—"

"What have they done to you?" Kris prompted.

"Beatings for the least little clumsiness—bread and barley-broth and moldy cheese, meal after meal. They own the biggest flock of hens in the town, and I haven't tasted an egg or a bit of chicken in half a year! My pledged clothing is *her* castoffs, and worn to nothing by the time I get them. When I'm not bruised, I'm hungry, when I'm not hungry, I'm cold! But I'll have my revenge—"

The look of mad hatred she turned on the two made them shrink back away from her, frightened at the transformation in her. And Talia clenched her hands until her nails bit into her palms, endeavoring to hold control in the storm of the rage and hatred she was experiencing.

"—oh, *yes,* I'll have my revenge! That's what the birds were for, you know. I've not been eating them. I've been sacrificing them—giving them to the wolves. They come to me every night now. Soon now, soon they'll teach me how to change my skin for one of theirs, and when I learn—when I learn—"

The mad light in her eyes told clearly what she expected to do to her employers when she'd learned to shift her shape. Talia went cold all over, shaking from head to foot. The beat of the girl's emotions against her crumbling barriers was almost enough to send her fleeing in panic. Her breath froze in her throat, and she could feel herself coming perilously close to insanity herself.

"—and after them, the rest. And my gray brothers and sisters will help, oh, yes—" The maid began to raise her voice, and her words disintegrated into babbling; raving fragments of hatred and imagination.

It was too much for Talia to bear. The girl was shattering her barriers, and about to draw *her* down into madness. She reached out blindly, without thinking, using her Gift in instinctive self-defense, and touched the girl, putting her into a sudden sleep.

The plaintiff couple was speechless; for a long moment, so was Kris.

"I think," Kris said carefully, at last, "That we had better take her and put her into the care of a Healer. I don't know how much of what she said about the way you treated her was the truth, and how much she imagined, but I think perhaps you'd better agree to pay all the Healer's expenses. And if you take another servant—you'd best be careful about her working conditions."

Kris was ominously silent as they rode back to the Station in the gathering dusk. The disposition of the mad girl had occupied all the rest of the afternoon. It had taken the Healer nearly a candlemark to wake her from the deep sleep Talia had thrown over her. And Talia was profoundly shamed, as much for her panicked, unthinking reaction as for the self-centered, willful irresponsibility that had led her to neglect her duty.

"Kris . . . I'm sorry," she said in a subdued, unhappy voice as soon as they were past the city gates. "I didn't mean—I—"

Kris said nothing, and Talia shrank back into herself, the last of her carefully-built self-confidence shattered.

He guesses—surely he guesses. I'm a failure; I can't even control myself enough to complete half a circuit. I can't do anything right.

But he made no reply, not even to condemn; she

could only sense that he was thinking, but not what he was thinking about. She rode silently at his side, waiting for the axe to fall, all the way back to the Station. And the fact that it did *not* fall only made things worse.

Kris rode in silence, only now beginning to realize that by not giving her a little comfort and encouragement that he had made a nearly fatal mistake. Her self-esteem was far more fragile than he had guessed. And her nerves were plainly gone. Now he thought he knew why she would venture no judgments at all, and gave him her opinions hesitantly, and only when directly asked for them. When he asked her, back at the Station, she avoided answering all questions about how she was feeling, answering only that she was "all right." He began to wonder if she'd ever recover from the incident . . . and he began to fear that he'd ruined her.

And then, deep in the darkness of the night, the disturbing thought occurred to him that she was slowly going mad, and perhaps taking him with her.

There was snow on the ground as they rode toward the tiny hamlet that bore the dubious distinction of being the settlement that was farthest north and nearest the Border, right up against the Forest of Sorrows itself. Talia, more used to having to exert herself to bolster what was left of her shields than to stretch out to sense the population centers, began wondering if her powers had finally failed her altogether. But, no—there was Kris, so clear to her raw mind that his proximity was almost painful. So it had to be something else.

She finally got up her courage and confided what she had not sensed to Kris. "There's just too much . . . well, 'silence' is the only way I can put it. I can hardly feel anything, and the little I can pick up is as if everyone were sleeping, or unconscious."

"You're certain that the cold's not affecting you?" he asked.

I only wish it would, she thought wistfully, then answered him. "No . . . I don't think so. It was no colder back at Greenhaven, and I could feel the people from a day away."

He considered. "All right then, we'd better pick up our pace to the fastest the chirras can maintain. If there's something wrong, the sooner we get there, the better."

The snow creaked underfoot, and the bridle-bells rang madly as they picked up the pace to a trot. The air was utterly still; the sky cloudless and an intense blue that almost hurt the eyes. Sun filtered through the bare branches of the trees, leaving shadows like blue lace on the snowbanks. It was a beautiful day, and the strange uneasiness Talia was feeling was entirely out of place in it.

The village itself was very quiet as they came within sight of it—too quiet by far. Sheltered between two hills, the cleared area in which it stood showed no tracks on the snow whatsoever, neither coming nor going. The gates stood open, and unattended. Kris' face showed his alarm so clearly that Talia knew without having his emotions battering her that he was as fearful as she. He ordered Talia to remain where she was, and descended the hill they were on to the village gates, taking his chirra inside with him.

He hadn't been inside long when she saw the gates slam shut, and heard the bar slide into its slots. Immediately following this, she saw an arrow arc over the palisade to land in the snow on her side of the wall.

She ran to where it had landed. It bore four rings; three were green, one was red. She checked the fletching pattern; it was Kris' without a doubt. It might have seemed silly for him to have patterned the arrow when she'd watched him enter the village with her own eyes, but this was truly the only way for her to be certain that when the gate slammed shut it had been because *he* had shut it, and not outlaws lairing within.

This could only mean one thing. The entire village had fallen victim to some kind of plague.

Lord and Lady—what do I do— she thought frantically, then staggered as Rolan pushed her impatiently with his nose. She felt his annoyance as plainly as if he'd spoken it. He'd had more than enough of her self-indulgent nerves; this required action, simple action. She knew very well what she had to do, and she'd damn well better get about doing it!

It was as if something within her that had been broken was being splinted together. She forced herself to regain calm, to plan. She wrote a note, telling Kris that she was leaving her chirra tethered to the gate, and that he should take it inside when he saw that she'd left. She took a plain white arrow of her own, tied the note to it, and sent it back across the wall. She went through her packs, removing a map, a skin of water, and a bag of meal for herself and Rolan to share.

Consulting the map, she saw that the nearest Healing Temple lay five days by horse to the east. That meant that she and Rolan could make it in two.

She tethered the chirra, swung herself onto Rolan's back, and they were off.

This was where the ground-devouring pace of the Herald's Companion was worth more than gold or gems. A Companion could travel at the equivalent of an ordinary horse's gallop for hours without tiring. If need be, he could subsist for several days at this punishing pace with little more than water and a handful or two of meal. He would need several days of heavy feeding and rest when the ordeal was over, but a Companion never faltered, and seldom even strained muscles or tendons under the conditions that would kill a horse. Any place a hooved animal could go, a Companion could go, including scrambling over icy, hazardous rock-falls only goats would dare. The only thing his Herald need worry about was whether he was capable of staying on his back!

Talia and Rolan pushed their pace far into the night; she ate and drank in the saddle, even dozed a bit. Their road was clear, and relatively dry; the footing was good, so Rolan exerted himself to the uttermost. There was even a full moon, so they could see their way quite clearly. The noise of their passing disturbed whatever wildlife there was, so they rode in a silence broken only by the sound of Rolan's hooves pounding on the frozen ground. It was an eerie journey, like something out of a dream, a wild ride that never seemed to get anywhere. Rolan was relatively fresh, so they continued on until even after the moon had set. Finally, however, even he had to take a brief rest. Not long before dawn, they broke their journey in a tiny clearing alongside the road, beside a stream crowned with an ice-covered waterfall.

Rolan halted right next to the pool below the waterfall, his flanks heaving, his sides steaming in the cold, his breath puffing out and frosting around his nostrils. Talia broke the ice for him, but the water was too cold for him to drink safely. She gave him water from her own waterskin instead, filling it when it was empty, warming it against her body, and letting him drink until he'd had enough. She filled the skin one last time, and had a long drink herself after giving him about a third of the meal she was carrying. Just as the sun rose, striking fire from the bejeweled waterfall, they were ready to resume the grueling run.

They stopped again near noon, for both of them had needs of nature to attend to. That did not take them long at all, and Talia took advantage of the daylight and relatively warm sun to strip his tack off him long enough for it to dry, rubbing him down with the towel she always kept in his saddlebag.

She leaned her head against his flank, knees feeling weak, and not just from the long ride.

Lady help me—Healers have my Gift—how am I ever going to face them? How can I face anyone, falling apart like this? Oh, gods—I can't bear it—

Rolan nudged her shoulder gently; she could almost hear him in words, so clearly did his message come to her. *I'll help you,* the feeling said.

"Oh, Gods—can you?"

The reply was an unqualified affirmative. She sighed, and relaxed, and reached out to him—

And felt her shields coming up, held up by a force from outside herself; felt a calm come over her, and a kind of numbness that was so much better than the pain and stress she'd been living with that she nearly cried.

"How long—?"

His regret seemed to say that he couldn't hold things for very long at all.

"Just make it long enough for us to get there and back. I'll work so hard I'll wear myself out, and *that* will keep things under control. I can't project if I don't have the strength to spare. I'll figure out what's gone wrong, I know I will—if I can just stay away from people for a while—"

Then let's go, his impatient headshake said.

The tack, including the saddle blanket, was dry to the touch, so she lost no time in getting him saddled again and getting on their way, with anxiety riding pillion behind her.

They galloped into the courtyard of the Healing Temple shortly after dusk. Her Whites and her Companion gave her instant attention; Rolan had not even halted when a green-clad novice Healer was at her stirrup to receive her orders. Immediately behind him came two more, one with hot wine with herbs in it for Talia, the other with fresh, warm gruel for Rolan. Both of them consumed their portions with gratitude, while a messenger went to arouse the two Heralds posted to this Temple. Meanwhile another novice lit torches all around the courtyard, and before Talia had finished her wine, a fragile, slender woman whose close-cropped hair flamed red even in the uncertain torchlight came at a dead run across the cobbled court. She had a heavy satchel slung over one shoulder, her green robes were flying, and she was tying a cloak on as she ran.

"I'm Kerithwyn;" she said as she reached Talia. "I'm the most experienced Healer here in plague diseases. The other two you asked for will follow as soon as our Heralds are ready, but I'm ready to leave now."

"All right, then; the sooner we get back to Kris the happier I'll be. You're used to riding pillion with a Herald?" Talia held out her hand to aid the Healer astride Rolan.

"You could say that," the woman replied, taking Talia's outstretched hand. She gave Talia an odd look when their hands touched, hesitated a moment, then set her foot on top of the Herald's, and lifted herself onto the pillion pad behind Talia with practiced ease.

"Rolan is a good bit faster than most Companions—so be prepared."

Despite the advance warning, Talia heard the woman gasp a little in surprise as Rolan launched himself back the way they had come.

It was obvious, however, that the woman was no stranger to this kind of transportation. She held her seat without losing her grip on her medicinals or on Talia's belt, but also without any panic-stricken clutching. She kept her cloak tucked in all around her, and kept her head down, taking advantage of the small shelter behind Talia from the wind of their passing. Talia was relieved to learn that she was prepared to eat and doze a-horse, and if anything, was even less willing than Rolan to stop for rest.

They reached the village shortly after midday of

the second day of their return. It was still utterly
lifeless, and Talia's unpredictable shields had shut
down on her, so that she couldn't even sense Kris
within.

She had the Healer dismount, then backed Rolan
up to the gate to beat a tattoo on it with one of his
hind hooves. No matter where Kris was, waking or
sleeping, so long as he hadn't fallen ill himself, he'd
hear *that*.

She fretted, hands clenching on the reins, when he
didn't appear immediately after the pounding. He
could so easily have caught the plague himself; they
were anything but immune. Kerithwyn stirred uneasily by her stirrup, the same thoughts obviously
occurring to her, by the worried look on her face.

But then she heard the bar slide back and the gate
cracked open just enough to admit them. She rode
straight in without stopping to dismount, the Healer
following, and only slid off when they were inside
the gates.

"The other two are less than a day behind us, but I
was ready immediately, so I came on ahead," Kerithwyn
told Kris briskly. "What is the situation?"

Kris was sliding the bar back into place, and when
he turned to face them, Talia wanted to weep with
pity for him. She could hardly believe how worn-
looking he was; he must have been on his feet since
she'd left.

"It's bad," Kris said wearily, "It looks like the entire population was hit within a day or two. There
were five dead when I got here, and I've lost three
more since."

"Symptoms?"

"High fever, delirium, a red rash, and swelling
under the jaw and the arms."

Kerithwyn nodded. "Snow fever—that's what we
call it anyway. It generally shows up right after the
first few snowfalls; after Midwinter it seems to vanish and it never appears in warm weather. How have
you been treating them?"

"Trying to get liquids down them, especially willowbark tea, although when the fever seemed to be getting too high, especially in the children, I packed them in snow for a bit to bring it down."

"Excellent job! I couldn't have done better myself," she applauded. "I've got some specific remedy with me, but it will take a little time to do any good, so we'll be doing more of the same with the ones not in immediate danger. I'll start with Healing the worst victims now. Have either of you ever assisted a Healer before?"

"I can't," Kris replied shaking his head, so that his lank hair fell onto his forehead. "The last Healer I spoke to said my Gifts were all wrong. I'm afraid I'll be of more use as a simple pair of hands."

Kerithwyn turned to look at Talia, her look oddly measuring.

She swallowed hard, but answered. "I've never tried, but my Gifts are Empathy and Mindhealing. My instructor said they were Healing types." *If I'm going to be assisting, I can't have shields up anyway, and this is going to take so much energy I won't be projecting either.*

"Empathy in a Herald?" Kerithwyn raised one eyebrow. "Well, you ought to be a great deal of help, then. We'll try it, anyway; the worst that can happen is nothing. Herald, have you isolated the worst cases?"

"They're all in here," Kris pointed to a small house immediately next to the gate. "When it didn't seem to harm them to move them, I put all of the worst of them together."

"Excellent." Kerithwyn gave him about a pound of an herbal mixture, instructing him to make a cauldron of tea with it. He was to give every victim at least a cupful, and drink some himself. As Kris left to follow her instructions and care for Rolan, Kerithwyn entered the house with Talia.

The house was cramped and dark, with the windows kept shuttered against the cold air. Kris had moved as many beds and pallets into the three rooms of the house as he could fit. He had done his best to keep his patients clean and had herbal incense burning on the hearth against the miasma of sickness, but there was still a faint but noticeable odor of illness. So many people crowded together made Talia feel claustrophobic, and the smell made her faintly nauseous. She was only grateful that these people were apparently so deeply unconscious that there was nothing for her to have to try to shield against. Kerithwyn appeared not to notice any of this.

The worst of the sick ones was a frail old woman whose bloated jaws looked grotesque on her thin face.

"Take a chair and sit next to me, Herald," the Healer instructed. "Make yourself comfortable, take my free hand, and drop your shielding—" Again that measuring look. "—and do whatever it is that you do when you prepare to Mindspeak. I'll take care of the rest."

Talia closed her eyes and forcibly ignored her surroundings and put her anxieties into abeyance by concentrating on an old breathing exercise.

It took her a long, considering moment to determine that she was still capable of going into deep-trance. With everything *else* going merrily to hell, she wasn't entirely certain she'd be able to perform even such a rudimentary exercise as deep-trancing.

Tentative trial proved that fear, at least, was groundless.

Once she achieved the appropriate level of trance-state, the Healer appeared to her inner eyes as a nearly solid core of calming green-and-gold energy.

Gods be thanked, she thought with detached gratitude, *Kerithwyn must be even more of an expert than she claimed.*

It wasn't just that the Healer possessed a controlled power the equal of any of the teaching Healers Talia had dealt with—it was also that Talia herself had nothing to fear from the Healer's presence. Kerithwyn was allowing *no* negative emotions to ruffle the surface of *her* mind!

The patient seemed to be roiling with something dark, muddy-red. Talia observed with detached fascination as the Healer sent lances of light into these sullen eddies, cleaning and dispersing them, and feeding the tiny, flickering sparks she uncovered beneath them until they burned strongly again. As Kerithwyn worked, Talia could both see and feel energy draining from herself to the Healer, replacing what Kerithwyn spent.

Now that she understood what the Healer required, she opened the channel between them to its fullest possible extent and reached for Rolan's support. Energy flowed to the Healer in a steady, powerful stream from the two of them, and the work picked up in pace and sureness. It was all finished in a moment, and Talia felt the contact between them break. She sped up her own breathing, turned her concentration outward, and opened her eyes.

The Healer's gray eyes were filled with approval. "*Very* good, Herald; you grasped the concept quite quickly. Can you continue as well as you have begun?"

"I'll give you all I have."

"In that case, I think that the plague will claim no more victims. As you can see, we have done quite well with this one."

The old woman bore little resemblance to the sick creature she had been when they started. The swelling in her jaws was already more than half gone, and it was clear that her fever was nearly broken. Talia was immensely cheered by the sight. This was the first time in so long that she'd done something right. . . .

They treated every person in the house before the Healer insisted that Talia rest. Talia sought out their packs, remembering that she had seen them when she had entered. Kris had left them all in a heap by the fire. She dug out some dried meat and fruit, but found she had so little appetite that she couldn't even raise enough interest to bite into the rations. Instead of eating, she sagged cross-legged on the hearthstone with her back to the fire, soaking up the heat with her eyes closed, too exhausted to sense anything, and so grateful for the respite that all she wanted to do was enjoy the stillness in her mind.

"Foolish girl! Didn't you learn anything about Gifts at that Collegium of yours?"

Talia opened her eyes in surprise; Kerithwyn was standing over her with a steaming mug in one hand and a bar of something in the other.

"You should know perfectly well that if you don't replenish your energy reserves, you'll be of no use to anyone!" She thrust both articles into Talia's hands. "I know you aren't hungry—eat anyway! Finish these, then go find your partner and make him eat and sleep. He doesn't look like he's done either for a week. Don't worry, when I want you, I'll find you. And make sure your Companions are all right as well."

The block proved to be dried fruit and nuts pressed together with honey. Under other conditions Talia would probably have found it to be revoltingly sweet, but once she'd forced down the first bite, it seemed to gain enormously in appeal and the rest followed rather quickly. She recognized the liquid for the tea Kris had been feeding the plague victims, and saved one bite of the bar to take the nasty taste out of her mouth.

She looked first for Rolan; Kris had removed his tack, thrown several blankets over him, and led him to the stabling area of the inn. Kris had left food and water within reach, but that was all he'd had time to do.

She groomed and cleaned him, grateful that Companions were intelligent creatures that could be trusted to walk themselves cool. He was obviously tired for the first time in her experience, and equally obviously hungry, but otherwise none the worse for the run. She blanketed him warmly against chill and hunted until she found the grain storage area. She added dried fruit to the sweet-feed and put plenty within easy reach, then made a pot of hot gruel, which Rolan slurped up greedily as soon as it had cooled enought to eat.

It occurred to her, tired as she was, that she ought to check on Tantris. Kris' Companion whickered a welcome and rattled his grain bucket entreatingly. She laughed—how long it had been since the last time she'd laughed!—he had hay, he wasn't about to starve, but he obviously wanted some of the same treatment Rolan was getting. She obliged him as he nuzzled her in thanks. The chirras, loose in a large enclosure that gave them access to the outside and which contained enough fodder for them for a week, were in fine fettle. She changed their water, and went to look for Kris.

It didn't take much persuasion on her part to get him into the bedroll she had laid out on the hearth. He actually fell asleep before he'd finished the rations she'd given him; she gently removed the half-finished meal from his hands and placed it where he would see it when he woke, then took up the task she'd pulled him away from.

All three of them worked like slaves far into the night, snatching food and sleep in stolen moments when no one seemed to need aid too urgently. Oddly enough, the frail-seeming Kerithwyn exhibited the least amount of wear. She showed incredible stamina and tirelessness; she frequently scolded them into taking a rest when she herself had taken fewer breaks than either of them.

All three of them were worn and wan when the longed-for sound of hooves pounding on the gate signaled the arrival of the other two Healers and their Herald-escorts.

The two new Healers—a great, hairy bear of a man, and a round-faced girl who seemed scarcly old enough to have attained full Greens—quickly assumed control from Kerithwyn, who found a flat space, a few blankets, and promptly went to sleep. Both Heralds were experienced in assisting Healers, and sent Talia and Kris to their bedrolls for their first steady night of sleep since they'd arrived here.

All of them were on their feet the next day, and back to the job at hand. They took it in turn to eat and sleep, and by the end of the week several of their former patients were in good enough shape to begin helping them care for their fellow victims. At that point Kerithwyn told Kris gently but firmly to be on their way.

"We don't need you anymore—no, not even for the usual," she insisted. "Our own Heralds can take care of any disputes; we get the laws and news at least once every month, and we're perfectly capable of relaying reports. I want you two *out* of here before you catch this plague yourselves."

"But—" Kris protested.

"*Out!*" she replied. "I've had this sort of thing happen to me six times already; this is the seventh. You are *not* shirking your duty. Loris and Herald Pelsin are going to be *staying* here until Midwinter; these people are *not* going to need you! Now go!"

Kris gathered his belongings, acquired some fresh food to supplement the dried—it would stay perfectly sound in the cold—left their reports with the Heralds who had brought the Healers, as well as giving them the written reports on the villages they had already visited to be sent back to the capital.

But Talia did not escape so easily. While Kris was conferring with the other two Heralds, Kerithwyn took her aside just before she was ready to mount

Rolan. "Child," she said bluntly, "Your shields are as full of holes as last week's target, and if you weren't exhausted, you'd be projecting everything under the sun! You're in such a state that if I had any time, I wouldn't let you leave this place. But I *don't* have either the time or the energy to spare. I don't know what you've been doing, or what you *think* you're doing, but whatever it is, it's dead wrong. You'd better get yourself in hand, girl, and quickly, or you'll be affecting even the unGifted. Now go—and start working on that control."

With those blunt words she turned on her heel and left; leaving Talia torn between running after her and begging her help, and slitting her wrists on the spot.

In the end, though, she gathered the ragged bits of her courage around her, and headed out the gate after Kris.

Kris consulted the map; Kerithwyn had ordered him to find a layover point where the two of them could take a long rest. He told Talia that he thought he'd found a particularly good Waystation for them to use as their resting-place. Talia nodded, sunk in her own misery; Kris was preoccupied with making certain of their current location, and hadn't noticed anything—or at least, he hadn't said anything to her about it. But after what Kerithwyn said . . .

Well, she was going to have to be twice as careful as before, that was all.

They were a full half-day from the village now, and well into the Forest of Sorrows itself. Kris had called a halt around midday, so that they could all get a bite to eat while he checked his bearings. There were several narrow roads through Sorrows, and if they had missed theirs, or mistaken the road for a herd-track, they could get into trouble before nightfall.

But they *were* on the right road, and the Waystation was within easy striking distance.

It was fortunate that it was not too far distant, for just after they had dismounted and taken rations from their packs, the chirras began whuffing, and dancing uneasily.

"Talia, chirras don't misbehave unless there's a good reason," Kris said with a frown of worry, as his jerked the lead rope from his hands for the third time. "Can you tell what's wrong?"

"I don't know . . ." she said doubtfully, still shaking from her confrontation with the Healer, and never having done a great deal of work with animals. "I'll give it a try, though."

She braced herself, and sent herself into the deep-trance in which she had been able to touch animals' minds before. The image of what was causing their unhappiness was clear and sharp—and enough to send her flying back to consciousness with speed. "Snow," she said succinctly, for the image had been crystal clear and highly sharpened by fear. "Lots of it—a big blizzard coming down out of the north. It'll hit us before dusk."

Kris swore. "Then we haven't much time. Let's get moving."

Seven

The chirras resumed their good behavior, as if they understood that Talia had learned what was troubling them. They all pushed on as quickly as they could, but the icy road made it hard for both chirras and Companions to keep their footing, and the clouds piling up from the north were making it as dark as if it were already dusk. Then a bitter wind began, cutting through the trees with an eerie moan. The road they were following had taken a turn to the north about a furlong back, which put the wind right in their faces. Kris and Talia dismounted and fought against it alongside the Companions and chirras. When the first fat flakes began falling, they were already in difficulty.

Within moments it was no longer possible for either Herald to see more than a few feet ahead, and the wind was strong enough to whip the edges of their cloaks out of their benumbed hands. It howled among the tree branches, and ravened on the ground, shrieking like the damned. The trees groaned and creaked in protest, the thinner branches whipping wildly above their heads. It was so hard to be heard above the storm that neither of them bothered to speak, using only hand signals when there was something that *had* to be communicated. This was like no

159

storm Talia had ever seen before, and she hoped (when she had any thoughts at all through the numbing cold) that it wasn't typical for this Sector.

The snow piled up with frightening speed; ankle-deep, then knee-deep. They completely lost track of distance and time in the simple struggle to place one foot in front of the other. Kris and Tantris found the lane that led to the Waystation more by accident than anything else, literally stumbling into it as they probed the bushes at the side of the road.

The lane soon plunged down between two shallow ridges where they were sheltered from the worst of the wind. They let go of the girths they'd clung to and stumbled along in their Companions' wake, trusting to their mounts' better senses to guide them all to the Station. By the time they achieved it, they could hardly see the path ahead of them. The bulk of the Station loomed up before them out of the gray-white wall of snow only when they were practically on top of it.

The Station probably hadn't been visited since the resupply team had last inspected and stocked it during the summer. A quick survey of the woodpile told them that there wasn't enough stockpiled there to last for as long as they were likely to be snowed in. In frantic haste, they left the chirras tied to the building, removed everything from the packs on their Companions, fastened lead ropes from their own belts to the snaffles on the saddles and went out with axes to look for deadfall.

It was grueling work, especially coming on top of the previous crisis. Talia's arms and shoulders ached with the unaccustomed work; what didn't ache, was nearly numb with cold. Her cloak was caked with snow to the point where it creaked and bits of snow fell off when she moved. Her world narrowed to the pain, the axe in her hands, and the deadfall in front of her. More than anything else, she longed to be able to lie down in the soft snow and rest, but she knew that this was the very last thing she should do. Instead, she continued to struggle against pain and the driving snow, using the numbing cold and the ache of overtaxed muscles as a bulwark against despair—the despair that Healer Kerithwyn had evoked with her brusque warning. She drove herself in the gathering gloom until she became aware that she could barely see where her axe was falling. It was nearly night now—true night.

It was time to give up. As Talia and Rolan hauled in the last load while full darkness fell, it was all she could do to cling to his girth as he dragged her and the wood back toward the station. The wind had picked up—something she wouldn't have believed possible—and it was all but tearing her cloak from her body. Her breath was sobbing in her lungs, sending needles of ice and pain through her throat and chest.

She opened the door of the Station, only to blink in surprise—for there was nothing before her but a gloom-shrouded little room with a door on the opposite wall. After a moment, her fatigue-fogged mind managed to grasp the fact that this Station, unlike any other she had seen previously, had an entranceway to buffer the effect of the outside chill.

She fumbled the second door open, Rolan crowding into the entrance after her. Kris had beaten her to the Station with his final load shortly before, and had fumigated it and started a fire in the fireplace. He unfastened her from Rolan; she stumbled thankfully toward the yellow beacon of the fire with half-frozen limbs. He led Rolan into the shelter of the Station itself, and as she collapsed next to the warmth of the flames she saw that he had brought in Tantris and the chirras as well. It made things a bit crowded until he got them all settled, but Talia knew that there was no way anything could live long in the howling winds outside.

She peeled off her snow-caked garments and hung

them beside Kris' on pegs above the fireplace. Kris was already taking care of meal preparations, so after she slipped into her woolen shift and old breeches (feeling far too exhausted for a complete change of clothing) she made a nest of the dun-colored blankets from both their bedrolls on top of dry straw in front of the fire. This way they could warm their aching, shivering bodies in comfort while waiting for whatever it was to cook.

She blinked stupidly at the fire, mind and body alike still numb and cold. She held to that numbness, stubbornly, not wanting to face the alternative to numbness. She succeeded; she remained sunk in exhausted apathy long after she normally would have begun to show some signs of life. Kris was standing over her for several minutes before she realized he was there.

"Talia . . ." he began awkwardly, "I know this isn't the time or the place, but there isn't likely to be a better one. I have to talk to you."

Without really realizing it, she rose slowly to her still-benumbed feet, feeling a cold that had nothing to do with the blizzard outside. "Ab-b-b-out what?" she stuttered, fearing the worst.

"Kerithwyn had some words with me before we left," he said, as the despair she'd been holding off with the last of her strength came down on her with the same overwhelming power as storm—and with it, oddly enough, a hopeless kind of rage. "Hell, Talia—she told me you've been holding back on me; that your Gift is totally out of control!"

Something within her shattered, letting loose the storm she'd held pent up for so long.

Kris was expecting anger, denial—*but not this!* He was battered by alternating waves of suicidal despair, and killing rage; the shock of it literally sent him to his knees. His eyes filmed with a red mist. There was a roaring in his ears, behind which he could dimly hear the squeal of an angry horse and the clatter of hooves on stone.

That was what brought him out, before he grabbed a weapon and killed himself, her, or both of them. He built up the strongest shield he could, fought his way to his feet, and rushed her, literally slamming her into the wall behind her with enough force to make his own teeth rattle.

"*Stop it!*" he shouted at the wild, inhuman thing struggling beneath his hands. "*Damn* you, *Stop* it! Look what you're doing to us!" He wrenched her around violently, so that she could see for herself the unbelievable sight of Rolan backing Tantris into a corner, teeth bared and eyes wild and red-rimmed. *"Look what you're doing to them!"*

She stared—and collapsed so suddenly he didn't even have time to catch her, for she fell right through his hands. She fell and curled into a limp ball on the cold stone floor of the Station, sobbing as if she had lost everything she ever held dear.

And the storm within the Station walls faded away to nothing.

He went to his knees beside her, and gathered her against his shoulder. She didn't resist—didn't even seem to know he was there. He held her while she cried, horrible, tearing sobs that seemed to be ripping her apart inside, while the fire he'd started burned lower and lower, and the storm outside echoed her heartbroken weeping.

Finally, when it seemed possible that the fire might die altogether, he picked her up and put her in the nest of blankets and hay. She curled up, facing away from him and still crying, while he built up the fire, finished the tasks he'd left undone, and returned to her.

He got in beside her, chilled to the bone, and took her equally cold body into his arms again. The violence of her grief seemed to have worn itself out; he shook her a little. "Come on—" he said, feeling more than awkward. "Talk to me, lady—"

"I–I—" she sobbed "I want to die!"

"Why? Because your Gift got out of control? What kind of attitude is that for a Herald?"

"I'm *no* kind of Herald."

"Like bloody hell!" he interrupted. "Who says?"

"Everyone—you told me—"

"Oh, hell. . . ." *Now* he realized what it was that triggered this whole mess in the first place—himself, telling her the rumors about her. Gods—he *knew* she hadn't a high level of self-esteem—what he'd said back at the start of this trip must have hit her like a punch in the kidneys. He must have started her on a round of self-examination and self-doubt that turned into a downturning spiral she hadn't the power to stop. Her Gift was the sort of thing that would feed on doubt and make it reality—which in turn would feed her doubts, reinforcing them as her loss of control turned rumor into truth.

And *this* was the result. A fully developed Gift without any controls on it whatsoever, and a young woman ready to kill herself the minute he turned his back.

"Listen to me—*dammit* Talia, *listen!*" He shook her again. "If things were that bad, Rolan would have left you. He'd have repudiated *anybody* not worthy of her Whites. Has he made any move like that at all?"

"N-n-n-no . . ."

"Has he even *warned* you?"

The sobs were fading. "N-n-no."

"He's *helped* you, hasn't he? He's kept your damned secret. *He* thinks you're still a Herald. So *act* like one, dammit! Stop emoting and start *thinking*. You're in a mess; now how can we get you out of it?"

She looked up at him for the first time, eyes swollen and red. "We?"

"We," he repeated. "I'm as much to blame for this as you are. I should never have told you those damned stories—should have believed you when you told me they weren't true. I'd be willing to bet it was *my* doubt that made all this worse. Hmm?"

She shook her head, then hid her face against his chest. He pulled her closer, and began stroking her hair and rocking her a little. "Poor baby—" he murmured, "—poor scared, lonely baby—here—try this." He reached out and seized a small leather bottle from the top of his pile of belongings beside them, and passed it to her. "One of the standard cures for sensitivity is wine. This ought to blunt your edges good!"

Talia accepted the bottle, took a gulp and almost choked. The stuff was like drinking sweet, liquid fire!

"What—*is*—that?" she asked when she'd stopped gasping for breath.

"Something the Healers make—spirits of wine, they call it. They make it by freezing the wine they make from honey, and throwing away the ice; that's what's left. The one that looks like a bear gave it to me before we left."

Talia took another drink, just a sip this time, and with more caution. It didn't burn the way the first mouthful had, and left behind a very pleasant sensation in her mouth and stomach. And it certainly *did* blunt the edges of both her sensitivity and her raw nerves. *That* was the best thing that had happened to her all day, so she took a third swallow.

"Easy there, little one," Kris laughed, sounding relieved. "That stuff's potent!"

"I can tell," she said, feeling a bit giddy. "But I feel a lot better. Not so raw."

"That was what I hoped," he replied, appropriating the bottle and drinking from it himself. "I suppose we shouldn't be drinking it on an empty stomach, but I figure you need it. Hell, after what I've been through, so do I!"

She had drunk enough that she was just aware of

Kris' mental presence; his proximity was no longer painful. "Thanks."

"Don't mention it."

She lay quietly in the circle of his arms, feeling utterly drained, as they continued to share sips of the bottle. The fire popped and crackled, with little bits of blue and green flame among the red and orange. She was finally beginning to feel warm all the way through—something she hadn't thought likely out there in the snow—and relaxed—something she hadn't thought likely ever again. The fire smelled of evergreens, like forest-green incense. The chirras and Companions shifted a little from time to time, rustling the straw Kris had laid down for them. Gods—what she'd almost done to them! She touched with Rolan just long enough to assure herself that he was all right. . . .

His forgiveness and love was so total that tears came to her eyes again.

"Hey," Kris said gently "I thought we'd agreed there'd be no more of that."

When she didn't reply, he put one hand under her chin, tilted it up, and kissed her.

It was *intended* to be a brotherly kiss.

It didn't stay brotherly for more than an instant.

"Bright Havens!" he breathed in surprise when they finally moved apart.

Talia leaned back into his shoulder; her desire had surprised her as much as it had him, although she knew that was a common enough reaction after great stress. She wasn't aware of him as her counselor or even as a Herald at this moment—only as a friend and an emotional shelter—and knew with certainty that he was as aware of her need as she was of his own. This time she reached for him.

As their mouths met and opened, he gently slipped the shift down past her waist. She shivered in delight as his mouth brushed the back of her neck, the line of her shoulders, as he kissed away her tears; he sighed as she nibbled his earlobe timidly. With her shields gone, they seemed to be feeling every tiny nuance of each other's reactions. As she traced the line of his spine with a feather-like touch, she felt it as much as he—when she tensed and gasped as he found an unexpectedly responsive spot, he tensed in sympathy as well.

Finally their mutual desires grew too impatient to be put off any longer; he slowly let her down on the blankets beside him, sank into her embrace, and entered her.

He was totally unprepared for the stab of pain that was shared as the pleasure had been. He would have withdrawn from her at once, but she clung to him with fierceness and would not let him go.

She'd expected pain, and endured it. What she had not expected was that he would curb his own desire, to bring her past the pain, and finally to patiently wait on her pleasure before taking his own.

She shifted over as he collapsed, then nestled into the curve of his arm again. They curled together in their warm nest, spent and replete, and feeling no urgent need to do anything other than savor the experience they'd shared. For long moments there was no sound at all but the sounds of the fire, and the tiny stirrings of the four at the other end of the station.

He turned his head to look into her dark eyes, wide and drowsy with content. "Why didn't you tell me you were a virgin?" he asked softly.

"You didn't ask," she said sleepily. "Why? Is it that important?"

"I don't think I'd have loved you if I'd known."

"All the more reason not to tell you," she pointed out logically. She nestled closer to him, her head on his chest, pulling blankets over both of them. "But I'm glad it was you."

"Why?"

"Among other things, my gossiping Heraldic sisters were right. It was . . . a lot nicer than I'd been led to believe first times usually are."

"A compliment?" he asked, amused.

"A compliment."

A thought occurred to him. "Wait a minute. I thought you and Skif . . ."

She smiled, the first real smile he'd gotten out of her in weeks. "That's what you were supposed to think. It was awful—we both had horrid schedules, and we were so exhausted that we kept falling asleep before we could get anywhere."

She told him the comic-frustrating tale of their abortive romance, and how it had finally culminated in their swearing blood-brotherhood, rather than bed.

"Poor Skif! And poor Talia," he chuckled. "You knew he'd be teased half to death if that tale got out, didn't you? So you let everyone think otherwise."

"Mm-hmm. Poor Skif . . ." she yawned, "victim of unrequited lust." She was falling asleep in his arms, and as much as he hated to disturb her, he knew that he'd better.

"Wake up, sleepy. If you don't want to greet the dawn with a headache, you'd better have some food in you, and something to drink besides that devil's brew. The last thing you need is a hangover in the morning, and as potent as that stuff is, you're likely to wish you had died if you let it give you one. And we may be warm *now*, but we're going to wake up cold and stiff in the middle of the night if we don't make up a better bed. After all we've weathered, I'd hate to see you cramped in knots for want of a little sense."

She yawned hugely but didn't protest. They both rummaged out clean bedclothes and pulled them on. While he ladled stew out of the pot over the fire, she remade their "nest" with everything she could find to use as a blanket. He made hot tea, and they drank it with their meal.

They bedded down in each other's arms after he'd banked the fire, seeing no reason now to return to their practice of separate beds.

"I'm awfully glad this happened now," she said before he drifted off to sleep.

"Why's that, little bird?"

"Two sleep warmer together than two alone . . . and it's getting a lot colder."

Kris was pleased to discover that (unlike some lovers he'd had) Talia was a quiet sleeper; not at all restless, and not inclined to steal the blankets (which was, in his opinion, the quickest way to ruin an otherwise satisfactory relationship). He found her presence oddly comforting, and an especially good antidote to the howl of the wind outside.

He woke once when Tantris tickled his mind into wakefulness; he and Rolan wanted out. He was very grateful for the tiny entranceway this Station possessed; it wasn't part of the usual design, but with crowding he could fit one Companion and one chirra inside and still close the door to the interior before opening the outer door. If the exterior door had opened directly into the station as was usually the case, every time he had to let them out he'd be letting most of the heat they'd built up out with them.

The wind hadn't slackened in the least, and the snow was still coming down as thickly as before. It was definitely daylight, but he couldn't even tell where the sun was, much less see how high it was. It took all his strength to keep the door from being blown out of his hands; he realized then that this was why they'd awakened him and not Talia. He'd left halters and lead-reins on the chirras, which the Companions used to lead them outside.

One more advantage of chirras, he reflected wryly. *You can't housebreak mules.*

The scrape of a hoof on the door signaled their

return. He managed to hold to the door and slammed it behind them, but in spite of the buffering of the entranceway, their exit and re-entrance had stolen a noticeable amount of the heat from the room. He built the fire back up after filling the biggest pot they had with clean snow, then carefully groomed all four of ice and snow. He made sure they were comfortable, and noticed with a smile that all four of them lay in a close-packed group, with chirras on the outside and Companions in the middle.

"You're too clever by half," he told Tantris, and smiled at the Companion's amusement-laden reply.

:Given the choice, would you *take the outside? They've got the coats for this, brother-in-soul—we haven't!:*

He was grateful for Tantris' nonchalance; both the Companions seemed to be taking the events of the previous night as simply one more obstacle to be met and dealt with, rather than an insurmountable disaster. That heartened him, for he expected to need their help.

He hung the pot full of half-melted snow over the fire, then banked it again before returning to the bed that was looking better by the moment.

When he slipped in beside Talia he got another delightful surprise. Instead of pulling away, Talia actually hugged his chilled body to her warm one until he was no longer shivering, despite being three-quarters asleep herself. *There never,* he reflected as he drifted back to dreams, *was a truer test of friendship!*

When he finally woke of his own accord, he judged that several hours had passed; it was probably late morning or early afternoon. There didn't seem to be any real reason to get up; the winds still howled with the same ferocity outside.

"I wish these Stations had a window," he said drowsily, "It's impossible to tell if it's still snowing or not."

"No, it isn't," Talia murmured sleepily in his ear.

He hadn't realized she was awake. "No, it isn't, what?"

"It's not impossible to tell if snow's still coming down. Listen, and you can hear it on the roof and windward walls. It has a different sound than wind alone. It kind of hisses."

Kris listened; she was right. There was a hissing undertone to the storm outside. "How did you know about that?" he asked, more than a little surprised.

"Comes of sleeping in the attic. There're no windows in the attic of a Hold house, and that's where all the littles sleep. If you wanted to know what kind of weather to dress for, you learned to recognize all the sounds that weather makes. Where are you going?"

"Now that we're awake, I'm going to get the fire built back up."

He got an armload of wood from the stack he'd brought inside earlier, exposed the banked coals, and soon had it blazing again. In spite of the heat given off by the banked coals, the room was icy; the chimney was cleverly baffled, but the wind was still succeeding in stealing some of their heat. He was quite chilled by the time he was satisfied with the state of the fire. When he slid back in beside her, Talia again snuggled up to warm him.

"That's definitely above and beyond the call of duty," he said, when he'd stopped shivering, "Thanks."

"You're welcome. Consider it payback for last night."

He deliberately misunderstood. "Bright Havens, little bird, you keep surprising me! I hadn't the least notion there was such a sensualist under that serene exterior."

She played along. "Why shouldn't there have been?"

"You surely didn't show any sign of it. And you certainly haven't been . . . practicing, shall we say?"

"I hadn't found anyone I was enough at ease with before this except Skif, and that liaison seemed to have a curse on it!" There was rueful laughter in her voice. "But it wasn't that I lacked interest; I never told you about Rolan."

"What's *Rolan* got to do with this?"

"Remember I told you that he's always in the back of my mind? That I always know what he's doing, and I can't shield him out at all?" Her expression was a little shadowed as she realized she couldn't shield anyone out at the moment.

"So?" he prompted, "Why would you want to?"

"Nighttime in Companion's Field gets very interesting . . . and Companion mares share another characteristic with humans besides the gestation period." When he looked blank, she sighed. "They're always 'in season,' oh, wise counselor."

"Good Lord. And if you can't shield him out . . ."

"That means exactly what your filthy mind is thinking."

"Secondhand experience?"

"Something like it."

He pulled her head to rest comfortably on his shoulder. "Talia, I'm sorry I didn't see the state you were in, and I'm sorrier I didn't do anything about it."

"Oh—I—" She sobered immediately when he mentioned her emotion-storm. "Gods, Kris, what am I going to do?"

"We."

"What?"

"We. You, me, Tantris and Rolan. This is not the total disaster you seem to think it is. Let's take the easy things. First of all, you've learned something you won't forget. Now let me tell you a little something, Queen's Own. The reason you're out here is that you'll see every kind of problem you're likely to run up against at Court—only out here it will be much more clear-cut, much simpler. You learn how to handle it where it's easy to deal with, instead of plunging right in and drowning. Take somebody who's held a grudge for so long it's an obsession. You've seen it once now, would you recognize it again?"

Talia thought about how she'd felt when the girl looked into her eyes; the odd chill she'd sensed. "Yes," she said at last.

"And do you think you could handle it?"

"Maybe . . . I think I'd have to get an assist though."

"Good for you. Before this you'd have said 'yes.' Now you realize you might need help. You're learning, greenie. Now the hard part. Your Gift has gone out of control; we have to get it back under control again. I'll be willing to bet part of the reason for it going was that nobody recognized you need special training—training to keep your own emotional state from feeding back on your Gift. I'm not even certain there *is* such a thing."

"Why do you say that?"

"Because I can't think of another Queen's Own in living memory that has had as powerful a Gift as yours. I've never heard of empathy strong enough to be used as a weapon. Talamir certainly didn't have it—nor Keighvin before him. I don't even know that there's a Healer around with empathy that strong. *Maybe* a Healer could train you, but I wouldn't care to bet money on the idea."

"Then what . . ."

"We'll bloody well *invent* the training. All four of us. First off, your shields are gone. That's likely to be the hardest for you to get back, but I think *maybe* we can deal with it in a different way for now. Hey, Fairyfoot—"

Tantris looked up and snorted. *:Yes, master of the world?:*

"Go ahead, *be* sarcastic."

:You started it.:

"This is serious, Hayburner. Can you impose shields on her from outside?"

Tantris looked at both of them thoughtfully. *:Yes,:* he said after a long pause, *:but not for very long.:*

"If you can, then Rolan can—"

:Has.:

Kris raised one eyebrow. "Huh. I should have anticipated that. All right, I know *I* can; I've reinforced shielding on the kids I was teaching. So if we take it turn and turn about, can we keep her buffered so long as it's just the three of us she's dealing with?"

:I would think so.: Tantris looked at the other Companion measuringly. *:Rolan says to tell you we can probably even handle small gatherings of people.:*

"Better than I'd hoped. Fine. I'll take first watch. When I flag . . ."

:I'll catch,: came the confident answer, *:My pleasure, brother-in-soul.:*

"Did you get the drift of that?" He turned to Talia, setting up shielding around her as he spoke.

"You're—oh, *Gods!*" The relief on her face was a revelation; until that moment he had not realized *how* much strain she was under.

"Right. Now . . . having gotten that taken care of temporarily, we'll deal with the half of the problem that's dangerous to others."

"The projecting—"

"But not now. You're too tired to project past the end of your nose unless I make the mistake of frightening you half to death again, so that can wait. I'm hungry, and I want a bath."

Although they had used the Waymeet village bathhouse frequently, choosing a scrub by way of restorative over the sleep they had had little time for, it had been well over a day since the last time they'd gotten clean. Since both of them had fastidious natures, they were feeling it.

"You go first, then. I want to groom the fourfeets, and I'll wash afterward. I can start to smell them now, and if I don't get them pretty well clean, things could get whiffy in here. Since I'm doing Rolan, I might as well do all four of them. There's no need in both of us getting filthy."

Kris sniffed; the air was faintly perfumed with an odor of wet wool and horse-sweat. "You don't have to do all four, but if you insist, I'll let you. You're ruining my lovely self-indulgence, though. If you're going to go all virtuous on me and work, I'll have to find something to do as well." He sighed heavily, and made sad eyes at her.

She made a face at him, feeling like her old self for the first time in weeks. She got dressed, threw her cloak on, then took the first chirra's lead-rein.

Chores kept them occupied for the rest of the day, housekeeping and tending to mending that had been left neglected while they ministered to the plague victims. Talia was just as happy; she was reluctant to face her problems just now when she was so emotionally raw. After a quiet bit of lunch, Kris went to take inventory of their supplies.

There was a half-height door opposite the entrance to the station; it led to a storage shed. Kris found far more supplies there than he had dared to hope—and found some unfamiliar jars and barrels as well. He brought some of those into the Station.

The jars held honey and oil. "Someone near here must have left these after winter set in," Kris said in surprise. "It wouldn't be safe or wise to leave them here in warm weather; they'd go bad or attract animals. That's why they're not standard stock. What's in the barrel?"

"The oil can be used in the lamp, too." Talia opened her barrel. It held what seemed to be dried beans. Kris was perplexed.

"Now why . . ." he began, when Talia remembered something Sherrill had told her.

"Sprouts!" she exclaimed. "To keep us from the winter sickness, if we get stuck here longer than the fruit lasts. We're supposed to soak those in water until they sprout, then eat the sprouts. They do that where Sherrill and Keren come from."

Kris looked sober. "We may need them, too. Even if the fruit holds out, it's dried; not as good for holding off winter-sickness as fresh." He made a mental tally of all their supplies. "I think we can hold out for a month or so," he decided, from experience with being snowed in before. "And from the looks of this storm, that's exactly what may happen. It's still going strong, and by the way the sky looked today, I don't think it's going to be slackening soon."

"Do we have enough fodder, though? Tantris and Rolan are big eaters, and we can't feed them on bark and twigs the way we can with the chirras if supplies run low."

"There's fodder and straw baled and stacked on the other side of the shed where you can't see it, besides on the near side," Kris reassured her. "It almost looks as though whoever was stocking this Station was expecting a storm this bad. It seems odd, but I don't know enough about this area to tell you whether or not this type of weather is typical for this time of year. Dirk would know that better than I."

"Whatever the reason for the abundance of supplies, it's a good thing for us that they're there."

They did something about supper, and Kris returned the harp. With an inquiring glance in her direction, he began with a song that she'd sung at the Herald's revel. Taking the glance as an invitation, she stretched herself next to him and began to sing quietly. He hummed the low harmonic under his breath; his voice, though no match for Dirk's, was reasonably melodic. Behind them the Companions and chirras pricked their ears up to listen with every evidence of interest.

Suddenly two new voices joined in, wordlessly crooning an eerie descant. Talia and Kris jumped, startled, and stopped—the new voices stopped with the music.

Puzzled, they began again, this time peering into the darkened side of the Station. After a moment, the descant resumed.

"Well, that's what I get for making fun of Dirk's

and Harthen's tales!" Kris said in surprise. "Chirras *do* sing!"

Rolan and Tantris were staring at their stable-mates with a kind of ironic astonishment. Evidently *they* hadn't expected the singing either. The chirras, oblivious to everything but the music around them, were reclining with their eyes closed and their heads and necks stretched upward as far as they could reach. Their throats were pulsing, and the humming was, without a doubt, coming from them.

"Don't feel badly. I wouldn't have believed it either," Talia replied. "I mean, they look like sheep, sort of, and sheep don't sing. Probably there aren't too many people playing or singing around them, which would be why more folks haven't heard them. *We* never did; they were always outside in the lean-to."

The chirras joined in happily on almost everything they played, but they particularly seemed to enjoy the livelier tunes. What was utterly amazing—apart from the simple fact that they sang at all—was *what* they sang. They crooned harmonics to the melody rather than following the melody itself, and usually chose the upper range in a descant. They would listen for a verse or two before joining in, but though very simple, their harmonizing always fit. Talia knew a great many human singers who couldn't boast that ability.

They continued on for some time, so fascinated by this inhuman choir that they forgot any worries they had. They continued until Kris' fingers were much too tired to play any more. Although he dearly wanted to go on, after a few fumblings, which caused the chirras to flatten their ears and stare like a pair of offended old women, he was forced to admit it was time to give his hands a rest.

"In that case . . ."

"What have I decided? This is going to be rather hard on you, little bird—"

"And the past few weeks haven't?" she replied bitterly.

"Not like this; it's going to be pretty cruel. The way I figure it, the two of us *not* shielding, and especially Rolan, are going to be watching you like cats at a mousehole. The least little indication of projection, and we're going to jump all over you. After a few days of that, I am willing to bet that you will by damn not be doing any projecting without knowing that you're doing it!"

"It doesn't sound pleasant," she said slowly, "but it does sound like it may work."

"Then once we've got you knowing when you're projecting, we'll move to handling the projection consciously. Then we'll work on you controlling the level of it. Finally we'll work on getting your shields back up."

"If you think I can. . . ."

"I bloody damn *know* you can!" he said. "But we are not going to be doing anything tonight. If you're as worn out as I am—and if you're not *more* worn out, you're a better man than I, after all you've been through—you won't be able to do anything, much less working something as delicate as a rogue Gift."

As he spoke, he became acutely aware of his own mental fatigue, and the strain of holding shields on her. Just as he felt his own control waver, he felt Tantris slip into his place.

:*My turn, brother,*: the mental voice said firmly. He sighed and sent a wordless thought of thanks.

Talia readied things for the morning, while he cared for their Companions. She had shed her clothing and was lazily reaching for the woolen shift she was using as a bedgown, when she found her wrist caught by Kris' hand.

He had come upon her quietly from behind, and now captured her other wrist, holding her with her back pressed into his chest. "Surely you're not sleepy already?" he breathed into her ear, sending delightful shivers up her back.

"No," she replied, leaning her head back as his lips touched the back of her neck and moved around to the hollow below her ear.

"Good," he drew her down beside him, on top of the blankets he'd spread on the hearthstone, right next to the fire. He stretched himself beside her so that she was between him and the fireplace, feeling truly relaxed for the first time since Elspeth was Chosen.

He cradled her shoulders while his free hand traced invisible patterns on her skin that seemed to tingle— she moved her own hands in half-instinctual response to what she felt from him; at first hesitantly, then with growing surety. Every inch of skin seemed to be doubly sensitive, and she murmured in surprise and delight as his hands did new and entrancing things. Just when she thought for certain that he'd roused her to the uttermost, he moved his seeking mouth elsewhere, and she learned how it was to be fully awakened to desire.

Learning from him, she followed his lead, as he roused her to fever pitch, let her cool a little, then aroused her senses again. Finally, when she was certain neither of them could bear any more, he sought her mouth again and joined with her.

The pain was less than nothing compared to what they shared.

When at last Kris disengaged himself from her, they lay twined together for a long, euphoric moment, still deeply in rapport. He half-rose and handed her the nearly-forgotten shift with one hand while pulling on his own robe. She slipped it on, lazily gathered up the blankets, and remade their bed. She curled up in it with utter contentment as he banked the fire against the night.

"That Gift of yours is not always a bad thing," he said, finally. "Should you ever choose a life-partner, I think I would envy him, little friend. Now I see what they mean about wedding or bedding Healers—

especially if all of them have the same kind of Empathy that you do."

"Oh?" Her ears all but perked up with interest. "And what do they say?"

"That you may not get much time with them because they're always likely to be called away—but what time you do get makes up for their frequent absences."

She reached up to pull the blankets more securely about the two of them, and something odd about her hand caught his attention. He captured her wrist again, and held it so that the palm would catch the last of the firelight, frowning a little as he did so.

Her palm was disfigured by a deep, roughly circular scar.

"That," she said quietly, answering the question he did not speak, "is the reason why I was afraid of men for so long—and why I don't trust handsome ones. My brother Justus, with the innocent face of a golden-haired angel and the heart of a demon, did that to me when I was nine years old."

"Why?" The word held a world of shock and dismay.

"He wanted . . . I don't know what he wanted; maybe just to see me hurting. He hated anything he couldn't control. He used to inflict as much pain as he could on the farm animals whenever something had to be done with them. He'd half-drown the sheep, dipping them for insects; he'd cut them terribly, shearing them. Horses he broke *were* broken; there was no spirit in them when he was done. I think it galled him that I could have an escape from the boredom of Hold life that he couldn't ruin—he couldn't stop my reading or dreaming. He ordered me one day to drown a sack of kittens; I tore the sack open instead so that they all escaped. I'm sure he knew that that was exactly what I would do. He backhanded me, knocked me down flat, stepped on my wrist, and used a red-hot poker on my hand. I think that one time he overstepped what he'd intended; I don't think he meant to burn me as badly as he did, at least not after he saw what he'd done. Gods, I'll never, ever forget his face while he was burning me, though." She shuddered, and he held her a little closer. "That—obscene *joy*—I still had nightmares about it right up through my second year at the Collegium. I know they heard me screaming, but no one came very fast because they knew he was setting a task for me and figured I was being punished for slacking. When I didn't stop after a couple minutes, though, one of the Underwives came to check. *After* all the damage was done. When she saw me, he'd already thrown the poker down. He told Keldar Firstwife that he'd hit me for disobedience and I'd grabbed the poker to hit him back, but it had been in the fire too long. He didn't even have to explain why it was that my palm was burned and not my fingers. They believed him, of course, and not me."

"Gods!" He was sickened—and a little more understanding of why she hadn't confided in him.

"It was . . . a long time ago. I'm almost over what it did to me. I think if he were still alive, and subjecting a wife or children to his sadism . . . well, he's not. He managed to get himself killed a year or two after I was Chosen. There was a raid, and he had to prove just how much braver he was than anyone else. And Keltev, who was bidding fair to grow up like him, seems to have learned better, so . . ." She shrugged.

"That's the one who used to tease you about wanting to be a Herald—Keltev? Now I know why you put up with the Blues for so long. You had practice; after Justus they must . . ."

"As far as physical tormenting, they were amateurs. Mental, though . . . they were quite . . . adept. But I'd learned from my sibs that if you give them the satisfaction of knowing they've hit home by acting as if they'd hurt you in any way, they only get worse. And how was I to know I'd be believed?"

"Oh, Talia—" he held her closely against his chest. "Poor little bird!"

"It wasn't so bad as all that," she said softly into his shoulder. "Besides, I've learned better now. I've got people I can love, friends I can trust—my year-mates, my teachers—and now—" She looked up at him a little shyly. "—you and Dirk."

"And everyone else in the Circle, little bird," he replied, kissing her softly on the forehead, "I'm just sorry I didn't trust *you*. But we'll fix it. We'll fix it."

She simply sighed assent.

The fire was now little more than glowing coals, and Kris stared at them while he let his mind drift, not yet ready to sleep.

"You know, you and Dirk will get along beautifully," he mused. "Your minds work almost the same way."

"Why do you say that?"

"You wouldn't do anything to save yourself pain, but you dared your brother's anger to save the kittens. That's so much like Dirk it isn't funny. Hurt him . . . he'll just go and hide in himself; but hurt a friend, or something helpless—Gods! He'll sacrifice himself to save it, or he'll rip your heart out because he couldn't. You're two of a kind; I really think you're going to be more than casual friends."

"Do you really think so?" she said, a little too eagerly.

All the pieces fell together, and the suspicion he'd had earlier became a certainty. "Why, Talia," he chuckled, "I do believe you're a bit smitten with my partner!"

He felt the cheek resting on his shoulder grow warm. "A little," she admitted, knowing that it would be useless to deny it.

"Only a little?"

"More than a little," she replied almost inaudibly.

"Serious?"

"I . . . don't know. It depends on him, mostly," she was blushing furiously now. "I'm afraid it could get that way very fast under the right conditions."

"But now?"

She sighed. "Kris, I don't know, I just don't know. And why am I bothering to get my hopes up? I don't know how he feels . . . whether or not he's likely to be the least bit interested in me. . . ."

"*You* may not. I think maybe I do. If I'm reading him right, he's already interested." Kris thought back on the way Dirk had acted right before he and Talia had left. He couldn't stop talking about how envious he was that Kris had gotten her as an intern, and he kept on at great length about her wonderful voice. Normally, since that bitch at the Court had hurt him, he'd paid very little attention to women, except for the occasional ribald remark.

Then he'd hinted that it would be a good notion if they'd all practice together so they could do more as a trio. Holy Stars, he'd never once suggested that they practice together with *anyone* before, not even Jadus.

"For one thing," Kris said slowly, "he wants us to play together on a regular basis. I mean, he wants *us* to play, and *you* to sing."

"He does?" she said in bemusement. "He plays?"

"As well as I do, or better. Since my voice isn't very good, though, and his is, he's kind enough to let me have the playing to myself. Out on the road we play together quite often, but outside of myself hardly anyone in the Circle knows he can."

"And he said I was full of surprises!"

"Oh, you are." He caressed her hair absently. Lord of Lights, they were so well suited to each other. There was a great deal more to both of them than would ever show on the surface. There were depths to both of them that *he* knew he'd never see.

He chuckled a little.

"What's so funny?"

"Bright Havens, I hardly dare think what you might be like in the arms of someone you truly loved! He'd better have a strong heart, or he might not survive the experience!"

"Kris!" she exclaimed indignantly, "You make me sound like the widowing-spider that eats her mate!"

He ruffled her hair. "Maybe I'd better make certain that you and Dirk make a pair of it. He's the strongest man I know."

"Keep this up much longer," she said warningly. "and I'll put snow down your back after you fall asleep."

"Cruel, too. On second thought, maybe I'd better warn him off."

"Do that, and I'll go directly to Nessa when we get back, tell her that you confided your everlasting passion for her to me, but that you're too shy to tell her yourself."

"Not just cruel—vicious!"

"Self-defense," she countered.

"Monster of iniquity," he replied, tugging at her hair until it fell into her eyes. "You know, of all the people I can think of, I can't imagine being able to stand being snowed in with any of them except you and Dirk—especially for as long as *we're* likely to be stuck here."

She grew serious. "Is it really likely to be that long?"

"If it doesn't stop snowing soon, it could easily be a month. This Station is down in a valley and protected by trees. We're not getting the worst of it. I tried to get past the trees earlier, and you can't. The snow has drifted as high as a chirra in some places. Even after the snow stops, we'll have to wait for the Guard to clear the road, because until they do we won't be going anywhere."

"How will anyone know where we are?"

"I told that Healer—the bearish one, I think his name is Loris—where I intended us to hole up.

Besides, little bird, this may be all to the good. We may well need all that time to get your Gift back under control again."

"That . . . that's true," she said soberly. "Oh, Kris—do you really think we can?"

He noted with a bit of pleasure, the "we," for it meant she was no longer thinking in terms of dealing with the problem on her own. "Not only do *I* think so, but Tantris and Rolan do. You're not going to argue with them, are you?"

"I . . . I guess not."

"I hear a doubt. No doubts—that's what got you into this mess in the first place. We *will* get you back in control. I may not be a Kyril or an Ylsa, but I *am* a Gift-teacher. I know what I'm doing."

"But—"

"I told you, but me no 'buts'! *Believe*, Talia. In yourself as much as in me. That's the weakest leg your Gift has to stand on right now."

She didn't reply to that; just stared thoughtfully at the fire until her eyes drooped and finally closed, and her slow, steady breathing told him she'd fallen asleep.

He remained awake for much longer, engaged in a struggle with himself he *had* to win, a struggle to set aside a Herald's impartiality and wholeheartedly believe in *her*.

For if he could not—she was certainly doomed, and quite probably so was he. The moment she sensed doubt in him, despair and betrayal would turn her wild Gift against both of them. And he had *no* doubt of how *that* would end.

Eight

Kris pursued an icy apparition through the storm-torn forest, a creature that was now wolf, now wind, now an unholy amalgam of both. It glared back over its shoulder at him through snow-swirls that half obscured it, baring icicle fangs and radiating cold and evil. He shivered, unable to control the trembling of his hands, though he clenched them on his weapons to still their shaking . . .

His weapons—he looked down, surprised to see that his bow was in his hands, an arrow nocked and ready. The beast ahead of him snarled, dissolved into a spin of air and sleet with hell-dark eyes, then transformed back into a leaping vulpine snow-drift. He sighted on it, and more than once, but the thing never gave him a clear target.

Talia was somewhere ahead of him, he could hear her weeping brokenly above the wailing of the wind and the howling of the wind-wolf, and when he looked down he could see her tracks—but he could not seem to spot her through the curtains of snow that swirled around him. He realized then that the wind-wolf was stalking *her*—

He quickened his pace, but the wind fought against him, throwing daggers of ice and blinding snow-swarms into his eyes. The thing ahead of him howled, a long note of triumph and insatiable hunger. It was outdistancing and outmaneuvering him—and it would have Talia before he could reach her. He tried to shout a warning—

And woke with a start. Outside the wind howled like a demented monster. Talia touched his shoulder, and he jumped involuntarily.

"Sorry," she said, "You—you were dreaming, I think."

He shook his head to clear it of the last shreds of nightmare. "Lord! I guess I was. Did I wake you?"

"Not really. I wasn't sleeping very well."

He tried to settle himself, and found that he couldn't. A vague sense of apprehension had him in its grip, and would not loose its hold on him. It had nothing to do with Talia's problems; a quick exchange of thought with Tantris confirmed that she was not at fault.

"Kris, do you think maybe we should move the supplies?" Talia said in a voice soft and full of hesitation.

"That doesn't sound like a bad idea," he replied, feeling at once that somehow his uneasiness was connected with just that. "Why? What made you think of that?"

"I kept dreaming about it, except I couldn't shift anything. It was all too heavy for me, and you wouldn't help. You just stood there staring at me."

"Well I won't just stand and stare at you now." He began unwinding himself from the blankets. "I don't know why, but I think we'd better follow up on your dream."

They moved everything from behind the Station to either side of the door on the front. Rather than diminishing, the sense of urgency kept growing as they worked, as if they had very little time. It was hard, chilling, bitter work, to manhandle the clumsy bundles of hay and straw through the snow, but neither of them made any move to give up until the last stick and bale was in place.

While there was still light left to see by, they took turns clearing the valley of deadfall. They finally had enough to satisfy Kris when they'd found the last scrap of wood that hadn't vanished into snow too deep to be searched. It would not outlast being snowed in, but there was more than enough to outlast the storm. If, when the storm died, they couldn't reach any more deadfall, they could cut one of the trees surrounding the station, evergreens with a resinous sap that would allow them to burn, even though green.

But when they returned to their shelter, their work wasn't complete. For though there seemed little rational reason to do so, they continued to follow their vague premonitions and moved all the supplies from the storage shed into the Waystation. It made things very crowded, but if they didn't plan on moving around much, it would do.

By the time they finished, they were as chilled and weary as they had been the first night.They huddled over the fire with their bowls of stew, too exhausted even for conversation. The wind howling beyond the door seemed to have settled into their minds, numbing and emptying them, chilling them to the marrow. They huddled in their bed in a kind of stupor until sleep took them.

The wind suddenly strengthened early the next morning, causing even the sturdy stone walls to vibrate. They woke simultaneously and cowered together, feeling very small and very vulnerable as they listened with awe and fear to the fury outside. Kris was very glad now that they'd trusted their instincts and moved everything to the leeward side of the Station and within easy reach.

"It's a good thing this isn't a thatched roof like the last Station we were in," Talia whispered to him, shivering against him, and plainly much subdued by the scream of the wind outside. "Thatch would have been shredded and blown away by now."

Kris nodded absently, listening mainly to the sound of the storm tearing at their walls like a beast wanting to dig them out of their shelter. He was half-frightened, half-fascinated; this was obviously a storm of legendary proportions and nothing he'd ever seen or read could have prepared him for its power. The Station was growing cold again, heat escaping with the wind.

"I'd better build up the fire now, and one of us should stay awake to watch it. Talia, make a three-sided enclosure out of some of our supplies or the fodder, and pile lots of straw in it. We need more between us and the cold stone floor than we've been sleeping on. Leave room for the four-feets; if it gets too cold they'll have to fit themselves in nearer the fire, somehow."

Talia followed his orders, building them a real nest; she also layered another two bedgowns on over the woolen shift. Kris uncovered the coals and built the fire back up—and when he saw the skin of ice forming on their water-kettles, he was glad he had done so.

They crept back into their remade bed and held each other for extra warmth, staring into the fire, mesmerized by the flames and the wail of the wind around the walls. There didn't seem to be any room for human thought, it was all swept away by that icy wind.

Their trance was broken by a hideous crashing sound. It sounded as though a giant out of legend was approaching the Station, knocking down trees as he came. The noise held them paralyzed, like rabbits frightened into immobility. There wasn't anywhere to run *to* in any event. If something brought the Station down, they'd freeze to death in hours without shelter. Neither of them could imagine what the cause could be. It seemed to take several minutes, approaching the Station inexorably from the rear, finally ending with a roar that shook the back wall and a splintering sound that came unmistakably from beyond the half-door.

They sat shocked into complete immobility, hearts in their throats, for a very long time.

Finally— "Bright Goddess! Was that where I thought it was?" Kris gulped and tried to unclench his hands.

"B-b-behind the Station," Talia stuttered nervously, pupils dilated with true fear. "Where the storage shed is."

Kris rose and tried the door. It wouldn't budge. "Was," he said, and crawled back in beside her.

She didn't venture to contradict him.

Twice more they heard trees crashing to the ground, but never again so close. And as if that show of force had finally worn it out, the wind began to slacken and die. By noon or thereabouts, it had gone completely, and all that remained were the faint ticking sounds of the falling snow. Without the wind to keep it off the roof, it soon built up to a point where even that could no longer be heard.

The Station stopped losing heat. The temperature within rose until it was comfortable again, and the rising warmth lulled them back into their interrupted sleep before they realized it.

The Companions prodded them awake. How long they'd been asleep they had no idea; the fire was dying, but by no means dead, and the silence gave no clue.

Rolan impressed Talia with his need to go out. Immediately. Talia could tell by Kris' face that Tantris was doing likewise.

He looked at her and shrugged. "Might as well find out now as later. We're still here, and under shelter at least," he said, and pulled on fresh clothing while she did the same.

It was not long till dark. The stacked fodder had kept the door clear of snow or they'd never have gotten it open. Beyond the shelter of the bales was a drift that reached higher than Kris' head.

The chirras were not at all perturbed by the sight; they plowed right into it, forcing their way almost as if they were swimming, their long necks keeping their heads free of the snow. The Companions followed and the two Heralds followed them. After making their way through drifts that rose from between the level of Talia's waist to the height of the first one, they suddenly broke into an area that had been scoured down to the grass by the wind.

The forest around them had a quality of age, of power held in check, that was raising the hair on the back of Talia's neck. There was *something* here . . . not quite alive, but not dead either. Something . . . waiting. Watching. Weighing them. Whatever it was, it brooded over them for several long moments. Talia found herself searching the shadows under the trees until her eyes ached, looking for some sign, and found nothing. But *something* was out there. Something inhuman, almost elemental, and—and at one, in some strange way she couldn't define and could only feel, with the forest itself. As if the *forest* were providing it with a thousand eyes, a thousand ears. . . .

"Where's the road?" Talia asked in a small, frightened squeak.

Kris started at the sound of her voice, looked around, then turned slowly, evidently getting his bearings. The Station from here seemed to be only one taller drift among many. There were new gaps in the circle of trees that surrounded it. "That way—" he finally pointed. "There *was* a tree just beside the pathway in—"

"Which is now across the pathway in."

"Once we get to it, we can have the chirras and Companions haul it clear . . . I hope."

"What about the back of the Station?" She was not certain that she wanted to find out.

"Let's see if we can get back there."

Working their way among the drifts in the deepening gloom, they managed to get to a point where they could see what had happened behind the Station, even though they couldn't get to it yet. Kris whistled.

Not one, but nearly a dozen trees had gone over, each sent crashing by the one behind it, the last landing hard against the side of the Station. The storage shed was gone; splintered.

"At least we'll have plenty of firewood," Talia said with a strained laugh.

"Talia—" there was awe in Kris's voice. "I never believed those stories about Sorrows and Vanyel's Curse before—but *look at the way the trees fell!*"

Talia subdued her near-hysterical fear and really took a good look. Sure enough, the trees had fallen in a straight line, all in the direction of the force of the wind—except the last. There was no reason why it should have deviated that she could see, and had it fallen as its fellows it would have pulverized the Station—and them. But it had not; it had fallen at an acute angle, missing the Station entirely and destroying only the empty shed. It had almost fallen *against* the wind.

"Gods," Kris said, "I—I never would have believed this. I never believed in miracles before." He looked around again. "I . . . this sounds stupid but, whatever you are . . . thanks."

The steady feeling of being watched vanished as he said it. Talia found she could breathe easily again.

"Look, we'd better get back inside. It's nearly dark," Kris gazed up at the sky, and the snow that still fell from it with no sign of slackening.

Subdued by their situation and the destruction

outside, they made their meal, ate, and cleaned up in silence. Finally Talia broached the subject that was troubling them both.

"*Can* we get out of here?"

"I'd like to be reassuring and optimistic, and say yes—but truthfully I don't know," Kris replied, resting his chin on his knees and staring into the fire. "It's a long way to the road, and as I've told you, it will be worse beyond the trees. It's going to take us a long time to cut a path there, with no certainty that the Guard will have gotten that far when we do make it."

"Should we try to force our way without cutting a path?"

He shook his head. "The chirras could do it, unburdened, but not Tantris and Rolan. Even if they could, we'd need the supplies. I just don't know."

"Maybe we'd better just concentrate on digging our way out."

"But how can we dig ourselves out with no tools?"

"There's the tree blocking the way, too."

Kris stared at the fire without speaking for a long time. "Talia," he said finally, "Holderfolk never buy anything if they can help it—their miserliness is legendary. What do you know about making shovels?"

"Not much," she replied ruefully, "But I'll try."

"Let's take an inventory of our materials."

They had plenty of rawhide for lashings, lots of straight, heavy tree limbs for handles and bracings, but nothing to use for blades. The unused bedboxes were so stoutly built that it would be next to impossible to pull the bottoms out, and the shelves were made of board too thick to be useful. There *had* been thinner wood used in the shelves of the shed— but they were fragmented now. Finally Talia sighed sadly and said with reluctance, "The only thing we have to use is the harp case."

"No!" Kris protested.

"There's nothing else. When we leave here we can

detune My Lady and wrap her in blankets and cloaks and she should be all right without the case. The wood is light and strong, and it's been waterproofed. It's nearly even the right size and shape. We haven't got a choice, Kris. Jadus wouldn't thank us for being sentimental fools."

"Damn!" He was silent for a moment. "You're right. We haven't any choice."

He got the case from the corner on top of Talia's packs where he'd left it. Wincing a little, he took his handaxe and carefully pried the front and back out of the frame, and handed them to Talia.

She fished a bit of charcoal out of the fireplace and drew something like the blade of a snow-shovel on each piece. She handed him one while she took up the other.

"Try and whittle it to that shape while I do the same."

She shaved delicately at the edges of the wood with the blade of her own axe, with shavings falling in curls next to her. Kris watched her with care until he felt he knew exactly what she was doing, then began on his own piece. There was one blessing; the grain was fine enough that with sharp axes it was relatively easy to shape. When both their pieces approximated the look of a shovel blade, Talia marked holes in the boards for them to drill out with their knives. By the time they'd finished, their wrists and hands were tired and sore.

Talia flexed her hands trying to get some feeling and movement back into them. "Now I need two pieces about so wide," she said, gesturing with her hands about two fingers' width apart, "And as long as the backs of the blades. I expect you'll have to cut them out of the frame."

While Kris further demolished the harpcase, she rummaged in her packs for her pot of glue. When she found it, she placed it in a pot half-filled with water, and put that container over the fire so the glue would melt. Meanwhile she went through the dozen or so branches that looked to be good handle material and picked out the two best.

Once the glue was ready, she showed Kris where to drill holes in the branches, and how to taper the end that was going to be fastened to the blade. Her wrists just weren't strong enough for the job. When he finished the first one, she lashed it to the blade with wet rawhide, stretching the thong as tightly as she could so that it would shrink and bind the shovel to blade as firmly as possible when it dried. Then she cross-braced the back of the blade with a smaller branch cut to fit, lashing it the same way to the handle. Lastly she glued the piece of frame to the back of the shovel blade to act as a stop to keep the snow from sliding off. She lashed another piece of branch to the handle behind the stop to act as a brace, then she glued every join on the whole make-shift shovel, saturating even the rawhide with glue. That finished all she knew how to do; she set the whole thing aside to cure overnight, and started in on the second.

"They're not going to hold up under much rough handling," she sighed wearily when she'd finished. "We're going to have to treat them with a great deal of care."

"It's better than trying to do it with bare hands," Kris replied, taking her hands in his own and massaging them.

"I guess so," she tried to force herself to relax. "Kris, just how does the Guard clear the roads off?"

"They recruit villagers. Then it's teams with shovels; they dig out the worst places, and pack down the rest."

"I don't imagine that it's a very fast process."

"No."

The single word hung in the air between him. Talia was afraid, but didn't want to put more of a burden on Kris than he already had by giving way to her fears.

The silence between them grew.

"I hate to say this" he broke it reluctantly "but you're projecting. I can feel it, and I know it isn't me, and Tantris just backed me up."

Anger flared a little, followed by despair—

"Dammit Talia, *lock it down!* You're not helping either of us!"

She gulped back a sob; bit her lip hard enough to draw blood, then steadied herself by beginning a breathing exercise; it calmed her, calmed her enough that she actually found the leakage, and blocked it. Kris heaved a sigh of relief, and smiled at her, and she felt a tiny stirring of hope and accomplishment.

Finally he let her hands go and went after the harp; she wasn't in a mood to sing by any means, but he chose nothing that she knew. He seemed more to be drifting from melody to melody, perhaps finding his own release from distress in the music he searched. She listened only; the chirras seemed to have caught the somber mood and did not sing either. She used the harpsong to reinforce her own ritual of calming and did not open her eyes until it stopped.

Kris had risen and was replacing the harp in its corner of the hearth. He returned to her side and stretched himself next to her without speaking.

She was the one who broke the silence.

"Kris, I'm scared. *Really* afraid. Not just because of what's happening to me, but because of all that—" she waved her hand "—out there."

"I know." A pause. "I'm scared, too. We . . . haven't got a good situation here. You—you could have killed us both the other night. You still could. And out there . . . I've never felt so helpless in my life. Between the two, I just wanted to give up. I just wanted to curl up in a ball and hope it all went away."

It cost him to admit that, Talia knew. "I wish I wasn't so messed up; I wish I was bigger and stronger.

Or a Farspeaker like Kyril," she replied in a very small voice.

"You can't help what happened. As for being a Farspeaker, I don't think both of us together could reach someone with the Gift to hear us, and if we could, I don't know that it would do any good," he sighed. "We just have to keep on as we have been, and hope we get out of here before the supplies run out. That's the real problem, when it comes down to it—the supplies. Otherwise I wouldn't worry. We've got about enough for a month, but not much more than that. If we run out . . ."

"Kris—you know, we *are* in Sorrows—remember the tree? Maybe—maybe we'll be sent game."

"You could be right," he mused, beginning to brighten. "It would take less magic to send a few rabbits within reach of our bows than it did to divert that tree."

"And maybe we'll get out before we have to worry about it. And you don't have to worry about me, you know. I'm Borderbred. I can do with a lot less than I've been used to eating."

"Let's not cut rations down unless we have to. We'll be using a lot of energy keeping warm."

Gloom settled back over them. Talia decided that it was her turn to dispel it.

"I wonder what things are like back at Court right now. It's almost Midwinter."

"Pandemonium; it's never less. Uncle hates Midwinter; there're so many people coming in for the celebrations who 'just incidentally' have petitions that there are Council meetings nearly every day."

She looked at him unhappily. "I don't get along with your uncle very well. No, that's a lie. I don't get along with him at all. I *know* he doesn't like me, but there's more to it than that. I keep having the feeling that he's looking for a way to get rid of me."

Kris looked flatly astonished. "Whoa—wait just a

minute here—you'd better start at the very beginning. I can hardly believe my ears—"

"All right," she replied hesitantly, "but only if you
promise to hear me out completely."

"That's only fair, I guess."

"All right; when I first got to the Collegium I had
a pretty miserable time of it as you know. Dirty
tricks, nasty anonymous notes, ambushes—it was the
unaffiliated students, the Blues, but they made it
seem as if it was other trainees that might be responsible so I wouldn't look inside the Collegium for
help. It all came to a head—"

"When they dumped you in the river just after
Midwinter—"

"And they meant to kill me."

"What?" he exclaimed.

"It isn't common knowledge. Elcarth and Kyril
know; and Sherrill, Keren, Skif, Teren, and Jeri.
Ylsa knew, so did Jadus; I think Alberich knows.
Mero guessed. I'm pretty sure one or more of the
others told Selenay some time later. One of the Blues
told me to 'give their greetings to Talamir' just after
they threw me in—I think the meaning there is pretty
clear. They expected me to drown, and if it hadn't
been that my bond with Rolan was strong enough
for him to know what had happened—well. But I
was delirious with fever when they were caught and I
couldn't tell anyone. They claimed it was all just a
joke, that they hadn't thought I'd get worse than a
ducking. Your uncle backed them up before the
Council. So instead of being charged with trying to
kill me, they got their wrists slapped and were sent
home to the familial bosoms."

"That's hardly an indication that—"

"You promised not to interrupt me."

"Sorry."

"The next time we got into it was over Skif. It was
right when Skif was helping me unmask Elspeth's
nurse Hulda. I needed to find out who had spon-

sored her into Valdemar besides Selenay and Elspeth's father. Skif went to the Provost-Marshal's office to find the immigration records, and Orthallen caught him there. He dragged him up in front of Selenay, accusing him of trying to alter the Misdemeanor Book. And he demanded that Skif be given the maximum punishment for it—stable duty with the Guard for the next two years on the Border. You know what *that* could have meant. At worst, he could have been killed; at best, he'd be two years behind the rest of us, and I'd have been without one of my two best friends all that time—as well as being without the only person in the Collegium who could possibly have helped me expose Hulda. I got Skif off, but I had to lie to do it; and I can tell you that Orthallen was *not* pleased."

Kris looked as if he wanted to interject something, but held his peace.

"Lastly there's the matter of my internship. Orthallen 'in view of my youth and inexperience' was trying to pressure the Council into ruling I should stay out in the field for three years—double the normal time. Fortunately, neither Selenay, Elcarth or Kyril were having any of that—and pointed out that internships are subject only to the will of the Circle, not the Council."

"Is that all?"

"Isn't it enough?"

"Talia, this all has very logical explanations if you know my uncle. Firstly he couldn't possibly have known about the students' malice—I'm certain of it. He's known most of them since they were in swaddling clothes; he even refers to people grown and with babes of their own as 'the youngsters.' And he probably felt obligated to act as their spokesperson. After all, you had *two* people to speak for you on the Council, Elcarth and Kyril."

"I suppose that's logical," Talia said reluctantly. "But Skif—"

"Oh, Skif—my uncle is a prude and a stickler for convention, I know that for a fact. Skif has been a thorn in his side ever since he was Chosen. Before Skif came, there was never any problem with Heraldic students getting involved in trouble down in town—the unaffiliates and the Bardics, and once in a great while the Healers, but never the Grays."

"Never?" Talia's right eyebrow rose markedly. "I find that rather hard to believe."

"Well, almost never. But after Skif started *his* little escapades—Lord and Lady, the Grays are as bad as the Bardics! It's like the younger ones feel they have to top him. Well, Uncle is not amused, not at all. He's a great believer in military discipline as a cure for high spirits, and I'm certain he never meant anything worse for Skif than that."

"What about me? Why does he keep trying to get between me and Selenay?"

"He's not. You *are* young; his idea of Queen's Own is someone like Talamir. I have no doubt he truly felt a long internship was appropriate in your case."

"I wish I could believe you."

"Holding a grudge is rather childish—and unlike you—"

"I am *not* holding a grudge!"

"Then why are you even refusing to consider what I've told you?"

Talia drew a deep breath and forced herself to calm down. "There is a third explanation for what he's been doing. It could be that he thinks of me as a threat to his influence with Selenay. And I might point out one other thing to you—and that is I am willing to bet the person who told you all about those 'rumors' is your uncle. *And* I'd be willing to bet he asked you to investigate them. *He* knows what my Gift is. He could well know what the effect of hearing that poison would be on me."

Instead of refuting her immediately, Kris looked thoughtful. "That is a possibility; at least over the internship thing. He's very fond of power, my uncle; he's been Selenay's chief advisor for a long time, and was her father's before that. And there isn't a great deal you can do to change the fact that Queen's Own is always going to have more influence than chief advisor. And I hate to admit it," he finished reluctantly, "but you're right about my source of information on the rumors."

Talia figured that now that she'd got him thinking instead of just reacting, it was time to change the subject. She would dearly have loved to have suggested that Orthallen might well have *originated* the rumors, but Kris would never have stood still for the implication that his uncle's conduct was less than honorable.

"Kris—let's try and forget about it, for a few hours, anyway. We've got other things to worry about."

He regarded her soberly. "Like the fact that you had enough energy to project; like the fact that you could do it again."

"Yes." She drew a deep breath. "I could even break down again; I was right on the verge of it this afternoon. If we hadn't had something to *do*, I might have. And I was—maybe hallucinating out there."

"Hell."

"I'll—try. But I thought you'd better be warned."

"Featherfoot?" He looked long at Tantris, then nodded in satisfaction. "He says he thinks he and Rolan can handle you, if it gets bad again. He says it was mostly that Rolan was caught off-guard that things got out of hand the first time."

She felt a heavy burden fall from her heart. "Good. And—thanks.'

He gave her a wink. "I'll get it out of you."

She made a face at him, and curled up in the blankets to sleep with a much lighter heart.

They woke at very close to their normal time; there would be no dallying today, nor for many days to come, not if they wanted to reach the road before their supplies ran out. They suited up in their warmest clothes, took the shovels, and began the long task of cutting a path to freedom.

The snow was wet and heavy—an advantage, since it stayed on their shovels better. But the very weight of it made shoveling exhausting work. They took a break at noon for a hot meal and a change of clothing, as what they'd put on this morning was now quite soaked through. They shoveled until it was almost too dark to see.

"We've got to get to that tree and get it moved out of the way while the snow's still like it is now," Kris said over supper. "If it should turn colder and freeze, we'll never be able to get that thing moved. It would be stuck in ice like a cork in a bottle."

"We'll be all right as long as the snow keeps falling a little," Talia replied, thinking back to her days watching the Hold flocks at lambing time. "We'll only have to worry about the temperature falling if the weather changes."

They turned in early, hoping to get to the tree before the end of the next day.

By late afternoon they had reached it, and decided, after looking the massive trunk over, that it would be best if they hacked it in half with their handaxes and hitched the chirras and Companions to the lighter half. When darkness fell, they were slightly more than halfway through the trunk.

Again they rose with the sun and returned to the tree. They managed to cut through it by noon, and after lunch made their attempt to move it.

They had decided the previous night to leave nothing to chance and had made a set of harnesses for themselves from spare rope. They hitched their own bodies right in beside the chirras and Rolan and Tantris.

It turned out that it was just as well that they had decided to do so. Only when all six of them dug in and strained with all their strength did it move at all.

All of them gasped and panted with the effort, and over-burdened muscles screamed out in protest, while the tree shifted fraction by minute fraction. It took until dark to haul it clear of their escape route.

As darkness fell, they dragged themselves back into the Station, nearly weeping with aches and exhaustion. Nevertheless, they rubbed the chirras dry and groomed their Companions, fed and watered and blanketed them. Only then did they strip off their own sodden garments and collapse on their bed. They were too bone-weary to think of anything but lying down—and their aching bodies.

Finally, "Do you really *want* supper?" Kris asked her dully; it was his turn to make it.

The very idea of food was nauseating "No," she replied in a voice fogged with exhaustion.

"Oh, good," he said with relief. "Neither do I."

"I can't seem—to get warm." It took an effort to get the words out.

"Me either." Kris sat up with a low moan. "If you'll get the tea, I'll dig out the honey."

"It's a bargain."

They'd left hot water for tea on the hearth, knowing they'd want it. Neither of them rose any farther than their knees as they dragged themselves to their goals. Talia poured water onto the herbal mixture, spilling half of it as her hands shook with weariness. Kris returned with the jar of honey in one hand, and something else in the other.

He put the jar down with exaggerated care, and Talia spooned three generous dollops into each mug. Fortunately, it was too thick to spill as the water had. She pushed one mug toward Kris, who handed her something in exchange for it.

It was one of the fruit and nut bars Kerithwyn had forced into them back at Waymeet. Talia felt sick at the sight of it.

"I know," Kris said apologetically. "I feel the same

way. But if we don't eat something, we'll pay for it
tomorrow."

She stirred the honey into her tea and drank it
even though it was still so hot it almost scorched her
tongue. As heat spread through her, the food began
to seem a bit more appealing. As she finished the
second mug of tea, she was actually feeling hungry.

Chewing the tough, sticky thing took the last of
her energy, though. From the look of things, Kris
was feeling the same way. The third cup of tea
settled the question entirely. She just barely managed to get underneath the blankets before she was
asleep.

She woke with every muscle screaming an angry
protest. She shifted position a little, and a groan
escaped.

"I wish I was dead—I wouldn't hurt so much,"
Kris moaned forlornly in her ear.

"Me, too. But I keep thinking of what Alberich
always told us."

"Must you remind me? 'The cure that is best for
the sore body is more of what made it sore.' Oh, how
I wish he was wrong!"

"At least we have to go out long enough to see
what we have to deal with beyond the tree."

"You're right." Kris uncoiled himself slowly and
painfully. "And we have to wrestle more wood inside."

"And more hay."

"And more hay, right. There's this much, little
bird. If you feel like I feel, you couldn't project past
your own nose right now!"

They helped each other wash and dress; there
were too many places they couldn't reach for themselves without their stiff muscles screaming at them.
Talia managed to concoct porridge with fruit in it,
making enough to feed them twice more, and tea as
well. They would probably be so tired they wouldn't
taste either, but it would be solid and warm, and

hopefully they wouldn't be so tired tonight that the very thought of food was revolting.

When they opened the door, the glare of the sunlight on all that snow drove them back—for the weather had changed overnight, and the sky was cloudless. Without some kind of protection for their eyes they'd be snowblind in moments.

"Now what?" Talia asked, never having had to deal with this kind of situation before.

Kris thought hard. "Keep your eyes shadowed from above by your cloak hood, and I'll see if I can rig something for the snowglare."

He rummaged through his pack, emerging with a roll of the thin gauze they used for bandages. "Wrap that around your head about twice. It should be thin enough to see through."

It wasn't easy to see through, but it was better than glaring light that brought tears to the eyes.

The tree lay where they had left it, and beyond it was the pathway out. Somewhere.

It was possible to see where it went by the lane between the trees and the absence of underbrush. The problem was that it lay beneath drifts that from where they were standing never seemed to be less than four feet deep.

"Well, at least there're no more downed trees," Talia said, trying to be cheerful.

Kris just sighed. "Let's get the shovels."

The drifts were deep, but at least they were not as wide as the ones in their valley had been. Though the snow was seldom less than two feet deep, it also was rarely more than six. They shoveled and trampled until dusk, then brought in more wood and fodder, ate, and fell into bed.

Talia woke in the middle of the night feeling very cold. Puzzled, she huddled closer to Kris, who murmured sleepily, but didn't wake. Despite this, she kept feeling colder. Eventually she moved warily out of bed; as soon as she did so, the chill of the air struck her like a hammer blow. She slipped her feet into her sheepskin slippers, wrapped her cloak around herself, and quickly moved to pile wood on the fire. When the flames rose, she could see the eyes of the chirras and Companions blinking at her—they had moved out of their corner and nearer to the heat.

" 'Smatter?" Kris asked sleepily. "Why's it so cold?"

"The weather changed again. The temperature's dropping," Talia said, thinking about how the wet snow outside must be freezing into drifts like outcroppings of white granite. "I think the luck-goddess just left us."

Nine

When at last they slept again, it was restlessly; they woke early, and with a premonition of the worst. The icy chill of the Station did not encourage dawdling; they dressed quickly and went out to discover just how bad the situation truly was.

It wasn't good, by any stretch of the imagination. The snow had frozen, thickly crusted on top, granular and hard underneath. The crust was capable of supporting their weight, and even the weight of the chirras unladen (providing that they held their pace to a snail's crawl), but it would never hold the chirras with even a small pack, or the Companions. And as if that weren't bad enough, it was obvious that their shovels were not sturdy enough to deal with snow this obdurate.

Both Heralds stared hopelessly at the rock-hard place where they'd left off digging the night before and at the now-useless shovels. Finally Talia swore passionately, kicked at a lump of snow, and bit her lip to hold back tears of frustration, and reminded herself *not* to let anything leak.

"Look, Talia, we're not getting anywhere like this," Kris said after a long moment of silence. "You're tired; so am I. One day isn't going to make any difference to us one way or the other—for that matter, neither will two or three. I'm your counselor; well, I counsel that we take a rest, and let our bodies recover, until we can think of a plan that has some chance of getting us out of here."

Talia agreed wearily.

Once back inside, she lit the little oil lamp and surveyed the shambles they'd made of the interior of the Station. "We're obviously going to be here a while, so it's time we stopped living in a goat pen. Look at this! We hardly have room to move."

Kris looked around, and ruefully agreed.

They began cleaning and rearranging with a vengeance. Working in the comparatively warm Station was by far and away easier than shoveling snow had been. Before noon, the Station was cleaned and swept and all was in good order.

"Had any ideas?" Kris ventured over lunch.

"Nothing that pertains to the problem. I did think of something that needs doing, though. Since we're stuck until we can think of a way to handle that snow, we ought to do something about washing our clothing. The only warm things that I have left to wear are what I've got on."

"There's saddle-soap in the Station supplies to clean the leathers," he said, thinking out loud, "and we could empty two of the barrels to wash in."

"I brought more than enough soap for all the rest," she told him, "And the Lord knows we don't have to scrimp on water!"

"All right then, we'll do it! I'm in no better shape than you—and I *hate* wearing filthy clothes."

Under the primitive conditions of the Station, cleaning white clothing was not an easy chore. Again, however, it was easier than the digging and hauling they'd been doing, and a great deal warmer as well. Eventually every clean surface sported a drying garment.

"I never thought I'd want to see another set of

student Grays again," Talia said, sitting back on her heels and surveying her handiwork.

"I know what you mean," Kris grinned, looking up from his last pair of boots. "At least the damn things didn't show dirt quite so badly. How are you doing?"

"I'm done, since I did my leathers while you were washing."

"This finishes it for me."

"Well, I still have hot water left—enough for two really good baths. It's too bad we can't fit ourselves into the barrels and soak, but at least we can get really clean."

"Good thinking, little bird. Although after all the soap and water I've been immersed in today, there isn't much that needs to soak!"

Things began to take on a more cheerful appearance once they were clean, especially since they weren't aching from the punishing cold and muscle strain of the past few days.

Talia combed her wet hair out in front of the fire, more than half mesmerized by the flickering flames and the movement of the comb through her hair. The Station had lost the slightly stale odor it had acquired during the blizzard, and now smelled of soap and leather—very pleasant. Bits of old tales began to flicker through her mind—unconnected images dealing with tales of battle, of all things. Battles, and how the Companions themselves used to fight alongside their Heralds. Or were those images unconnected?

"Kris," she said slowly, an idea beginning to form, "the main problem is the hard snow and the ice crust. Our shovels aren't strong enough to break it into pieces. But if we wrapped their legs to keep them from being cut, Rolan and Tantris could—like they were fighting."

"By the Stars of the Lady, you're right!" he exclaimed with excitement. "Not only that, remember how you wondered what good those huge claws did the chirras? They dig themselves hollows to lie in, in dirt *or* in snow. If we could make them understand what we wanted, we could have them dig out chunks of a size we could manage!"

"Havens, Rolan and Tantris can do that!"

Tantris snorted, and Rolan sent Talia a little mental caress.

Kris laughed. "All right, granther—" he said to his Companion, looking happier than he had all day. He turned back to Talia. "The Source of all Wisdom over there seems to think we'll be able to work faster than we did before. He wanted to know why we hadn't thought of this until now."

"Well *you* two wouldn't have done us much good with the wet snow, now, would you?" Talia asked the two sets of backward-pointing ears. Rolan tossed his head.

"And the chirras would have made more of a mess than they'd have cleared. The snowdrifts weren't stable enough until they froze," Kris added, a little smugly. "So there."

"Did he say anything else?" Talia asked, a little envious of Kris' ability to Mindspeak with his Companion.

"He just told me he's been worried about how hard we've been working—but then he actually *ordered* me to rest tomorrow. You'd think we were trainees."

Talia shook her head ruefully, for there was no doubt that Rolan considered this to be an excellent idea. There was a distinct undertone to *his* mental sending of worry that both of them had been overworking.

"Rolan says the same. I don't think I want to argue. Oh, Bright Havens, I hurt!" Talia stretched aching arms and shoulders. "This has hardly been the rest stop we were ordered to take."

Kris groaned good-naturedly, stretching his own weary muscles. "If anything, I'm more exhausted than I was when we stopped, if that's possible. I'm certainly a lot sorer."

"Then I'll make you an offer; want a backrub?"

"Do you?"

"Oh, Lord, yes," she sighed.

"I'll work on you, then you work on me. Strip, wench—I can't work through four shirts and a tunic!"

"It's only two," she protested with a laugh, "And they're summer-weight at that. While I was cleaning, I wanted to clean everything!" Nevertheless, she complied, stretching out on a pallet of blankets on the hearth. Kris seemed to find every last ache, and drove each one out with deft fingers. Soothed by the gentle hands, she drifted into a half-sleep.

He woke her by tickling the back of her neck. "My turn," he said, as she lazily turned her head.

She sighed with content and rose to her knees, and slipped on a shift (blessedly clean, and warm from the fire) while he took her place on the hearth. She tried to copy what he'd done to her, and hunted for the muscles that were the most tense, and so hurt the most. Before very long she had him as soothed and relaxed as she was, and they basked in the heat of the fire like a couple of contented cats.

"I'll do anything you ask," he murmured happily, "Anything, so long as you don't ask me to move. And as long as you don't stop."

She giggled at the tone of his voice as she gently rubbed his shoulders. "All right, then—tell me about Dirk."

"Promise not to stop what you're doing?"

"Surely."

"Good," he said with satisfaction. "Because it's a very long story. For one thing, I have to start with his grandfather."

"Oh, come now—" she said, raising an eyebrow. "Is this really necessary, or are you just trying to prolong the backrub?"

"I promise you, it's absolutely necessary. Now, 'once

upon a time' when Dirk's grandfather settled his Steading, he lived on the very Border itself. He was quite ambitious, so he added a little more to his lands every year, and only stopped when he had as much as one man could reasonably expect to keep under cultivation with the aid of a moderate number of hands. By then the Border had been pushed back by him and others like him. So now that it was a safer place to live, he married."

"Logical, seeing as he had to have produced at least one offspring to be Dirk's father."

"Quiet, wench. As it happened, their only child was female, but it didn't perturb him that he would be leaving the Steading to her; he fully expected that she would marry in due course, and the place would still be in the bloodline. However, the gods had other ideas in mind."

"Don't they always?"

"First of all, it turned out that his daughter had a really powerful Gift of Healing. Now this was as welcome as it was unexpected, since it's hard to get Healers to station themselves near the Border. There's always more work there than they can handle successfully unless they're stationed with a Temple, and you know how Healers are—they'd rather die than leave something half-done. At any rate, Borderbred Healers always seem to feel they have a duty to serve where they were born, so there was little chance she'd end up anywhere else. Her proud and happy father sent her off to Healer's Collegium, and in due course she returned in her Greens. So far everything had gone according to expectation. However, being the Healer put a crimp in her father's original plans for her. It seemed that the young men of the area were somewhat reluctant to court a person whose attentions could, because of her Gift, never be entirely devoted to any one person. And this despite the tale I told you about them. Healers are, after all, Healers first and anything else second."

"Like Heralds, or priests. Look at us."

"Point taken. At any rate, not even the rather substantial inducement of her inheritance could lure any of the neighboring farmers or their sons to the nuptial table. The old man began to despair of having his hard-won acreage remain in the family. Then there came the second twist to the plot. Late one autumn night there was a terrible storm."

"I've had my fill of storms."

"Hush, this is a required storm. In fact, it was the worst autumnal storm that part of the Kingdom had ever seen. It began after sunset, and lightning downed so many trees that it was completely unnecessary to cut any for firewood that fall. Freezing rail fell from the heavens in sheets rather than drops. There was so much thunder that it was impossible to hold a conversation and impossible to sleep. And in the midst of all this chaos and confusion, there came a knocking on the farmstead door." Kris was very obviously enjoying himself to the hilt.

"A tall, dark, mysterious stranger, no doubt."

"Who's telling this story, you or me? As a matter of actual fact, it *was* a stranger; half-drowned, half-frozen, half-dead and very much bedraggled, but blond, and hardly mysterious. It was a young Bard, only recently graduated from *his* Collegium and starting his journeyman period. He'd lost his way in the storm, fallen into a river, and had all manner of uncomfortable things happen to him. When he pounded on their door, he was already fevered, delirious, and well on his way to a full-blown case of pneumonia."

"I smell a romance."

"You have an accurate nose. Naturally, the young Healer took him in and nursed him back to health. Just as naturally, they fell head over heels in love. Being a man of honor, as well as having his head stuffed full of all those romantic ballads, the Bard begged the old man's permission to wed his daughter in true heroic style. He needn't have worried, because by now the old fellow was beginning to think that *any* son-in-law was better than none. However, he made it a condition of his agreement that they remain on the Steading.

It rather surprised the old farmer when the—he thought—feckless, footloose Bard agreed with all his heart—subject to the agreement of his Circle of course. How could the old man have known that our Bard was born a farmer, and that entwined with his love of music and his love of the daughter was his love and deep understanding of the land? Well, the Circle agreed—provided he compose a Master's ballad about the storm, courtship, and all; and he settled down happily with all three of his loves—land, lady, and music. Then before the year was out, he had a fourth."

"Dirk. So that's where he got that wonderful voice!"

"And where he learned to play so well. Actually, though, you're a bit ahead of the tale. The first child wasn't Dirk. He has three older sisters, two younger, and a baby brother. When they can be sorted into some semblance of order and organization, they have family concerts. You should hear them all singing together, it's wonderful; I swear even the babies cry in the right keys! Well, grandfather passed to his reward content in the knowledge that the land would remain in the bloodline, since by the time he departed, two of the girls had begun enthusiastically producing enormous broods of their own."

"I was asking about Dirk."

"Talia, my little bird, you can't separate Dirk from his family. They're all alike; see one, you know what the rest are like. How things ever get done in that household I have no idea, since it seems to be formed entirely of chaotic elements."

"Just like a Bard."

"Actually, he's the most organized of the lot. If it weren't for him and the husbands of the sisters, they'd spend all their time flying in circles. There's an incredible amount of love there, though; and it overflows generously on anyone who happens to find himself dragged unwittingly into their midst."

"Like you."

"Like me. Dirk insisted on hauling me home with him the first holiday after we'd met when he found out there wasn't going to be anyone home with me but the servitors. They treated me *exactly* like one of the family, from bathing babies to teary farewell kisses. I was rather overwhelmed. I certainly hadn't expected anything like them!"

Talia chuckled, picturing to herself the reserved, slightly shy young boy that Kris must have been, finding himself in the hands of what must have seemed like a family of madmen.

"Once I got used to them, I had a lot of fun. That's why, every chance I've had, I've gone home with Dirk when he went. Right now four of his sisters are married. Three of them live in extensions to the original house and their husbands share the work on the Steading, because Dirk's father has developed bad knees. The last has his own land to look after, but they're still on hand for every holiday in the calendar. It's a good thing they all get along so well."

"We were talking about Dirk."

"Right." Kris' eyes gleamed with mischief at the impatience in her voice. "He was Chosen even younger than I—only eleven; probably because at eleven he was more mature in a lot of ways than I was at thirteen. We were Chosen the same year, and almost the same month. He told me that Ahrodie Chose him in the middle of the marketplace on Fair Day, and he kept trying to direct her attention to his sister because he thought he was too ugly to be a Herald!"

"Poor child."

"So we went through the Collegium as year-mates. He saw how lonely I was there, and how unused to dealing with other children, and decided that I needed a friend. And since I couldn't seem to make one by myself, he was going to do it for me! In classes, though, I had to help him along, and he was never better than average. It was pretty well accepted by all of us that after our internships he was going to work Border Sectors and I was going to teach. Then we found out how our Gifts dovetailed, and how incredibly well we work together, and everyone's plans were rather abruptly changed."

"And you began working as a team."

"Oh, yes. *And* we discovered that we have a kind of Gift for intrigue as well. The number of situations we've gotten ourselves into would astound you, yet we always seem to extricate ourselves and come home covered in glory."

"Kris, what's he really like?"

"Behind the jester-mask? Very sensitive—that's his heritage coming out. Endlessly kind to the helpless; you should see him some time with a lap full of kittens or babies. Don't think he's soft and sentimental, though. I've seen him slit people's throats in cold blood when they deserved it, and do it from behind in the dark without a pretext of fair play. He says that if they're intending to do the same to him, it doesn't make sense to give them warning. He can be totally ruthless in the cause of Queen, Kingdom, and Circle. Let's see, what else is there? You've danced with him, so you know that his bumbling farmer look is totally deceiving. He's one of the few people that Alberich will accept to act as a substitute with his advanced pupils when Alberich is sick. And for all that, he's terribly vulnerable in certain areas. I helped him get over his broken heart, and I promise you, Talia, that I will personally break the neck of anyone who hurts him like that again."

He was lying with his head turned to one side and pillowed on his arms; Talia could not help but see the fierce, cold hatred in his expression at that moment.

Kris's fierce tone as he spoke the last few words was completely unfeigned. He remembered only too well what Dirk had been like then—broken, defeated—it had been horrible to compare what that bitch had made him into with what he had been before she'd worked her wiles on him. Dirk seldom shed a tear—but he had wept helplessly on Kris' shoulder when she'd ruined his life and his hopes for him. It was a thing he never wanted to witness again. And if he had any say about it, he never would.

Then a painful thought occurred to him. He *knew* Dirk was more than interested in Talia . . . and she *had* been showing evidence of the same sort of feeling. But he and Talia had most of a year to go on her internship, and now that they were intimate, it was damned unlikely they'd go back to their earlier relationship. What the *hell* was he going to do if she started getting infatuated with *him?*

It was more than a possibility; after all, nearly every other female he'd spent any time with had ended up in the same state.

He didn't want to think about it. . . .

"I think it's time to do something about your problem," he said, thinking that trouble might be less likely if he reasserted his position as a figure of authority.

"Like what?" She sat up slowly, and shook her hair out of her eyes, her expression in the flickering firelight a sober one.

"I'm going to take you absolutely back to basics. Back to the very first thing they taught me."

"Shielding?"

"Hell, no, girl," he replied, astounded. "More basic than that—and if shielding was what they taught you first, maybe that's one reason why you're having this problem. I'm taking you right back to the first steps. Ground and center."

She looked puzzled, and shifted a little, curling her legs under her. "Ground and *what?*"

"Oh, Gods," he groaned. "How the hell did you get away with—of course. Ylsa must have thought you knew the basics. Maybe you did . . . instinctively." He bit his lip, thinking hard, staring off into the space beyond his internee. Talia just sat quietly, peering anxiously at him through the half-dark of the Station. "Trouble is, as *my* teacher used to say, instinct is *no* substitute for conscious control."

"I—I guess I've rather well proved that, haven't I?" she replied bitterly.

"Well, once instinct goes, there's no basis for reorganizing yourself." He took a deep breath, acutely aware of the faint smell of soap, straw, and animal that pervaded the Station.

"Gods." She sighed, and rubbed her temple with one hand. "All right—do your worst."

"Don't laugh," he replied grimly, "Before I'm through it may well seem like just that. All right, are you comfortable? Absolutely comfortable?"

She frowned, shifted a little, then nodded.

He settled himself, folding his own legs under him, shifting until the straw under his blanket moved to a more comfortable place. "Close your eyes. You can't sort out what's coming in at you unless you can recognize what's *you* and what *isn't*. That's what my teacher used to call 'the shape inside your skin.' Find the place inside you that feels the most stable, and work out from there. Feel *everything*—then put what you've felt away, because you can recognize it as you."

He was using what he called "teaching voice" with her, a kind of soothing monotone. She'd gone quite naturally into a half-trance, fairly well relaxed. By unfocusing his eyes and depending on Sight rather than vision, he could See every move she made by the shifting energy patterns within her. Sight was a good Gift to have for this situation, maybe better than her own would have been. By looking/not-looking in a peculiar sort of way that made his eyes feel strained, he could see energy fields and fluxes. What he Saw was difficult to describe; it was something like seeing multiple images or "ghosts" of Talia, each one haloed in a different "color." When he Looked at the unGifted or Gifted but untrained, the images didn't quite mesh and the edges were fuzzy and indistinct. In Talia's case the edges were almost painfully sharp and the images were given to flaring at unpredictable intervals—and they were so unconnected they almost seemed to belong to more than one person. If she could find her center, they would fuse into one; if she could ground, the flaring would stop.

"All right, once you've found that stable place, there's a similar place outside of you—in the earth itself. When you feel that, connect yourself to it. Finding the stable place is called 'centering,' connecting yourself to the earth is called 'grounding.' "

He could tell, although his own Gift wasn't anything like hers, that she had *almost* managed both actions. Almost—but not quite. The images were overlapping, but not fusing; and they dimmed and brightened and dimmed again. And he could see that she was off-balance and not-connected, although to *her* it probably seemed as if she'd done exactly as he asked. Poor lady—he was about to do a very cruel thing to her.

He sighed, and signaled Tantris—who gave her a rude mental shove.

A shove that translated into a very physical toppling over.

"Not good enough," he said coldly, as she stared up at him from where she was sprawled with a dazed expression on her face. "If you'd done the thing properly, he wouldn't have been able to budge you. Again. Ground and center."

She tried—much shaken, this time. If anything,

she was worse off than before. Tantris hardly flicked her, and she lost internal balance. This time she did not lose physical control, although it was a near thing. She visibly swayed as if beneath a blow.

"Ground and center, girl. This is a baby-lesson, it ought to be reflex. *Reflex,* not instinct. Do it again."

She was exhausted, sweat-drenched, knotted up all over, and shaking with the effort of holding back tears before he let up on her. There *had* been progress, though, and he told her so.

"You're not there yet," he said. "But you're closer. You got a little closer to your true center each time you tried for it—except for the last time; you missed it altogether. That's why we're quitting for a little."

She buried her face in her hands, trembling all over. "I think," she said after a moment, her voice muffled, "that I could come to hate you with very little effort."

"So why don't you?" he asked, masking his apprehension and the cold chill he felt at her words.

She looked up at him, and lowered her hands away from her face, slowly. "Because you're trying to help me, and this is the only way you know how."

He let out the breath he'd been holding in a long sigh of relief. "Lord of Lights," he said thankfully, "you would not believe how glad I am to hear you say that."

"Because if I did hate you, I could quite easily kill you."

"Exactly so. And all the easier while I was working with you—because I have to be completely unshielded to See what you're doing."

She shuddered, and he moved forward to put his arms around her. She tensed for a moment, then relaxed onto his shoulder. "How much more of this. . . ?"

"Until you get it right."

"Gods. And this is only the very beginning?"

"Just the first steps."

She bit back a sob of frustration; he felt it, more than heard it, and ached for her.

And said the cruelest thing yet. "All right, you've had your wallow in self-pity. Now let's get back to work."

And when she stared at him in disbelief, he snapped an order at her like any drill-instructor. "Ground and center, girl, *ground and center.*"

When he finally let up on her, it was so late that he'd had to mend the fire twice; she was physically as well as emotionally drained. She crawled into bed and huddled among the blankets, too spent even to cry.

He was almost as exhausted as she.

He staggered over to the fire and banked it with painful precision, controlling the shaking of his hands with effort. "You almost had it," he said, finally. "You came so close. I think you might have had it, if you'd just had the energy to get there."

She lost the bleak emptiness that had been in her eyes. "I—I thought maybe—"

"Tomorrow we'll try something different; we'll try it in link. Once you *find* your center, you won't lose it again. Gods, it is so frustrating watching you . . . I can *See* you coming close and missing, and I want to scream."

"Well, it's no Festival from inside either," she retorted, then managed a wan smile. "The least you can do, after torturing me all night, is to get in with me and keep me warm."

"Oh, I think I could manage something more personal than that," he replied, dredging up a smile of his own.

Talia fell asleep almost immediately, every last bit

of energy exhausted by the efforts of the day. Kris remained awake a bit longer, trying to figure how he was going to fit in the training with the all-too-necessary effort of digging out. Just before he finally slept, Tantris had the last word.

:Not one day,: Tantris ordered. *:You're more tired than you thought. You rest tomorrow, too.:*

"I'm fine," Kris objected in a whisper.

:Hah! You only think *you are. Wait until tomorrow. Besides, if you can get her centered, you'll be on the way to solving* that *problem. That takes precedence, I think.:*

"I hate to admit it," Kris yawned, "But you're right, Featherfoot."

Kris had not realized how truly bone-weary they were until he woke first the next day to discover that it was well past noon. He woke Talia, and they finished mending all the now-dry garments, putting off the inevitable "lesson" as long as possible by mutual unspoken accord.

Finally it was she who said, reluctantly, "I suppose we'd better . . ."

"Unfortunate, but true. Here—" he sat on the blankets of their "bed," and patted a place in front of him. "—I told you I was going to try a different tactic. You've linked in with me before, so you know what it's like."

She seated herself cross-legged, their knees touching, and looked at him warily. "I think I remember. Why?"

"I'm going to try and show you your center. Now, just relax, and let me do the work this time." He waited until she had achieved that half-trance, closed his own eyes long enough to trance down himself, then rested his hands lightly on her wrists. It was little more than a moment's work to bring her into rapport; *that* part of her Gift was still working, almost *too* well. He opened his eyes slowly, and Looked, knowing she could see what he Saw.

She looked, gasped, and grabbed—throwing both of them out of trance and out of rapport.

He had been expecting something of the sort and had been prepared for a "fall." She had *not* been, and sat shaking her head to clear it afterward.

"That was a damnfool move," she said, when at last she could speak.

"I won't argue with that statement," he replied evenly. "Ready to try again?"

She sighed, nodded, and settled herself once more. This time she did not grab; she hardly moved at all.

Finally she broke the trance herself, unable to take the strain. "It's like trying to draw by watching a mirror," she said through clenched teeth.

"So?" he replied, giving her no encouragement to pity herself.

"So I try again."

It was hours later when she met with victory; as Kris had suspected, when she centered properly, it was with a nearly audible *snap,* a great deal like having a dislocated joint pop back into place. There was a flare of energy—and a flash of something almost like pain—followed by a flood of relief. Kris had Tantris nudge her—then shove her, with no effect.

"Ground!" he ordered; she fumbled her way into a clumsy grounding with such an utter lack of finesse that his other suspicion—that she'd never done grounding and centering properly before—were pretty much confirmed. It was then that he realized that her shields hadn't just gone erratic, they'd collapsed; and the reason they'd collapsed was that they'd never been properly based in the first place.

"All right," he said quietly, "Now you're properly set up. Can you see now why it's important?"

"Because," she answered slowly, "You have to have something to use as a base to build on?"

'Right," he agreed. "Now come out of there."

"But—"

"You're going to find it yourself, this time. *Without* my help. Ground and center, greenie."

"Ground and center. Dammit, that's *not* right." "Do it again. Ground and center." "Again, and faster." "Dammit, it should be *reflex* by now! Again."

Talia held to her temper by the most tenuous of holds. If it hadn't been for the concern he was feeling, so overwhelming that she could sense it with no effort at all, she'd have lost her temper hours ago. Ground and center, over and over, faster and faster— with Tantris and Rolan shoving at her when she least expected it.

The first time they'd pushed her before she was properly settled, she'd literally been knocked out for a moment; she came to with Kris propping her up, expression impassive.

"Tantris *hit* me," she said indignantly.

"He was supposed to," Kris replied, letting her go.

"But I wasn't ready! It wasn't *fair!*" She stared at him, losing the tenuous hold she'd had on her emotions. It felt like betrayal; it felt horribly like betrayal—

"Damn right, it wasn't fair." He answered the anger and hurt in her voice with cool contempt. "Life isn't fair. You learned that a long time ago." He felt the anger then—hers; it couldn't be coming from anywhere else, since beneath his veneer of contempt, he was worried and no little frightened. He was taking his life in his hands by provoking her, and was all too conscious of the fact. "Dammit, you're leaking again. *Lock it down!*" The anger died; she flushed with shame. He didn't give her a chance to get back into the cycle of doubt and self-pity. "Now; ground and center—and get centered *before* they can knock you over."

He didn't even let her stop when they ate; snapping at her to center at unexpected moments, letting

Tantris or Rolan judge when she was most off-guard and choosing then to push at her. It wasn't until *he* was exhausted, so exhausted he couldn't properly See anymore, that he called it quits for the night.

She undressed for bed in total silence; so barricaded that there was nothing to read in her face or eyes. He waited for her to say something; waited in vain.

"I'm not sorry," he said finally. "I know it's not your fault you got out of Grays half-trained, but I'm not sorry I'm doing this to you. If you don't learn this the hard way, you won't learn it right."

"I know that," she replied, looking up at him sharply. "And I'm *not* angry at you—not now, anyway. I'm mostly tired, and Gods, my head hurts so I can hardly think."

He relaxed, and reached for the container of willowbark on the mantlepiece, handing it to her with a rueful smile. "In that case, I can assume it's safe to come to bed?"

"I wouldn't murder you there, anyway," she replied with a hint of her old sense of humor. "It would get the blankets all sticky."

He laughed, and settled himself, watching her make herself a cup of herbal tea for her headache. Before today he hadn't been sure—but now he dared to believe she *would* tame that wild Gift of hers. It wouldn't be too much longer before centering *would* be reflex. Then it was only a matter of time, to build back what she'd lost.

"Kris? Are you still awake?"

"Sort of," he answered drowsily, lulled by the warmth and his own weariness.

"I just want to say that I appreciate this. At least, I do when you're not pounding on me."

He chuckled, but made no other reply.

"I need you, Kris," she finished softly. "That's something I don't forget even when I'm angriest. I really need you."

It took a while for the sense of that to penetrate—
and when it did, it almost shocked him awake again.
If he hadn't been so tired—

As it was, guilt followed him down into sleep. She
needed him. Good Gods; what if it was something
more than need?

Talia waited until Kris' deep and even breathing
told her he really had fallen asleep, and carefully
extricated herself from the bed without waking him.
She always thought better with some task in her
hands, a holdover from her childhood, so she took
her cup of willowbark tea and set about polishing
some of the bright bits of metalwork on Rolan's tack.
The cloak she'd wrapped around herself kept the
chill off her back, and the fire in front of her gave
off just enough heat to be pleasant. Thusly settled
in, she put her mind to the myriad of problems at
hand.

The fire crackled cheerfully; she wished *she* could
feel cheerful. Lord and Lady, what an unholy mess
she'd gotten into! The storm alone would have been
bad enough; *any* of the problems would have been
bad enough. To have to deal with all of them together . . .

At least she'd made a start, some kind of start, on
getting herself retrained. Kris seemed happier, after
this afternoon's work. He had been right about one
thing; now that she knew what "being centered" felt
like, she'd never lose the ability to find that firm base
again. She'd wanted to kill him this afternoon, and
more than once—but she was learning in a way that
would make her stronger, and now that she was
calmer, she could appreciate that.

She needed him, more than she'd ever needed
anyone else.

But—Lord and Lady—what if it was something
more complicated than need, or even need and the
kind of feeling she had for Skif?

He *was* handsome; handsome as an angel. And despite a certain smug vanity, a man she'd be more than proud to have as a friend. Look at the way he was taking his life in his hands—literally—for the sake of getting her back in control of herself and her Gift. He was kind, he was gentle, he was considerate, and with the way her mind had been playing tricks on her lately, it was more than a possibility that she'd unconsciously used her Gift to influence the way he thought about her. Even to the point of getting him into bed with her—

Lady knew *she* was no beauty. And if she had influenced him in that, she could have caused an even deeper attraction.

She clenched her hands on her mug so hard they ached. That was one thing she had *not* wanted. At least not originally. But now?

She liked Kris well enough. Well enough—but not *that* well.

She *was* attracted to Dirk, there was no question about that. And strongly; more strongly than she'd ever felt about anyone.

It was almost, she decided a bit reluctantly, as if Dirk was some hitherto-unrecognized, hitherto-unmissed, other half of herself, and that she'd never again feel whole after having met him unless—

Unless what?

Heralds seldom made any kind of long-term commitment; contenting themselves with the close friendship of the Circle, casual, strictly physical liaisons, and the bonds of their Companions. And truly, few Heralds she knew were at all dissatisfied with that kind of life. Realistically speaking, the job was far too dangerous to make a lifebond possible or desirable. Look what had happened to Keren when Ylsa died; if Sherrill hadn't had exactly what she needed *and* been right on the spot, she might very well have death-willed herself in bereavement.

And she'd only seen Dirk a handful of times.

But for Heralds, sometimes only once was enough. Her mind drifted back years.

It was late one night that they'd all been gathered in Keren's room over hot mulled wine and sometimes ribald conversation. Somehow the subject turned from bawdy jokes to the truth behind some of the legends and tales told by outsiders about Heralds: they were laughing at some of the more absurd exaggerations.

"Take that love-at-one-glance nonsense," Talia had giggled. "Someone ought to really take the Bards to task over that one. How could anyone know from the first meeting that someone they've just met will be a lifepartner?"

"Oddly enough, that's not an exaggeration," Sherrill had replied soberly. "When it happens with Heralds, that's generally exactly the way it happens. It's almost as if there were something, something even deeper than instinct, that recognizes the other soul." She'd shrugged. "Metaphysical, sentimental, but still true."

"Do you mean to tell me that both of you had that happen?" Talia had been incredulous.

"As a matter of fact, the very first time I set eyes on Keren," Sherrill replied. "Notwithstanding the fact that I was just under fourteen at the time."

Keren nodded. "Ylsa and I knew when we met midway through our third year—until then we'd never done more than wave at each other across the room since we had had very different schedules. We did wait, though, until we were both sure that it was something solid and not ephemeral, and until we'd completed our internships, before commiting to each other."

"And I didn't want to intrude on what was obviously a lifebond."

"You would have been welcome. To tell you the truth, we'd wondered a little—"

"But I didn't know that at the time, did I?" Sherrill had laughed. "Truly, though, Talia, anyone I've ever talked to that has seen a lifebond has said the same thing; that was the way it was for Selenay's parents, for instance. It either happens the first time you meet, or never."

"And if it's not a lifebond, there's nothing you can do to make it one—to make it more than a temporary relationship, no matter how much you want it to be something more," Keren had continued. "My twin found that out."

Talia must have looked intensely curious, although she hadn't actually asked anything, because Keren continued after a moment.

"Remember I've told you once or twice that I've got a niece and nephew almost your age? Well, they're Teren's. Not only were we not Chosen at the same time, but it took seven years for his Companion to come for him. By then I was a field Herald—and he was married and working the sponge-boat. Then it happened. He was Chosen. And the wife he had thought he was contented with turned out to mean less to him than he'd ever dreamed. He *wanted* to love her, he really did. He tried to make himself love her—it didn't work. He went through an incredible amount of soul-searching and guilt before concluding that the emotion wasn't there and wasn't going to be, and that his real life was with the Circle and his Companion. And to tell the truth, his wife—now ex-wife—didn't really seem to care. His children were adopted into our family and she turned around and married into another with no sign of regret that *I* could see. So you see," she had concluded, "if you're a Herald, you either have a lifebond and recognize it at once, or you live your life without one."

Talia sighed.

If she were going to be honest with herself, she had to admit that this seemed to be exactly what had happened to her with regard to Dirk. *Seemed* to be—that was the key. How did she know that this wasn't some fantasy she was building in her own mind?

It didn't feel much like a fantasy, though. It was more like a toothache; or perhaps the way Jadus had felt about his missing leg. He'd said it had often seemed as if it were still there, and aching.

Well, there was something in Talia that ached, too. Fine. What about Kris?

What she felt for Kris . . . just wasn't that deep. Yes, she needed him—his support, his expertise, his encouragement. But "need" was just not the same as "love." Or rather, the emotion she felt for him was a different kind of love; a comradeship—actually closer to what she felt for Rolan or Skif or even Keren than anything else.

But if *Kris* had become infatuated with *her*—Gods, it almost didn't bear thinking about.

Granted, he certainly wasn't acting very lover-like. And earlier—he almost seemed to be throwing Dirk at her. Outside of bed he was treating her more like Alberich treated a trainee who had gotten some bad early lessoning and needed to have it beaten out of him. Except in the digging out, when he treated her as an absolute equal; neither cosseting her nor allowing her to take more than her share of the work.

Provided her mind hadn't been tricking both of them—which was a very real possibility.

"Oh, hellfire," she sighed.

At least she'd managed to clarify *some* of her feelings. And there wasn't anything she could do about it anyway—not until she had her Gift under full control, and could sort out what was "real" and what wasn't. She drank the last of the stone-cold tea, and put up the harness, then slipped back into bed. Right now the only thing to do was to enforce the sleep she knew she needed badly. It was best to just try and take things a day at a time.

Because at this point, she had more pressing problems to deal with. If she couldn't get her Gift back under control, this would all be very moot. . . .

For she was quite well aware of how close she'd come to driving both Kris and herself over the edge. It could happen again, especially if he did something to badly frighten her—and if it did—

If it did, it could end, only too easily, in his death, hers, or both.

Ten

Well, there was one way, Talia knew, to keep herself under control—and that was to work herself into a state of total exhaustion. So in the morning she rose early, almost before the sun, and she began pressing herself to her limits—making each day blur into the next in a haze of fatigue. It became impossible to tell what day it was, or even how long they'd been there.

Talia usually woke first, at dawn, and would prod Kris into wakefulness. One or the other of them would prepare not only breakfast, but unleavened cakes with some form of soup or stew: something that could remain untended most of the day without scorching, simply because they both knew that by the time they came in, they would have barely enough energy to eat and perform a sketchy sort of wash before collapsing into bed.

After a hearty breakfast of fruit and porridge, she would wrap the Companions' legs against the sharp edges of the ice-crust while Kris haltered the chirras, and all six occupants of the Station would troop out into the cold to begin the day's work.

Rolan and Tantris would move up first, and break the crust of ice and the hard snow beneath by rearing to their full heights and crashing down on it with their forelegs, or backing up to it and kicking as hard as they could. They would move back, and Talia and Kris would then take their places; picking up the chunks that had broken off and heaving them to either side of the trail they were cutting. The chirras would use their powerful foreclaws on what remained until they were halted by snow too packed for them to dig or crust too slippery to get a grip on. Then the Heralds would move the chunks they'd dislodged, scoop up the loose snow, and let the Companions take over again.

They would work without a break until the sun reached its zenith, then take begrudged time for a hasty lunch. On their return, they would work until darkness. Each day the trips to and from the Station got longer; sometimes it was only that which kept Talia working. There were times, too many times, when their progress was limited to a few feet for a whole day of back-breaking labor; and she knew the Station itself was furlongs from the road. It was when their measured progress amounted to little more than a dozen paces that the temptation to give up was the strongest.

When darkness fell, Kris would tend the Companions while Talia groomed the chirras, checking them thoroughly for any sign of injury or muscle strain during the process of grooming them. Rolan and Tantris, of course, could be relied upon to tell their Chosen if *they'd* been hurt, but the chirras were another story. And if one of the chirras had to drop out of the work, their progress would be halved.

Finally Kris or Talia—usually Talia—would ensure that everyone was well supplied with food and water and blanketed against the night chill before they wolfed down their own dinners and sought their bed.

It was the hardest physical labor either of them had ever performed. The constant cold seeped into their very bones, and their muscles never stopped aching. It wore them down, a little more each day. They had strictly rationed their own supplies, and

the food they were taking in was not equaling the
energy they were expending. They were getting thinner, both of them, and tougher, physically. It was a
change Talia hardly noticed, because it was so grad-
ual, but once in a while she would think vaguely that
her friends would have been surprised to the point
of shock by the way she looked.

Kris continued to hammer at her through the first
week of digging out, until centering and grounding
had become reflexive. After that, he left her in peace,
only offering an occasional bit of weary advice. Talia's
control over Empathic projection came and went, at
unpredictable intervals. although Kris evidently never
noticed her projecting involuntarily. If he had, he
would have pounced on her, of that she was certain.
Her shielding *was* returning now that she had something to form a firm base for it, but it was the
thinnest of veils, hardly even enough to know that it
was there. She worked at control with nearly the
same single-minded obsession she was giving the physical labor of digging out.

The only pauses in their routine were the two
occasions when they again ran out of clean clothing.
Those two days were given over to a repeat of their
washday, and to brave attempts to revive one another's faltering spirits. As tired as Talia was, it was easy
to become depressed. Kris wasn't quite so much the
pawn of his emotions, but there were times Talia
found herself having to pull him out of despair. The
endless cold did not help matters any, nor did the
fact that they had, indeed, needed to cut green wood
to use in their fire. The green wood, even when
mixed with seasoned, gave off much less heat. Talia
felt as if she'd never be warm again.

But one afternoon, nearly a month from the time
they'd first reached the Station, she looked up from
their task in sudden bewilderment to realize that
they'd finally reached the road.

And the road was as drift-covered as the path out had been.

"Now what?" Talia asked dully.

"Oh, Gods." Kris sat down on a chunk of snow with none of his usual grace. This was a scenario he'd never contemplated; he'd always assumed that once they broke out, the main road would be cleared as well. He stared at the icy wilderness in front of them and tried to think.

"The storm—it must have spread farther than I thought," he said at last. "The road crews should have been within sensing distance by now, otherwise."

He felt utterly bewildered and profoundly shaken— for once at a total loss for a course of action. He just gazed numbly at the unbroken expanse of snow covering the road, unable to even think clearly.

Talia tried to clear her mind—to stay calm—but the uncanny silence echoed in her ears. And that feeling of someone watching was back.

She glanced apprehensively at Kris, wondering if *he* was sensing the same thing she was—and in the next breath, certain it was all originating in *her* mind.

The feeling of being watched was, if anything, more intense than it had been before. And ever-so-slightly ominous. It was very much akin to the uneasy queasiness she used to have whenever Keldar would stand over her at some chore, waiting and watching for her to make the tiniest mistake. Something out there was unsure of her—mistrusted her— and was waiting for her to slip, somehow. And when she did— Panic rose in her, and choked off the words she had intended to say.

Kris stared at the unbroken ice crust as if entranced, unable to muster enough energy to say anything more. Gradually, though, he became aware of a feeling of uneasiness—exactly as if someone were watching him from under cover of the brush beneath the snow-laden trees. He tried to dismiss the feeling, but it continued to grow, until it was only by sheer force of will that he was able to keep from whipping around to *see* who was staring at the back of his neck—

It wasn't entirely an unfriendly regard . . . but it was a wary one. As if whatever it was that was watching him wasn't quite sure of him.

He tried to shield, to clear his mind of the strange sensations, only to have them intensify when he invoked shielding.

And now he was seeing and hearing things as well— slight forms that could only be caught out of the corner of his eye, and slipped into invisibility when he tried to look at them directly. And there seemed to be sibilant whisperings just on the edges of his hearing—

All of which could well be from a single source. Talia had told him once already that she thought she was hallucinating; she could well be drawing him into an irrational little nightmare-world of her making.

"Talia!" he snapped angrily, more than a little frightened. *"Lock it down!"*

And he whipped around to glare at her, enraged, and just about ready to strike out at her for her lack of control.

Talia forgot the strange watcher; forgot everything except Kris' angry—and untrue—accusation. She flushed, then paled—then reacted.

"It's *not* me!" she snapped. Then, when he continued to stare at her with utter disbelief, she lost the control she had been holding to with her psychic teeth and toenails.

This time, at least, the Companions were prepared, and shielded themselves quickly. Kris, however, got the full brunt of her fear of the situation and her anger at him. He rose involuntarily to his feet and staggered back five or six paces, to trip and fall backward into the hard snow, his face as white as hers, and unable to do more than raise his arms in front of his face in a futile gesture of warding.

And the watcher stirred—

Talia froze; the feeling that some power was uncoiling and contemplating striking her down was so powerful that she was unable even to breathe. Somehow she cut off the emotion-storm—and simultaneous with her resumption of control, Rolan paced forward slowly, to stand beside her. He faced, not her, but the watching forest, his whole posture a silent challenge.

There was a feeling of vague surprise—and the sensation of being watched vanished.

Talia felt released from her paralysis and wanted to die of shame for what she'd nearly done to Kris. As he blinked in surprise, she turned blindly away from him, leaned against a tree-trunk and wept, her face buried in her arms.

Kris stumbled to his feet, and put both arms around her. "Talia, little bird, please don't—" he begged. "I'm sorry; I didn't mean—I lost my temper. It'll be all right. It's got to be all right—I'm sorry. I'm sorry—"

But dreary days of grinding labor and nights of too little rest had taken their toll of his spirit as well. It was only when the tears started to freeze on both their faces that they were able to stop sobbing in dejection and despair.

"It—that thing watching—"

She shook with more than cold. "I—don't want to talk about it," she said, looking uneasily over her shoulder. "Not here—not now."

"It wasn't you—"

"No. I swear on my life."

He believed her. "All right, let's handle what we've got; the storm was worse than we thought," he said, getting control of himself again. "This is the very

northernmost end of the road. They can't be more
than a few days away, and we aren't running short of
food yet. We'll be all right—especially if we start
rationing ourselves."

"We won't need as much food if we rest," Talia
said, drying her eyes on the gauze she'd used to
protect them from sunglare.

"And we can plant a signal so that they know we're
here. I can get the crust to hold me a good distance,
and you're lighter than I am; about an hour's scramble will do. Wait here."

He mounted Tantris and the two of them headed
back to the Station, vanishing from sight down the
narrow little valley they'd cut. Talia waited for their
return, occasionally looking warily over her shoulder. Whatever had been watching her had been within
a hair of striking her; why she was certain of this,
she had no idea, but she could not rid herself of the
thought. She had no idea what had deterred it, but
she did not want it to catch her unaware. She clung
to Rolan's neck, and waited, exerting every bit of
control she had. For it seemed to her that the watcher
had only acted when it appeared that she was attack-
ing Kris. If that *was* the case, she had no intention of
inadvertently invoking it agin.

It was at least a candlemark—and far too long for
her peace of mind—before she saw Kris and Tantris
trotting back. He carried four white arrows, two long
branches, and some bright blue rags.

"These will show up at a distance. Here, pattern
these, will you?" He dismounted and handed her
two of the arrows, and began working on his two.
"We tie the arrows to the stick, and plant the stick
out in the middle of where the road is. When the
crews find them, they'll know we're here, and still
alive. They'll even know for certain it's us if they
happen to have a Herald with them—surely anyone with them will have been given our patterns."

"Why are we doing this?"

"If we don't, they might not clear the road this far. This is just the northernmost loop; it isn't strictly needed to get between Waymeet and Berrybay. It takes longer to go around than to cut through Sorrows, but nobody travels much in the winter except Heralds. And nobody knows *where* we've been 'lost.'"

He handed her one of his arrows in exchange for hers. Both of them tied the arrows to one of the branches, and made them as conspicuous as possible with fluttering rags.

"You go toward Waymeet, I'll go toward Berrybay," he said, preparing to climb up on the snow crust. "Plant yours at the first crossroads you come to. I'll do the same. Hopefully the road crews will find *one* of them before they give up."

"Kris—what if it snows again?"

"Talia, for the love of the Goddess, don't even *think* that. Walk as far as you can, but be back here by dusk."

Talia had never felt so lonely. There was scarcely a sound from the white woods on either side. She could hear the creaking sounds of Kris carefully making his way across the snow crust behind her, sliding his feet so as not to break it. Even so, she heard the crunch that meant he'd fallen through at least once before he got too far away for the sounds to carry to her. It was a measure of his own dejection that he didn't even have the spirit to swear.

She set out herself, often having to detour around high drifts that she didn't dare try and climb. Her eyes ached from tears and snowglare, and she was as tired as she'd ever been in her life. She was grateful that she was lighter than Kris; the snow crust was holding beneath her without any such mishaps as he had had.

The silence was eerie—frightening. As frightening

in its way as the howl of the storm had been. Talia
was shivering long before she reached her turnaround
point, and not just from cold. There were no sounds
of birds or animals, no indication that anything else
lived and moved here besides herself. That horrible
feeling of something watching might be gone, but
there was still something uncanny about the Forest
of Sorrows, something touched with the chill of death
and the ice of despair. Whatever power held sway
here, it was unsleeping and brooding; she *knew* it
beyond doubt, and somehow knew she was feeling
only the barest touch of its power—and she didn't
really want to trust to the supposed protection of her
Whites by venturing too far alone. She was more
than relieved to find a half-buried crossroads sign;
that meant she could plant her gaudy staff in the
snowcrust at the peak of a drift and retrace her
steps.

She was never so glad to see another human being
as she was to see Kris, picking his way across the
snow, coming toward her.

Back in the Station, Talia surveyed what was left
of their supplies. "They'd better come soon," she
said, trying to keep doubt out of her voice. "Even if
we're careful, we don't have much. It'll probably last
for a week, but not much more."

"If they're as worried as I think—as I hope—they'll
be working around the clock, even by torchlight,"
Kris said, sheer exhaustion making his voice tone-
less. "It just can't be too much longer."

"They may not recognize us as Heralds at all," she
replied, trying to joke a little. "I doubt they've ever
seen Heralds looking so shabby. I've had to practically rub holes in my things to get them white again.
Our appearance is hardly going to enhance the Heraldic image."

She screwed her face up in imitation of an old
man's grimace, and croaked; "Heralds? Yer be not

Heralds! Yer be imposters, for certain sure! Gypsies! Scalawags! And where got ye them whitewashed nags, eh? Eh?"

Kris just stared at her for a long moment, then suddenly began to laugh as helplessly as he'd wept earlier. Perhaps it was their weariness that made them as prone to near-hysterical hilarity as to tears. Talia began to giggle herself, then crow with laughter. They collapsed into their bed-nest together, legs too weak to stand up, and for a long time could hardly stop laughing long enough to breathe. No sooner would one of them get himself under control, and the other start to follow suit, when one look would set them both off again.

"Enough—please—" Kris gasped at last.

"Then don't keep looking at me," Talia replied, resolutely staring at a stain on her boots until she got her breath back.

"Berrybay has a Resupply Station," Kris said, doing his best to maintain a serious subject. "We *can* get new uniforms there, and we can get our leathers bleached and re-treated. I'll warn you, though, the sizes will only be approximate."

"Just so that the Whites *are* white and not gray, or full of holes."

"I don't suppose you know enough sewing to alter what we get?" Kris asked wistfully. She could tell by his expression that his fastidious nature was mildly disturbed by the notion that he would be looking considerably less than immaculate in outsize uniforms.

Talia raised an eyebrow in his direction. "My dear Herald, I'll have you know that by my third year at the Collegium I was *making* Whites. I may very well have made some of *your* wardrobe."

"Strange thought." He pulled off his boots, slowly. "It—it *wasn't* you playing tricks on my mind?"

"No," she replied. "Not until you shouted at me."

"Gods—I think I must be going mad."

She was rubbing her white, cold feet, trying to

restore circulation. "Don't—please—it's the isolation, the worry," she responded, with a clutching of fear in her chest. "Not enough rest, not enough food—"

"Are making me see things? Are *you* seeing things?"

"No," she admitted, "But—it seems like the forest is—watching. Almost all the time."

Kris started. Talia saw him jump, and bit her lip.

"It's nothing," he said. "Just—Tantris says you're right. He says the forest *is* watching us. Dammit—I thought it was you, doing things to me. Sorry."

"Kris—I lost it again—" Tears stung her eyes.

"Hey, not as bad as last time—and you got control back by yourself. Right?"

"Sort of. Whatever it was—when I turned on you, it suddenly felt like it was going to do something to *me* if I touched you. That was when I got scared back into sense."

"And you got control back. However it happened, *you* got control back. Don't give up on me, little bird. And don't give up on yourself, either."

"I'll try," she said, a faint tremor in her voice. "I'll try."

Leaden silence hung between them, until he took it upon himself to break it. "Jadus left you his harp, so I assume that you know how to play it, but I've never once heard you do so. Would you?"

"I'm nowhere near as good as you are," she protested.

"Humor me," he insisted.

"All right, but you may be sorry," she curled into the blankets to try and keep a little warmth in her legs and back and took the harp from him when he brought it from its corner.

This was the first time she'd played in front of anyone but Jadus. The way the firelight caught the golden grain of the wood brought back those days with a poignant sadness. She rested her hands on the strings for a moment, then began playing the first thing that came to memory.

*   *   *

The song was "Sun and Shadow," and Kris was very much aware from the first few notes that she performed it quite differently than he did. Where he and Dirk emphasized the optimistic foreshadowing of the ultimate solution to the lovers' trials, and made the piece almost hopeful in spite of its somber quality, she wandered the lonely paths of the song's "present," where their respective curses seemed to be dooming the pair to live forever just out of one another's reach. She was correct in insisting that she wasn't as technically adept a player as Kris, but she played as she sang—with feeling, feeling that she made you hear. In her hands "Sun and Shadow" could tear your heart.

The last notes hung in the air between them for long moments before he could clear his throat enough to say something.

"I keep telling you," he managed at last, "that you underestimate yourself."

"You're a remarkably uncritical audience," she replied. "Would you like her back, or shall I murder something else?"

"I'd like you to play more, if you would."

She shrugged, but secretly was rather pleased that he hadn't reclaimed My Lady. Her mood was melancholy, and it was possible to find solitude by losing herself in the music—solitude that it wasn't possible to create when he was playing or she was singing. She continued, closing her eyes and letting her hands wander through whatever came to mind, sometimes singing, sometimes not. Kris listened quietly, without comment. The few times she looked up, his face was so shadowed that she couldn't read his expression. Eventually she ran out of music fitting her mood, and her hands fell from the harpstrings.

"That's all I know," she said into the silence that followed.

"Then that," he replied, taking the harp from her,

"is enough for one night. I think it is more than time enough for bed."

She had doubted she'd be able to sleep, but the moment she relaxed, she was lost to slumber.

Three days later the Station seemed to have shrunk around them and felt very confining, especially to Talia, who had always had a touch of claustrophobia. Her temper was shortened to near nonexistence . . . and she feared losing it. Greatly feared it.

"Kris—" she said, when his pacing became too much for her to bear. "Will you go out? Will you *please* go somewhere?"

He stopped in midstep, and turned to eye her with speculation. "Am I driving you out of patience?"

"It's more than that. It's—"

"That feeling of being watched. Is it back?"

She sagged with relief. "You feel it, too?"

"Not now. I did a little while back."

"Am—I sending both of us mad?" She clenched her hands so hard that her nails left marks in her palms.

He sat on the floor at her feet, took her hands in his, and made her relax them. "I don't think so. If you'll remember, *Tantris* told me that the forest was watching us."

"What *is* it?"

"I only have a guess; it's Vanyel's Curse. It's made the whole forest aware somehow."

"I don't think it likes me," she said, biting her lip.

Kris had the "listening" look he wore when Tantris Mindspoke him. "Tantris says that *he* thinks it's disturbed by you; you're a Herald, but you're a danger to me, another Herald. It isn't sure what to do with you."

"So as long as I stay in control, it will leave me alone . . ."

"I would surmise." He rose to his feet. "And to keep you from losing control, *I* am going out."

*   *   *

Kris had decided to flounder his way down the road toward Waymeet, in hopes of meeting with a road crew. He entered the Station to have an entirely unexpected and mouthwatering aroma hit him full in the face.

"I'm hallucinating," he said, half-afraid that once again he really *was*. "I'm smelling fresh meat cooking."

"Pretty substantial hallucinations, then, since you're going to have them for supper," Talia replied, with a sober face. Then, unable to restrain herself, she jumped up from the hearth to throw her arms around him in a joyful hug. "Two squirrels and a rabbit, Kris! I got them *all!* And there'll be more—the fodder is attracting them! I didn't even lose or break any arrows!"

"Bright Havens—" he said, sitting down with a thump, hardly daring to believe it.

There was no denying the stewed meat and broth Talia ladled out to him, however. They ate every scrap, the first fresh food they'd had in weeks, sucking the tiny bones dry, then celebrated with exuberant loving. They fell asleep with untroubled hearts for the first time in many days.

They were awakened the next morning very early; the chirras were stirring restlessly, and both Companions seemed to be listening to something.

Rolan was overwhelmingly relieved and joyful, and Talia went deeper to find out why.

"Tantris says—" Kris began.

"There're people coming!" Talia finished excitedly. "Kris, it's the road crew!"

"There's a Herald with them, too. Tantris thinks they'll reach us sometime after noon."

"Have they reached our marker yet?"

"Yes. The Herald had his Companion broadcast a Mindcall to ours when he found it. I might even have met them yesterday, if I hadn't gone in the wrong direction—idiot that I am!"

"How were you to know? How many are there?"

"Ten, not counting the Herald."

"Should we go out and try to dig the path out farther to meet them?"

"No," Kris said firmly. "The little we can do won't make much difference, and I'm still tired. We'll pack up, straighten things up here, and meet them where the path meets the road."

It seemed strange to see the Station barren of their belongings, with only the empty containers that the supplies had been stored in to tell of their presence there this past month. It took longer than Talia had thought it would to repack everything; they did not leave the Station until almost noon.

When they reached the road, they could see the newcomers in the far distance. They waved and shouted, and could tell by the agitated movements of the other figures that they'd been spotted. The work crew redoubled their efforts, and before too long— though not soon enough for Talia and Kris—the paths met.

"Heralds Talia and Kris?" The white-clad figure that was first through the gap was unfamiliar to both of them, though his immaculate uniform made them uncomfortably conscious of the pitiful condition of their own.

"Yes, Herald," Kris answered for both of them.

"Praise the Lady! When the Guard learned that you hadn't stayed at Waymeet and hadn't arrived at Berrybay, and that you'd left on the very eve of the storm, we all feared the worst. Had you been caught in it, I doubt you would have survived even one night. This was the worst blizzard in these parts in recorded history. Oh, I'm Tedric. How on earth did you manage?"

"We were warned by our chirras in time to make

the Waystation, but I doubt that we'd be in any shape to greet you now if it hadn't been stocked by someone other than the regular Resupply crew," Kris replied. "Whoever it was, he seems to have had an uncannily accurate idea of how much provender we'd need, and what kinds."

"That's the Weatherwitch's doing," said one of the work crew, a stolid-looking farmer. "Kept at us this fall till we got it stocked to her liking. Even made us go back after first snow with some odd bits—honey 'n oil, salted meat 'n fish. We had it to spare, praise Kernos, and she's never yet been wrong when she gets one o' these notions, so we went along with it. Happen it was a good thing."

"Praise Kernos, in very deed! I see you've got your gear. Come along with me and I'll have you warm and dry and fed before nightfall. I'm with the Resupply Station outside of Berrybay. I've got plenty of room for both of you, if you don't mind sharing a bed."

"Not at all," Kris replied gravely, sensing Talia struggling with the effort of maintaining what little shielding she had against the pressure of fifteen minds. "We've been sleeping on straw next to the hearth for warmth. Right now a camp cot would sound like heaven, even if I had to share it with Tantris!"

"Good. Excellent!" Herald Tedric replied. "I'll guide you both back; these good people know what they're doing, and they certainly don't need me in the way now that we've found you."

The members of the work crew made polite noises, but they obviously agreed with him.

"Fact is, Herald," the red-faced farmer whispered to Kris, "Old Tedric's a good enough sort, but he don't belong out here. He's too old, and his heart's more'n a mite touchy. Waystation Supply post was supposed to be a pensioning-out position, if you catch my meaning. He ain't the kind to sit idle, even though he hasn't the health to ride circuit no more. We're supposed to be keepin' an eye on him, make sure he don't overdo—job's set up so's he could feel useful, but wouldn't have to do anything straining. Guard's supposed to do all his fetching and carrying for him. But what with this storm and all, Guard's busy clearing the roads, seein' to the emergencies— when he found out you two was missin', nothing would do but that he go out with us. Gave us a real fright a time or two, gettin' short of breath and blue-like when we thought we might've found bodies. Good thing you turned up all right, or I reckon we'd have had a third body on our hands."

This put things in an altogether different light. Kris felt a sudden increase in respect for the talkative and seemingly feckless Herald. On closer examination he saw that Tedric was a great deal older than he had first appeared, partially because he was bald as an egg, and partially because he had the kind of baby-soft face that tends not to wrinkle with age. His Companion cosseted him tenderly, flatly refusing to race headlong down the road so that he could prepare the Station for his guests.

Talia and Kris took turns telling him what had transpired from the time they discovered the plague in Waymeet.

"So you're the Queen's Own, the one with the Gift for emotions and mindHealing?" he asked Talia, peering at her short-sightedly. She could sense his faint unease around her, even through the shields Rolan was holding, and mentally shrank into herself. "I wonder if you could do something for the Weatherwitch?"

"Considering that we obviously owe her our lives, I'll certainly be glad to try," Talia replied, trying not to show her own unease and her real dismay at being asked to *use* her wayward Gift. "Just who is she, and why do you call her the Weatherwitch?"

"Ah, it's a sad story, that," he sighed. "A few years ago, it would be, when I'd only just been assigned this post, there was a young woman named Maeven in Berrybay who'd gone and had herself a Festival child—that's a babe that no one will claim, and whose mother hasn't the faintest notion who the father might be. People being what they are, there was a certain amount of tsk-ing, and finger-pointing, until the poor girl heartily wished the babe had never been conceived, much less born. That's what made what happened to her all the worse, you see. You know, 'be careful what you ask for, you might get it'? I'm sure she often wished the child gone, and when the accident happened, she blamed herself. She was taking her turn working at the mill, and she left the little one alone for longer than she should have. Poor mite was just beginning to crawl about, and it managed to wriggle free of the basket she'd left it in. It crawled straight to the millrace, fell in, and drowned. She was the one to find the body, and she went quite mad."

"But why 'Weatherwitch'?" Kris asked.

"She must have had a Gift, and her going off her head freed it altogether, because she started being able to predict the weather. She'd be acting just as usual, dandling that rag-doll she got in place of her babe—then out of nowhere she'd look straight *through* you, and tell you that you'd better see that the beans got taken in because it was going to hail that night. Then, sure enough, it would. People in Berrybay and for a bit around took to coming to her any time the weather looked uncertain. She began to be able to See the weather that was coming days, then weeks, then months in advance. That's why the villagers heeded her when she told them to stock the Station. I wish they'd told me, I'd have laid in a good deal more on my own."

"You stocked it very well, and we've nothing to find fault with," Kris replied reassuringly. "I'm afraid, though, that you'll find we've used up just about everything that was there."

"That will be no problem," Tedric said cheerfully. "I'll be glad to have a little task to turn my hand to. Most of my work's done in the summer, and winter's a bit of a slow time for me. But it looks to me as if you could use a full resupply yourselves."

"I'm afraid so," Talia said as Tedric shook his head over the state of their uniforms. "I don't think the fabric is going to be good for much except rags."

"I've got plenty of stock back at the Station, and I'm no bad hand with a needle," Tedric replied. "I think I can refit you well enough so that you won't be looking like crow-scares. I've got all the necessaries for bleaching and refinishing your leathers, so we won't have to replace those, and your cloaks still look in fairly good shape, or will be after we clean them. If you don't mind staying a bit, I can turn you out looking almost like the day you left to take this sector."

"That sounds fantastic!" Kris said with obvious thankfulness.

"I can help with the altering, sir," Talia added.

The old Herald twinkled at her. "But who tailors the tailor, then? And surely you wouldn't deny an old man the pleasure of helping fit a pretty young lady, would you?"

Talia blushed, and to cover it, settled My Lady wrapped in her blankets in a new position on her lap. Without the harpcase to protect her, Talia elected to carry her personally.

"What's this?" Tedric asked and brightened to learn it was a harp.

"Which of you is the musician?" he asked eagerly.

"We both are, sir," Kris replied.

"But he really plays a great deal better than I do," Talia added. "And Herald Tedric, we'd truly appreciate it if you could find someone to make a new traveling case for her while we're here. We had to destroy the old one to make snow shovels."

"The cabinetmaker would be proud to oblige you," Tedric said with certainty. "In fact, he may even have something already made that will fit. Midwinter Fair is at the Sector capital in a few weeks, and he's been readying a few instrument cases to take there, as well as his little carved boxes and similar trumperies. He's known for his work on small pieces as well as furniture, you see. I'll make a note to start stocking shovels in our Stations from now on. Not every Herald has harpcases to sacrifice."

They passed the village of Berrybay just before sunset, Talia finding herself grateful for the shielding Rolan was supplying her, and reached the Resupply Station with the coming of the dark. The place was much larger than Talia had expected.

"Bright Havens!" she exclaimed. "You could house half the Collegium here!"

"Oh, most of it isn't living quarters—it's mostly haybarn, warehouse, and granary. I do have three extra rooms in case some need should bring a number of Heralds this far north, but only one of those rooms has a bed; any more than two would have to make up beds on the floor. But let's take first things first. I expect you'd both appreciate a hot bath. It will pleasure both of you to know I have a real bathing-room, just like the ones at the Palace and Collegium. While you're getting washed, I'll find some clean clothing for you to wear until we get your new outfits altered and your leathers cleaned. As soon as you're feeling ready, there'll be supper. How does that strike you?"

"It sounds wonderful—especially the part about the hot bath!" Talia replied fervently, as they dismounted in the station's stable.

"Then take yourselves right in that door over there—I'll tend to your beasts and friends. Go up the staircase, then take a sharp right. The copper's all fired up. I've been doing it every day on the chance that we'd find you. The room you'll be using is sharp left."

They each took a small pack and Talia took her harp, and entered the door he'd indicated. Tedric hadn't exaggerated, though it only held a single tub, the bathing-room was identical in every other way to the ones at the Palace.

"Which of us goes first?" Talia asked, thinking longingly of clean hair and a good long soak.

"You. You look ready to die," Kris replied.

"I'm feeling the strain a bit," she admitted.

"Then get your bath. I can wait."

When tight muscles were finally relaxed, and the grime that had accumulated despite her best efforts ruthlessly scrubbed away, she wrapped herself in towels and sought their room. She found that Tedric had preceded them there; on the bed were laid out fabric breeches and shirts of something approximating their sizes.

The approximation was far from exact. It was obvious that if these articles were representative of the kinds of clothing held in storage, there was a great deal of work that was going to have to be done.

She stretched out on the bed for just a moment . . . only to fall completely asleep.

Kris had taken himself downstairs again to talk in private with Tedric. He hadn't missed the older man's initial unease around Talia—nor the fact that he had already know that Talia was Queen's Own and what her Gift was. The identity of an internee was not supposed to be generally known, and the Gift of the Queen's Own wasn't generally even a matter of public knowledge among the Heralds themselves.

He decided that he was a bit too tired for diplomacy, and bluntly asked the older man where he'd gotten his information about Talia.

"Why . . . rumors, mostly," Tedric supplied in astonishment. "Although I didn't credit the half of them. I can't imagine a *Herald* misusing a Gift, and I can't believe the Collegium would allow anyone out who was poorly trained. And I've said so. But I must tell you, there are a lot of eyes and thoughts up here—and, I regret to say, some of them hoping to catch a Herald in failure."

After a covering exchange of pleasantries, Kris climbed the stairs with a worried soul. He found Talia asleep on the bed, and took his towels without waking her.

He lay back in his hot bath to soak, his mind anything but relaxed. If anyone discovered the state Talia was in, not only her reputation would be finished, but the reputation of Heralds as a whole and that of the Collegium would be badly damaged. The faith Heralds themselves had in the Collegium would be shaken if they knew how poorly counseled she'd been.

For that reason, they *dared* not abort the circuit and head back; that would be the signal of failure certain critics of the system had been waiting for. Nor could Kris himself let any senior Herald know the true state of things and how poorly controlled Talia was—for that would lead to a profound disturbance in the ranks of the Heralds themselves, a disturbance that could only roll all the way back to Selenay and Elspeth, with all the attendant problems it would cause them.

It would be up to Kris, and to Talia herself, to get her back to the functional level she had before this whole mess blew up in their faces.

It was with that sobering reflection he finished his bath, and went to get dressed and wake her.

She woke from her nap in a fairly good mood, giggling a little at the way she looked in the outsized garments Tedric had supplied.

"It's because two-thirds of the Heralds are men, little bird," Kris replied. "And all the Resupply Stations get the same goods. So most of the clothing stored here will be made to fit men. I expect when he gets a chance to look, he'll find some things closer to your size. If you think you look silly, look at me!"

The waist of his breeches was a closer fit than hers, but the legs were huge and baggy and much too long, and the sleeves of his shirt fell down far past his fingertips.

"I expect most of what he has is in two categories— large, and 'tent.' At any rate, it's better to have to cut down than try to piece on more fabric."

They descended the staircase to join their host; Kris barefoot and Talia in her sheepskin slippers, since their boots were so stiff from repeated soaking and drying that it was too much of an effort to try to pull them on. In any case, the dwelling was very well heated, and Kris' bare feet caused him no discomfort.

They found the old Herald puttering about in a room that seemed to combine the functions of kitchen and common room. He chuckled to see them, looking like two children clothed in their parents' cast-offs.

"I just took what was nearest to hand" he said apologetically. "I hope you don't mind."

"They're clean, and dry, and warm," Kris smiled, "And right now, that's all we care about. I must say that what I smell would have me pleased to come to table in a grain sack, if that's all there was to wear."

Tedric looked very flattered, and seemed to have no recollection of Kris's earlier interrogation. "When one lives alone, one acquires hobbies. Mine is cooking. I hope you don't find it inferior to what you're used to."

Talia laughed. "Sir, what we're 'used to' has been porridge, stew made with dried meat and old roots, half-burned bannocks, and more porridge. I have no doubt after the past month that your meal will taste as wonderful as your bathtub felt!"

Venison with herbs and mushrooms was a definite improvement over the meals they'd been making. A mental check assured them that Tedric had seen to Rolan, Tantris, and the chirras in the same generous fashion. Both the Companions were half-asleep, with filled bellies, drowsing in heated stalls.

When their own hunger was truly satisfied, Kris helped Tedric clear away the remains of the meal while Talia ran back upstairs for My Lady.

"You seemed so interested in which of us was the musician that I thought we'd repay you for your hospitality," Kris said, taking the harp and beginning to tune her.

"One doesn't hear a great deal of music out here." Tedric replied, not troubling to keep the eagerness from his eyes. "I think it's the one thing that I really miss by being stationed here. When I rode circuit I was always running into Bards."

The old Herald listened with a face full of quiet happiness as they played and sang. It was quite plain that he had missed the company of other Heralds, and equally evident that he had told the simple truth about missing music out here on the Border. Of course, it was very possible that the traveling Bards had simply not noticed this Station, half-hidden off the road and placed at a bit of a distance from Berrybay. It was just as possible that Tedric's work kept him so busy during the summer (the only time journeyman Bards were likely to come this way) that he could not spare the time to seek the village when Bards came through. Kris made a mental note to send a few words to that effect when they sent their next reports. Old Tedric should not have to do without song again if he could help it.

When they finally confessed themselves played out, Tedric instantly rose and insisted that they seek their bed.

"I don't know what possessed me, keeping you up like this," he said. "After all, I'll have you here for as long as it takes to outfit you. **Perhaps I'll hide all the needles for a week or two!**"

When they rose the next morning—somewhat reluctantly, as the featherbed they'd shared had been warm and soft and hard to leave—they discovered that he had already put their leathers and boots to soak in his vats of bleaching and softening solution. Talia helped him take some of their ruined garments apart to use as patterns, and they began altering the standard stock. Tedric was every bit as good with a needle as he'd claimed. By day's end they were well on the way to having their wardrobes replenished, and it was not possible to tell that the garments had not been made at the Collegium; by week's end they were totally re-outfitted.

Once their outfitting was complete, they set about discharging their duties to the populace of Berrybay.

The rest and the tranquillity had been profoundly helpful in enabling Talia to firm up what control she had gotten back over her Gift. She had enough shielding now to hold against the worst of outside pressure on her own; that wasn't much, but it was better than nothing. And she felt her control over her projective ability would hold good unless she were frightened or startled—or attacked. If any of those three eventualities took place, she wasn't entirely certain *what* she'd do. But worrying about it wouldn't accomplish anything.

She almost lost her frail bulwarks when they entered the village. Kris had warned her that the rumors had reached this far north, but the knowledge had not prepared her.

When they set up in the village hall, she caught no few of the inhabitants giving her sidelong, cautious glances. But what was worse, was that the very first petitioners wore charms against dark magic into her presence.

She tried to keep up a pleasant, calm front, but the villagers' suspicion and even fear battered at her thin shields and made her want to weep with vexation.

Finally it became too much to stand. "Kris—I've got to take a walk," she whispered. He took one look at the lines of pain around her eyes, and nodded. He might not be an Empath, but it didn't take *that* Gift to read what the people were thinking when they wore evil-eye talismans around one particular Herald.

"Go—come back when you're ready, and not until."

She and Rolan went out past the outskirts of the village. Once away from people, she swore and wept and kicked snow-hummocks until her feet were bruised and her mind exhausted.

Then she returned, and took up the thread of her duties.

By the second day the unease was less. By the third, the evil-eye talismans were gone.

But she wondered what the reaction of the villagers was going to be when they sought out the Weatherwitch on the morning of the fourth.

The depression surrounding the Weatherwitch's unkempt little cottage was so heavy as to be nearly palpable to Talia, and to move through it was like groping through a dark cloud. The Weatherwitch sat in one cobwebbed, dark, cold corner, crooning to herself and rocking a bedraggled rag doll. She paid no heed at all to the three who stood before her. Tedric whispered that the villagers brought her food and cared for her cottage—that she was scarcely enough aware of her surroundings to know when a meal was placed before her. Kris shook his head in pity, feeling certain that there was little, if anything, that Talia could do for her.

Talia was half-attracted, half-repelled by that shadowed mind. If this encounter had taken place a year ago, she would have had no doubt but that she could have accomplished something, but now?

But having come, and having sensed this for herself, she could *not* turn away.

She half knelt, and half crouched, just within touching distance, on the dirty wooden floor beside the woman. She let go of her frail barriers with a physical shudder of apprehension, and let herself be drawn in.

Kris was more than a little afraid for her—knowing nothing, really, of how her Gift worked, he feared it would be only too easy for her to be trapped by the madwoman's mind—and *then* what would he do? Talia remained in that half-kneeling stance for so long that Kris' own knees began to ache in sympathy. At length, her breathing began to resume a more normal pace and her eyes slowly opened. When she raised her head, Kris extended his hand to her and helped her to her feet again.

"Well?" Tedric asked, not very hopefully.

"The gypsy family who died of snow-sickness two months ago—the ones in the Domesday Book report; wasn't there a child left living?" she asked, her eyes still a little glazed.

"A little boy, yes," Kris answered, as Tedric nodded.

"Who has him?"

"Ifor Smithwright; he wasn't particularly pleased, but *somebody* had to take the mite in," Tedric said.

"Can you bring him here? Would this Smithwright have any objection if you found another home for the child?"

"*He* wouldn't object—but *here*? Forgive me, but that sounds a bit mad."

"It *is* a bit mad," Talia said, slumping with weariness so that Kris couldn't make out her expression in the shadows, "but it may take madness to cure the mad. Just . . . bring him here, would you? We'll see if my notion works."

Tedric looked rather doubtful, but rode off and returned less than an hour later with a warmly-wrapped toddler. The child was colicky and crying to himself.

"Now get her out of the house; I don't care how," she told Tedric wearily, taking the baby from him and soothing it into quiet. "But make sure that she leaves that doll behind."

Tedric coaxed the Weatherwitch to follow him out with a bit of sweet, after persuading her to leave her "infant" behind in the cradle by the smokey fire. Talia slipped in when her back was turned. Seconds after that, a baby's wail penetrated the walls of the cottage, and the madwoman started as if she'd been struck.

It was the most incredible transformation Kris had ever seen. The half-crazed, wild animal look left her eyes, and sense and intelligence flooded back in. In a few seconds, she made the transition from "thing" to human.

"J-Jethry?" she faltered.

The baby cried again, louder this time.

"Jethry!" she cried in answer, and ran through the door.

In the cradle was the child Tedric had brought, perhaps something under a year old, crying lustily. She scooped the child up and held it to her breast, holding it as if it were her own soul given back to her, laughing and weeping at the same time.

No sooner did her hands touch the child, when the last, and perhaps strangest thing of all, happened. It stopped crying immediately, and began cooing back at the woman.

Talia was not even watching; just sagging against the lintel, rubbing her temples. The other two could only watch the transformation in bemusement.

At last the woman took her attention from the baby she held and focused on Talia. She moved toward her hesitantly, and halted when she was a few steps away.

"Herald," she said with absolute certainty, "*you* did

this—you brought me my baby back. He was dead, but you found him again for me!"

Talia looked up at that, eyes like darker shadows on her face, and shook her head in denial. "Not I, my lady. If anyone brought him back, it was you. And it was you who showed me where to find him."

The woman reached out to touch Talia's cheek. Kris made as if to interfere, but Talia motioned him away, signaling him that she was in no danger.

"You *will* reclaim what was yours," the Weatherwitch said tonelessly, her eyes focused on something none of them could see, "and no one will ever shake it from you again. You will find your heart's desire, but not until you have seen the Havens. The Havens will call you, but duty and love will bar you from them. Love will challenge death to reclaim you. Your greatest joy will be preceded by your greatest sorrow, and your fulfillment will not be unshadowed by grief."

" 'There is no joy that has not tasted first of grief,' " Talia quoted softly, as if to herself, so softly that Kris could barely hear the words. The woman's eyes refocused.

"Did I say something? Did I see something?" she asked, confusion evident in her eyes. "Was it the answer you were looking for?"

"It was answer enough," Talia replied with a smile. "But haven't you more important things to think of?"

"My Jethry, my little love!" she exclaimed, holding the child closely, her eyes bright with tears. "There's so much I have to do—to make it up to you. Oh, Herald, how can I ever thank you enough?"

"By loving and caring for Jethry as much as you do now; and not worrying what others may say about it," Talia told her, motioning to the other two to leave, and following them quickly.

"Bright Havens!" Tedric exclaimed, a little uneasily, when they were out of earshot of the cottage.

"That was like old tales of witchcraft and curse-lifting! What kind of strange magic did you work back there?"

"To tell you the truth, I'm not very sure myself," Talia said, rubbing tired eyes with the back of her hand. "When I touched her this morning, I seemed to see a kind of—cord? tie?—something like that, anyway. It was binding her to something, and I seemed to see that page in the report about the gypsies. I know outlanders aren't terribly welcome here, so I took a chance that the survivor wouldn't find a new home very easily. You confirmed what I guessed, Tedric. And it just seemed to me that what she needed was a second chance to make everything right. Am I making sense?"

"More sense than I hoped for. It's hardly possible that he could be—hers? Is it?" Kris said hesitantly.

"Kris, I'm no priest! How on earth can I answer that? All I can tell you is what I saw and felt. The little one is about the same age as hers would have been and they certainly seem to recognize each other, if only as two lost ones needing love. I won't hazard a guess after that."

"This is a terribly callous thing to ask, I know," Tedric said, looking a good bit less anxious now that the "magic" was explained away as rational common sense. "But—she won't lose her powers now that her mind is back, will she?"

"Set your fears at rest; I think you and the people of Berrybay can count on their Weatherwitch yet," Talia replied. "Speaking from personal experience, I can tell you that such Gifts rarely lie back down to rest once you've roused them. Look at what she said to me!"

" 'Love will challenge death to reclaim you,' " Kris quoted. "Strange—and rather ambiguous, it seems to me."

"Prophecy has a habit of being ambiguous," Tedric said wryly. "It's fortunate that she's able to be more exact when it comes to giving us weather-warnings. Come now; you and Rolan are tired and hungry, Talia, both of you. You deserve a good meal, and a good night's rest before you take the road again."

"And prophecy to the contrary, my heart's desire at the moment is one of your venison pies followed by a convivial quiet evening and a good sleep in your featherbed, and I hardly think I need to seek out the Havens to find *that!*" Talia laughed tiredly, linking arms with Tedric and Kris, while Rolan followed behind.

Well, she had weathered *this* one. Now all she had to do was continue to survive.

Eleven

"Well, little bird," Kris said lazily. "It's almost Midsummer. You're halfway done. Evaluation, please."

Talia picked idly at the grass beside her. "Is this serious, or facetious?"

"Quite serious."

The sun approached zenith, and a warm spot created when the white-gold rays found a gap in the leaves of the tree overhead was planted just on Talia's right shoulder blade. Insects droned in the long grass; occasionally a bird called, sleepily. They were at the Station at the bottom of their Sector where they had first entered, back last autumn. Today or the next day a courier-Herald would make a rendezvous with them, bringing them the latest laws and news; until then, their time was their own. They had been spending it in unaccustomed leisure.

She thought, long and hard, while Kris chewed on a grass stem, lying on his back in the shade, eyes narrowed to slits.

"It's been horrid," she said finally, lying back and pillowing her head on her arm. "I wish this past nine months had never happened. It's been awful, especially when we first get into a town, and they've heard about me, but . . ."

"Hmm?" he prompted when the silence had gone on too long.

"But . . . what if this . . . my Gift going rogue . . . had happened at Court? It would have been worse."

"You would have been able to get help there," he pointed out, "better than you've gotten from me."

"Only after I'd wrecked something. Gods, I hate to think—letting loose that storm in a packed Court. . ." she shuddered. "At least I've got projection under control *consciously* now, rather than instinctively. Even if my shields aren't completely back."

"Still having shield problems?"

"You know so, you've seen me in crowds. There are times when I hate you for keeping me out here, but then I realize that I *can't* go back until I have my shields back. And we can't let anyone know about this mess until it's fixed; not even Heralds."

"So you figured that out for yourself."

"It didn't take much; if people knew that the rumors were at least partially true, they'd believe the rest of it. I've watched you playing protector for me every time we meet another Herald. And there's something else. I can't go back until I figure something out."

"What?"

"Not just the 'how' of my Gift, but the 'why' and the 'when.' It's obsessing me, because those rumors about manipulation come so close to the truth. I *have* used my Gift to evaluate Councilors, and I *have* acted on that information. When does it start becoming manipulation?"

"I don't know . . ."

"Now I'm more than half afraid to use the Gift."

"Oh, hell!" He flopped over onto his side, hair blowing into his eyes. "Now *that* bothers me. Hellfire, none of this would have happened to you if I'd just kept my mouth shut."

"And it might well have happened at a worse time—"

"And might *not* have." Those blue eyes bored into hers. "What's gone wrong is as much my fault as yours."

She had no answer for him.

"Well, the situation went wrong, but I *think* we're turning it around," he said at last.

"I hope so. I think so."

"Well, you're handling everything else fine."

There was an uneasiness under his words; she was sensitive enough now to tell that it had something to do with her, personally, not her as a Herald.

Oh, Gods. She did her best to hide her dismay. She had done her level best to keep their relationship on a friend/lover basis, and *not* let her Gift manipulate him into infatuation, or worse. Most of the time she thought she'd succeeded—but then came the times like these, the times when he looked at her with a shadowed expression. She knew, now, that she didn't want anything more from him, for as her need of him grew less, her feelings had mellowed into something very like what she shared with Skif.

But what of him?

"I wonder what Dirk's up to," he said, out of the blue. "He's Sector-riding this term, too."

"If he has any sense, being glad he's not having to eat your cooking." She threw a handful of grass at him; he grinned back. "Tell me something, why do you keep calling me 'little bird'?"

"Good question; it's Dirk's name for you. You remind him of a woodlark."

"What's a woodlark?" she asked curiously. "I've never seen one."

"You normally don't see them; you only hear them. Woodlarks are very shy, and you have to know exactly what you're looking for when you're trying to spot one. They're very small, brown, and blend almost perfectly with the bushes. For all that they're not very striking, they're remarkably pretty in their own quiet way. But he wasn't thinking about that when he named you; woodlarks have the most beautiful voices in the forest."

"Oh," she said, surprised by the compliment, and not knowing quite how to respond.

"I can even tell you when he started using it. It was just after you'd fainted, and he'd picked you up to carry you to your room. 'Bright Havens,' said he, 'she weighs no more than a little bird.' Then the night of the celebration, when we all sang together, I caught him staring at you when you were watching the dancers, and muttering under his breath—'A woodlark. She's a shy little woodlark!' Then he saw me watching him, and glared for a minute, and said, 'Well, she is!' Not wanting to get my eyes blackened, I agreed. I would have agreed anyway; I always do when he's right."

"You two," she said, "are crazy."

"No milady, we're Heralds. It's close, but not quite to the point of actual craziness."

"That makes me crazy, too."

"You said it," he pointed out. "I didn't."

Before she could think of a suitable reply, they heard a hail from the path that led to their Station and scrambled to their feet. It was their courier— and their courier was Skif.

"Welladay!" he said, dismounting as they approached him. "You two certainly look hale and healthy! Very much so, for a pair who were supposed to have come near perishing in that Midwinter blizzard. Dirk was damned worried when I talked to him."

"If you're going to be seeing him sometime soon, or can find a Bard to pass the message, you can tell him that we're both fine, and the worst we suffered was the loss of Talia's harpcase," Kris said with a laugh.

"If? Bright Havens, I haven't got any *choice!* I've been flat ordered to find him when I'm done with briefing you, on pain of unspecified torture. You'd have thought from the way he was acting that neither of you had the mother-wit to save yourselves from a wetting, much less a blizzard."

Kris gave Talia another odd, sidelong glance.

"You'd best bring your Companion and whatever you've brought for us on up to the Waystation," she said. "It's going to take you a while to pass everything to us, and to make sure we've got it right."

"A while, O modest Talia? With you, I've got no fear that it'll take long," Skif grinned. "I know quite well that you can memorize faster than I can, and Kris was my Farseeing teacher, so I know he's just as quick. I'll turn Cymry loose and let her kick her heels up a little; I can lead the pack mule afoot."

"We'll take her tack for you," Kris offered. "No use in you carrying it when we're unburdened."

Skif accepted the offer gladly, and they strolled up the path toward the Station together; Kris with the saddle and blanket balanced over one shoulder, Talia with the rest of the tack, Skif with the saddlebags.

"I've brought you two quite a load," he told them as they approached the station, "Both material and news. Hope you're ready."

"More than ready," Talia told him. "I'm getting pretty tired of telling the same old tales."

"Don't I just know! Well, I've got plenty of news, personal and public, and more than you may guess. Do you want your news first, or your packs?"

"Both," Kris said with the charming smile of a child. "You can tell us the personal news while we gloat over our goodies."

"Why not?" Skif chuckled. "I'll start with the Collegium and work my way outward."

The first bit of news was that Gaytha and Mero had surprised nearly everyone by suddenly deciding to wed. They had had themselves handfasted just before Skif had left, and were to be wedded in the fall. Kris' jaw sagged over that piece of news, but

Talia, recalling things she'd seen over holidays while still a student, nodded without much surprise.

Keren had broken her hip during the past winter. She'd slipped and taken a bad fall trying to rescue a Companion foal from beneath a downed tree (the foal was frightened silly, but otherwise emerged from the ordeal unscathed. The same—obviously— could not be said for poor Keren). Sherrill had taken on Keren's duties as riding instructor as well as her own scheduled classes. When Keren's bones were healed, she decided that it was getting to be time to think about training a successor anyway, so they were currently sharing the classes.

Alberich had at last retired from teaching all but the most advanced students; to no one's surprise, he had appointed Jeri to take his place.

Companions had Chosen twenty youngsters this spring, the largest number yet. For the first time in years the Collegium was completely full. No one knew whether there should be rejoicing or apprehension over this sudden influx of Chosen; the last time that the Collegium had been full had been in Selenay's father's time; there had been the Tedrel Wars with Karse on the Eastern Border shortly thereafter and every one of the students had been needed to replace those Heralds that had sought the Havens when it was over.

Elspeth was doing unexpectedly well, and Talia rejoiced to hear it. Elcarth had taken her heavy schedule and lightened it by a considerable amount, and she had responded by working like a fiend incarnate on those classes that were left. She seemed determined to prove that she was not ungrateful for the respite, and that she did not intend to shirk her remaining responsibilities.

There was little news of the Court, but none of that was good. The rumor-mills had been churning away; mostly working on the grist of Elspeth and the absent Talia. About half of it was elaboration on the rumors they already knew, the rest concerned Elspeth's supposed unfitness for the Crown—that she was too pliant, too much of a hoyden, not bright enough— and too dependent on the Heralds in general and Talia in particular to make all her decisions for her.

Kris noted without comment the brief shadow of pain that veiled her face.

"But I've told anybody who's bothered to bring up the subject that whoever started these tales had holes in his skull. Elspeth's nothing but a normal tomboy— like Jeri, and they were perfectly willing to consider Jer as Heir! And I told 'em nobody who knows you would even consider the idea that you might be misusing your Gift! So that's that. All right, it's your turn," Skif ordered. "You two have to tell me the whole tale of your blizzard. I've been strictly charged by half the Circle to bring back every detail. If you leave one thing out, I'm not entirely certain of my safety when I get back!"

Kris told most of it, from the plague at Waymeet to the arrival of Tedric—leaving out the disintegration of Talia's control.

"Sounds grim," Skif said when they'd finished. "I'm surprised you didn't tear each other's throats out—from boredom if nothing else. Of course, you were too busy digging out to have time to be bored."

Kris inhaled his wine, and nearly choked to death trying to keep from laughing.

Talia covered her blushes by pounding his back— then took over the conversation with a stern glance in his direction that almost sent him into another fit.

"It was a good thing we had the harp with us," she said, firmly restraining the urge to set both her hands around his throat and strangle him. "Music did a lot to keep us going. And we discovered something really strange, Skif. Did you know that those stories the Northerners kept telling us about how chirras sing are true?"

"You've been on circuit too long," he replied with a disbelieving grin.

"She's telling the truth, Skif," Kris asserted. "Chirras do sing—well, hum is more like it. They do it intentionally, though, and I've heard worse harmonics coming from human throats."

"Can you prove this? Otherwise I'm going to have a hard time convincing anyone else, much less myself."

"Are you planning on spending the night with us?"

"So long as I'm not in the way."

"You can stay if you clean up dinner," Talia teased. "We'll cook for you, but you'd better do your share of the work."

"Anything is better than having to eat my own cooking!" Skiff replied with a hearty sigh. "When I was interning, Dirk absolutely refused to let me cook anything after the first two meals I ruined. I don't blame him. I'm the only person I know that can boil an egg for an hour, and have it turn out half scorched and half raw."

"Then you'll get your demonstration after dinner."

When they had finished their evening meal, Talia called the chirras up from the lake to the Waystation and gave the demonstration Skif had demanded. As the first notes rose from the packbeasts' long throats, Skif's eyes widened in disbelief. A quick look around, however, soon proved to him that there was no trickery involved. After the first two songs he relaxed and admitted that he found the wierd harmonics quite pleasant, if at first startling.

When they tired of singing, they began trading road-tales. Skif had by far the largest stock of funny stories, since his assignment as courier put him in contact with a wide variety of situations (in one case, he'd had to rescue his contactee at the meeting point from an amorous and overly enthusiastic cow). But in the midst of what Skif had thought was one of his more amusing anecdotes, Talia suddenly excused herself and walked out into the night with some haste.

"Did I say something wrong?" Skif said, bewildered, since she had been giving every evidence of enjoying the story until then. "What's the matter with her?"

"I have no more idea than you—" Kris started to say. Then he thought of something.

"Just wait a moment." He closed his eyes and Mindcalled to Tantris. The answer he got made him half-smile, although he spared a flash of pity for Talia.

"She'll be back in a little while," he told the puzzled Skif. "When she's less—shall we say—uncomfortable."

Skif was annoyed. "Just what is that supposed to mean?"

"Skif, your Cymry's a mare."

"That was fairly obvious."

"Rolan's a stallion, a stallion that hasn't been near a Companion mare for several months. Talia's Gift, in case you've forgotten, is Empathy; and unlike most of us, she tells me that Rolan is *always* with her—'in the back of her head,' she calls it."

"What?" Skif was bewildered; then realization dawned. "Oh-ho. I forgot a little experiment we did. You can't shield out your Companion with a bond that tight, can you?"

"That's it—not on that level, you can't. And with her Gift thrown in, it's even more . . . overpowering. As I recall, you can barely Mindspeak, right? So you're protected from Cymry's sporting. Needless to say, the same is not true for Talia."

Skif's chuckle was just a touch heartless. "Too bad your Tantris isn't a mare."

"I've had that thought a time or two myself," Kris admitted, joining the chuckle.

Skif sobered abruptly. "Look—Kris, I know it's

none of my business, but are you and Talia—you know—?"

"Damned right it's none of your business," Kris said calmly. He'd been expecting the question, assuming that Skif was only waiting to get him alone. "So why are you asking?"

"Kris, it's part of my job to notice things. And I've noticed that while you aren't cuddled up like courting doves, you're both a lot easier with each other than I've ever seen either of you around anyone else." Skif paused, then remained silent.

"You were obviously planning on saying more; go on."

"I owe Dirk. I owe him my life; by all rights he should have left us when Cymry and I fell into that ravine while I was interning. He had no way of knowing we were still alive, and the trail was washing out under him with every second he stayed. But he didn't leave; he searched all through that downpour until he found us, and if he hadn't, we wouldn't be here now. He's been acting damned peculiar whenever anybody mentions Talia. He was starting to act that way when you two left, and it's gotten worse since then. Dear old 'I'm-indifferent-to-women' Dirk came close to tearing my heart out and feeding it to me when I couldn't give him any more information about you two than rumor—and I would bet my hope of the Havens that it wasn't over *your* welfare. So if you two are more than friends, I want to know. Maybe I can break it to him gently."

"Oh, Gods," Kris said weakly. "Oh *Gods*. I don't know, Skif—I mean, I know how I feel, which is that I'm quite fond of her, and that's all; but I don't know how she feels. I'm afraid to find out."

"I have the suspicion that there's a lot more going on here than you've told me," Skif replied. "You want to make a full confession?"

"Gods—I'd better go back a few years—look, the reason Dirk pretends to be indifferent to women is because he was so badly hurt by one that he came within a hair of killing himself. It was that bitch, Lady Naril; it was when we were first assigned to Court. She wanted me, I wasn't having any. So she used Dirk to get at me."

"Don't tell me—she played the sweet innocent on him. She tried working that one on me, but I'd had warning."

"I wish Dirk had. By the time I knew what was happening, it was too late. He was flopping like a stranded fish. She used him to set up a meeting between us; and at that point she handed me an ultimatum; either I became her lap-dog, or she would make Dirk's life hell for him. Unfortunately she hadn't counted on the fact that Dirk was jealous as well as devoted. He'd stayed within earshot, and he heard the whole thing."

"Good Gods!" Skif couldn't manage more than that.

"Verily." Kris closed his eyes, trying to shut out the memory of how Dirk had looked when he confronted them. It had been ghastly. Even his eyes had been dead. But what had followed had been worse. Kris had made a hasty exit, and when he'd gone, Naril had taken Dirk to pieces. If only he'd known, he'd *never* have left them alone—

"But—"

"He was shattered; absolutely shattered. I think it was only Ahrodie that kept him from throwing himself in the river that night. Now you tell me he's acting like—"

"Like a man with a lifebond, if you want to know the truth. He's close to being obsessed."

"Talia *was* showing signs of the same thing, but now—I just don't *know*, Skif. We—started sleeping together during that blizzard. There were a lot of other complications that I can't go into, and now I don't know *how* she feels. But I'm mortally afraid she's gotten fixated on me."

And he was Dirk's best friend. Gods, Gods, it was happening all over again—

"Well, what are you going to do about it?" Skif asked.

"I'm going to break it off, that's what, before it gets too serious to be broken off. If it *is* a lifebond, once the infatuation is nipped in the bud, she'll swing back to Dirk like a compass needle. But for Lord's sake, don't let Dirk know about any of this." Kris rubbed his forehead, feeling almost sick with remorse.

"No fear of that—" Skif broke off what he was saying to nod significantly in the direction of the door behind Kris.

Talia entered and resumed her abandoned seat, looking much cooler and more composed.

"Better?" Kris asked in a sympathetic undertone.

"Much," she sighed, then faced Skif. "As for you, you troublemaker, I hope you're prepared to cosset a pregnant Companion in another couple of months!"

"Now Talia," he chortled heartlessly, "Cymry's been at her games with every stallion I've rendezvoused with, and nothing like that has happened yet."

"Every other stallion wasn't Rolan," she said with a wry twist to her lips. "Serves you right, too, for not warning me, you smug sadist. Or don't you remember your history, and the extraordinary fertility of Grove stallions—*particularly* the Companion of the Queen's Own?"

"Kernos' Spear! I never once thought of that!"

Both Kris and Talia laughed at the expression on Skif's face.

"I'd be willing to bet a full wineskin that Cymry didn't think of that either," Kris added.

"You just won," Skif said, reaching behind him into his pile of belongings, and throwing a leather bottle at the other Herald. "Oh, well—no harm without a trace of good. This will keep me off the road, but it will also keep me from having to do my own cooking. I'd better start thinking of ways to make myself useful around the Court and Collegium. Hope Teren likes being courier—he's the only one free at the moment, now that the new babies are done with Orientation."

He settled into his bedroll with a much bemused expression.

The next day was involved in memorizing all Skif had to impart to them. When both of them were letter-perfect, in the early afternoon, Skif packed up the few bits he had of his own personal gear and supplies, and headed back the way he'd come.

"How much did you tell him?" Talia asked, watching him depart.

"Only that we've had some complications I can't go into; I had to tell him, he noticed you weren't looking too well. That's all." He gave her yet another of those odd, sidelong glances.

"Lord—poor Elspeth, facing those damned rumormongers all by herself! Gods—I *need* to be there— and I *can't* be there—"

"That's right. You can't. Going back now won't do you any good, and might do her harm."

"I know, but it doesn't stop me from wanting to—"

"Look at it this way—with all the rumors that are bound to start about *me* and you, maybe they'll forget about the others."

"Oh, Gods—" she blushed, "—have I *no* privacy?"

"Not as a Herald, you don't."

They walked back to the Station; Kris was brooding about something, Talia could see it in the closed expression he wore, and sense it in the unhappy unease that lurked below the surface of his thoughts.

It was an unease she shared. She couldn't tell exactly what was bothering him—except that it had to do with her *and* with Dirk. She wondered if this was a sign that her worst fear was true, that he *had* become far more involved with her than he'd intended.

She didn't want to hurt his feelings—but damn it all, it wasn't *him* she wanted! If only he'd *talk* to her. . . .

They read their letter-packets in silence; Talia's was mostly brief notes, and not very many of them. But the last letter had Talia very puzzled; it was enormous, from the thickness of the packet, and yet she couldn't recognize the handwriting on the outside. She frowned at it, recalling for a moment the evil days when virulent and anonymous letters were a daily occurrence. Then she steeled herself and broke open the seal, telling herself that there was no reason why she shouldn't pitch it into the fire if it turned out to be of that ilk.

To her shock and delight, it was from Dirk.

The actual letter was not very long, and the phrasing was stilted and formal, yet just to know that he'd written it gave her a delightfully shivery feeling. The content was simple enough; he hoped that her close association with his partner would lead to a closer friendship among the three of them, since they all shared the common interest of music. It was in light of this common interest that he had (he said) made bold to write her. He had been assigned to the Sector that contained most of the Kingdom's papermills and printing houses and was the headquarters of the Printer's and Engraver's Guild. This meant that music and books that were difficult to obtain elsewhere were relatively common there. He had bought himself a great deal of new music, and had thought that Talia and Kris should have copies also.

It was what he hadn't said that both excited and worried Talia. The letter was so bland that it could have reflected either polite indifference to her, or been an attempt to conceal the same sort of obsession that she was feeling.

Still, it was definitely odd for him to have sent the music manuscripts to Talia instead of to Kris.

Kris coughed uneasily, and she looked up to meet his eyes.

"What's the matter?" she asked.

"Dirk's letter," he replied, "I'm usually lucky to get a page, maybe two—but this approaches perilously the size of an epic!"

"That's odd."

"That's an understatement. He rattles on about nothing like a granny-gossip at a Fair, and it's what he *doesn't* write about that's the most interesting. He dances verbally about doing his very best to avoid the subject of my internee. That's not easy to do in a letter this size! He doesn't mention you until the very end, and then only to say that he's sent you some music that we all might like to try together some time. It's as if he's afraid to write your name for fear he'll give something away."

Talia swallowed a lump that had suddenly appeared in her throat.

"Here's the music he sent," she replied, handing him the packet.

"Bright Havens, this must have cost him a fortune!" Kris began sorting it into two piles, one for each of them—when something slipped out from amid the music manuscripts.

"Hm? What's this?" He picked it up; it seemed to be a slim book bound in brown leather. He leafed through it.

"This—without any doubt—is intended for you," he said soberly, handing it to her.

It was a book of ballads, among them, the long version of "Sun and Shadow."

"How do you know he didn't buy it for himself?" she asked doubtfully. "Or you?"

"Because I happen to know he has two copies of that same book, both bound in blue, which happens to be *his* favorite color. One he keeps at his room, the other travels with him. And he knows I have the book, I'm the one that showed it to him. No, it's no accident that this was among the manuscripts—and it's undoubtedly the reason why he sent them to you instead of me."

"But—"

"Talia, I have to talk to you. Seriously."

Gods—here it came.

"I—" he began, looking almost tortured. "Look, I like you a lot. I think you're one of the sweetest ladies to wear Whites. And I probably should never have let you get involved with me."

"What?" she said, unable for a moment to comprehend what he was trying to say.

"Dirk is worth twenty of me," he continued doggedly, "and if you stop to think about it, you'll realize I'm right about that. You're seeing more in our relationship than exists—than *can* exist. I just can't give you anything more than friendship, Talia. And I can't let you ruin your life and Dirk's by letting you go on thinking—"

"Wait just a damned minute here," she interrupted him. "You think that *I'm* infatuated with *you*?"

He looked surprised by her reaction. "Of course," he replied—in an insultingly matter-of-fact tone.

All the tension that had been building up inside her came to a head. She'd been putting up with his occasional air of superiority, the slight condescension he used whenever later evidence proved that some decision of his that she'd opposed turned out to be right. And there was an underlying resentment on her part at his unvoiced attitude that getting her Gift under control was now largely a matter of "will" and not the slow rebuilding of something that had been shattered past recognition.

It was that "of course" that had been the spark to set the pyre alight. She turned on him angrily, fists clenching unconsciously. "Of course? Just because every other female falls languishing at your feet? You think I've no mind of my own?"

"Well," he replied, taken aback, and obviously intending to try to say something to placate her.

"You—you—" she was at a total loss for words. All this time, she'd been wasting, worrying about *him*, about hurting *his* feelings. And he had been blithely assuming that just because she'd been sleeping with him, she was *obviously* going to be fixated on him. Even now, he was still bewildered, perfect features blank with perfect astonishment.

She pulled back her right arm, and landed a perfect punch right on the end of that perfect chin.

Kris found himself staring up at her from the ground in front of the Station door, with a jaw that felt dislocated.

"You conceited *peacock! Humor* me, will you? At least—" she snarled "—you can't accuse me of misusing my Gift *this* time!"

He lifted one hand and felt along his jawline, a little dazed. "No. That was a physical attack, all right . . ."

But by the time he answered, she had turned on her heel and stalked off toward the tiny lake, into the darkness. By the time he gathered his wits and came after her, there was no sign of her beyond a little pile of clothing next to the blankets they'd spread there earlier in the day.

Now he was beginning to become angry—after all, he hadn't meant to insult her!—and a little worried, as well. He began stripping off his own clothing to go in after her. As he waded in through the shallows, he saw something moving across the lake, coming toward him. Before he had any idea of what she intended, she pulled both his legs out from beneath him and yanked him under the water. Coughing and spluttering, he broke the surface again to see her bobbing just out of reach.

She was laughing at him.

"Bitch!" he yelled, and dove furiously after her.

But when he reached the place where she had been, she was gone, and the surface of the pond was undisturbed. He peered around in the dim light, trying to locate her, when hands grasping his ankles gave him just enough warning to hold his breath this time. Once again he was pulled under, and once again she escaped without his laying a finger on her.

This time when he surfaced and gasped for air, he did not immediately set out after her. When he didn't move, she called mockingly, "That's not going to save you, you know," and dove under, vanishing.

He waited for her to surface, ready to catch her before she'd fully located him. When she didn't, he waited for currents that would tell him she was somewhere nearby, beneath the water.

Nothing happened, and he began to be a little concerned. She'd been under an awfully long time. He struck out for the spot where he'd last seen her.

He had no sooner begun to move when she erupted from the water immediately behind him. Hands on his shoulders drove him under. He kicked free and came thrashing back up, to find her a bare fingerlength out of reach.

"Infatuated fool, am I? *Stupid*, am I? Then why can't you catch me?"

He kicked off after her, windmilling the surface energetically. She didn't seem to be expending half the effort he was, yet she sped through the water with ease, remaining out of reach with a laziness that galled. From time to time she'd vanish altogether, and this was the signal that he'd better hold his breath, because shortly after her disappearance he would find himself pushed or pulled under the surface again.

And no matter how hard he tried, he couldn't catch her even then.

Finally he took refuge in the shallows, and waited

for her to follow. Now *he* was angry; humiliated, and angry, and ready to take her apart.

She rose, dripping, out of the water just out of reach. He glared at her—

And suddenly realized he'd put himself in a worse position than before. He was stark naked—he could probably pound her into the ground like a tent peg if he could get his hands on her—but if she could get even the tiniest amount of leverage to get a knee in—

Oh, she could *hurt* him.

Anger, frustration, and acute embarrassment chased each other around inside of him until he was nearly vibrating with conflicting impulses—while she glared back, just as angry as he was. Until something of his inner confusion communicated itself to her—and she collapsed to her knees, laughing helplessly.

His anger ran away like water.

He was completely exhausted; when anger stopped giving him an energy boost, he felt it. He turned his back on her, climbed out of the water, and dragged himself onto the waiting blanket without bothering to reach for a towel or his clothing.

As he lay face down, panting, he heard footsteps behind him.

"No more—please!" he groaned. "You've won; I've lost. I'm an idiot. And a boor. Truce!"

"You give up too easily." Talia laughed deep in her throat, like a cat purring, "And you deserved what you got. Keren's right; every so often you start to think you can have everything your own way, and you ought to have a lesson."

She sat down beside him, and he moved his head enough to see that she'd donned her short undershift and was toweling her hair vigorously.

"Where did you ever learn to swim like that?"

"Sherrill," she replied. "Oh, I've been able to swim since I was very little, but my efforts were a lot like yours; loads of thrashing to little purpose. After the

time I was dumped in the river, Alberich detailed
Sherrill to teach me the efficient way to swim, and
how to keep from drowning under most conditions.
Next winter she gave me a 'final exam' by pushing
me off the bridge fully clothed. Obviously, I passed—
though a pair of my boots is still probably residing at
the bottom of the river. Good thing I'd almost out-
grown them."

"Remind me never to anger either of you while
swimming."

"Count Keren in on that, too. She's just as good.
Poor, abused Kris." He could almost see her eyes
sparkling with mischief. "Are you half-drowned?"

"Three-quarters. And completely worn out."

"Forgive me, but I doubt that." She ran a delicate
finger along his spine.

He gritted his teeth and remained unmoving, trying
his best to ignore the shivery-pleasant sensations she
was causing. When he didn't respond, except for
goose bumps, she simply laughed again, and began
stroking him delicately from neck to knees.

He was determined not to yield, and held himself
as quiet as possible.

"Stubborn, hmm?" she chuckled.

Before he had any notion of what she intended,
she began fondling him in such a way that his original intentions went flying off in every direction.

"Witch!" he said fiercely, and flipped over so quickly
that he managed to get her pinned beneath him.

"I thought you were supposed to be worn out."

"I'll show you how worn out I am," he muttered,
and began tormenting her in return, playing teas-
ingly with every part of her that he could reach. She
simply chuckled throatily and returned kind for kind.
He held out as long as he physically could—but the
conclusion was foregone. It left them both dripping
with sweat, and drained as well as sated.

"Lord of Lights," he said when he was able to
speak. "If that's an example of what Rolan does to

you, I'm glad Tantris *isn't* a mare! By the time we finished this circuit, I'd be worn to a shadow."

Instead of replying, she sighed, rose, and took the few steps to the water's edge, plunging gracefully back into the pond.

When she returned, clean and dripping, she seemed to have regained a more tranquil mood. Kris took a brief dip himself, and by the time he got back she was dry again, wearing her sleeveless tunic against the cooling breeze. He dried himself off and handed her the bottle Skif had left with them. She took a long pull at it and gave it back.

"So it's Midsummer's Eve, hmm? We never celebrated Midsummer on the Holdings," she said, "And I was always at the Collegium during holidays after I was Chosen."

"Not celebrate Midsummer? Why not?" he asked in surprise.

"Because, according to the Elders, it has no religious significance and is only a frivolous and lewd excuse for licentiousness. That's a quote, by the way. What do people usually do, Midsummer's Eve?"

"Your Elders have a little right on their side." He couldn't help smiling. "On Midsummer's Eve at sunset, there are picnics in the woods. People always *begin* in large groups, but by this time of night they've usually paired off. The excuse to sleep out tonight is that you need to sleep in the forest in order to find the freshest flowers in the morning. Believe it or not, when morning arrives, people *do* manage to pick flowers."

She took a long pull on the bottle. "For their lady-loves?" She probably hadn't meant it to sound cynical, but it did.

Kris was too tired to take offense. "No, for every female, no matter who. There's no female of any age that lacks a garland or bouquet; those that have no relatives get them from anyone that can claim the remotest acquaintance with them. No one is left out, old or young. Women who have been or are about to be mothers get baskets of fruit as well. That day there are more picnics in the woods—family picnics, this time, with a bit more decorum—and music and tales in the evening. Bards love it; they're sure to leave with their pockets full of coin, their hair full of flowers, and a young lady or gentleman on each arm. It's rather like a Birthing-Day celebration, but on a bigger scale."

"Holderfolk don't celebrate Birthing-Days either— except to deliver a lecture on responsibility," she said tonelessly.

"When *is* your Birthing-Day?" he asked curiously.

"Midsummer's Eve. Tonight. Which is no doubt why I'm such a demon-child, having had the bad taste to be born on such a licentious night."

"So *that's* why you've been so off-color!" Kris snatched at the excuse to turn her mood around. "You should have told me!"

"I'm being more than a bit of a bitch, aren't I? I'm sorry. First I get mad and knock you down, then I make a fool out of you, knowing damn well that I could probably swim rings around you, then I half-drown you, and I conclude by doing my best to ruin the rest of the evening by being sour. I'm being rotten, and I apologize."

"You've put up with my moods often enough. You're entitled to have off times yourself."

"Well I think I've caught up for the next hundred years or so."

"I'm sorry I didn't talk to you about—you and me—before," he said, as the bottle came and went.

"I wish you had. You've been leaving me in knots because *I* was afraid I'd manipulated you into being fixated on *me*. I couldn't imagine why you'd be making love to me unless it was because my Gift had warped you. I'm not exactly the gods' gift to men. And I've been mostly a problem to you on this trip."

"Oh, Gods—" He was at a complete loss for words

for a long time. Finally he handed her the bottle, and caught her hand when she moved to take it. "Talia, you are a completely lovable and lovely person; I care for you because you deserve it, not because your Gift manipulated me. Dirk may well be lifebonded to you—and if that's true, I couldn't be happier. It would satisfy one of *my* dearest wishes, that both of you should find partners who deserve you. And if those partners should be each other— that would make me one of the happiest people in this Kingdom."

"I—" she said hesitantly, "I don't know quite what to say."

"Just don't hit me again. That's one response to being at a loss for words I'd rather you didn't repeat. Now, what else is bothering you?"

"I'm tired. I'm tired of having to struggle for what seems to come easily to everyone else. I'm tired of having responsibility for the whole damned Kingdom on my back. I'm tired of being alone, and fighting my battles alone."

"Well—"

"Look, I know it has to be this way, but I don't have to smile and pretend I *like* it! And last of all, I'm feeling rotten because nobody has ever given me a Midsummer garland or a Birthing-Day present."

"Makes sense."

The bottle was more than half empty; they'd shared it equally, and Kris was beginning to see things through a very delightful haze.

"How does it make sense?" she demanded irritably.

"Because if you could have what you wanted, you wouldn't be upset, but you can't so you are." It seemed like a brilliant deduction to Kris, and he examined the statement with delight.

Talia shook her head as she tried to reason it out. "That just doesn't come out right, somehow," she complained.

"It will after another drink." He passed her the bottle.

When the last drop of liquor was gone, so was her ill temper.

"I—am fairy—very—glad that we've got something to shleep— sleep on right here," Kris said carefully, "Ish—it's much nicer, you can see the stars, and I can't walk anymore anyway."

"Stars are nice," she agreed. "Not moving's nicer."

"See the Wain?"

"Who?"

"The Wain—those stars jusht over the big pine there. Five for the bed 'n the axle, two for th' wheels, three for th' tongue."

"Wait a minute," she peered at the stars, trying to get them to form up properly, and was delighted when she finally did. "What's the rest of 'em?"

"Right next t' the Wain's the Hunter. There's the two little stars for his belt, two more for 's shoulders, four for's legs—" He realized by her steady breathing that she had fallen asleep.

He reached over for the second blanket and covered them both with it, without disturbing his floating head much. He lay back, intending to think a little—but a little thinking was all he managed, since he, too, was soon drowsing.

The next morning he woke before she did, and remembered the conversation of the night before. He moved very carefully, hoping that he wouldn't wake her, and on being successful moved off into the woods on a private search.

Talia woke to an incredibly subtle perfume wreathing around her. She opened sleep-blurred eyes to see where it was coming from, to discover that someone had placed a bouquet by her head.

"What?" she said sleepily, trying to think why there should be flowers beside her. "Who?"

"A joyous Midsummer to you, Herald Talia, and a

wonderful Birthing-Day as well," Kris said cheerfully from a point behind her. "It's a pity that more of your friends couldn't deliver trifles, but you'll have to admit that we *are* a bit far from most of them. I trust you'll accept this one as a token of my profound apology for insulting you last night. I didn't intend to."

"Kris!" she exclaimed, as she sat up and took up the flowers, breathing the exquisite fragrance with hedonistic delight. "You didn't need to do this—"

"Ah, but I did. It wouldn't be Midsummer unless I gathered at least one bouquet. Besides, that scent you're enjoying is supposed to be a sovereign remedy for hangover."

"Is it?" she laughed.

"I have no idea," he admitted. "Part of my hangover always includes a stopped-up nose. Look at the stems, why don't you?"

Holding the bouquet together was a silver ring, of a design of two hands clasped together. It was the token a Herald only gave to the friends he loved best.

"Kris—I don't know what to say—"

"Then say 'Thank you, Kris, and I accept your apology.' "

"Thank you, love, and I *do* accept your apology—if you'll accept mine."

"I would be only too pleased to," he said, giving her a cheerful grin. "Dear heart, I'd intended to give you that at Midwinter, but since you said you'd never had a Birthing-Day gift, the opportunity was too good to pass by. And it had damn well better fit— you wouldn't believe how hard it is to get someone's ring size without them knowing! It goes on the right hand, little bird; the left is reserved for another purpose."

Talia slipped it on, vowing to discover when Kris' Birthing-Day was so as to return the gesture with interest. "It's perfect," she said as he sat down next to her with a very pleased expression.

She threw her arms around him, completely happy for the first time in months, and opened a tiny channel of rapport deliberately so that he could know what she couldn't say in words.

"Hoo—that's as intoxicating as what we were drinking last night, little bird!"

She took the hint and closed the channel down again, but she could tell that he had enjoyed the brief thrill.

"What are these flowers? I've never smelled anything so wonderful in my life! I think I could live on the scent alone."

"A little deep-woods northern flower that only blooms at this time of year. It's called 'Maiden's Hope.' I thought you might like it."

"I love it." She continued to breathe in the scent of the flowers with her eyes half-shut. Kris thought with amusement that she looked rather like a young cat in her first encounter with catmint, and told her so.

"I can't explain it—it smells like sunrise, like a perfect spring day, like the heart's desire—"

"How about like breakfast?" he replied comically.

"*Breakfast?* Oh well, if that's your heart's desire—" She laughed at him and rose smoothly to her feet. "It is my turn, so I guess I'd better reward you for being so outrageously nice to me after I tried to murder you last night."

"And since you seem so enamored of those flowers, I'll see that you have some in your wedding garland if I have to nurture them in a hothouse myself."

"I thought you had a black thumb." She removed one of the creamy white blossoms and tucked it behind one ear.

"For you, little bird, my thumb will turn green. I

never break my promises if I can help it, and this is one I definitely intend to keep."

"Then I'd better keep my promise of breakfast. Where will I get my flowers if I let you wither away of starvation?"

They gathered their scattered belongings and returned arm-in-arm to the Waystation.

Twelve

Geese honked overhead, heading south. It had been one of those rare, glorious golden autumn days—far too lovely a day to spend indoors, so Talia and Kris had been hearing petitions stationed behind a wooden trestle table set out in front of the inn door. Their last petitioner had been a small boy leading a very large plowhorse, and he had given them a message.

Talia scanned the letter, and handed it without comment to Kris. He read it in silence, while the scruffy child who had brought it scuffed his feet uneasily through the pile of golden leaves at his feet.

Kris returned the message to her, as she braced her arm on the rough wood of the trestle table and leaned her chin on one hand. "How long ago did all this happen?" she asked the boy.

" 'Bout two days," he said, combing dark hair out of his eyes with his fingers. "Feud, though, tha's been on years. Wouldn't be s'bad this time 'cept fer th' poisoned well. Tha's why granther sent me. Reckons in settlin' now, 'for somebody gets killed."

Talia looked up at the position of the sun, and added figures in her head. "I'm for riding out now," she said, finally. "Advice?"

Kris brushed more leaves off the table, and glanced back over his shoulder at the inn behind them. "We don't have any more petitions to be heard, but riding out to a place that isolated is going to take the rest of the afternoon. We'll have to ride half the night to make up the time, and we won't have the chance to reprovision until we get to Knowles Crossing."

Talia's shields chose that moment to go down; she felt the boy's anxiety with enough force to make her nauseous while she fought them back into place. She couldn't manage more than half strength; could still feel the child fretting after they were up. "I take it that means you think we should reprovision now, and wait until tomorrow morning."

"More or less."

"Well, I don't agree; let's wrap things up here and move out."

She could feel *his* disapproval as they followed behind the child, perched like a toy on the back of an enormous, thick-legged horse that was more used to pulling a plow than being ridden.

"You let the boy manipulate you," he said, finally, as their mounts and chirras kicked up swirls of leaves.

"I didn't. A poisoned well is a serious business out here. It indicates a situation gone out of control. Are you willing to have deaths on your conscience because we dallied a day, buying supplies?" She whispered, but her tone was angry.

He shrugged. "My opinion doesn't matter. *You* are the one giving the orders."

She seethed. They argued frequently these days—now and again it was something a bit more violent than an argument. Kris often seemed to take a stand opposing hers just for sheer obstinacy.

"You bastard," she said as the reason occurred to her. The boy looked back at her, startled. She lowered her voice. "You are just opposing me to see if I *can* be manipulated, aren't you?"

He grinned, ruefully. "Sorry, love. It was part of my orders. Including manufacturing emotions, since you can sense them. Face it, if anybody is going to be able to warp your decisions, it would be your counselor. But now that you know—"

"You can stop giving me headaches," she replied tartly. "Now, let's get down to business."

"You could have used your Gift back there," he said, as they settled at last into their bed. It had taken a long, hard ride through the moonless, frosty night to reach their Station once the feud had been settled. And it had taken a lot of negotiating to *get* it settled.

"I—I still haven't figured out the ethics of it," she answered slowly. "Having it, and having people's emotional states shoved in my face is bad enough. I *still* don't really know when it's right to use it."

"Damn. What if it had been the only way to take care of the problem? Then what would you have done?" Kris was worried about this; he was afraid that if an emergency arose and the only way to deal with it was by exercising that Gift, she might well freeze. And if it came to using it offensively, the likelihood of her freezing was all the greater.

"I don't know." A long pause, as she settled her head on his shoulder. "The only other people I know of with Empathy are Healers—and they are never going to come into contact with the situations *I* have to deal with. *Where* are the boundaries?"

He sighed, and held her; that being the only comfort he could offer her. "I don't know either, little bird. I just don't know."

Kris leaned his aching head against the cold stone mantelpiece of the Station fireplace. This had *not* been a good day. By now the rumors about her had spread everywhere they went. Although this was *not* their first visit to Langenfield, the villagers met Talia with unease and a little fear—and often wearing evil-eye talismans; they were obviously uncomfortable with her judgment and her abilities.

Talia had given no impression of anything but confidence, intelligence, and rock-steady trustworthiness, despite the fact that Kris knew that she had been trembling inside from the moment she passed the village gates.

This situation had been one she'd had to face over and over again, every time they entered a new town.

He felt Talia's hand touch his shoulder. "I'm the one that should have the headache," she said softly, "not you."

"Dammit, I *wish* you'd let me do something about this—"

"What? What can you do? Give them a lecture? I have to *win* their trust, and win it so firmly that all their mistrust starts to look foolish in their *own* eyes."

"I could make it seem like I'm the one taking the lead."

"Oh, that's a *great* idea. Then all they'll do is wonder if I'm manipulating you like a puppet," she retorted bitingly.

"Then I could back you up, dammit!" He met her anger with anger of his own. They glared at each other like a pair of angry cats, until Talia broke the tension by glancing down. Kris followed her glance to see that her hands were clenched into tight fists.

"Damn. I was all set to give you another love-pat, wasn't I?" she asked, chagrined. "This—Gods, between my shields being erratic, and having to face this same situation over and over—I'm like a harpstring tuned too high."

Kris forcibly relaxed his own tight muscles, including *his* fists. "I should know better than to provoke you. Intellectually, I understand. You have to face the battle and win it *on your own*. But emotionally— it's a strain on both of us, and I can't stop wanting to help."

"That's why I love you, peacock," she said, putting both hands around his face and kissing him. "And—

Havens! Wait here—it's been such a rotten day, I totally forgot!"

He stared after her in puzzlement, as she dashed out the Station door and returned, brushing snow from her shoulders. "I left this in a pocket on my saddle so I wouldn't forget it—and then I go and forget it!" She pressed a tiny, wrapped parcel in his hand. "Happy Birthing-Day."

"How did you—" He *was* surprised. "I—"

"Unwrap it, silly." She looked inordinately pleased with herself.

It was a ring, identical to the one he'd given her months ago. "I—" He swallowed the lump that had appeared in his throat. "I don't deserve this."

"In a pig's eye! You've earned it a dozen times, and more, even if you *do* tempt me to kill you once a week."

"Only once a week?" He managed a grin to match hers.

"You're improving—or I am. Now I *did* remember to get a nice fresh pair of quail, honeycake, and a very good bottle of wine." She slid her arms around his, stood on tiptoe, and kissed the end of his nose. "Now, shall we make this a proper Birthing-Day celebration, or not?"

Now came the stop she was dreading above all the others; Hevenbeck.

There hadn't been a more pleasant winter afternoon on this entire trip; cold, crystal-clear air, sunlight so pure it seemed white, a cloudless and vibrant blue sky above the leafless, white boughs of the grove of birch they were passing through. Snow on the ground sparkled; the air felt so clean and crisp it was almost like drinking chilled wine. Talia let the cheer of the day and of the others elevate her own spirits; after all, there was no reason to think that the people of Hevenbeck would be any worse than the rest of what she'd dealt with. It was unlikely in the extreme that anyone except the old miser and his wife would remember her or that she'd nearly let her own troubles distract her from what could have become a serious situation.

They were several miles from Hevenbeck, when Talia was suddenly struck by a wall of fear, pain, and rage. She reeled in her saddle, actually graying out as Kris steadied her. She came back to herself feeling as if she'd been hit with a warhammer.

Kris was still holding her, keeping her from falling off of Rolan's back. "Kris—" she gasped, "FarSee to Hevenbeck—"

Then it was her turn to steady him, as he willed himself into deep trance. Her head still rang with the fierce anguish of the emotions she'd encountered; she breathed deeply of the crisp air to try and clear it, and clamped down her shields—and for once, they actually worked, right up to full strength.

It hardly seemed as if he'd dropped into his trance before he was struggling up out of it again, blinking his eyes in confusion.

"Northern raiders—" he said with difficulty, still fogged with trance, "—though how they got past Sorrows—"

"Damn! And no help nearer than two days. How many?"

"Fifteen, maybe twenty."

"Not *too* many for us to handle, I don't think—"

"I'd hoped you would ride your internship without seeing any fighting," he said hesitantly.

She jumped down off Rolan and headed for the chirras, her feet cruching in the snow. "Well, we haven't got a choice; trouble's there, we'd better deal with it."

"Talia, I'm just a Herald, but you're the only Queen's Own we've got—"

"I also shoot better than you do," she said crisply, sliding his sword and dagger out of his pack and reaching over the chirra's furry back to hand them to him. "If it'll make you feel any better, I promise not to close in for hand-to-hand unless I have to. But you handed over responsibility, and unless you overrule me, I say I'm going. Ten to fifteen aren't too many for both of us—but they could be for one alone."

"All right." Kris began strapping his weapons on, while Talia led the chirras off the road entirely. With snow creaking beneath her feet, she took them into the heart of a tangled evergreen thicket out of view of the roadway. There she tethered them lightly, the scent of bruised needles sharp in her nostrils, and backed out, breaking the snow-cake to powder and brushing it clear of footprints with a broken branch.

She laid a gloved hand lightly on Rolan's neck, as his breath steamed in the cold air. "Tell them to stay there until dark, loverling," she murmured. "If we're not back by then, they can pull themselves loose and head back to the last village."

Rolan snorted, his breath puffing out to hang in front of his nose, and stared fixedly at the thicket.

"Ready?"

He tossed his head.

"How about you?" She looked to Kris, whose face was pale, and whose mouth was set and grim.

"We'd better hurry. They were about to break down the gate."

She stripped the bridle bells from both sets of harness, and vaulted into the saddle with a creaking of leather. "Let's do it."

They made no effort to come up quietly, just set both Companions to a full gallop and hung on for dear life. White hills and black trees flashed past them; twice the Companions vaulted over fallen tree-trunks that the villagers had not yet cleared away from the roadbed. As they galloped up over the last hill, the sun revealed the plight of the village in merciless detail; black of ash, red of blood, orange of flame, all in high contrast against the trampled snow.

The raiders were just breaking through the palisade gate as they came galloping up. Enormous iron axes swung high, impacting against the tough iron-oak of the gate with hollow thuds. The noise the bandits were making covered the approach of the two Heralds entirely, between the sound of the axes against the wood and the war-cries they were shrieking. Three or four of their number lay dead outside the palisade, blood soaking into the snow about them. The gate came down just as the Heralds got into arrow-range—most of the rest surged through the gates and into the village. There were still a handful of reivers outside; to her relief, Talia saw nothing among them but hand-weapons—no bows of any kind.

Rolan skidded to a halt, hooves sending up a shower of snow, as Talia pulled an arrow from the quiver at her saddle-bow without looking, and nocked it. She aimed along the shaft, feeling her own hands strangely calm and steady, and shouted—her high, young voice carrying over the baritone growls of the raiders. They turned; she found her target almost without thinking about it, a flash of pale skin above a shaggy dark fur—and loosed.

One of the raiders took her arrow squarely in the throat; he clutched at it, crimson blood welling round his fingers and spotting the snow at his feet. Then he fell, and she was choosing a second target; there was no time to think, only to let trained reflexes take over.

Talia's next two arrows bounced harmlessly off leather chest-armor and a battered wooden shield; Kris had not stopped when she had, but had sent Tantris hurtling past her, charging headlong into the gap where the gate had been while the reivers were busy protecting themselves from her covering fire. That seemed to decide the ones still left outside; they rushed her.

She got off one more shot, picking off her second

man with a hit in his right eye. He went down; then Rolan warned her he was going to move. She clamped her legs tight around his barrel, as he pivoted and scrambled through the churned-up mud and snow along the palisade. When they were still within arrow-range he pivoted again, hindquarters slewing sideways a little, mane whipping her chest. She already had an arrow nocked; she sighted again, and brought down a third with a solid hit in his chest where an armor plate had fallen off and not been replaced.

A puff of breeze blew a cloud of acrid smoke over the palisade; she coughed and her eyes watered as she groped for another arrow. The remaining three men came on, howling, spittle flecking beards and lips, as her fingers found another shaft in the rapidly emptying quiver.

The nearest, bundled in greasy bearskins, stopped and poised to throw his axe. That was long enough for her to sight and loose. Her arrow took him in the throat, and he flung the axe wildly, hitting only the palisade, as he collapsed. Then Rolan charged the two that were left.

Talia clung with aching legs and arrow-hand while he reared to his full height and smashed in the head of the first one in his path. It was a horrible sound, like a melon splitting open; Talia felt the shock as Rolan's hooves connected, heard the surprised little grunt the man made. Blood and fear and stale grease-and-sweat smell stank in their nostrils. The last one was too close for arrow shot. Talia felt at her belt for her throwing dagger, pulled it loose, and cast it at short range. This one had worn no chest-armor at all. He stopped short, his eyes surprised; his sword dropped from his hand and his free hand felt at his chest. He looked down stupidly at the dagger protruding from his ribs, then his eyes glazed over, and he fell.

Talia and Rolan raced for the gate; she glanced

behind her for possible foes and saw they were leaving red hoofprints behind them.

She was met with a chaos of burning buildings and screaming people; they thundered inside, and skidded to a halt, confused for a moment by the fear and smoke. Talia felt, more than saw, a fear-maddened ox charging down the single street; saw out of the corner of her eye a child running straight into its path. Rolan responded to her unspoken signal; whirled with joint-wrenching suddenness and leapt forward; she leaned out of the saddle, clinging to the saddle-bow, and scooped up the child as Rolan shouldered the oncoming animal aside. Then he leapt again, giving Talia the chance to deposit the baby on a doorstep. Kris was nowhere to be seen—but neither were the raiders.

Talia vaulted off Rolan's back and began grabbing hysterical townspeople; without stopping to think about it she began forcibly calming them with her Gift, and organizing them into a fire brigade. All the while she fought the urge to flee away, to somewhere dark and quiet, and be sick. She kept seeing those surprised eyes—*feeling* the fear and pain just outside of her shields.

But there was no time to think—just to act. And pray that her shields stayed up—or she had no idea of what might happen under such a load.

Kris appeared when the fires were almost out; face smudged with smoke, Whites liberally splashed with blood, eyes dull. Tantris stumbled along beside him. Talia left her fire-brigade to deal with what was left, just as cheering villagers appeared in his wake, waving gore-encrusted scythes and mattocks. She limped to his side; only now was she noticing she'd sprained her left ankle, and wrenched her right shoulder when she'd caught up that child. He lifted his eyes to meet hers and she saw reflected in them her own bleak heart-sickness.

She took the bloody sword from his unresisting hand, fought down her own revulsion, and touched his hand; hoping to give him the ease she could not yet feel.

He sighed, and swayed; and leaned against Tantris for support. Tantris was as blood-speckled as Rolan, and had a shallow cut along one shoulder. "They wouldn't surrender, and wouldn't run," he said, voice harsh from the smoke and the shouting. "I don't know why. The Healer's dead; that poor mad girl with him. There's about ten more dead and twice as many wounded. Thank Gods, thank Gods, no children. That couple—burned to death trying to save their damned chickens. Three houses burned out at the other end of the village—" He stared at the townsfolk cheering and laughing and dancing awkwardly in the bloody snow and churned-up mud. "They think the battle's over. Goddess, it's just beginning—the ruined foodstores, the burned out houses, and the worst of winter yet to come—"

"It—it's not like in the ballads, is it?"

"No," he sighed, rubbing his eyes with a filthy hand. "It never is—and we have a job to do."

"Then let's get the chirras back and set about it."

Their second stopover at Waymeet, by contrast, was almost embarrassing, Kris being hailed as the village's hero for having remained behind to tend the ill while Talia went for help. It became necessary to remind the grateful people of the rules that governed a Herald's behavior on circuit, else they would have been feasted at a different house every night, slept in the best beds in the village, and come away with more gifts than the chirras could carry.

That stop went a long way toward raising their spirits. *Both* their spirits—for there were no evil-eye talismans on display in Waymeet, and there were no odd sidelong glances at Talia. And her shields were holding—were still holding—

They stopped with Tedric at Berrybay; he proved to be more than delighted to welcome them, and a two-day rest with him—and a chance to cry out their heart-sickness on the shoulder of someone who would truly understand—completed their cure.

When they were back to making normal conversation Tedric mentioned, with the pleasure of a child in a new toy, that since their visit, the wandering Bards had taken to stopping overnight with him, and that scarcely a month went by now without at least one arriving on his doorstep.

Kris thought of his report, and smiled to himself.

Maeven Weatherwitch and her adopted child were thriving. Her ability to Foresee had actually grown. The grateful people of Berrybay allocated a portion of their harvests to her so that she need not take the chance of losing the Gift to hunger or an accident in the fields. Best of all, the local priestess of Astera was training her to become her own successor.

And Talia's shields continued to hold.

They rode through the early Spring leaves (scarcely more than buds) on their last few stops for this circuit. Come Vernal Equinox, scarcely more than a month away, they would turn their chirras over to the next Herald assigned to this circuit and would be on their way back to the Collegium.

It was over—it was almost over. Talia felt her control was back, and more certain than before. Her shields were back, and stronger. Now if only . . .

If only she could ease the aching doubt in her mind . . . the rights and the wrongs. . . .

The unanswered questions kept her up nights, staring into the darkness long after Kris had fallen asleep at her side. For if she could not find an answer for herself, how could she ever again dare *use* the Gift she'd been born with, except in utterly circumscribed circumstances?

Birds newly-arrived from the south sang in the budding bushes all around them; trees seemed to be covered with a mist of green. Talia was not expecting trouble, so when Kris asked her to deliberately drop her shields and cast her senses ahead to Westmark, what she encountered caught her completely off-guard. The force of emotion she felt sent her slumping forward as if from a blow to the head. Kris urged Tantris in close beside her and steadied her in the saddle as she shook her head to clear it.

"What is it?" he asked anxiously. "It can't be—"

"It's not raiders, but it's bad. There's death, and there's going to be more unless I get there fast," she said. "You bring on the chirras while I go ahead."

She sent Rolan into his fastest gallop, leaving Kris and the packbeasts far behind. They flashed through beams of sunlight cutting between the trees like spirits of winter come to invade the spring. She narrowed her eyes against the rush of greening wind in her face, and the whipping of Rolan's mane, trying to sort out the images she'd gotten. She had touched the terrible, mindless violence of a mob, and two sources of fear—one, the fear of the hunted; the other, the fear of the hopeless. Underneath it, like a thin stream of something vile, had lurked a source of true and gloating evil.

Even above the pounding of Rolan's hooves, she heard the mob as she neared the outer wall of Westmark, a sturdy and skilled piece of brick-layer's work, dull red behind the pale mist of opening leaves. She heard the hair-raising growl long before she saw the mob itself. She had no need to be in trance to feel the turmoil of emotions, though by the grace of the Lady they hadn't yet found their victim. She could almost taste his fear, but it wasn't the panic of the caught creature yet.

As she came within sight of the mob, a single figure burst from under cover of the town gates and ran for his life straight toward her, his feet kicking up yellow road-dust as he ran toward her. At the sight of him, the people hunting him howled and plunged through the gates after him.

He seemed determined to cast himself under Rolan's hooves if it was necessary to do so in order to reach her. With all the skill burned into both of them by Keren, she and Rolan avoided him and wheeled around in a wrenchingly tight circle, putting Rolan's bulk between the fugitive and his hunters.

The stranger seized the pommel of her saddle in a white-knuckled death-grip and gasped: "Justice—"

She remained in the saddle, certain that if all else failed, she could have him up behind her and be away before any of the mob could react. But at the sight of her Companion and her unmistakable uniform, the crowd slowed, began muttering uncertainly, and finally stopped several feet away.

When she spoke, a silence fell upon them. "Why do you hound this man to his death?" she demanded, pitching her voice to be carrying and trumpet-clear.

The crowd before her, no longer the mindless mob now that their momentum was broken, stirred uneasily. Finally one man stepped forward; by his fine dark umber wool and linen clothing, prosperous, and no farmer.

"That trader's a murderer, Herald," he said. "A foreigner and a murderer. We reckon on giving him his due."

"Nay—" the man at her saddle panted, olive skin gone yellow-pale, large dark eyes wide with fear. "Trader, yes, and foreign. But no murderer. This I swear."

An angry growl arose at his words.

"Hold!" she shouted, pitching her voice to command before they could regain their mob unity. "It is no crime to be a foreigner, and the Queen's word

grants Herald's justice to anyone within the bounds of this Kingdom who would claim it. This man has claimed justice of me; I *will* give it to him. You who call him a murderer—did any of you see him kill?"

"The body was in his wagon, and still warm!" the spokesman protested, rubbing his mustache uneasily.

"So? And was the wagon then so secured that none could enter it but he? No? Then how can you be certain that the body was not put there to turn suspicion upon this one—already suspect because of being foreign?"

The dismay she felt told her that they had not considered the possibility. These were not evil people— that thread of viciousness she had sensed was not coming from one of *them*—they were only thoughtless, and easily led while in the herd-mentality of the mob. Confronted with someone who made them think, they lost their taste for blood.

"This will be done by the law, or not at all," she said firmly. "Let every man, woman and child not bedridden assemble in the square. At this point there is not one of you above suspicion. Let the body be brought to me there."

The man clinging to her pommel was slowly regaining his courage and his breath. "I have heard of your kind, Lady Herald," he said, obviously nervous, by the sweat only now beginning to bead his generous forehead; but equally obviously willing to trust her. "I swear to you that I did not do this evil deed. You may put me to the ordeal, if you will."

"There will be no 'ordeal,' and nothing to fear if you are truly innocent," Talia told him quietly. "I do not know what you have heard of us, but I pledge you that you shall have exactly what you asked of me—justice."

The trader walked beside her as she rode Rolan into the town gates, past the substantial bulks of the brick houses, and on to the cobblestoned square. Exactly as she had ordered, every ambulatory person in the town that day was assembled there. They had left an empty space for her in the middle, and in this space there lay a long, dark-draped bundle—plainly, the victim.

Talia picked out two dozen robust-looking, mortar-bespeckled citizens, and ascertained by questioning them under her Gift that they could not have had anything whatsoever to do with the crime, as they had all been engaged in moving the town wall outward. She set these men, armed with cudgels, to guarding the exits to the square, since once the killer realized that he or she was about to be uncovered, he might try for an escape and Talia did not intend that he should succeed.

Then she removed the blanket. The young woman—girl, almost—had been beaten severely, and her neck was broken. She had been pretty; her clothing was well-made, not badly worn, but had been ripped in many places. Whoever was guilty of this was brutal and violent, and nothing Talia sensed in the trader corresponded to the kind of mind that could batter a young girl to death. The crime *did* match that thread of evil she'd sensed before she confronted the mob, however.

"Who was this child?" she asked, after giving her own nerves a moment to steady.

"My stepdaughter." A square-jawed, bearded man stepped forward, his face hard, his brown eyes unreadable. Talia noted that he did not address her with the honorific "Herald." This might mean much, or nothing.

"When was she found, and by whom?"

"About an hour ago, Herald," a thin, graying woman in a floury apron spoke up. "My boy found her. I'd sent him to the trader with the money for some things I'd asked him to set aside for me." She pushed forward a lanky blond lad of about fifteen with a sick expression and greenish face.

"Tell me what you found, as exactly as you can

remember it," Talia ordered, pity making her move to shield him from view of the body.

"Ma," he gulped, eyes fixed on her face, "Ma, she sent me like she said, with egg money for some fripperies she'd asked the trader to hold for her. When I got to the wagon, the trader weren't there, but he's told us to go in and wait for him times afore when he weren't there, so I did. It were kinda dark inside, and I stumbled over something. I flung the door open to see what I were a-fallin' over. It were Karli—" he swallowed hard, his face growing greener. "I thought maybe she were sick, maybe drunk even, so I shook her. But her head rolled so funny—" He scrubbed his hand against his tunic in an unconscious effort to rid it of the contamination he'd felt from touching a corpse.

"Enough," Talia said gently. The poor child could never have seen violent death before, much less touched it. She remembered how she had felt after the fight at Hevenbeck, and tried to put her sympathy in her eyes. "Have any of you ever seen this girl with the trader before?"

Several people had, volunteering that she'd had huddled, whispered conferences with him, conferences that broke off if any came near. Feet scuffled uneasily on the cobblestones as she continued her interrogations as thoroughly and patiently as she could, and she could hear little whispers at the edge of the crowd. She wished she could hear them clearly, for they might tell her a great deal.

The man who claimed to be the murdered girl's stepfather spat angrily and interrupted. "We're wasting time! Anyone with eyes and ears knows the scum killed her! He wanted her, no doubt, then killed her when she refused him—or if she did not refuse, for fear she'd make him wed her after."

Talia's eyes narrowed. This hardly sounded like a grief-stricken parent.

"*I* am the instrument of the Queen's Justice, and it

is I and no one else who will decide when we are wasting time," she said coldly. "Thus far I have seen nothing to implicate this man, beyond him speaking with the girl. I am sure she spoke to many. Did she not speak daily even to you? Does this make you a suspect?"

Was it her imagination, or did he pale a trifle?

"Trader, what say you?"

"May I speak all the truth?" he asked.

Now *that* was an odd way to answer. "Why need you ask?"

"Because I would not malign the dead before her kith and kin, but what I would say may not meet with the approval of those here."

"Wait but a moment, trader," she answered, and closed her eyes. She took a moment to pass deeply into trance and invoke once again the "Truth Spell." There were two stages of this spell. The first stage could be cast by any Herald, even those with only a touch of a Gift. It caused a glow, invisible to the speaker, but quite apparent to anyone else, to form about the speaker's head and shoulders. The second stage, (and one which required not just a Gift, but a powerful "communication" Gift), could, when invoked, force the speaker to tell *only* the truth, regardless of his intentions. Talia's Gift was sufficient to enable her to bring both forms of the Truth Spell into play, and she invoked them now. As the blue glow formed about the trader's head, she could hear a sudden intake of breath, then sighs of relief. These people might never have seen Truth Spell in action in their lives, but they knew what it was, and they trusted in the power of the spell and the honesty of the wielder.

"Tell all the truth freely. You cannot hurt her in the Havens, and it is your own life you are defending."

"She came to me several times, yes," he said. "She wished me to take her with me when I left here."

"Why?" Talia asked.

"Because she wished to escape—what and why she would not say. She said that no one would believe her if she were to say what it was. She first offered me money, but I dared not risk the damage to my trade if these people were made wroth. Still, she persisted. In the end, she agreed that she would 'disappear' a day before I was to leave so that it would seem I had naught to do with it, and as payment she offered herself," he sighed. "It was wrong, surely, but I am only flesh, and she was comely. It did not seem so evil that I should have pleasure of her in return for an escape she desired so badly. I was to have met her on the road outside of town tomorrow night, after dusk. After I spoke to her this morning, I did not see her again alive."

The glow did not falter, nor did Talia feel the drain of energy that would have indicated that the trader was being forced to tell the truth. The crowd, which had been watching the glow intently, sighed again. Now it was obvious to everyone that the trader could not be guilty—but then, who was?

"Lies! All lies!" The stepfather broke free of his neighbors and plunged forward with the apparent intent of strangling the trader with his bare hands. Rolan reared, ears laid back, and snapped at him, keeping him away, as Talia herself drew her dagger with a hiss of metal—and in the rush of his anger and—and yes, *fear*—Talia Saw the scene his emotions carried and knew the truth.

"Hold him!" she ordered, and several strong men rushed him and pinioned his arms against his sides, despite his struggles.

Despite what she knew, she could not accuse him solely on the basis of what she'd Seen. But from the rest of what she'd picked up, she might not need to.

"Karli's sister—where is she?" Talia demanded, and many hands pushed the pale, shrinking girl forward, a girl of about fourteen, with a sweet, timid face and dark eyes and hair.

"I don't want to force you to speak," Talia told her in a soft voice no one else could hear, "but I will if I have to. Will you tell us the truth about this man who calls himself your father, and be free?"

She had cringed when shoved before Talia, but the Herald's kindly voice and the reassurance she was trying to show revived her—and the last words, "be free," seemed to set new courage in her. She stood up straighter, and stared at her stepfather with hate.

"Yes. Yes!" Her voice was shrill with defiance. "I'll tell the truth. It was *him*—our so-kind father—that Karli wanted to escape from! And why? Because he has been making us lie with him every night since mother died!"

The accusing words rang in the sudden silence. The villagers stared at the girl and her stepfather in stunned amazement.

"Lying slut!" the man screamed into the shocked quietude, struggling against the hands that held him.

"I speak nothing but the truth!" she shouted back, her eyes dilated with fear—and something more, something of anger and rage and shame. "When we cried, when we fought, he beat us, then he raped us. Karli swore she'd escape somehow, but he found out, said he'd teach her to mend her ways."

"She lies!"

"Do I? Then hold him for six months and wait," she laughed wildly. "You all know he hasn't let a male older than five near me since last winter. I would have gone with Karli, but how could I earn a copper, bulging with child? *His* child—*his* bastard!" She broke down, sobbing hysterically, and one of the women darted forward without hesitation to throw a shawl around her in a protective maternal gesture, followed by others, who formed a comforting circle around the girl, shielding her from the sight of her

ravisher and glaring at him with hate-filled and dis-
gusted eyes.

Talia confronted him, shaking with outrage, but
somehow controlling her own revulsion. "You went
seeking the child, and found her with the trader.
You decided to confront her, teach her a lesson. You
became angry when she defied you, thinking herself
safe because she was in a public place. You beat her,
and killed her, then hid her body in the trader's
wagon, knowing he'd be blamed, knowing that if he
was killed before I arrived no one would ever look
farther for the real murderer."

She was transferring the Truth Spell to him even
as she accused him, forcing him to speak his real
thoughts when next he opened his mouth.

It worked more thoroughly than she had imagined it would. "Yes—and why not? Do I not feed and
clothe them? Am I not their owner? They are mine,
like their slut of a mother! She died without giving
me my money's worth, and by the Gods, it is their
duty to fill her place!"

Talia was nauseated by the mind behind those
words. No punishment seemed adequate to her to fit
what he had done. An odd, disinterested corner of
her weighed all the facts—and coldly made a thought-
out, logical decision.

Her revulsion and anger built until she could no
longer contain it—and then it found the outlet that
matched the decision she'd come to. She *forced* rapport on him—not the gentle sharing she had had
with Kris, but a brutal, mental rape such as she had
not dreamed she was capable of. Then with a sidewise
twist, she pulled the stepdaughter into the union—
and forced her memories into his mind, forced him
to *be* her through all her pain-filled and horrified
experiences.

He gave a single gargling howl, stiffened, then
dropped to his knees. His startled captors released
him, but he was in no shape to take advantage of the

situation. When they pulled him to his feet, his mouth hung slack and drooling, and there was no trace of sanity left in his eyes. Talia had locked him into a never-ending loop, as he re-lived, over and over, every waking moment that his stepdaughter had spent as his victim.

The villagers moved away from her, one involuntary pace.

Now she'd just shown them what she could do.

"Herald?" one of the men said timidly, looking at her with respect tinged with fear. They knew that she had punished him herself even if they had no idea how. "What must we do with him?"

"What you please," she said wearily, "and according to your own customs. Whether he lives or dies, he has been dealt with."

As they took him away, one of the women caught her attention. "Herald, we have heard you have a mind-magic. Is there aught you can do for this girl? And—I am a midwife. Would you take it amiss if she should 'lose' the child? Though I am not Gifted, I learned my craft among Healers. It can be done with no harm to her."

In for a lamb—she thought, and nodded.

The people were dispersing, too shocked and appalled even to whisper among themselves. Talia stumbled wearily to the knot of women, and knelt beside the shivering, sobbing girl. She eased into trance, and probed as Kerithwyn had taught her. She could "read," though she could not act on what she read. It was as she had suspected; the girl was too young, the not-born malformed. She transferred her attention to the girl's mind and began laying the foundation for a healing that time and courage could complete without any further intervention on Talia's part— imprinting as forcefully as she could that none of this had been the girl's own fault. Lastly, she sent the girl into a half-trance which would last for several days, during which the damage done to her body, at least, could be mended.

She stood, bone-weary, and faced the midwife. "What you suggest would happen eventually, and it will be easier on her body if it were to happen now. She hates what she bears as much as she hates the father, and the cleansing of her body may bring some ease to her heart. And—tell her that *she* was never to blame for this. Tell her until she believes it."

The midwife nodded without speaking, and she and the others led the half-aware girl to her house.

Only the trader was left. His eyes brimmed with tears and gratitude; the proximity of his clean, normal mind was infinitely comforting to Talia. After the running sewer of the stepfather he seemed like a clear, sparkling stream.

"Lady Herald—" he faltered at last, "—my life is yours."

"Then take it, and do good with it, trader," she replied, burying her face in Rolan's neck, feeling her Companion's gentle touch slowly cleansing her of contamination.

The trader's footsteps receded.

And the sound of three sets of hooves was approaching. They rang with the unmistakable chime of Companion hooves on stone—and were accompanied by the soft sound of gently-moving bridle bells.

Oh, Goddess, help me! she thought. *No more—I can't bear any more.*

But the hooves continued to approach, and then she heard footsteps and felt hands take her shoulders. She looked up. It was Kris.

"I saw the end, and I heard the rest from the midwife," he said quietly. "But—"

"But—you made a judgment *and* a punishment, Herald," said a strange voice, a female voice, age-roughened, but strong. Talia looked beyond Kris to see two unfamiliar faces; a woman about Keren's age, but strongly and squarely-built, and a young man perhaps a year or two older than Kris, with mouse-brown hair. Both wore the arrows of Special Messengers on the sleeves of their Whites.

Special couriers—their Companions must have sensed the trouble, and brought them to help.

And they were senior Heralds. "You *did* use your Gift on that man, did you not?" the young man asked, somberly.

"Yes," she replied, meeting their eyes. "I did. And I would do the same if the circumstances warranted it."

"Do you judge that to be an ethical use of your Gift?"

"Is shooting raiders an ethical use of my hands?" she countered. "It's part of me; it is totally in my control, it does not control me. I made a reasoned and thought-out decision—*if* the man ever accepts his own guilt and the fact that what he did was *wrong*, he'll break free of the compulsion I put on him. Until then he will suffer exactly as he made his victims suffer. That seemed to me to be far more in keeping with his crime than imprisoning or executing him. So I judged, and meted out punishment; I stand by it—and I would do it again."

She regarded them both with a certain defiance, and somewhat to her surprise, they both nodded with a certain amount of satisfaction.

"Then I think that *we* are not needed here after all," said the woman. "Clear roads to you, brother—sister—"

They wheeled their Companions and rode back out the gates without a single backward glance.

That left only Kris.

"You did very well, Herald Talia," he said gently.

She stood wearily in the firm grasp of his hands, with his voice recalling her to duty. She longed beyond telling to lay that duty on him, and she knew that if she asked, he would take it.

But if she laid it on anyone, she would be proving false to her calling. If this were a normal circuit, there would be no Kris to take up the burden of her tasks because she felt too worn, too sickened, too exhausted—and yes, too cowardly, too cowardly to face all those people and prove again to them that their trust was not misplaced, that a Herald could bring healing as well as punishment. And they must be shown yet again that though a Herald had powers the guilty had to fear, the innocent would never feel them. She must face the fear in those faces and turn it back into trust. Kris could not do that for her, and if he were not here, she would not even have the brief luxury of imagining that he could.

She sighed, and hearing the weariness, the pain in that sigh, Kris almost wished that she'd ask for him to take over. His heart ached for her, but this was the trial by fire that every Herald had to face, soon or late, and she most of all. No matter what the personal cost, a Herald's duty must come first. She had proven that her Gift was under her control. She had proven that she was willing to accept the ethical and moral responsibilities that particular Gift laid upon her. Now she must prove she had the emotional and mental strength to carry any job she undertook to its end.

She had no choice, and neither did he. They had accepted this responsibility along with every other aspect of becoming a Herald. But—he hurt for her.

She looked up, and must have seen his thoughts writ plainly in his eyes.

"I'd better locate the Town Council, the Mayor and the Clerk," she said, pulling herself up straight and schooling her face into calm. "There's work to do."

As Kris watched her walk away, head high, carriage confident, nothing reflecting her inner agony, he felt a glow of pride.

Now she was truly a Herald.

*   *   *

Kris preceded her to the Waystation nearest the town and had all in readiness when she rode up, shoulders slumped in exhaustion. The rules governing both of them allowed him to do that much for her, at least. She sought their bed long before he, and was apparently asleep by the time he joined her, but in the darkness he felt her shaken with silent tears, and gathered her into his arms to weep herself to sleep on his shoulder.

The second day she took reports and news, and began settling grievances. Kris winced to see how warily the townsfolk regarded her, like some creature from legend—powerful, and not necessarily to be trusted. It was well that this was such a large place, for after her performance of the previous day, it might have been difficult to find those willing to have her sit in judgment over them—except that there was no choice in the matter here. Anyone with a grievance to settle before a Herald in a place this size must register that fact in writing; with the witness of their own words, there was not one of them bold enough to deny his original will.

Talia had the right to choose the order of their judgments; normally she did not exercise that right, but she chose otherwise this time. Wisely, she picked those cases to settle that required tact, understanding, and gentleness to come first. Gradually the townsfolk began to relax in her presence, began to lose their fear of her. By the third day, they were laughing at the occasional wry jest she inserted into her comments. By day's end, the fear was forgotten. By the fourth day, when she took her leave of them, she had regained their trust in Heralds, and more. Kris was so proud of her that he fairly shone with it as they rode on to their next stop.

The gods must have agreed with him, for they were kind to Talia in this much, at least. There were no further crises for the rest of the circuit.

"I can't believe it's over."

"You'd better," Kris laughed, "since that's the rendezvous point ahead of us. And unless my eyes are deceiving me—"

"They're not. That's a Companion grazing, and I think I see two mules."

"So tonight is the last we'll spend in a Waystation for a while. Sorry?"

"That I won't be eating your cooking or mine, or sleeping on straw? Be serious!"

Kris chuckled, and squinted against the light of the westering sun. "Hark!" he intoned melodramatically. "Methinks our relief hath heard the silver sound of our Companions' hooves."

"Or the rattling of your few thoughts in your empty head—" Talia kneed Rolan and they galloped into the lead. "It's Griffon!"

Sure enough, it was Talia's year-mate, who had gotten into Whites at the same time, but evidently finished his own internship early. She slid off Rolan's back after both of them had pulled up beside him with a clattering of hooves and jangling of bridle bells, and delivered a hearty kiss and embrace that sent him blushing as red as ever she had. He greeted Kris with such obvious relief that both of them were hard put to keep from chuckling at his bashfulness.

"There's an inn just a half hour down the road from here," he told them, stammering a trifle. "They're expecting you. I thought you'd probably rather sleep soft tonight, so when Farist caught the edges of Rolan's sending, I rode down there and warned them."

"Right, and thanks!" Kris answered for both of them, touched by the unexpected courtesy. "Seems like it's been forever since we had real beds."

"Not true," Talia interrupted him. "We had a real bed just a bit over four months ago, with Tedric."

"So we did, but it still seems like forever. That

reminds me though; my first bit of advice to you is to always plan to stop at the northernmost Resupply Station; it's right near Berrybay. Tedric is a good host, loves having company, and his cooking—!" Kris rolled his eyes heavenward in mock ecstasy.

"And *my* first bit of advice is to watch out for the other northernmost surprise—" Briefly Talia outlined the plague's symptoms and described how it had decimated Waymeet.

They took turns detailing some of the hazards and pitfalls of this circuit, then turned their chirras and their remaining supplies over to him. Griffon helped them load their own gear on his mules, and by the time it was dusk, he was well settled into the Station and they were ready to be on their way.

As the lights of the inn shone through the darkness ahead of them, Kris sensed Talia's involuntary shiver.

"I know," he told her softly. "Now it's over—and now is when it *really* starts to get hard. But you're ready. Trust me, little bird, you *are* ready."

"You're sure?" she replied in a small, doubtful voice.

"As sure as I've ever been of anything in my life. You've been ready since Westmark. If you can handle that, you can handle anything; touchy nobles, Heirs with adolescent traumas, heart-wounded Heralds—"

"Mooncalf Heralds with lifebonds?" she asked with a tinge of sarcasm.

"Even that. *Especially* that. You haven't let it get in the way of anything yet, and you won't now. You're ready, dearheart. And if you *dare* make a liar out of me—"

"You'll what?"

"I'll—I'll commission a Bard to write you into something scathing."

"Great Goddess!" she reeled in the saddle, clutching her heart as if stabbed, her high spirits restored. "A death worse than Fate!"

"See that you behave yourself then," he grinned. "Now come on—there's dinner waiting, and soft feather beds; and after that—"

"Yes," she sighed, staring down the road to the south. "Home. At last."

DAW

DAW Presents
Epic Adventures in Magical Realms

MERCEDES LACKEY
THE VALDEMAR TRILOGY

Chosen by one of the mysterious Companions, Talia is awakened
to her own unique mental powers and abilities, and becomes one
of the Queen's Heralds. But in this realm, beset by dangerous
unrest and treachery in high places, it will take all of her special
powers, courage and skill to fight enemy armies and the
sorcerous doom that is now reaching out to engulf the land.

- [ ] ARROWS OF THE QUEEN: Book 1   (UE2189—$2.95)
- [ ] ARROW'S FLIGHT: Book 2   (UE2222—$3.50)
- [ ] ARROW'S FALL: Book 3   (UE2255—$3.50)

VOWS AND HONOR

- [ ] THE OATHBOUND: Book 1   (UE2285—$3.50)
- [ ] OATHBREAKERS: Book 2 (Jan. '89)   (UE2319—$3.50)

PETER MORWOOD
THE BOOK OF YEARS

An ambitious lord has meddled with dark forces, and an ancient
evil stirs again in the land of Alba. Rescued by an aging wizard
Aldric seeks revenge on the sorcerous foe who has slain his
clan and stolen his birthright. Betrayed by a treacherous king,
can even his powerful friends save him as he faces demons,
dragons, and wrathful fiends?

- [ ] THE HORSE LORD: Book 1   (UE2178—$3.50)
- [ ] THE DEMON LORD: Book 2   (UE2204—$3.50)
- [ ] THE DRAGON LORD: Book 3   (UE2252—$3.50)

NEW AMERICAN LIBRARY
P.O. Box 999, Bergenfield, New Jersey 07621

Please send me the DAW BOOKS I have checked above. I am enclosing $_____
(check or money order—no currency or C.O.D.'s). Please include the list price plus
$1.00 per order to cover handling costs. Prices and numbers are subject to change
without notice. (Prices slightly higher in Canada.)

Name_____

Address_____

City _____ State _____ Zip Code _____
Please allow 4-6 weeks for delivery.

DAW

A note from the publisher concerning:

QUEEN'S OWN

An organization of readers and fans of the works of Mercedes Lackey is now being formed. Presently called "Queen's Own," the new Mercedes Lackey appreciation society is loosely structured and has no formal dues.

"Queen's Own" functions as an information center about Mercedes Lackey's books and music, and provides a network of pen friends for those who wish to share their enjoyment of her work.

For more information, please send a self-addressed stamped envelope to:

"Queen's Own"
P.O. Box 43143
Upper Montclair, NJ 07043

(This notice is inserted gratis as a service to readers. DAW Books is in no way connected with this organization professionally or commercially.)